M000200649

THE
EX
HUSBAND

BOOKS BY SAMANTHA HAYES

The Reunion

Tell Me A Secret

The Liar's Wife

Date Night

The Happy Couple

Single Mother

The Trapped Wife

THE
EX
HUSBAND

SAMANTHA HAYES

bookouture

Published by Bookouture in 2022

An imprint of Storyfire Ltd.
Carmelite House
50 Victoria Embankment
London EC4Y 0DZ

www.bookouture.com

Copyright © Samantha Hayes, 2022

Samantha Hayes has asserted her right to be identified as the author of this work.

All rights reserved. No part of this publication may be reproduced, stored in any retrieval system, or transmitted, in any form or by any means, electronic, mechanical, photocopying, recording or otherwise, without the prior written permission of the publishers.

ISBN: 978-1-80314-525-9
eBook ISBN: 978-1-80314-524-2

This book is a work of fiction. Names, characters, businesses, organizations, places and events other than those clearly in the public domain are either the product of the author's imagination or are used fictitiously. Any resemblance to actual persons, living or dead, events or locales is entirely coincidental.

*This book is dedicated to Martyn Eagles
Many thanks for your generous winning bid in
the Book Aid for Ukraine charity auction*

PROLOGUE

The bonfire smoulders in the chill autumn air, the charred arm sticking out of the garden rubbish as if the blackened fingers are reaching for something. Thin plumes of smoke twist up into the overcast sky, a light breeze carrying the acrid smell over the wall into the neighbour's garden. Several bronzed leaves spiral to the ground, landing at the feet of DI Carla Nelson as she stares down at the fire – what's left of it.

Fleetingly, her mind casts forward to Bonfire Night next week – wondering whether she, Dan and the kids will trudge down to the recreation ground as they always do, stuffing their faces with hot dogs and toffee apples as their twins stare expectantly into the night sky, the fireworks glittering in their eyes. Even though they're thirteen now, they still love the excitement, the anticipation, wrapping themselves up warm and snug. Then she imagines Dan glued to his phone, angling it away from her and missing the display entirely, thinking she hasn't noticed the secret smile on his face as he texts *her* back.

'What do you reckon?' the DI says, refocusing her attention on the body in the fire, studying the one or two patches of skin that have escaped incineration. 'Twenties? Early thirties?' She crouches down for a closer look. It's like he's wearing a mask, his melted features barely human any more and his skin swollen and taut.

'Hard to tell,' DC Flynn Marshall replies, shrugging. 'Could be older. Or much younger.'

Carla winces as she stands up, her bad knee clicking. 'Helpful,' she says, rolling her eyes. Though everyone seems young to her these days, even a charred corpse. She squints at the blackened arm. There's a watch still on the wrist – impossible to tell what make it is, or if it's expensive or cheap. She notices there's no wedding band on the ring finger, and a molten film – once clothing – is stuck to his chest.

When they'd first arrived, Carla had noticed that the body appeared to have been dragged halfway out of what was left of the bonfire and, from what they'd gathered so far – which wasn't much – it was his partner who'd discovered him. The woman's screams had alerted one of the neighbours and she'd dashed out of her house; between them, they'd tried to haul the remains from the fire.

Carla stands, hands on hips, staring down, coughing as the smoke suddenly surges up into her face. The body is burnt to an extent that will make the task of identification difficult rather than impossible for the forensic pathologists to complete. Though, given the distraught state of the woman next door, his identity is likely already known.

Craig Forbes, of the same address, was reported missing less than twenty-four hours ago.

'Poor fucker,' Flynn says, shifting from one foot to the other. He yawns. 'Forensics are on their way.'

'And the liaison officer?' Carla replies, stifling her own yawn. It's been a long shift. She hears another wail coming from the neighbouring property and then a distant male voice trying to calm her down – PC Wentworth. Being local, he was first on the scene and took the woman back to her house until the specially trained liaison officer arrived. Carla had assumed the woman to be the deceased's wife, though she supposed she could be his girlfriend, partner, lover, mistress. Who knew these days? Her mind flashes forward to Bonfire Night again – Dan with his nose in his phone, his smug smile. She imagines herself knocking it from his hands, sending it flying into the huge fire, sparks raining upwards as she watches it melt. But then the evidence she needs would be gone too.

Evidence... Jesus, she thinks, wincing inside. *This is your husband, not some case to be pored over, picked apart and analysed.*

'The FLO is also on the way,' Flynn says, inclining his head in the direction of the big house on the other side of the old Victorian garden wall.

DI Nelson nods and shifts from one foot to the other, staring down. God, she hates these shoes, but they're the only type that get her through a twelve-hour shift and beyond. She can't remember the last time she wore a pair of heels. *A dress and heels,* she thinks to herself. *Maybe the lack of them is the reason for Dan's self-satisfied smiles.*

Another guttural scream from next door.

'Doesn't seem right, just standing here,' Flynn says, walking around to the other side of the smouldering fire to escape another plume of smoke. 'I feel like I want to chuck water over him or something.' He takes a packet of mints from his pocket and pops one in his mouth, crunching it.

'Too late for that,' Carla says through a sigh, staring at his charred head again. No sign of any remaining hair, if there was any there in the first place. Fleetingly, Dan is on her mind again. 'Anyway, I don't want this scene disturbed until the others get here.' She points to the dwindling pyre with her foot, catching sight of her ugly shoe again. 'There'll be evidence in there.'

She casts her eyes around the walled garden, wondering what the hell has gone on. It's clearly a vegetable garden with a few remaining raised beds, raspberry cages and cordons of fruit trees wired neatly to the old brick wall – or rather, it *was* a vegetable garden. She spots a chicken run in one corner, but part of it has collapsed, with the side of the wooden coop in a similar state. There are no chickens now, and the structure looks as though it's been smashed up. In fact, the entire garden appears as if it's been recently vandalised by... 'By a bulldozer,' Carla says, eyeing the line-up of diggers by the gateway. Another machine stands closer to the fire, beside a trench, as if abandoned midway through digging, its bucket raised about six feet. The whole area looks more like a building site now.

She walks over to the five-bar gate – the only boundary in the rectangular-shaped garden adjoining the road. The hawthorn either side of it appears to have been recently chopped back to reveal the gateway – its edges freshly clipped and sharp. She notices that about six feet of the hedgerow has been professionally laid, though the work appears unfinished. When she looks down at the ground, muddy caterpillar tracks are imprinted in the churned-up earth. Around the site, areas of ground have been dug, leaving trenches and mounds of turf and earth, while remaining vegetables from the summer months lie pulled up and destroyed, chucked away from their growing site.

'Ma'am...' Flynn says. Carla turns, faced with a team of forensics officers arriving at the scene.

'Afternoon, lads,' she says, striding back towards the arched gateway in the brick wall across the other side of the site. Behind it is a small courtyard garden belonging to the little house, which neighbours the bigger, adjoining property. She hears a female-sounding voice from beneath the hood of a white coverall suit and mask making a disgruntled sound. 'And ladies,' she adds. 'Just hold off a moment here, if that's OK,' she says to the only face she recognises from the group. She's worked with Dave Simmons many times before and knows he's damn good at

his job. 'There are a few things I want to check out before you
kick off.'

Maybe I'll surprise him, she thinks as she walks over to the
chicken coop, watching every footfall for fear of treading on
precious evidence.

'Flynn?' she says, beckoning him over with a flick of her
head. 'Walk with me.'

*Buy a pair of impossible-to-walk-in scarlet heels, some stock-
ings and one of those sexy corset things I once clicked on by accident. Get dressed up for when he comes to bed.*

'What's so funny?' Flynn asks, glancing over at her and
seeing her expression.

'I wasn't laughing,' Carla replies sourly, pacing along the
perimeter wall, scanning the ground. It's when she's looped
right back round again that she slips – but not because of
the mud.

'Oh Jesus,' she mutters, staring at her foot before wiping her
shoe on a patch of long grass. 'Someone couldn't keep it in.' She
stares down at the vomit – a browny-beige patch that has settled
on an area of flat mud, making her already unattractive shoe
now appear disgusting.

Then she spots it, lying in the grass near to where she wiped
her foot – a small scrap of paper about two inches by four, old
and crinkled with something written on it in faded black
marker. 'Flynn,' Carla says, pointing down. 'It looks like a
sticker.'

'Petrol,' they both read in unison, each of them glancing
around to see if they can spot what it was obviously once
stuck to.

CHAPTER ONE

TWO MONTHS EARLIER

Leah grabbed the top of the stepladder with one hand, holding the wallpaper stripper in the other. The machine sighed its final breaths as the water tank ran out again, though that wasn't the reason for pausing. No, she'd heard something outside.

An unfamiliar noise. Rumbling.

A slight vibration of the walls and floor that she'd not experienced yet. Having only lived there a few weeks, she was still learning the old house's many groans and creaks and foibles – as well as being in tune with the comings and goings of her various neighbours, getting to know who they were, which car belonged to which house, who had children and who went out to work or was home-based.

Then louder rumbling, which caused her to step down backwards off the ladder and place the flat wide head of the stripper back on its base. She brushed down her front to rid her overalls of little pieces of woodchip that she'd been scraping away at for the last three hours. It was a slow job, but she was determined to get the room ready for painting by the end of the day. After everything that had happened, she'd promised Zoey a beautiful bedroom, and that was what her daughter was going to get.

She heard someone yell out in the street below.

Whoa... Stop there!

Then the rasp of brakes.

Leah went up to the window and pulled back the dusty old net curtains. They'd be going in the bin before long, but for now they afforded a little privacy.

'Oh...' she whispered, catching sight of the huge pantechnicon parked in the street below. The dark green removals lorry easily spanned the width of her small house, plus a portion of the big house next door that her little place was joined onto – the house that had been sold soon after she and the kids had moved in. The previous couple had been relocated overseas at short notice. 'New neighbours already,' she whispered again, quite used to talking to herself while Zoey and Henry were at school.

She couldn't help the inner smile. There was no one to hear her now, no one to judge any more. No one to tell her what to wear – implying that she was 'asking for it' if she dared to go out wearing a dress an inch above her knee. No one to tell her what to cook or how to cook it. No one to monitor what time she got home from work, or bombard her with hundreds of messages if she decided to go for an impromptu drink with the girls. No one to guilt-trip her into having sex if she wasn't in the mood, and no one to tell her how much of her hard-earned money she could spend on herself or the kids.

There was simply no one in her life to judge what she did – and she vowed there never would be again. Not like that, anyway. She'd had a few dates with a guy, but he didn't really count.

Not yet, she thought, her smile widening.

He seemed nice, but a handful of meets and a few texts and FaceTime calls were a long way off a relationship, and if there was even a sniff of him being controlling or demanding, then she'd run a mile. Leah loved every last drop of her new-found safety and freedom far too much, even if it had come at a huge cost – emotionally as well as financially.

In the street below, two removals men wearing dark green uniforms stood on the pavement, their hands on their hips while they waited for the driver to park the vehicle as close to the kerb as possible. When the noisy engine fell silent, the driver and another colleague jumped out of the cab and the men began unlatching the side of the vehicle. Leah wasn't bothered that they'd parked right in front of her house – she'd had to park her vintage 1970s Mini further up the street anyway – and it'd only be for a few hours. She could see by the ramp they were setting up that they'd be unloading straight up the front path of the Old Vicarage next door. Her eyes cast around the street, looking out for any sign of the new neighbours arriving, but there was no one else there yet.

Leah let the net curtains fall closed and stepped away from the window. She didn't want to be a curtain-twitcher. If Craig were here, he'd have been outside like a shot, demanding that they move the van away from the front of their property, telling them off for blocking their light or being too noisy. Steam would have been virtually coming out of his ears, while his posturing and pent-up aggression would have made a terrible impression on the people moving in.

Leah shuddered as she went downstairs into her kitchen to fill the kettle, counting her blessings that she was finally free.

'*My* kitchen,' she said with a smile. It would never get old.

She didn't even care that her new place was small and old-fashioned, needing a refit that she could barely afford. She wasn't bothered, either, that the windows needed repainting or that the back door had seen better days. She didn't mind a jot that the original quarry tiles needed scrubbing on her hands and knees, or that she couldn't have the kettle and the oven on at the same time without the electricity going off. Another job for the long list, she thought, making a mental note to call Jimmy, the grandson of one of her clients. He was a decent lad and was training as a builder so always welcomed the extra cash.

No, all Leah cared about was that Craig wasn't here with her, criticising her every move, making her hardly dare breathe. Making her life seem not like her own.

She shook her head, ridding herself of the bad memories. They had no place in her new life. She was over her marriage ending and would now only look to the future.

She filled the kettle and flicked it on. Anyway, Craig would never live in a run-down little place like this; never subject himself to being the 'poorer neighbour' compared to the grand house next door. And for that, she was grateful. As an estate agent, he'd be constantly coveting the Old Vicarage, never shutting up about how he deserved to live there, no doubt making the neighbours' lives hell because of his jealousy. No – he'd rather die than live in a house like this, Leah thought smugly as she dropped a teabag into a mug.

'Which is exactly why I bought it,' she chirped to herself as the warm feeling inside grew again – the feeling that she was still getting used to since the divorce. In the last few months, her life had changed beyond recognition. 'And nothing,' she said, bending down to stroke Cecil, her tabby cat, 'is going to take my happiness away from me.'

From *us*, she added in her head, knowing that her children had also gone through enough upheaval to last a lifetime – or at least a childhood. At fourteen, Zoey appeared stoic and impassive, as though she didn't care one way or the other if her parents were together or not. Though Leah knew this was a front – a 'too cool for school' attitude that occasionally got her into trouble at *actual* school. Seven-year-old Henry on the other hand, to her dismay, had become withdrawn and anxious since the split, taking the weight of the divorce on his shoulders even though she'd tried to protect the kids from the gory details and legal battles. It was high time her children finally felt settled and able to look forward to their futures. Even if their father refused to be a stable presence in their lives, one thing was for certain: she was going be.

While she waited for the kettle to boil, Leah opened the back door to let in some fresh air. It had been a warm start to the autumn so far, but the last week had seen constant rain, only brightening up this morning. It was why she'd abandoned work in the vegetable plot and begun tackling Zoey's bedroom. The secret vegetable garden was one of the main reasons she'd bought the Wash House.

'Are you *sure?*' she'd asked several times when the young estate agent had shown her round several months ago. An incredulous expression had spread over her face as she'd stood in the arched gateway in the brick wall of the little courtyard directly behind the house, her mouth hanging open as she'd set eyes on it. A sharp shove of the old, warped door and it burst open, as though it was revealing a new world beyond in the form of the overgrown plot. 'Like, all of *this* belongs to the prop-erty? Really?' She couldn't believe it. The potential was huge.

The agent, a woman in her early twenties, had nodded, tapping something into her phone. 'Think so,' she'd said in a way that made Leah wonder if she was listening – or if she'd fallen foul of Craig's maligning of her. They were in the same business, after all. She shuddered at the thought of her ex getting wind of her house-hunting. She didn't want him to know anything about her. As far as she was concerned, the only reason they ever needed to communicate was about the chil-dren, and unless it was an emergency, then that could be done by email.

Leah had viewed so many houses over the last few months that the local estate agents probably all thought she was a time-waster by now. Her house-buying endeavours had become a standing joke with her friends as well as her parents – though they were entirely good-natured about it.

She and the kids had been staying with her mum and dad since they'd moved out of the family home twelve months ago when things had become intolerable with Craig. Over the years, he had refused to be the one to leave, making threats that she'd never see a penny from the house, that he'd go for full residency of the kids, that she'd never get to see them because she was mentally unstable. At the time, she'd believed him.

While her mum and dad had been lifesavers, she couldn't deny that the five of them living in their small two-bedroomed semi was beginning to have its drawbacks, not to mention that all their stuff was in storage. But once the gruelling rounds of court hearings and financial battles had come to a head, and the sale and split of the family home was ordered by a judge, buying a place for her and the children had become critical.

'So you're definitely sure?' Leah had checked again with the young estate agent, knowing that by the end of the day she'd be making an offer. The place did something to her – something inexplicable that none of the other properties she'd viewed had. It was as though its wonky walls and leaky roof were giving her a hug, drawing her in, telling her it was home. And the Victorian walled garden being part of the property was most certainly the cherry on top. She knew she had to have it.

'I can phone Barry at the office to confirm if you like?' she'd said, glancing down at her heels as they sank into the soft earth. Leah had walked on into the large muddy plot beyond the courtyard garden of the Wash House, her practical trainers making light work of the uneven ground. It didn't look as though anything had been grown in the garden for several decades, though she could vaguely see the outline of where raised beds once were, the wires along the mellow, south-facing brick wall where cordons of fruit trees would once have sunned themselves.

'Yes, yes, please do,' Leah had excitedly called back over her shoulder, marvelling at the potential. She envisaged asparagus beds and free-range hens, fruit cages and a strawberry patch. The kids would help her, and they'd grow everything organically. In an instant, she had a dream firmly wedged in her mind. When she'd booked the viewing, she assumed the Wash House only came with the little courtyard garden shown in the details and now, standing here, she couldn't understand why the agent hadn't included pictures of the walled garden. It was surely a selling point. But now she was relieved that they'd overlooked advertising it. She didn't want any competition or to be outbid.

'Yes, Barry says as far as he knows it definitely comes with the house,' the young estate agent said, hanging up from a phone call to the office. 'Though if you go ahead, he says you'll need your solicitor to check and confirm this. Apparently, the state of the garden has been putting people off, so that's why we haven't made much of it in the sales particulars. The wall is listed and will probably need rebuilding in the near future. It's an expensive job.'

'Yes, yes, it would be, as well as getting the garden under control,' Leah had said, trying to tone down her enthusiasm. 'Not to mention all the work on the house that needs to be done.' She'd shaken her head, but beneath her poker face her heart was doing cartwheels and her mind whizzing at a thousand miles an hour as she imagined making the little house into a forever home for her and the kids.

By the end of the day, she had an offer on the table; twenty-four hours later, the offer was accepted and the property removed from the market.

Mug of tea in hand, Leah went into her living room before heading upstairs to continue with the wallpaper stripping. The room seemed darker with the huge removals van parked directly outside – as though thunderclouds had gathered. Unlike the big house next door, her sliver of the original building only had a small front garden. As it was, the magnolia tree blocked out some of the light but, having noticed the creamy, hand-sized blooms when she'd driven down the street in the past, there was no way she would ever chop it down.

She peered out of the paned window, craning her neck to see if there was any sign of the new neighbours yet. The removals men lugged box after box of possessions up the front path like giant ants, occasionally stopping for a swig of water. But there was no sign of the occupants. She wondered if she'd have time to whip up some chocolate brownies to take round as a welcome gift later. She'd been touched when the previous people next door had done the same for her when she'd moved in. It was a shame that she'd barely got to know Josh and Carrie before they suddenly moved away. They'd seemed like good neighbours.

Back in Zoey's bedroom, Leah filled the wallpaper stripper with more water and waited for it to heat up. She sipped on her tea as she gazed around the room, mug in one hand and paint colour chart in the other. Zoey had taken only a minute to choose the colour when Leah showed her the samples.

'That one,' she'd said, jabbing her finger at the little square of sage green. She'd gone back to watching Netflix then.

'Good choice,' Leah had agreed. 'It'll look lovely with some crisp white bedding and all your plants.'

She smiled as she thought of her daughter, straight-talking and no-nonsense, though Leah knew that deep down things had affected her more than she'd ever let on. Such as her dad not always bothering to turn up for their arranged contact time.

A car horn blared in the street below, sending Leah to the window again. An expensive-looking grey four-wheel drive vehicle was reverse-parking, albeit badly, in front of the removals van. The driver of another passing car slowed down and shook his fist as the door of the grey vehicle opened. Leah watched as a woman with blond hair got out, seemingly impervious to the abuse yelled out by the other driver as he sped off. In fact, there was a big smile on the woman's face as she stared up at the Old Vicarage, one hand on her hip and the other sliding her huge dark sunglasses onto the top of her head.

Leah was expecting the other door of the car to open and perhaps a husband or partner or some kids to get out – but it seemed to be just the woman. 'My new neighbour,' she whispered to herself, pulling back from the window so she wasn't spotted. The rest of the family must be following on, she thought, waiting for another car to pull up. But in the next few minutes at least, as Leah peeked between the curtains a couple more times, no other car arrived. It was just the blond woman standing there, directing the removals men as they lugged boxes from the van.

CHAPTER TWO

'Hel-*lo*...' Leah said an hour later, brushing sticky flakes of woodchip off her overalls as she trotted out of her front gate and onto the street. 'And welcome!' she added brightly, giving the new neighbour a wide grin as she turned at the sound of Leah's voice.

'That one is for the living room,' the woman said to a removals man as he came down the ramp with a box. 'And be careful, please, there are fragile ornaments in it.'

'I'm Leah,' Leah said, holding out a hand as she approached. 'I live next door and thought I'd just come out and say hi quickly. Excuse the state of me, I've been decorating.'

'Hi... hello, Leah,' the woman said, giving her a look up and down. The smile seemed like an afterthought. 'And thanks so much for the kind welcome. Looks as though you've been hard at it.' The smile turned into a grin.

She seems nice enough, Leah thought, even if she is a little overdressed for moving-in day. Cream-coloured patent court shoes and a pale-grey pencil skirt didn't seem very practical.

'I'm Gillian. Pleased to meet you.' She smiled again, easier this time. 'I hope the van isn't in your way – it's taking up half the street. Lucky they didn't hit that old car behind it when they parked. It looks as though it would fall apart!' Her eyes flicked down the street, past the end of the lorry.

'Oh, that's my Min—'

'I was hoping to get into the office later, depending on how long this lot takes to unload,' Gillian went on, sweeping a hand up and down herself to explain what Leah had already been thinking about her clothes. 'A bit ambitious of me to think there'd be time on moving-in day.' She laughed again – a slight nervous edge to her tone.

'Looks like you've got a whole load of stuff in there,' Leah continued, deciding to ignore the comment about her car. Her dad had kindly given her his Mini when her previous one had packed up and, while it was old and almost a classic, it still ran well enough. Instead, Leah peered through the wide opening in the side of the huge van, seeing it was tightly packed with boxes and various pieces of furniture wrapped in grey protection blankets. 'That's the biggest game of Jenga I've ever seen. Could take a while to get it all out.'

'Tell me about it,' Gillian said with another laugh. 'They've been packing boxes for several days. Mind you, it was from two homes, so...' She trailed off, catching sight of a glass-fronted cupboard coming down the ramp. 'Oh, do be careful,' she called out. 'That was my grandmother's. It's an antique. She'd turn in her grave if anything happened to it.' She covered her eyes briefly.

'Moving's so stressful,' Leah said, feeling she ought to leave her to it. She seemed rather on edge. 'I've only been here a short while myself, so I know what it's like.'

Gillian turned back to Leah then glanced over at her little place. 'It's... cute,' she said, her eyes flicking back to her own, much larger and grander house. 'It would have all been one property once upon a time, of course.'

'Indeed,' Leah replied. 'Mine used to be the old wash

house. It's where the servants did the laundry for the family living in your new home, as well as some of the other big houses in the area.' She pointed to the slate name plaque next to her rickety old wooden gate. Whenever the postman came through it, she heard him cursing to himself as he tried to stop it falling off its hinges completely. Another job for Jimmy, she thought.

'I'll be bringing all our dirty clothes round, then,' Gillian said with a laugh, pulling her sunglasses back over her eyes again. 'Well, I'd better get on with supervising this lot, but nice to meet you, Leah. My partner is away on business at the moment, but when he's back, we must all get together. Do you have children?' Gillian cleared her throat and briefly looked away.

'Yes, yes, two little mischief-makers,' Leah said with a laugh as a removals man huffed past them. 'Not that they're that little any more. But don't worry, they're not noisy. They're as good as gold, in fact. And I don't have any yapping dogs either,' she added, wanting to make a good impression.

Gillian stared at her for a moment, making Leah wonder if she was talking too much. 'Great. We'll invite you and your better half around for drinks when we're settled. Good luck with the decorating!' she chirped before turning away and heading up her front path, calling out something to one of the removals men about where to put the piano.

Leah wondered whether to stop and correct her, tell her that there was no 'better half', but decided against it. Gillian was out of earshot now and she didn't want to broadcast her marital status to the entire street. Anyway, she was quite used to attending gatherings solo – not that she'd been to many of those since being single. After she and Craig first separated, social-ising had been the last thing on her mind, and she'd enjoyed spending her evenings alone with her children. And once the divorce was finally over, she'd needed recovery time more than ever. It felt as though she'd been sucked dry with nothing left inside to give anyone.

'Right, Cecil,' Leah said to the cat when she was back inside. 'Let's crack on with this stripping. I want it finished before the kids get home from school.'

———

'That'll be your sister back,' Leah said, hearing the front door bang as she washed her hands at the old Belfast sink later that afternoon. Henry had been getting on with learning his spellings since they'd walked home from school an hour ago, while Leah had scraped the last remnants of paper off the walls ready for rubbing down and then decorating. It was so tempting to call Jimmy to see if he had a few hours spare to finish the job, but every penny counted right now.

'Hi, darling,' Leah called out. There was a mumbled reply from the hallway then the sound of feet galloping up the stairs. 'How was swimming club?'

Silence.

'When's tea, Mum? I'm starving,' Henry said, sitting slumped over his spelling book.

'Coming *riiight* up, my dear boy,' Leah replied in a silly voice, ruffling her son's hair as she squeezed past the kitchen table. 'You need a trim, young man. I'll have to get you into the salon.'

'It's for old ladies,' Henry mumbled, kicking his feet against the chair leg. 'Can't you just do it at home?'

Leah laughed. 'I dare you to say that to my customers, you cheeky monkey,' she said, taking a packet of sausages from the fridge. She and Henry had popped into the local butcher on the way home and her son had chosen his favourite ones, with Leah promising to make toad-in-the-hole, though that seemed ambitious now. She was exhausted, but a promise was a promise. Her kids had seen too many broken ones in their lives recently, so if making what her son wanted for dinner helped him feel even an ounce more settled, then that was what she would do. 'I'll cut your hair at home instead,' she added.

'Watcha, Sprat,' Zoey said, giving her brother a poke as she blustered into the room. He squealed before throwing his rubber at her, which Zoey dodged, turning it into a silly dance move. Henry aimed his pencil at his sister then, his scowl breaking into a grin.

'Enough, guys,' Leah warned. 'And no stabbing your sister, Henry.'

Henry stared down at his exercise book again, covering his ears and mouthing letters to himself.

'Good day?' Leah asked her daughter. 'How was swimming training?'

'Fine,' Zoey said, staring between her phone and the inside of the cupboard as she hunted for the biscuits. 'Dad never replied to my text about coming to the end-of-term gala.' Her tone was flat, her eyes heavy.

Leah reached out to her, stroking her shoulder. She felt her strong swimmer's muscles beneath, knowing how much it would mean to her daughter if her father was at the event to cheer her on.

Twice, Leah thought, shaking her head.

That was the number of times Craig had bothered to show up at Zoey's races since she began training a couple of years ago. Both times she'd won. In fact, she *always* won. She had real talent, and dreamt of one day trying out for the Olympic swimming team. Whether it was realistic or not didn't matter. What mattered was that her parents supported her.

At the time, Leah simply couldn't understand her husband's lack of interest in Zoey's achievements, especially something that was so important to her. But hindsight now told her that Craig's mind had been on other things – or rather, other *women*

– and knowing that Leah was tied up poolside for several hours in the evening cheering their daughter on had simply facilitated the deceit.

'I'm sure Dad's just busy with work, love,' Leah told her, fishing out a packet of chocolate digestives from behind some tins of tomatoes. She gave them to Zoey. 'He'll reply soon enough. Maybe you could phone him later?'

Zoey shrugged as she tore into the packet, elbowing Henry out of the way as he leapt up and tried to grab them off her. 'Wait, Sprat,' she said, turning her back on him as she removed a couple. Then she handed her brother the packet. 'Bet he won't answer. Just like he didn't turn up on Saturday,' she directed quietly at her mum.

Leah's heart clenched. As ever, she'd dropped the kids at her parents' house in plenty of time at the weekend for the prearranged pick-up at 11 a.m. It allowed the three of them time to have a quick drink and snack after Zoey's swimming club training first thing, and also gave Leah and Henry some time together while they waited for the session to finish. The two of them usually ambled around the shops in town, and Leah had found a pair of jeans and a couple of T-shirts in a charity shop that fit her son, plus a denim jacket she knew Zoey would love.

After they'd picked up Zoey – wet-haired and fresh-faced – they'd driven over to her parents' house on the edge of town and Leah had left the kids there for Craig to collect. They'd been doing it this way since the court-ordered contact was finalised, and her mother didn't seem to mind. In fact, it had been Rita who'd proposed the arrangement, stating that she wasn't afraid to deal with Craig and whatever mood he might be in. Leah was grateful that she didn't have to be faced with her ex every other weekend, plus a regular weekday evening. Though she sometimes wondered if her mother had a job on her hands preventing her father, Ronald, from strangling Craig on the doorstep. As it was, Leah had concealed the depths of her ex's deceit from them both, though her father was intuitive and still mad as hell at his ex-son-in-law – perhaps *more* mad than was warranted, she sometimes thought, considering what she'd held back from telling him.

The phone call from her mum had come about two hours after she'd dropped off Zoey and Henry, and wasn't much of a surprise. Craig had managed to show up once out of the last three of his allotted weekends with the children, and since they'd moved into the Wash House he'd yet to bother to fetch them for their overnight stay midweek. Leah always made sure they were at their grandparents' house at the right time, figuring that if nothing else it was time well spent with Nana and Pops.

'I'm sure there was a good reason for him not showing up,' Leah told her daughter, knowing she was going to have to email her ex. He'd made such a fuss in court about setting regular times for contact, yet now he couldn't be bothered. She didn't see why the kids should suffer because he couldn't prioritise them. And she could hardly explain to Zoey and Henry that it was probably because he was besotted with his new woman. As soon as they'd separated, Leah had learnt that they'd wasted no time in making things public.

Not that she's that new any more, Leah reminded herself. God knows how long that particular affair at work had been going on – though she'd lost track of all her ex's dalliances over the years, resigning herself to never knowing the full extent. In the end, ignorance had given her some kind of peace and, oddly, rather than feeling bitter, she'd almost felt grateful to the woman she'd never met who'd finally brought their sham of a marriage to a close. It had been no way to live.

'Maybe,' Zoey said, also sounding resigned about her father. Leah knew how much it hurt her, feeling abandoned.

'I met the new neighbour earlier,' Leah said, hoping the change of subject would lighten the mood.

Zoey glanced at her, giving a quick nod as she sat down at the table next to her brother. She swiped his exercise book from him. 'I'll test you on your words, Sprat,' she said, biting into a biscuit.

'She seemed really friendly,' Leah added.

Zoey smiled up at her mum before turning back to Henry's schoolbook. 'Right, Sprat,' she said. 'First word... Spell "deceit".'

CHAPTER THREE

'Lucky for some,' Gabe said with a wry smile as he picked up both their drinks from the bar.

Leah glanced back over her shoulder as she led the way to the free table in the window. 'Lucky... as in?' She pulled out the stools while Gabe put the drinks on beer mats before heading back to the bar to fetch the two packets of crisps he'd bought. She was pleased he'd called earlier, asking if she was free for an impromptu drink.

'Date number seven.' He grinned as he sat down. 'Lucky... as in the number.'

Leah stared at him, trying not to laugh as she took off her jacket. She wondered when, exactly, he'd started counting the number of times they'd seen each other.

'Have you never played bingo, Miss Ward?' he asked, pulling open the packet of beef and onion and laying it between them.

'Let me think.' Leah rubbed her chin while making a silly face. 'Nope.'

Date number seven, she thought, taking a sip of her gin and tonic. '*Actual* dates, you mean?' she said, crunching on a crisp.

Gabe nodded. 'Mm-hh.'

'Time flies when you're having fun,' she said, noticing a flicker of agitation. It was one of the things Craig had had the audacity to say when she'd found out the extent of his cheating – and just how far back in their married life it had started.

'Coffee at Rabble in town, a drink at the Golden Lion, dinner at Pho Shizz, a walk along the canal towpath and afternoon tea, the castle gardens and a picnic, a chug on *Blue Moon* to the pub until the prop got tangled with weed, and now this.' Gabe spread his palms to indicate the pub, while Leah counted up on her fingers.

'Yup, I suppose that's seven actual dates,' she said with a wink.

'In the same number of weeks since your divorce went through, if that makes you feel better.' He wiped beer froth from his top lip. 'No rush.'

'Did you get the boat going again?' she asked.

She couldn't deny that Gabe living on a boat, being something of an alternative, free spirit, was an attraction for her. But she wasn't kidding herself either – dating someone who was the complete opposite to Craig in every way imaginable was always going to be appealing.

The only thing Gabe and her ex had in common was their good looks. But even then, that was in completely opposite ways. Craig with his chiselled features and precisely cut blond hair, his shaved and gym-honed athletic body had, to anyone who didn't know him, a Greek god thing going on – and he took every opportunity to flaunt it. To Leah, any feeling of attraction to his technical good looks had long since been lost in the wake of his betrayals.

Gabriel, however, was handsome in an understated way – he had an air about him, as though he exuded something alluring and mysterious, as if his soul had flavour. His wavy brown hair – shoulder-length and often tied back in a ponytail – always smelt nice. His clothes, while never designer or tailored like Craig's, were unique and messily stylish, somehow seeming to fit just right even though they were mainly from vintage shops or things he said he'd had for years. Levi's and a check shirt with sturdy tan boots was his go-to look, with an old army-style jacket on top. With his chestnut beard and broad shoulders, his landscaping and tree surgeon job completed the lumberjack vibe. But the undeniable attraction Leah felt was way more layered than that. She saw something in his eyes, as though his mind was constantly searching and, in turn, he seemed as intrigued by her as she was by him.

'I did indeed get it going,' Gabe replied, referring to the boat. 'Weed gets tangled round the prop all the time. I'm quite used to being waist-deep in the canal to get it off. All part of life on the water.'

'Seven years, you said?' Leah was sure that was how long he'd said he'd lived aboard *Blue Moon*, his fifty-five-foot narrowboat. 'There's your lucky number again.' Though not quite so lucky for me, Leah thought. It was the number of affairs Craig had had during their marriage. Well, the ones she knew about, anyway. She batted away the intrusive thoughts about her ex.

'Not to mention I'm the middle child of seven siblings.'

Leah stared at him, drink halfway to her mouth. He'd mentioned various brothers and sisters before, but she hadn't realised there were so many.

'Shocked?'

'I'm just imagining what Christmas must be like.'

'Put it this way, I don't host it. The boat would sink,' he said. 'But it's fun. I like it. I have fourteen nieces and nephews.'

'Seven times two,' Leah quipped, forcing the length of her marriage from her mind – fourteen years.

'So have you met your new neighbours yet?' Gabe asked. He pushed the packet of crisps closer to Leah.

'A couple of times now, but only the woman, Gillian. She seems... really nice.'

'Nice is good,' Gabe said. 'You don't want wild, crazy or eccentric when it comes to neighbours.'

'Is that why you live on a boat?' Leah asked, play-kicking his leg with her foot. 'So you don't have any neighbours to moan about?'

'Partly,' he replied. 'But more so my neighbours don't moan about *me*.'

'Ah, the music,' she said, remembering when they'd moored and fired up the barbecue on the rear deck when they hadn't made it to the pub. Debussy had been resounding from the external speakers and, rather than disturb the beautiful and remote scenery around them, the violins had somehow enhanced it, as though the countryside had its own soundtrack. But other people may not have felt the same way – especially when he switched it up a gear and blasted out Iron Maiden.

'Anyway, Gillian has asked me round for a coffee in the morning, so I'll get more of a chance to suss her out. I don't know what she does, but she's been going out to work smartly dressed each morning.'

'Seen any sign of a partner yet?' Gabe's Dublin accent suddenly seemed more pronounced. 'Or any kids?'

'No and no,' Leah said, glancing out of the pub window. There was a group of lads hanging about in the car park, smoking, with Jimmy among them. He flicked Leah a wave, grinning when he saw her. 'I'm not sure she seems the type to have kids,' she said, turning back to Gabe, feeling bad for making assumptions. 'Or maybe they go to boarding school. They've clearly got money.' She didn't mean to sound bitter, but however hard she tried, her mind always swung back to her ex. Her *loaded* ex, who had somehow managed to convince the judge that he had nothing.

'I can believe that,' Gabe said, laughing and slipping off his jacket. He touched his beard, his dark brown eyes twinkling. 'And they probably have servants and a butler. And a chauffeur, too.'

'Don't forget the groundsman,' Leah joked, given Gabe's line of work.

'Their house must be worth what, a cool million? Probably the type to send their kids off to school.'

'One point two million, to be precise,' Leah said. 'Not that I've looked at online valuations or anything,' she added with a laugh.

'To be honest,' Gabe said, 'I'd much rather live in your house than theirs. Yours has charm. Next door is... well, it's rather grand. Not very homely.'

'And how would you know what my place is like?' she asked, pulling a silly face. 'You've not been inside yet.' Leah remembered the night he'd walked her home from the Thai restaurant in town. *Do you want to come in for a coffee* had been on the tip of her tongue as they'd stood at the garden gate, but knowing that Zoey and Henry were upstairs asleep (with Zoey probably not even asleep, given it wasn't quite ten o'clock), she'd decided against it. The kiss he'd given her at the doorstep had been enough – just as it had been the first time.

'Only a hunch from seeing the outside. Don't worry, I've... I've not been spying on you.' His turn to glance out of the window then as he took a sip of his pint. 'I like the colour of your bedroom, by way,' he added, grinning.

Leah prodded him in the ribs, rocking on the little stool as she laughed. 'If you'd been spying on me then you'd know exactly why I always have paint under my fingernails,' she said. 'Every room needs decorating and—'

Leah stopped suddenly, her eyes drawn to the bar. A couple had just come in – a tall blond woman and a shorter bald man. She stared at them, doing a double take as she turned back to

Gabe. 'Talk of the devil,' she whispered. 'My new neighbours are here. Gillian's partner must be back from his work trip.'

Gabe turned slowly, trying not to make it obvious he was staring. 'I wouldn't have put them together as a couple,' he said in a low voice, drawing in closer to Leah.

She watched the pair for a moment – though it was harder to see them now as the group of lads had also come in, crowding around the bar.

'Hi, Mrs F,' Jimmy called out, hitching up his jeans. He grinned, his dazzling eyes sparkling beneath his floppy fringe. Everyone in their little town knew Jimmy and his family – they were well liked and his grandmother, Margaret, ran the local WI.

'I'll call you about some work, Jimmy,' Leah mouthed at him, making a phone gesture with her hand. The lad gave a nod in return and stepped away from the bar with his mates, allowing Leah to see Gillian again.

She'd slipped off her jacket to reveal a knee-length wrap dress. Her legs were long and slim, tanned too, and her wavy blond hair fell around her shoulders, rippling as she laughed at something the man had said. His hand was positioned lightly in the small of her back, as though he was staking his claim on her, and his bald pate glistened from sweat. He was a few inches shorter than Gillian, Leah noticed, fidgeting from one foot to the other, as though he knew he didn't quite belong next to her. When he turned, Leah saw that he was also a good deal older.

'No, I wouldn't have put them together either,' Leah said, wondering if people had thought the same about her and Craig.

CHAPTER FOUR

'Come in, come in...' Gillian said, holding the front door wide. 'Welcome to my humble abode.'

Leah stood on the doorstep a moment, wondering if she was being sarcastic. She didn't think she was. 'Thanks for inviting me round,' she said. 'And it was nice to see you in the pub briefly last night,' she added, going into the hallway. 'It's a friendly place.' There was a vase of fresh lilies on the hall table and the black and white chequerboard floor tiles were partially covered by a large, expensive-looking Chinese rug. When Carrie and Josh had lived there, they'd left them bare, showing them off in all their glory.

'I have cake,' Gillian said, smiling as she led the way through to the kitchen. Not that Leah didn't know the way already – she'd been round several times when the old neighbours lived there, either for coffee with Carrie or for the couple's barbecues, drinks and Sunday brunches. They'd enjoyed hosting for their friends. But perhaps Gillian and her partner would become friends too, she thought hopefully.

'Never say no to cake,' Leah replied, looking around. The kitchen seemed so different with Gillian's belongings in place.

The cupboards were the same, of course – tall, cream wall cabinets, with the handmade base units painted a thundercloud shade of grey. The worktop was made of thick slabs of veined marble. The old flagstones on the floor were the same, but Gillian's glass and chrome table gave off a modern vibe compared to Carrie's rustic farmhouse one. It didn't suit the room at all. Gillian had put it on top of a very impractical white rug, Leah noticed, perhaps to cover up the floor's imperfections.

'Shows up every fingerprint,' Gillian remarked, spotting where Leah's gaze had fallen. 'I had a modern penthouse apartment in the city centre before, so apart from a couple of things I've inherited, my furniture doesn't really suit this house.' She shrugged. 'But Rex had his heart set on an old place. Something different this time round for him.'

'Rex?' Leah asked. 'Your partner?'

Gillian laughed and nodded. 'Everyone calls him that. He's still away on business.'

'Ahh...' Leah said, wondering who the man in the pub last night was. She didn't want to pry. 'Well, I think you've got the place looking very homely already.' She pulled out a chair to sit down and was about to lean forward on the table but thought better of it, folding her hands in her lap instead. 'And I'm with Rex. I love old houses.'

'Coffee?' Gillian asked, pressing some buttons on a huge machine that wouldn't look out of place in a trendy café. 'I can do you a latte, a cappuccino, a flat white, espresso, a macchiato, soy, skinny or regular, decaf or fully loaded or—'

'Just a black coffee is fine by me,' Leah said, feeling overwhelmed. 'No sugar.' She watched as the machine ground and hissed and frothed, finally producing Leah's plain coffee and a cappuccino for Gillian.

'I can't believe how organised you are after only a few days,' Leah commented as Gillian opened several kitchen cupboards to retrieve a couple of plates, and some forks from a drawer. 'My place is still chaos.'

Everything was unpacked and put away neatly – with pictures and curtains already hung, knick-knacks and house-plants adorning the deep windowsills, the huge walk-in pantry well stocked, and the big built-in dresser adorned with a collection of ultra-modern crockery. It looked as though she and Rex had lived there for years.

'I paid for an unpacking service and a stylist,' Gillian said, bringing the coffees over and sitting down opposite Leah. 'Honestly, with my other half travelling a lot lately, I'd never have had the time, especially as it's mad in the office at the moment. I work for Rexie, you see.' She grabbed a long knife and sank it into the loaf cake. 'You'll have a slice? It's coffee and walnut.'

'And I can't believe you've been baking so soon after moving house either,' Leah said, indicating that she'd like some. 'I still have no idea where my baking tins are. It looks delicious.'

'I didn't actually make it. It's from the patisserie in town. You know, the one next door to that slightly depressing-looking little hairdresser's. They delivered it earlier along with some artisan bread.' She laughed then, her silky hair rippling over her shoulders.

'Oh... yes, I know the place,' Leah said, feeling herself bristle.

'So, tell me, what do you do for work, Leah? Apart from a lot of DIY, by the sound of things.' Gillian paused, the knife still clenched in her fist as she glanced up. 'I've heard a lot of scraping on the walls in the evening.'

'Oh, I'm *so* sorry,' Leah replied. 'I had no idea you could hear. I assumed the walls were really thick, being such an old property.' She felt herself blush. 'If it's any consolation, I've finished wallpaper-stripping for now.'

'Let me guess,' Gillian went on, ignoring what Leah had just said. 'I'd say something manual... Are you a gardener?'

Leah suddenly felt self-conscious as Gillian glanced at her hands. However hard she scrubbed, there always seemed to be a crescent of mud or paint under her nails.

'I've seen you digging about in that patch of land from the upstairs window.'

'Oh, it's not a patch of land, it's actually my—'

'Or maybe you don't work? Lady of leisure, perhaps?' She made a dry, rasping sound in her throat.

Leah forced herself to pause before replying. 'I'm a hairdresser, actually. I own a salon in town.' She took a breath. 'The one next door to the cake shop.'

Silence for a moment.

Gillian took a bite of her cake and chewed slowly, washing it down with a large mouthful of coffee. When she finally spoke, Leah didn't mention the froth on her top lip.

'God, you must think me *so* rude.' She made a display of covering her face. 'When I said depressing, I meant... well, I just meant the shopfront could do with a lick of paint, that's all. I've heard really amazing things about it, actually. Good for you.'

Leah didn't react immediately – something she'd learnt to do from listening to Craig's passive-aggressive monologues picking on her every fault over the years. Waiting a moment, even just a brief pause for thought, gave her brain the space to neutralise his remarks. It took her a while to realise it, but what irked Craig the most was not to get a rise out of her.

'Oh, you're quite right,' Leah replied. 'The shopfront is rather dowdy. I'm getting it painted next spring. Funds are a bit tight at the moment, but our ladies don't seem to mind.'

'Ladies?' Gillian said, appearing relieved that she'd got away with the inadvertent insult.

'My customers. Most of them are pensioners.'

'Ahh,' Gillian said. 'A niche market. Clever.'

Leah was tempted to ask if Gillian wanted to make an appointment but saw no reason to get petty or fall out with the neighbour. The opposite was true, in fact. Despite her poor taste in kitchen tables and glaring faux pas, she rather liked her. Her forthright manner and directness were strangely refreshing.

'Have you been hairdressing long?'

'Since I left school,' Leah said between mouthfuls. 'As soon as I took to my first Barbie doll with the scissors aged ten, I knew that's what I wanted to do.'

In the past, she'd always worked for others, but when the salon in town came up for sale a couple of years ago, her dad had been overly generous and lent her the money to buy it. She'd never have been able to afford it otherwise, and Craig wasn't interested in supporting her career. Once Zoey and Henry had been born, it became clear he wanted her to be a stay-at-home mum – a stay-at-home everything, in fact.

'After I bought it, I had big plans to refurbish it, turn it into a super-trendy place with a nail bar and beauty treatments. I inherited my clients, and once I got to know them, I honestly hadn't got the heart to change a single thing. The bus service to the city isn't great and some of my ladies aren't as mobile as they once were. Plus, the cost of a city salon is out of reach for many of them, not to mention that for some, it's their only social contact. So that's why Waves is exactly the same as when I bought it.'

'That's so lovely,' Gillian said. 'Business shouldn't be all about profit and expansion.'

'Exactly,' Leah replied, noticing Gillian appeared uncomfortable for a moment. 'And we do OK. I pay the bills and staff on time. I just about break even, but I can honestly say I look forward to going into work, and that's what's important. Before I took over Waves, I was working in a busy city salon, but the commute was hard with the kids. My husband was...' She trailed off, not wanting to correct herself and say 'ex'. She didn't want to have to explain about her divorce. Not yet, anyway. 'Well, his working hours were long, and childcare was proving tricky at the time. Waves was a godsend, really. I even manage a day or two off a week – including today.'

'I can understand about the long hours,' Gillian said, giving Leah a look. 'My partner is always at the office or working on his laptop at home. We don't have any children, although Rexie has some from his previous marriage.'

Leah couldn't be sure, but she thought Gillian had a wistful look in her eyes as a hand slipped down onto her flat stomach and she glanced away.

After they'd finished their coffees, Gillian insisted on giving Leah a guided tour of the house.

'I fell in love with it the moment I set foot inside. Rex surprised me and had already bought it, insisting he had to have it.'

Leah wondered what would have happened if Gillian *hadn't* liked the property.

'I'm sorry I didn't get to say hello last night in the pub,' Leah said, trailing after Gillian as she strode off to the large drawing room. 'After we bumped into each other in the loos, I went straight out the back door to the car park. Gabe was waiting out there for me.'

'Oh... no problem. I was with a frie— A cli— It was a business meeting, actually,' she added, not seeming quite sure herself as she opened the wooden shutters in the huge front bay window. The room flooded with light. Then she dragged back the curtains that were drawn across the French doors that led out on to the terrace at the rear. Gone were Carrie and Josh's comfy velvet sofas, replaced with a rather uncomfortable-looking tapestry suite. Leah decided not to press further on who the man in the pub was.

'We don't really sit in here,' Gillian remarked. 'Well – we haven't really sat anywhere yet with Rexie away,' she laughed. 'But this will be our formal living room, for drinks receptions and entertaining.'

Crikey, Leah thought, knowing that just the other side of this wall, with its ornate marble fireplace and grand oil paintings and piano, was her cosy little sitting room. *You could fit four of my rooms in here*, she thought. She'd just about squeezed her own saggy old sofa into her living room, along with a couple of floor cushions and a beanbag for the kids and their friends. Her stripped boards with soft sheepskin rugs seemed a far cry from Gillian's plush almost-white carpet. She couldn't imagine having a room just for entertaining – not any more, anyway. Her and Craig's family home had been comfortable, for sure – an estate agent was always going to want a decent home, after all – but the detached executive new-build they'd bought off-plan in an exclusive cul-de-sac was nothing compared to Gillian and Rex's place.

'And this is where we'll have our movie nights. Rexie loves his films,' Gillian said, leading Leah through to the next room.

'You've got it looking lovely,' Leah said. She forced down the lump building in her throat, swallowing down what still felt a lot like... *grief*. However much she hated Craig for what he'd done, the divorce was still the end of their marriage. And that had come as a huge emotional loss. Was *still* a huge loss.

Craig had loved his movies too – he was a total film buff, with a Friday-night binge a regular occurrence, the pair of them cuddled up together once the kids were in bed, watching anything and everything, from new blockbusters to classic French art-house movies. It was the one night he was almost always home – her night on a rota of many, it had turned out. A token event to make him seem like the devoted family man everyone believed him to be. And what's more, Craig had always coveted a big leather corner sofa just like the one she was now staring at in Gillian and Rex's TV room.

'It'll be so cosy in winter with the stove lit,' Gillian went on, plumping one of the scatter cushions. 'Come on upstairs. I could use your advice on curtains.'

Leah followed Gillian up the sweeping staircase, wondering if she should have taken off her shoes. She didn't want to mark the immaculate carpet. Somehow, it seemed to matter more with Gillian living here than it ever did with Carrie and Josh. While they had loved their home, they'd made sure it was properly lived in.

'This is mine and Rex's room,' Gillian said, going into the largest of the five bedrooms. 'But I simply detest the curtain fabric. I have a phobia of birds, and certainly don't want them in here while I sleep.'

'That's a William Morris print,' Leah said, going up to the window and running her hand over one of the long curtains, admiring it. 'They're beautiful. Are you sure they won't grow on you? New ones will cost a fortune.'

Leah peered out of the bay window between the slats of the shutters. The neat front garden below – all clipped box hedges, lavender bushes and ornamental bay trees – was a contrast to her own tiny patch of mud and broken paving slabs.

'Well, whatever print it is, I can't abide those birds and their beady eyes watching me. They give me the creeps. You're welcome to them, if you want them.'

'Thanks,' she said with a laugh. 'I could probably make curtains for all my windows with the fabric.' She placed a hand on her back pocket, feeling her phone vibrate with a message. She didn't read it, not wanting to appear rude as Gillian showed off her en suite bathroom, telling her about the water softener she was going to get, how it was so much better for her hair. Leah's eyes flicked around the pristine, white-tiled room. The expensive gold-coloured fittings were gleaming, the shower glass barely visible it was so sparkling clean, and the towels looked plush, soft and brand new.

How the other half live, Leah thought, wishing she could afford stuff like this. On the shelves above the his-and-hers marble basins, various toiletries and glass bottles were lined up

– the tall ones at the back and the smaller ones to the front. Many were brands Leah had never heard of, and they looked expensive in their pastel-coloured boxes and tinted glass. Then she spotted a couple of items that made her do a double take.

Damn, she thought, turning to go back into the bedroom, hating that a tear was gathering in the corner of one eye. *Why did I have to see that?* But the triggers, as she'd learnt over the months, were everywhere. The distinctive gold Paco Rabanne packaging might not be that uncommon, but it was Craig's favourite cologne. Indeed, the Christmas before last, she'd lovingly wrapped a gift set for him and placed it under the tree not knowing that in another couple of months, life as she and the kids knew it would be blown apart. She closed the bathroom door and gathered herself. No point getting emotional. Things were different now.

Gillian suddenly whipped up her phone from the bedside table as it vibrated. 'Excuse me a moment,' she mouthed at Leah. 'Hello, *darling*, how are you? And *where* are you?' She giggled coyly, twiddling her hair round her left forefinger. While she was talking, Leah retrieved her own phone from her pocket, checking the text that had come in.

Henry's puked. What's for lunch, starving Z x

As big sister, Leah knew Zoey was perfectly capable of watching Henry while she had a coffee next door, and even in the evening when she went out with Gabe for a couple of hours, but she also knew that her daughter would never clean up any kind of mess, especially one made by her brother. It was time to go.

'Oh that's *wonderful!*' Gillian said, turning to face Leah again and making an expectant face. 'Yes, yes, will do, my darling. See you very soon! Love you... no, love *you* more... mwah... mwah.' Her voice got higher and higher until she finally hung up. 'Talk of the devil,' Gillian said, putting her phone back down. 'You'll get to meet the person responsible for all this very soon!' She swept her hand around the bedroom. 'Rexie is coming home later, a whole two days early. 'You and your husband must come for cocktails. I'll make some canapés and we can sit on the terrace and...'

Leah swallowed, spotting a pair of men's slippers neatly tucked beside the built-in wardrobes as Gillian went on excitedly. And on the opposite side of the bed to Gillian's, on the matching nightstand, she saw a book – *How to Get Your Own Way* – presumably being read by Rex.

'Sure, that... that'd be lovely, thank you.' So far, she'd managed to avoid talking about her ex and the fifteen sickening months between separating and divorcing. Anyway, explaining why there *was* no better half, that it was just her and the kids and the cat, would take more time than she had now. 'I'd better go. Henry's not very well,' she said, holding out her phone. 'Kids, eh?' She rolled her eyes.

'Let's swap numbers,' Gillian said. 'I'll text you about drinks.'

While Leah waited for her to enter her details in her phone, she spotted several miniature photos in little silver frames on the mantelpiece above the ornate fireplace on the opposite wall to the bed.

'Here you go,' Gillian said, handing it back.

Leah did the same in return on her phone and, as she turned to leave, she noticed that the grinning blond woman in the photos was Gillian. She couldn't quite make out the man's face as he was in shadow and turned away, but something niggled in her mind as she went down the stairs and said goodbye before heading back next door to take care of her son.

CHAPTER FIVE

'Hi, Mum,' Leah said, rushing through the salon door later that day. 'How are you?' She bent down to give her a kiss on the cheek. Rita Ward – in her early sixties, wiry and tall with long iridescent silver hair – gave her daughter a fond smile and wrapped a spindly arm around Leah's neck, the bell sleeve of her loose kimono revealing her sun and moon tattoo. As usual, Pixie, her little white terrier, was perched on her lap. There was no denying that, despite her unusual style, Rita had looked after herself and still turned heads.

'Thanks so much for helping me out on your day off, love,' she said, lifting a chunk of her thick, wayward hair and pouting through scarlet lipstick.

Even Leah admitted that styling and taming her mother's long locks was a challenge.

'You have no idea how grateful I am. Dad has sprung some official "do" on me tonight, and I need to look my best. Some army reunion he failed to mention.' She rolled her eyes and shook her head.

It still amazed Leah that she even existed – the unlikely product of an army officer and a leftover hippy who still believed it was the 1970s. It came as no surprise that she was an only child.

'Ooh, sounds like fun,' Leah said with a wink, knowing her mum would only be going out of loyalty to her father. Even though they were different in every way, they'd always been inseparable and were still as much in love now as they were when they'd first met aged sixteen at a village dance.

'Anyway, it's no problem at all,' Leah continued, grateful that her mum had phoned earlier. The kids were in grouchy moods, with Henry still feeling queasy from bingeing on too much ice cream. And Zoe was annoyed because she'd still not heard from her dad. She hoped that being in their grandad's company for an hour or two would perk them both up. 'I'll just set up my stuff,' Leah added, dashing over to her workstation.

A few minutes later, Rita was sitting in the shampooing area, head bent back over the basin while Leah gently massaged her head. She made soft purring noises, which, in turn, caused Pixie to gently whine as he rested his chin on Rita's legs. The salon had been busy all day, apparently, though things were winding down now. Sally and Charlotte, her two other stylists, plus Tom, the lad who helped on a Saturday, were having a well-earned cup of tea out the back before they closed for the weekend.

'How's the decorating going, love?' Rita asked, her eyes still closed. 'I wish you'd get someone in to do it for you. Isn't Margaret's grandson free to help? He's a good worker.'

'It's going slowly,' Leah replied. 'And I can't really afford even Jimmy's low rates at the moment. But guess what? I had a coffee with my new next-door neighbour earlier. The one I told you about, remember? She seems... well, she seems really nice.' She thought back to this morning, when she'd dashed home to Henry after he'd been sick.

'Oh, love, you look so pale,' she'd said, dropping to her knees beside the sofa and placing a hand on his forehead.

'Yuk, *Mum*, you've just *knelt* in it,' Zoey had said from the doorway, pinching her nostrils while making a retching sound.

Sure enough, Leah had felt something damp seep through her jeans, though she was more concerned about Henry than anything. He looked awful. 'What did you eat last?'

'She made me do it,' Henry had whined, clutching his stomach with one hand, while jabbing a finger at Zoey with the other.

'I did not!' Zoey shot back. 'I told you *not* to eat it all, stupid.'

As the kids bickered, Leah had felt her phone vibrate in the back pocket of her jeans.

Free tomorrow? How about a Blue Moon sundowner? G x

She'd smiled inwardly.

'Here's the evidence, Mum,' Zoey had said, reaching down behind the sofa and retrieving an empty ice cream tub. Henry had covered his mouth at the sight of it.

'Oh, Sprat,' Leah said, giving him a hug and trying not to laugh. 'I only bought it yesterday. You ate the whole thing?'

Henry had nodded, hanging his head. 'She dared me,' he'd whined again as Leah headed off to the kitchen to fetch the cleaning things. But she'd stopped, taken her phone from her pocket and read the text again.

He's nice, she'd thought. *Gabe. Thoughtful, calm and... and different.* She'd sensed as much on their first ever meet-up. She'd been about to text back that yes, she'd love to come for a drink on the boat tomorrow when another text flashed onto her screen.

Cocktails tomorrow at ours, 6 p.m.? Can't wait to meet your hubby. Gilly xx

'And what about that tree man you've been seeing?' Rita continued as Leah wrapped her hair up in a soft towel and led her back to the styling station, positioning her in front of the big mirror. 'Dave, isn't it?'

'Gabe,' she replied, glancing at her mum in the mirror, trying not to smile. 'He's asked me for a drink on his narrowboat tomorrow.'

'Is that wise, darling? I mean, you don't know him that well. He could push you overboard or take advantage of you.'

'Chill, Mum,' Leah said, squirting a dose of anti-frizz serum onto her hands before applying it to her hair. 'Gabe's fine.' *He might even be more than fine*, she thought but didn't say.

Despite her mother's concern, she knew she was keen for her to be paired off and settled down again – though in her eyes, nothing short of getting back with Craig would suffice. A reflection of her own relationship, she reckoned. It would take her dad committing murder for Rita to ever leave him, and even then, Leah was pretty sure she'd stand by him.

'I'm just looking out for you, darling, that's all. After everything you've left behind, all the things you've given up and sacrificed by leaving Craig, it's important to make sure he's the right one.' Rita looked at her daughter in the mirror, a pained expression on her face.

Leah closed her eyes for a second, refusing to rise to her mother's bait. 'Gabe and I are... just good friends for now, Mum. I'm not looking to get tied down again. A few outings here and there, a drink every now and again. That's all.' She'd learnt to be selective with what she told her mother and would never let on that every time her phone pinged with a message from Gabe, or he popped into her head in a random thought, her heart did a couple of cartwheels.

'Quite romantic, living on a boat,' Rita went on. 'Though it doesn't sound very settled or stable. Just put the layers back in, darling. I don't want anything off the length.'

Leah nodded, ignoring her comment about Gabe as she combed out her mum's hair. Even wet, it sprang into wayward silver coils that refused to be styled. *Just like Mum*, Leah thought. Stubborn and determined.

'All I'm saying is, don't give yourself too easily, OK? Men like the mystery and intrigue. That's the mistake you made with Craig, if you ask me.'

'Mum!' Leah said, seeing her own eyes widen as she glanced in the mirror. 'I think you'll find it was *Craig* who made the mistakes in our marriage. And he made them all by himself, regardless of anything I did.' She hadn't told her mother even close to the full extent of what she'd been through with her ex, but her words still cut deep.

'I know, I know, darling, that's not what I'm saying.' Rita adjusted Pixie on her lap, making the little dog shudder and growl as her many bracelets jangled on her wrists. 'But men are funny creatures, and don't always like a strong woman to—'

'Enough, Mum,' Leah said, holding up one hand in a stop sign while giving her a light tap on the shoulder with her scissors. 'It's not the 1950s. You and Dad have a special kind of weird in your relationship, and—'

'What about this new man's aspirations, darling?' she asked, wiping a drip of water from her neck. 'I mean, at the end of the day he's just a gardener.' Rita pulled a face in the mirror, making Leah realise just how similar they looked. At that moment, she wished they didn't.

'Mum, will you stop!' Leah sighed in exasperation. 'Gabe is a tree surgeon and landscaper, actually. And even if he was "just a gardener", that's more than fine by me.' She focused on snipping the layers on her mother's hair, unclipping several more strands to work on. She popped the clip between her lips to prevent herself saying something she'd regret.

'Do trees need doctors, then?' Rita replied, raising her plucked and redrawn eyebrows.

Then Leah did that thing she'd always done, even when she was a child – tune out of her mother's monologues.

'You just make sure that you're... and if he ever... not like this in my day... watch he doesn't...' She went on and on.

Leah had never been certain if it was anxiety or some long-held beliefs that made Rita lecture on various topics with authority – ironic, given that she was an expert in nothing. But she'd eventually decided it was deeply rooted in insecurity and designed to make herself somehow seem... *useful.*

From the moment she'd married her father, Rita had spent her days taking pottery classes or painting, learning yoga or going on meditation retreats, joining choirs and hillwalking groups. Her latest fad had been attending martial arts classes, and she'd been going to the dojo twice a week for the last year to study self-defence with 'my sensei', as she called the instructor.

As far back as she could remember, Leah had never known her mother to have a paid job (though she'd had stints volunteering over the years), and she'd never wanted a career, being quite content following her husband, Ronald, around the country when he was reposted regularly, trailing in his wake in a haze of sandalwood.

Admittedly, being the wife of a serviceman was hard and had made it almost impossible for her to forge a path of her own, especially with a child. But since her father had retired from the forces and they'd put down roots in their little semi in Alvington, it was as though her mother didn't quite fit... as though her soul wasn't the right shape for suburban life and was still searching and restless. In that respect, being an itinerant army wife had suited her well.

Leah reached for the hairdryer, flicking the switch and aiming the nozzle at her mother's hair. In the mirror, she saw Rita's mouth moving, the frown between her eyes deepening, but now at least she couldn't hear what she was saying. Leah simply nodded, adding an occasional smile here and there as she blow-dried Rita's hair, deciding she wouldn't be asking her mum's advice about inviting Gabe to be her plus one at Gillian's for drinks tomorrow night.

'Fortune favours the brave, darling,' she heard her mother say as she finally flicked off the hairdryer, pleased with the outcome. And, as Rita admired herself in the mirror, asking Pixie what he thought of her new style as she cuddled him close, Leah shuddered: it was another of Craig's expressions. Though also probably one of the more helpful things her mother had said lately.

CHAPTER SIX

Leah opened the front door with the security chain on, peeking out through the narrow gap, even though she knew exactly who it would be. Old habits died hard. Since the divorce, she was wary about who she let into her home. 'Hey,' she said warmly. 'Won't be a moment.' She closed the door again before Gabe had a chance to say anything.

'Right,' she said, opening the door fully with her handbag slung over her shoulder, ready to leave. 'Laurel and Hardy in there are under strict orders not to move a muscle for a couple of hours, let alone go anywhere near the freezer. And don't ask,' she added, holding up a hand when Gabe pulled a puzzled face. 'Henry fell out with a tub of cookie dough ice cream yesterday. I bluffed that I can hear every single thing he does through the walls, so he'd better behave.'

Gabe laughed and gave Leah a kiss – a lingering one on her lips. 'Good to see you,' he said. 'You look lovely.'

Leah stopped on the front step, staring up at him, noticing the appreciative look in his eyes – the same warm, kind look that had drawn her to him from the first moment they'd met.

'Looking pretty dapper yourself,' she replied, eyeing his

slim-fitting navy shirt, how his broad shoulders filled out the seams perfectly. 'And thank you again for agreeing to this.' She flapped a hand towards her neighbour's house. 'I hope you don't think it's too much of an imposition, asking you to come with me. To be honest, a drink on your boat watching the sunset would be far preferable, but I felt I should get off to a good start with the new neighbours. Gillian made such a thing about me coming with someone... and you were the obvious choice.'

She decided to leave out the bit where Gillian had mentioned coming with her husband, intending to drop into conversation later that she was divorced. She didn't want it to be awkward.

'Date number eight – making it official by finally attending a function as your boyfriend.' Gabe swept his long hair back off his face, grinning an endearing smile through his neat beard.

'Boyfriend?' Leah said, almost tripping as she went down the steps. She grabbed his arm and looked up at him. Something inside her did a little dance.

It suddenly felt as though she was someone else entirely, not living her own life. With her kids happy and content inside her cosy new home, a thoughtful, generous and kind man beside her, the horrors of court and her messy divorce fading from her mind daily – surely this kind of thing didn't happen to people like her?

'Partner? Significant other? I agree... boyfriend and girl-friend make us sound about fifteen.' Gabe laughed, opening the wonky gate of Leah's little front garden and letting her through first.

'Oh no... I didn't mean *that*. I meant... you want us to be... like... a couple?' Leah stopped in the street between the two houses, forcing her mother's words of warning from her mind. Even though it hadn't been in her life's plan just yet, she suddenly felt like dancing, spinning round in circles or leaping in the air. *Fortune favours the brave...*

Gabe waited a moment, rubbing his beard with an amused look on his face. He looked left then right, then back at Leah. 'I can't think of anyone else I'd—'

'Leah...' came a voice from the front garden next door. 'Hel-*lo!*'

Leah looked round and saw Gillian standing in her doorway, peering over the fence and shrubs which separated her much larger front garden from the road, and staring expectantly up the street towards town. 'Do come on in,' she said, beckoning them with her hand. 'I sent Rex out for some maraschino cherries half an hour ago, and he's *still* not back.' She made an exasperated sound.

'You'll be lucky to find those in Alvington,' Leah told her with a laugh. Somehow her hand had slipped into Gabe's – or his into hers – and she felt the little squeeze he gave her as they headed up the front path to her neighbour's house.

'This is Gabe,' Leah said once they were in the hallway. It had been surprisingly warm and sunny all day for early September, but the temperature dropped as soon they went inside the old Victorian manse.

'Ahh, the elusive husband! So very pleased to meet you, Gabe,' Gillian said, extending a hand.

'Oh, no, we're not—'

'Come on through to the terrace,' Gillian said, cutting Leah short. 'I've got everything set up outside. It's such a glorious evening, isn't it? A shame to waste the last of the warmth.' She wafted through her drawing room in a multicoloured maxi skirt with bright pink manicured toenails poking out from strappy white sandals.

Gabe gave Leah a nudge and a wink as they passed through the huge room with its grand furniture and plush rugs. 'From new couple to husband and wife in the space of two minutes,' he whispered as they followed on.

'Well, everything is set up – apart from the maraschino

cherries for the whisky sours, that is,' Gillian said, showing them the table adorned with long-stemmed glasses, tumblers, and half a dozen or so bottles of spirits and mixers plus a couple of cocktail shakers. There was also an ice bucket containing a bottle of champagne.

'I'm impressed, Gillian,' Leah said, noticing the spray of fresh flowers in a vase at one end of the table. Petals adorned the white cloth between the selection of canapés she'd put out. 'You've gone to so much trouble.'

'Nonsense, this really isn't any trouble at all. Just a neighbourly drink to get to know you both.' She grinned and took a bottle from the bucket. 'Bubbles while we wait for Rexie?' She glanced expectantly towards the open French doors again. 'He's probably stopped off at the pub for a quick pint and forgotten the time. Isn't there a game on?'

Leah noticed the nervous twitch under her left eye; the way she briefly frowned and touched her temple. It reminded her of how she'd waited up countless nights for Craig to come home, with him often sauntering in the next day, refusing to say where he'd been.

'Cricket, I think,' Gabe said. 'England versus Australia.'

'He may well be hunting around several shops,' Leah offered, not wanting Gillian to feel awkward. 'Maraschinos are counted as rare and exotic around here. If the shops are even still open, that is.'

Gillian peeled off the foil and unwound the wire on the champagne and, when she struggled to take out the cork, Gabe stepped in and gently twisted it out. It made a satisfying pop, and then Gillian poured three glasses.

'To new neighbours,' she said, raising her drink. Leah and Gabe reciprocated, each taking a couple of the dainty canapés that Gillian offered.

. . .

'Beautiful garden you have here,' Gabe said half an hour later when the general chit-chat barrel was almost empty. He was leaning on the stone balustrade that separated the large terrace from the lawn. 'Rexie' still wasn't back, while Gillian was growing ever more anxious. She'd texted and called him several times, but there'd been no reply.

'We have big plans for it,' Leah heard Gillian say as she excused herself for the bathroom. 'Oh, it's off the hallway, next to the front door,' Gillian called out to her as she went inside, though Leah already knew the way from previous visits to the house.

In the hall, Leah paused, her eyes lingering on a cluster of black and white photographs on the wall at the bottom of the stairs. In each of the prints was a much younger Gillian posing in what looked to be a professional studio. She was straddling a chair, sitting with her arms on the back as she pouted at the camera. In another couple she was sitting barefoot and cross-legged on the floor, her baggy cropped sweater showing off a few inches of her flat stomach above her jeans. And in the final one, she was leaning back against a white wall, her head tipped upwards, one knee bent as she stared wistfully at the ceiling, appearing to be deep in thought.

Leah went into the toilet. She couldn't ever imagine wanting to hang a collection of posed photographs of herself in her hallway for everyone to see, but then she'd never had the chance of a photo shoot either. She had a collection of the kids' school photo mugshots from over the years that were all still packed away in a box somewhere, not even framed, let alone hung on the wall.

It saddened her to think that Craig hadn't even made mention of photographs when he'd fought her tooth and nail, not only for the family finances in their divorce, but most of their furniture and belongings too. She knew for a fact that he'd immediately sold the items he'd been awarded and not kept a single thing, only wanting them so she couldn't have them. He'd taken delight in admitting it – off the record, of course. But he'd never once mentioned the school photos or the large collection of family snaps that Leah had taken and lovingly placed in albums over the years. It simply hadn't occurred to him to keep the memories – presumably because he couldn't sell them.

Leah was drying her hands when she heard the front door open, along with the sound of keys dropping onto the hall table. Rex back from the shops, she assumed. Taking a quick look in the mirror and fluffing up her hair, Leah opened the toilet door and stepped out into the hallway to finally meet her new neighbour.

A man was standing there, dressed in jeans and a white shirt, his back to her as he leant over the hall table flicking through a pile of mail.

'Hi,' Leah said, not instantly noticing that her heartbeat had quickened and her palms were sweating. 'I'm Leah, your neighbour.'

It was only when he turned round, almost as if in slow motion, that she realised why she was trembling and her cheeks were burning red.

'*Craig?*' she croaked, her voice barely working as she grabbed onto the door frame for support.

CHAPTER SEVEN

Craig stared at Leah, his all-too-familiar piercing look shooting chills through her.

'What are *you* doing here?' she asked, trying to stop herself from shaking. Her face contorted from one shocked expression to another.

'I was about to ask you exactly the same thing,' Craig replied, squaring back his shoulders and jutting forward his angular jaw. 'Why the hell are you in my house?'

His voice was deep and commanding, sending shockwaves through Leah. She felt as though she'd been transported back into the courtroom, the judge staring at her, her knees feeling as though they were about to buckle as she was grilled by Craig's barrister.

She tried to speak but couldn't. Instead, she glanced down at the polished hall table with the vase of lilies, noticing the discarded pile of mail next to a set of house keys – and a small glass jar of maraschino cherries.

Her mouth dropped open.

'You're *Rex*?' She stared up at him, shuddering as his eyes latched onto hers, the piercing pale grey of them triggering a thousand bad memories.

'If you've come here to harass me, Leah, forget it. I've moved on. And so should you. I suggest you get out and leave me and my partner alone. We've got company this evening and she's gone to a lot of trouble. I don't want you ruining it. If you've something to say, go through my solicitor.'

Each clipped sentence was a bullet fired. Leah visibly flinched, unable to help the slightly hysterical-sounding laugh that came out of her. She took a step back as Craig approached her.

'I *am* the company,' she spat. Her eyes flicked around the hall as she tried to make sense of the situation, tried to latch onto a reasonable explanation for him being there. But she couldn't think of one. 'You're Gillian's... *partner*? You *live* here?' She leant against the wall to steady herself. There was no way she'd accept that *Craig* was her new neighbour. In just a few seconds, her happy new life – everything she'd fought so hard for over the last couple of years – had the potential to be blown apart.

Leah turned away from him. She couldn't stand looking at him a moment longer. *Don't worry, this isn't real, it's not happening...* she screamed in her head as she went back through the house to the terrace. She even let out a little laugh, verging on hysteria. If she just kept on walking, rejoined Gabe and Gillian outside, had a drink to calm her nerves, then everything would be OK. When she turned round again, it wouldn't be Craig following her with a jar of cherries in his hand, it'd be Gillian's lovely husband. She'd be introduced and then she'd apologise to him for being a bit odd in the hall just now, blaming it on social anxiety or something. Then everything would be fine.

'Here, try one of these,' Gillian said as Leah drew up beside Gabe, taking hold of his arm. Gillian held out a plate of mini chicken skewers coated in a glistening layer of marinade. 'I made them myself. And drink this,' she added, holding out a cocktail. 'Oh, and please tell me my house isn't haunted! You look as though you've just seen a ghost.'

'We were just talking about gardens,' Gabe said, placing his hand on Leah's. 'I'm going to quote for cutting back the big sycamores at the end of...' He trailed off, staring down at her. 'Are you OK?' he asked her quietly. 'You have gone really pale.'

Leah knotted her fingers around the fabric of Gabe's sleeve as she stared down the garden, her expression blank. She didn't know what to do. What was it – fight, flight or freeze? She'd done all the fighting she had in her, and certainly didn't think her body was up to fleeing. So that just left freezing. It felt as though she was doing a pretty good job of that.

'Oh, there you are, Rexie,' she heard Gillian say behind her. When Leah looked over, she saw her slipping an arm around Craig as he came out onto the terrace. The two couples faced each other squarely, the table – heavy with its cocktails and canapés – forming a barrier between them.

'My hero for finding cherries,' Gillian trilled, seemingly unaware of the daggers shooting between her partner and Leah. She took the jar from his hand and popped it open. 'Who's for another cocktail with...' Her voice faded away as she stared first at Craig, then at Leah as she finally picked up on something. Craig's expression was one of pure hate, with a single muscle twitching repeatedly under one eye – a warning sign Leah had learnt not to ignore.

'Have you two done introductions already?' Gillian asked, followed by a little laugh. Her good nature told her to carry on regardless of the palpable tension. 'Darling, this is Leah and her husband, Gabe. He's a tree surg—'

'Leah and I have already met,' Craig said sourly. Then he glared at Gabe, his scowl deepening further.

Yes, eighteen long years ago, Leah thought wearily, wanting to thump him for even being here. How *dare* he show up in her life like this, just when she thought she was finally free? Was he even going to explain to Gillian that they'd been married, that they have two children together – two children who were in the house next door?

'And this is Leah's husband, you say,' Craig said, one eyebrow curling upwards as he glared at Gabe. 'I had no idea...' A look swept over his face that could have been amusement or anger, followed by another of his warning stares directed at Leah – the type he'd always used in public to let her know that she'd stepped out of line.

'We're not marr—' Leah's voice croaked as she attempted to explain, but she stopped herself. She knew reasoning with him was futile. All she wanted to do was get out, go home, lock the door and never come out again.

'Hello,' Gabe said with a nod, extending his hand. Leah wondered if he'd picked up on the tension – something in his expression told her that he felt uncomfortable too. 'You have a beautiful home,' Gabe continued regardless, lowering his hand when Craig ignored the gesture. 'I was just talking to Gillian about the sycamores, how I'd be happy to give you a quote for taking down those branches overhanging Leah's garden. My rates are very... reasonable.' Gabe cleared his throat drily.

'That won't be necessary,' Craig said. 'The trees are just fine as they are.'

'Gabe...' Leah whispered to him. 'I... I've got a migraine coming on. I think it's best if we call it a night.' She touched her temple in an attempt to convince him they needed to go. 'I... I need to lie down.' *In a dark room for the rest of my life.*

She heard Craig make a scoffing sound.

'Yes, yes of course,' Gabe said, his stare still fixed on Craig as he slipped an arm around her. Leah silently thanked him. She'd explain everything later – *somehow* – but for now the only thing she needed to do was get out.

'I'm so sorry, Gillian,' Leah managed to say as she turned to go, blocking Craig out of her line of sight with a hand tilted over her brow. It wasn't her fault, after all. 'I've not had a migraine in a long while but... but something has set me off.'

Craig made another scoffing sound.

'Oh no, poor you,' Gillian said, sounding genuinely disappointed. She swept back her hair and turned to Craig, giving him an expectant look as though he might have some magical cure up his sleeve. 'I have paracetamol, if that would help?' A last-ditch attempt to save the evening as she glanced back at the food- and drinks-laden table. She let out a little sigh.

'Thanks, but I really need to lie down. I really appreciate all the trouble you've gone to. I'm so sorry.'

'Nonsense,' Gillian replied, resigned to her guests leaving. 'Go and rest. We'll do this another time, won't we, Rexie? After all, we'll be neighbours for a long while.' And it was when Gillian let out a beaming grin, latching onto Craig's arm, that Leah thought she might throw up for real.

CHAPTER EIGHT

'I'm *so* sorry about all that,' Leah said once they were back next door. She flopped down onto the sofa and let out a sigh that felt as though it contained her entire life. Even though it was warm and balmy for early September, she felt chilled to the bone.

'I'm worried about you,' Gabe said, hands on hips as he stood over her. 'How can I help? I know your children are upstairs, so I can leave you to rest if you prefer.' His eyes flicked towards the living room door.

In the urgency of getting home, Leah had completely forgotten that Gabe hadn't even set foot in her house before now, let alone met her kids, who, by the sound of it, were in Henry's room playing on his PlayStation. They'd just about acknowledged her return with a brief call down, while Leah hadn't let go of Gabe's arm until she was well and truly shut inside her living room.

'They'll be engrossed upstairs for a while,' Leah said, leaning forward on her knees and dropping her head into her hands. 'I'll just say you're a friend, if they ask. It's fine.'

Gabe sat down beside Leah, frowning. He stared at her for a moment. 'Something tells me that a migraine wasn't the real reason that sent you running from next door like a kitten on hot coals.' He placed a hand on her leg, giving it a gentle rub. 'Want to talk about it?'

Leah looked up at him. 'That obvious, was it?' She fell back against the sofa cushions.

'Just a bit. I felt quite sorry for Gillian, actually.'

Leah nodded. 'Me too. She'd gone to a lot of trouble.' She tipped her head back, looked at the ceiling and groaned loudly, covering her face. 'Oh Go-*oddd*...'

'Leah, I can't help with your "migraine" if you don't give me a bit of a clue.' Gabe had a soothing look in his eyes, but also a concerned one. 'Did something happen to upset you?' He trailed off, pensive for a moment. 'Was it Rex? Did he say something in the hallway?'

Leah sat upright again. She had to get it out. 'For a start, his name isn't Rex. It's Craig. Craig Forbes. God only knows where Rex has come from. Some nickname Gillian calls him, I presume.'

'OK-aay,' Gabe said, listening intently.

'Craig is my... he's... Well, he's...' She felt tears of frustration collecting in her eyes, praying that they wouldn't spill over. She didn't want to cry in front of Gabe.

'Leah...?'

She placed her hand on top of Gabe's in what felt like a vague attempt to hold onto him, because once the truth was out, she anticipated he'd run a mile. She screwed up her eyes.

'Craig is my ex-husband.'

There, it was out. The words said. No going back.

After a few moments' silence, she heard a sigh. Only a quiet one, but there nonetheless.

She opened her eyes.

'Oh God,' he said. 'I never saw *any* of this coming.' Gabe shook his head, frowning and thinking for a moment. There was a sad look in his eyes, as if whatever he'd imagined between them going forward had just been knocked out of him. 'What a shock.' He leant over and gave her a squeeze. 'Why didn't you say anything while we were there? Why didn't *Craig* say anything?'

'You don't know Craig,' Leah said, trying to remember that Gabe knew nothing about her past. Craig keeping quiet about the situation was so very typical of him – wielding a silent power over her.

'So... let me get this straight,' Gabe said. 'You didn't know Craig was your new neighbour until tonight? And Gillian didn't know about it either?'

Leah almost heard Gabe's mind whirring as he worked out what this meant for them – the potential consequences of having her ex living next door. Or at least what it would mean once he learnt the gory details of their marriage, separation and divorce. She doubted Gabe was the jealous or possessive type, but finding out that his new partner lived next door to her abusive ex-husband would test even a saint's mettle. She'd not had a chance to figure out the full implications herself yet, how it had even happened, though a voice inside her head screamed at her to put the house on the market first thing in the morning. She was terrified by the prospect of Craig living so close by.

'I literally had no idea,' Leah replied, burying her head in her hands again. Her mind raced, trying to work out what she should do – how she could even exist from one minute to the next knowing *he* was only a few feet away, just the other side of the wall. She shuddered. Her safe space didn't feel at all safe any more.

'There's no way it'll sell for a decent price in this state...' she mumbled, her thoughts racing ahead and all over the place as she flung her head back against the cushions again. 'I'll have to finish the renovations fast... and then there's the garden.' When she looked down at her hands, they were shaking – as was her voice when she spoke. 'But it'll all take ages.' She let out a frustrated sob.

'Whoa, whoa... slow down,' Gabe said. 'You need something to calm your nerves.' She was aware of him leaving the room then returning a few minutes later with an inch of something in a glass that looked a lot like whisky.

'Drink this,' he said, sitting back down beside her and stroking her hair. 'You're in shock.'

Leah stared at her drink, then at Gabe. She couldn't deny that he looked shocked too – more than she'd anticipated. This didn't bode well for them. 'Thanks,' she said. 'I didn't even know I had any whisky.'

'Your daughter found it, actually. She was in the kitchen and dug it out of an unpacked box in your utility room.'

'Zoey?' she said, managing a laugh, not knowing whether it was worse that her daughter knew where a bottle of alcohol was packed away, or that Gabe had now met her by accident.

'I told her I was a friend and that I'd brought you home because you weren't feeling well. She seems really nice, by the way. The gentle, sensitive type.'

Leah's first reaction was to laugh – she didn't think anyone had described her hot-headed, feisty daughter that way before. But if she was honest, she knew that it was true. Zoey *was* gentle and sensitive, taking things to heart far more than she let on. *Like me*, she thought, despairing again.

'She's a good kid,' Leah said, knowing that the children were the only decent things she and Craig had ever achieved together.

'Now, look. My advice is to try to switch off for tonight. You've had a shock and the evening didn't go as planned. See how you feel tomorrow.'

Leah groaned. 'I wish I'd come over to your boat like you'd suggested in the first place. Then none of this would have happened.'

'Well, it would have – just not tonight. And coming over to mine, that's something to look forward to another...' He trailed off, making a pained face. 'Look, just try to distract yourself. I mean, maybe it won't be as bad as you think? You'll have babysitting on tap, for one thing. And it'll be easy for the kids to see their dad.'

Leah knew he was trying to help, but she let out another groan anyway.

'You don't know Craig. He's failed to turn up for his contact time with the kids lately. He hasn't replied to Zoey about coming to watch her swim. He never pays child maintenance on time and what he does give me is way less than it should be. The divorce was a shitshow from start to finish because he contested every single reasonable suggestion about a financial settlement or child contact my solicitor put to him, and he delayed every one of our court hearings because...' Leah stopped to catch her breath, '...because, can you believe, he was on bloody holiday with his new woman. *Three times.* He blatantly lied to the judge about everything. I tell you, that man was not going to be happy until he saw me in the gutter. *And now he lives next door...*' She let out another wail. She'd never revealed any of this stuff to Gabe before. There'd been no point. It was all in her past and she'd wanted to leave it there. Life at the Wash House was meant to be a new start, but it was suddenly feeling quite the opposite.

Gabe stared out of the window, silent for a moment. He cleared his throat.

'I'm *really* sorry to hear all that, Leah,' he said, turning back to her. He brushed his fingers against her cheek. 'I had no idea how things had been.'

For some reason, Leah thought he almost had a guilty look about him, as though he could have somehow prevented it.

'No, no *I'm* sorry. I shouldn't be spewing all this stuff out to you.'

If you scare him off, it's another win for Craig... a voice inside her warned.

'Look, I should go now,' Gabe said, turning away. 'Give you some time to take it all in. Try to eat and get an early night.' He stood up, fishing his keys from his jeans pocket. 'I'll call you in the morning to see how you are.'

'Sure, OK,' Leah replied, looking up at him. Was it too late? Had her outburst already turned him off her? Part of her wanted to launch herself at him, beg him not to go, have him spend the night with her even if they just lay in each other's arms all night long. But of course, that was impossible with the kids home – not to mention the thought of Craig being nearby. She shuddered and felt a wave of nausea again. As long as *he* was next door, she didn't think she'd ever be able to relax in her own home again.

'I'm so sorry tonight was ruined,' she said, wiping a finger under her eye. She reached up and squeezed Gabe's fingers before he pulled away and left.

CHAPTER NINE

Leah jolted awake. A noise. She was a light sleeper at the best of times, stirring at even the slightest sound – a relic from married life with Craig. If he believed she'd wronged him in some way, and when he deemed the silent treatment not enough punishment, he'd take to waking her in the night, making his move when she'd just nodded off by prodding her or making a loud noise, or pacing about the bedroom. A process he'd have no problem repeating all night long and, somehow, he'd still appear refreshed and breezy the next day, while Leah would barely be able to keep her eyes open as she looked after the children.

She held her breath in her pitch-dark bedroom, aware of the deep thrum inside her skull. After Gabe had left and she'd spent some time with the kids in front of the TV – trying not to appear too agitated – she'd hunted down the rest of the whisky when they'd gone to bed, pouring a couple more shots for herself. She rarely drank alone but had figured that under the circumstances, she needed something to take the edge off life.

There. A noise again. A bang. She fumbled around on her bedside table for her phone, pressing the home button to light up the screen. One thirty-four a.m. She'd only been asleep an hour and a half. Well – lying in bed for an hour and a half. Despite the drinks, sleep hadn't come easily.

Bang, bang, bang...

She sat up, trying to pinpoint the sound exactly. Was it coming from downstairs? Someone at the back door? She remembered going round checking all the locks, as well as making sure the windows were closed. With it just being her and the kids here, she was always extra security conscious, but even more so after tonight's shock. God knows what Craig was capable of now he knew they were neighbours.

Neighbours... She let out a stifled sob.

Leah suddenly startled, leaping out of bed as she heard the loudest series of bangs yet. She grabbed her dressing gown from the hook on the back of the door and threw it on, creeping over to the wall that adjoined Gillian's bedroom. Gillian and *Craig's* bedroom. There was no doubt in her mind now – that was where the sound was coming from.

'Dear God, don't let it be what I think it is,' she whispered, listening out as she put her ear against the wall. Everything was silent for a moment but then there was no mistaking the loud moans followed by more banging – the sound of something heavy knocking against the wall. Furniture, perhaps. The headboard of a bed.

Leah stepped away, feeling sickened as she heard more noises coming from next door – a man groaning. She covered her ears and headed for her bedroom door, knowing she wouldn't sleep with that going on. Checking in on the kids, who were both fast asleep, she went to the kitchen and grabbed the milk carton from the fridge, sloshing some into a mug and putting it in the microwave.

As it was heating up, she leant on the worktop, staring out of the kitchen window into her little courtyard garden. She imagined herself sitting outside in the autumn sun at the weekend with a cup of coffee as she scrolled the news on her phone –

something she enjoyed doing. Or watering her pots of herbs, jasmine and other plants she'd collected over the last couple of months. She also imagined Gabe coming round for a barbecue in the summer, perhaps meeting the kids, her parents, her friends – then the two of them sitting outside with a glass of wine once they were alone, sharing a kiss under the moonlight as the evening drew to a close.

But none of that seemed possible any more – not now she knew Craig would be watching her every move from an upstairs window next door. Looking down on her.

'It's OK, it's OK,' she tried to convince herself as the microwave pinged. She added a chai teabag to the mug and a dollop of honey, stirring it in before sitting down at the kitchen table and sipping the drink in the hope it might make her sleepy. Though she doubted anything less than half a packet of diazepam would achieve that right now.

'*Please* tell me I'm going to wake up in the morning and this will all have been a bad dream.'

She laughed bitterly, cupping her hands round her mug. Her ex-husband lived next door. Then it struck her: did he *know* she'd moved here before he bought the Old Vicarage? Had he done it on purpose? She'd not noticed him or Gillian viewing the property before Josh and Carrie had left, but then it had all happened so quickly and she'd not even seen a 'For Sale' board go up. Was Craig moving next door all part of a plan to continue making her life a misery, to control her, even though the divorce was over? It only took her a second to realise the answer to this.

'Of *course* it was planned. He *must* have done it on purpose,' she said, forcing herself to remain calm as she sipped her hot drink. He was mad as hell that the judge had been fair in his final decision, awarding Leah a settlement that allowed her to house herself and her children along with ongoing child maintenance payments. Impinging on her new life, positioning himself in plain sight – it was the ultimate sting in the tail, the best revenge. It was Craig wielding his power to show her he was still in control.

From now on, she was going to need every scrap of energy and resolve to get through this. If she only knew what getting through it would entail.

————

'You look like death, me duck,' was the first comment Leah received from her client at exactly 9 a.m. the next morning. Followed by 'Heavy night?' and 'Not been sleeping well, love?' and from her latest client, 'When did you last have a holiday, Leah?'

At 11.15 a.m., after drifting through her customers in a daze, Leah took a ten-minute break – the first chance she'd had to call Jodi, her best friend, since finding out about Craig. Over the last few years, she'd confided in her friend about the way Craig had treated her, some of the things he'd done – though no one knew the full extent of how things had been. Leah had been too ashamed to reveal everything. But if anyone knew what to do, it'd be Jodi.

'You'll never guess,' Leah said as soon as Jodi answered.

'You're pregnant?' Jodi quipped back. Her toddler made a shrieking noise in the background.

'Way worse,' Leah said flatly.

'The salon's gone bust? You're ill? Gabe's finished things with you? Or maybe he proposed? You won the lottery? Aliens abducted you in the night?'

'I wish they had,' Leah said. 'And no to all of those.' She sat in the tiny staff room at the back of Waves, sipping on a strong black coffee.

'Are you actually going to tell me?'

Silence as Leah built herself up to saying the words, just in case she'd imagined everything. But she knew she hadn't – there was an empty glass in the sink this morning and it smelt of whisky, and the half-finished bottle was in the pantry cupboard. Evidence of her distress.

'Craig is my new neighbour. He's moved in next door.'

They say a problem shared is a problem halved, but to Leah, it now felt like twice the size because it was occupying two people's brains.

'Sorry, say that again,' Jodi replied. 'Charlie emptied his tub of bricks just as you spoke.'

'I said, Craig is my new neighbour, Jode. His new partner is Gillian, the woman I told you about. Him, his stuff, his evil ways... it's all slap-bang next door to me as if I never even got away.' Leah felt her voice waver. 'I'm breathing the same *air* as him, for Christ's sake. I mean why... *why* did this have to happen?'

'Bloody hell,' Jodi, who was never stuck for words, said. 'Did he know you lived there? Has he done it on purpose?'

'It's Craig. Of *course* he's done it on purpose. But I don't see how he could have known where I'd moved to. I used Mum and Dad's address for court service and all the legal stuff, and he always picks the kids up from there too. Not that he bothers to turn up very often. I never gave him my new address.'

'I think that's your answer, then,' Jodi replied.

'Answer?'

'The kids. He'll have got it out of them somehow. Even if they didn't give him your address, he probably worked it out from things they've said. A few sly, probing questions from him and he'd have it figured out.'

'You think?' Leah said, pondering the possibility. 'I gently explained to them that where they live with me is private, that I'd prefer it if they didn't tell their dad. But I guess I was deluding myself, expecting them to take on that burden.'

'Yup,' Jodi replied. 'It was a bit naive of you to think he

wouldn't find out. Plus, he's an estate agent, Lee. He probably knows every property that's been on the market in the last ten years within a fifty-mile radius. And don't forget, he knows *you* inside out. Even if the kids just mentioned one or two things over the last couple of months, he'd have filed their comments away and eventually put two and two together. Or maybe he followed you or hired a private detective. It's the sort of thing he'd do.'

'But *why?*' Leah asked, already knowing the answer to that question. 'Why would he want to live next door to me any more than I want him there? And why hasn't he told the kids about it? So far, they seem oblivious.'

'Perhaps that's why he did it,' Jodi suggested. 'To make it easier to see them?'

'That's how he'll spin it,' Leah said, knowing the reality was way more sinister. 'I know he loves them, but he's had less and less time for them lately. It's heartbreaking. Nope. Craig moving in next door must either be a total coincidence, or he's done it to get at me. And my vote is firmly on the latter.'

CHAPTER TEN

At lunchtime, Leah headed out to grab a sandwich and clear her head. Not that she felt like eating, but she'd got half an hour until her next client arrived and needed something inside her. She was feeling light-headed. On a whim, she walked further into town, along the street lined with professional offices – a street she'd come to know well during her divorce.

She shuddered as she walked past several estate agents' windows on the way, reminded of Craig and his business premises in Birmingham – their nearest city and where he'd concealed several affairs with employees. But then she lurched to a stop as a previously empty unit caught her eye. Her hand came up slowly over her mouth as she recognised the familiar black and yellow branding on the properties displayed in the window, the familiar decor beyond the window inside. *Surely not...*

She scanned the details of several dozen properties and photographs lined up behind the glass, seeing her own stunned reflection on top of them. As if she needed confirmation of what she'd just read, her eyes were drawn to the sign above the window.

FORBES & CO. – RUN BY OUR FAMILY FOR YOUR FAMILY

'You've got to be kidding me,' she whispered from behind her hand, her eyes focusing through the glass into the office again. She saw three desks set at angles to each other with two of them occupied by attractive blond women in their twenties, each dressed in the signature uniform Craig insisted his staff wear. 'He's opened a new branch... in *my* town.' A feeling of dread surged through her – fingers tightening around her throat.

She'd figured she'd be safe from any random encounters with him by staying in Alvington, the town where her parents lived – but how wrong could she have been? Not only had he moved in next door to her, he'd set up a new office just a couple of streets away from her hair salon.

Leah turned and strode down the street with a new destination in mind. She had just enough time before her next client. None of this was coincidence, she told herself as she climbed the creaky old stairs that led from the street up to her solicitor's office.

'Hello,' she said to the receptionist, who sat in the small waiting area behind what looked like an old school desk. 'Is Liz Morgan available? I'd just like a quick word. It's... well, it's quite urgent.' Leah shifted from one foot to the other.

'Oh, hi Mrs Forbes,' the girl said, remembering her. 'I'll just check her schedule, one second.'

It's Miss Ward now, Leah wanted to yell, but decided against it. Instead, she took a couple of breaths to calm herself.

'You're in luck,' the receptionist said, picking up the phone and pressing a couple of buttons. 'She's got a few minutes before she heads out— Oh hi, sorry to bother you, Liz, but I've got Mrs Forbes in reception, and she'd like a quick word.'

A moment later, Leah was making her way down the dingy corridor to an office at the back of the building she was all too familiar with. A sick feeling swelled in the pit of her stomach as she remembered lugging a small suitcase along the same corridor before the court hearings, stuffed full of papers and other evidence that would form the many files of her court bundle. A bundle that set out to prove that pretty much everything her ex-husband had claimed in his forms was a lie.

From the moment Craig had received the initial divorce petition – with Liz advising a toned-down list of unreasonable behaviours rather than adultery so as not to antagonise him – he'd instructed the most expensive law firm in the Midlands to represent him. He'd subsequently been obstructive and difficult during every step of the process, leaving Leah drained and broke.

'Leah, hello,' Liz said, coming round from behind her desk and holding out her hand. She tripped on a stack of files that Leah seemed to remember being there when she was last in the office. 'How are you doing?' She pulled out a chair for Leah to sit down.

'Well, I was fine until last night,' Leah replied with a blank expression, sitting down heavily. Liz perched on the corner of her desk, which had an old monitor on it, dwarfed by more stacks of papers and files piled around it. There was a half-finished mug of coffee among the papers. Liz's office was small, with much of the space taken up by a bank of grey metal filing cabinets, no doubt stuffed with files containing the stories of other failed marriages and child residency battles.

Apart from a legal assistant, who Leah had never actually met, and her receptionist, Liz was a one-woman outfit and only dealt with conveyancing and family law cases. Despite her rather shabby surroundings, she was an elegant and well-groomed woman with delicate yet determined features framed by a mass of red hair, and a body that reeked of a six-times-a-week gym habit, as if physical perfection would make up for her less than salubrious office. But Leah hadn't cared about any of that when she'd hired her. She had the cheapest rates in the area and was all Leah could afford.

'Go on,' Liz said, frowning and wide-eyed as she pushed her large-framed black glasses on top of her head. 'What's happened?'

'Craig has bought the house next door to me. He's my neighbour. My ex is literally living a few feet away from me, and we're separated only by a brick wall. It may as well be made of paper.' Leah couldn't help the hiccup-like sob as her voice wavered.

Liz pulled a face, raising her eyebrows high on her forehead as she blew out a disbelieving sigh. She slid off the desk and lowered herself into her swivel chair, leaning forward on her forearms.

'Now there's a curveball I didn't see coming.' She picked up a pen from her desk, fiddling with it nervously. 'Tell me you're not serious,' she said, deadpan, tucking a strand of fiery hair behind her ears.

Leah gave a little nod. She looked away then looked back again. 'Sadly, I'm very serious.'

'The *nerve* of the man,' Liz said, making a concerned face. Leah knew that she'd got the full measure of Craig over the time she'd represented Leah, seeming to know his character well. 'I'm so sorry to hear this. After everything, you deserve some peace. The man has no shame.'

'Can he do this? Is it allowed? Surely there's some law against it. It must be stalking or harassment or invasion of privacy or... or *something*?' Leah heard her voice getting higher and higher, almost begging Liz to come up with something that would force Craig to move away.

'There weren't any particular orders made by the court, were there?' Liz moved her mouse, clicking and cursing as she waited for her computer to catch up. When the documents finally loaded, she speed-read to remind herself of the case, her eyes flicking over the text. They both knew it was a rhetorical question; while Leah had chosen not to have dealings with Craig during handover of the children, there was no order – non-molestation or otherwise – made by the judge stating that Craig must keep a certain distance away from Leah or not contact her. Liz paused for a second, frowning, raising her eyebrows at something – but then looked up. Again, that concerned look on her face.

'No, it appears there weren't,' she said eventually, answering her own question. 'And he didn't know you lived there before he moved in?' She tapped the pen against her lip.

'I have no idea,' Leah replied, explaining how she'd met Gillian first, how she seemed pleasant and had invited her round for coffee, then for drinks last night, and that's when the bombshell had dropped. 'Is there anything you can do to make him leave?'

Liz sighed, sitting back in her chair. She steepled her fingers under her chin. 'Could you perhaps try to put a positive spin on it? It'll be great for your kids, for a start. And if an estate agent has bought property in your street, then you know it's a solid area, likely a good investment.'

Leah scoffed. 'I admire your optimism,' she said. 'As far as I'm concerned, property values have just *plummeted* in my street. But I'll be putting the house back on the market as soon as possible. There's no way I can live next door to him.'

'I'd not be too hasty, Leah. Especially as you'll have penalties on your mortgage to consider, and all the extra fees of moving. Can you really afford to do that?'

'I can port the mortgage, buy somewhere else entirely. I'll go to the coast, the wilds of Scotland. Maybe I'll go to Europe, perhaps set up a salon in the South of France.'

Liz curled her lips inwards in a sort of pitying smile, her head tilted to one side. 'As I said, I don't think rash decisions are going to help right now. Besides, if you were to take the children too far away from here, you'd need Craig's permission.'

'What?' Leah spat, wondering whose side Liz was on. 'Don't be ridiculous.'

'You have a shared custody arrangement, and while Craig sees the children on his set weekends and during the week, knowing him as I do, then I'd say there's every chance he'd object to you moving too far away. He can get a "prohibited steps order" through court.'

'Surely he can't do that. He rarely even bothers to collect them. He's hardly going for father-of-the-year award.' Leah balled her fists.

'There's no saying he'd actually do anything, no, but let's be real, Leah – and I'm speaking from experience here – this is Craig we're dealing with.' Liz peered over the rim of her glasses. 'But he does have rights and options with the courts. Imagine how it would feel if it were the other way around.'

But Leah couldn't. She knew Craig would never take the children away from her full time, even though he knew it would virtually kill her. Having to care for them twenty-four seven would interfere with his lifestyle too much – school runs, packed lunches, washing, homework, sleepovers, various activities to ferry them to and from. Let alone having to spend one-on-one time with them. No, Craig had opted for the second-best way to ruin her life: by moving in next door.

'Leah?' she heard Liz say. Then she felt the warmth of a hand on hers as her solicitor reached out, passing her a box of tissues.

'Oh... thanks,' Leah said, taking one. She dabbed her cheeks.

'Look, my advice is to hold fire and do nothing right now. Fortune favours the brave, as they say. See how it pans out. If it's any consolation, my partner and I have lived in our house for nearly ten years and we've never said more than a passing hello to our neighbours. You don't have to interact with him. Just get on with your life as normal and pretend he's not there. Give it three months or so, and see how you feel about moving then, OK?'

Leah stared at her. Three months. It might as well be three decades. But she knew Liz was right. If there was nothing legal that could make Craig move, then why should she be forced out of what she'd believed was her dream home? She'd get some earplugs for night-time and grow some tall plants up against the brick wall separating their rear gardens. Hell, she might even get some trellis too. Ignoring him shouldn't be that hard, should it? After all, until she'd found the strength and courage to finally leave him, she'd been forced to turn a blind eye to his behaviour for years. She was well practised.

'Look, here are the contact details of a counsellor who's experienced in this area. I recommend her to some of my clients. It might help. You've been through a lot.'

Leah watched as Liz jotted down a number on a Post-it note, copying it from her computer screen. But it wasn't Liz thinking that she needed therapy that bothered her – no, it was something else that rattled her. Like the flame of a candle flickering in a draught.

'OK, thanks for the advice,' Leah replied, taking the piece of paper and standing up, knowing there wasn't much more to say. All she knew for certain was that Craig would not win whatever battle he was hoping to fight. It was as she turned to go that her eyes were drawn to Liz's black and yellow pen again, the familiar company logo on it causing her to trip over a stack of files piled up on the floor as she left.

CHAPTER ELEVEN

'Mummy, Mummy, look what Daddy gave me!' Henry came skidding into the hallway in his socks, holding out a box. 'It's Lego, my favourite!'

Leah clattered her keys and bag down on the little hall table, shaking her wet umbrella out of the door behind her. She left it propped on the doormat, realising that her mouth was hanging open as she slipped off her jacket.

'Oh...' she heard herself say, unnerved by hearing the word 'Daddy' as soon as she walked in the door.

'Hello, darling,' her mother said, appearing in the living room doorway. 'Good day at the salon?' The yellow rubber gloves Rita wore somehow complemented her brightly coloured ankle-length dress, cinched in at her small waist with a scarlet belt.

'Hi, Mum,' Leah said, her eyes fixed on the box her son was excitedly holding out. 'That's lovely, darling,' she managed, giving his hair a ruffle. 'But... but haven't you already got that set?' As if Craig would know what toys his children had, she thought. He'd struggle to remember the names of their schools.

'This is the new spaceship one. I've wanted it, like, for*ever*.

My other one is ancient and has bits missing. I'm going to put it together now.'

'It's dinner time soon,' Leah heard herself saying. 'Why don't you save it until the weekend?'

'No!' Henry said. 'I want to do it *now*.' He pulled a face and ran up the stairs with the box of Lego, leaving Leah standing face to face with her mother.

'A word,' the older woman said, beckoning Leah through into the living room. She saw that her mother had put a vase of flowers on the coffee table and plumped up all the cushions, as well as tidying up the general mess that had accumulated over the weekend. And there was a comforting smell coming from the kitchen – one of her chicken casseroles.

Her mum snapped off the rubber gloves and stood there, hands on hips. 'So when were you going to tell me?'

'Tell you what?' Leah wasn't sure if the look on her mother's face was concern or relief.

'Him. Next door.'

Leah let out a sigh. 'So it *is* real then,' she said, flopping down onto a chair. 'Thought I'd had a bad dream.'

'Oh darling,' her mum said, sitting down beside her.

'Don't,' Leah said, holding up a hand to prevent the engulfing hug she knew was about to follow. 'I don't need sympathy, I just need a way to get rid of him.'

'New patio?' her mother said with a wry smile, flashing her straight white teeth that Leah knew had cost a small fortune.

'Don't tempt me.'

'Joking, obvs,' Rita sang.

'Don't say "obvs", Mum.'

'Well, you can blame Zo-zo for that.' Leah's mum squeezed her leg. 'It's what all the kids say, apparently. Or should I say, *appaz*.'

'Blame me for what?' Zoey said, bounding down the narrow

staircase and into the living room. 'What's for dinner? I'm starving.'

'Go and get a snack, love,' Leah said, not wanting her daughter to overhear their conversation. 'So have you seen him?' she continued once Zoey was out of earshot.

'What do you mean *seen*?' her mum replied, almost defensively. She grabbed a cushion and clutched it to her body.

'As in, seen him sniffing around my house. In the garden or... well, wherever.' Leah shuddered. 'God, I can't believe I'm even asking that question.'

When she'd arrived home, she'd parked her car on the street and hurried up her front path, keeping her head down and making a point of not looking over at next door. She wasn't sure how many cars were on the Old Vicarage's large driveway, but she thought she'd seen at least one from the corner of her eye. She didn't want to live her life like this – avoiding everything about next door, hiding herself away, pretending the place didn't exist. She wanted to wave and smile at her neighbours, stop and chat over the fence, take round mince pies at Christmas and have them over for barbecues in the summer.

'*Goddammit!*' she whimpered, thumping the arm of the sofa. 'Why the hell did this have to happen?'

One–nil to Craig. No, a *thousand*–nil to him.

'Try to look on the bright side, darling,' Rita said. 'It'll be lovely for the kids, won't it?'

'Why does everyone keep saying that?' Leah snapped. 'The person I detest most in the world now lives a mere few feet from me. I even heard him having sex last night. It was disgusting.'

'You did?' Rita's eyes widened as she slowly lowered the cushion, allowing it to drop to the floor. 'Now that *is* ghastly,' she said, standing up and slowly walking to the hallway to get her coat.

. . .

'Would you take this out to the dustbin for me, love,' Leah said to Zoey once they'd eaten the casserole her mum had made. It had hit the spot and Leah was grateful for it, as well as for her mum picking up the kids from school earlier. Rita had headed off in a pensive mood before they'd eaten – her quiet goodbye reflecting the reality of having Craig living next door once she'd assimilated the implications. Her parents had been instrumental in her escape from an unhappy marriage – though her mother had tried everything to convince her to work things out – but she knew all they wanted was for her and the kids to be settled and content.

'Yuck, it stinks,' Zoey replied as her mum squashed the chicken bones into the overflowing bin bag.

'Which is exactly why it needs taking out. It's the big black plastic thing in the courtyard, in case you didn't know.' Leah gave her daughter a friendly poke and handed her the tied-up bag.

'Ha ha, very funny,' Zoey replied, sloping off while Leah began washing up.

'This is awesome,' Henry said, going back to his Lego model spread out on the table after he'd cleared his plate.

Leah glanced over. 'Did... did your dad drop it off at school for you?' She'd not even dared ask yet, and it wouldn't be the first time he'd left gifts for them at the school reception to make up for not seeing them.

'No, he came here,' Henry replied, licking his lips as he assembled the intricate parts of the spaceship.

'Here?' Leah closed her eyes briefly, not meaning to sound so snappy. 'Did he come inside?'

'Just in the hallway,' Henry replied. 'Nana asked him in.'

'I see,' Leah said, steadying herself against the sink. Her mother had been trying to protect her feelings by not mentioning it. She had to hold herself together for Henry's sake, even though she wanted to scream and shout and rage and storm next door to yell at her ex.

The back door opened. 'Can't find the dustbin,' Zoey said, still holding the rubbish bag.

Leah sighed. 'I'm sure I brought it in from the street the other day,' she said, going outside into the little courtyard. She stared at the partitioned-off bin storage area near the small lean-to brick outbuilding where she kept her gardening tools. Zoey was right. There was no dustbin. Confused, she went back inside and through the house to the front window to check the street, in case she'd forgotten to bring it in after all.

'Odd,' she said, not seeing it there either. She slipped on her shoes and ventured outside to check further up and down the street. And that's what it felt like – venturing. As though she was being watched from next door, laughed at by her ex as she stood there, puzzled.

There were no dustbins in the street at all.

'Well, that's a mystery,' Leah muttered to herself, going back inside and getting on with the washing-up.

'Why didn't you tell me Daddy lives next door now, Mummy,' Henry suddenly blurted out. 'Are we all going to live together again, like we used to? Is that why he's sharing our dustbin?'

Leah froze, her hand shoved in the dishwasher tablet box.

'What do you mean, sharing the dustbin?' She turned, watching as her son was engrossed in his Lego. 'And no, we're not living together again, love. I... I didn't know Daddy was going to move next door to us.'

'After he gave me the Lego, I saw him take our bin into his garden. It was on the pavement.'

'Right... OK, thanks, love,' Leah said, trying to hide her frown. She went out the back again, dragging a garden chair over to the wall that separated her courtyard from the big garden next door. Cautiously, she stepped up onto it and slowly raised her eyes above the slate coping stones. Beyond was the expanse of Gillian's lawn – Gillian and *Craig's* lawn – and the terrace where the short-lived cocktails had been set out. No one was out there, thankfully, though Leah saw lights on in the kitchen through the slatted blinds. It was twilight – but still light enough for her to spot the dustbin store right below her wall. She'd caught the odd whiff of next door's bins in the warmer months when she'd first moved in, but hadn't complained to the previous neighbours as they'd all got on so well. To know now that it would be her ex's rubbish she was smelling made it even more noxious.

'The *bastard*,' she whispered, noticing the familiar white paint splat on the lid of her black bin. While she didn't have her house name or number marked on it, she always knew which bin was hers because of the spilt paint.

Leah jumped down off the chair and marched back inside. 'Watch Henry for a moment,' she called up the stairs to Zoey as she went out of the front door, onto the street and then up the path of the Old Vicarage. She rang the doorbell several times, hearing the old-fashioned bell chime inside the large hallway. Nothing, so she knocked hard with her fist, ringing the bell several more times. Eventually, she heard footsteps and the door opened.

'Hello, Leah,' Craig said flatly, looking down at her. He had a glass of red wine in one hand, and he was wearing tartan slippers. Something he *never* wore when he was with her. She'd never known him to relax once, ever. His expression was blank, save for the glimmer of a smirk.

Leah gripped her hands behind her back, willing herself not to thump him. 'You have my dustbin. I've come to get it back,' she said as politely as she could manage.

Craig pulled a puzzled face. 'No, we don't have your bin, Leah.'

'You do. I saw it. Please bring it round onto the street.'

'Didn't you hear me? I said we don't have it.'

'Craig, you have taken my dustbin and I want it back.' Leah clamped her teeth together.

'There must be another one in the street somewhere. Take that instead.'

'There isn't. My bin has paint on the lid. I saw it in your garden.'

'No need to raise your voice, Leah. Chill out, will you?'

'I'm not rais—'

'Everything OK?' a voice said. Gillian's face appeared over Craig's shoulder. She wrapped her arms around his middle, making them look like a two-headed person.

'I think you've taken my bin by mistake, Gillian,' Leah said, wishing she'd answered the door instead of Craig. 'I've come to get it back.'

'Oh no, Rexie brought ours in earlier. Didn't you, darling?' Gillian nuzzled herself against him.

Leah stared at the pair of them looming above her on the top step – Craig with his wine and stupid slippers, Gillian fawning over him and dressed in a cream silk robe. She felt the dizziness building inside her, her heartbeat quickening and her throat constricting. Her vision blurred as memories flashed before her eyes – messages from the other women, Craig's red-faced rage, the countless hours Leah had waited up for him only for him stop out all night, the never-ending lies, him convincing her that she was crazy, that she'd imagined everything... Then the sting of his hand as he'd swiped it across her cheek.

Leah drew in a sharp breath as she snapped back to the present. 'Craig, just give me my dustbin back, will you? Please.'

Craig and Gillian stared at her for a moment, shaking their heads – Gillian with a pitying expression on her face. She looked as though she was about to say something, but it was Craig who closed the door, followed by the sound of him laughing behind it.

Leah couldn't help herself. It was as though something inside her had split, letting all the pent-up rage burst out as the dam broke. She lunged at the door, shoving her weight against the wood, thumping on it as she yelled obscenities.

'How dare you, you cheating, lying rat! You're nothing but a thief and... and...' Her throat burned as she screamed out, her face pressed close to the door, 'I'd rather burn in hell than let you get away with what you've done!'

'Leah?'

She heard the voice through her choked-up sobs but didn't register who it was at first. Her fist banged on the door a few more times, then she jabbed the doorbell long and hard. Tears streamed down her face, her hair getting matted and caught all over her face.

'Leah, are you OK?'

The voice again. *Shit.*

She turned round slowly. 'Gabe,' she said. He was standing on her front path the other side of the low fence separating the front gardens, a concerned and wary look on his face. 'I'm... yes, I'm fine, thanks. Just a misunderstanding.' Her croaky laugh made it worse.

Gabe frowned as Leah came back into her own garden, wiping her face as best she could. 'You seem really... upset and *angry*,' he said, taking a step back as she approached him for a kiss.

'Oh, no, not really,' she said, trying to sound breezy. 'It's nice to see you. Come on in,' she said, opening her front door, her hand shaking as she fumbled with the lock.

'No... no, I won't stop.' Gabe remained on the path. 'I just came round to pick up my black and white scarf. You know the checked one I often wear? I think I might have left it here.'

'Oh... OK,' Leah said, feeling miffed that he wouldn't come inside. But then, she could hardly blame him after her display just now. 'I'll go and look for it.'

Gabe nodded and waited outside while Leah went from room to room, searching for the tasselled scarf she'd often seen him wear loosely wound around his neck. He'd had it for many years, he'd previously told her, the only souvenir he'd bought from his backpacking tour of Egypt. She'd always thought it suited him. But she couldn't find it anywhere – not even in Zoey or Henry's rooms or the laundry basket in the bathroom.

'So sorry, but it's not inside,' she said breathlessly, coming out again. 'I'll check my car,' she added, going out onto the street.

'But I've never been in your car,' Gabe said as he followed her. 'Look, don't worry. It's fine. I can see you have other things on your mind.'

Leah twisted round, still half bent through the Mini's passenger door, banging her head as she looked up at Gabe. Her mouth hung open as he turned to go, walking off with just a quick flick of his hand instead of a proper goodbye.

CHAPTER TWELVE

Leah woke with a start. She sat up, panting and sweating as she reached for the glass of water beside her bed. Bleary-eyed, she jabbed the button on her phone. Six twenty-three a.m. Not long until her alarm went off. She'd been dreaming about the dentist... the painful whine of a drill deep inside her mouth as though it was boring right into her brain.

But wait... there it was again – the drill screaming and hammering into her head. She groaned, still half asleep as she pulled the pillow over her ears. What was going on? Not only could she hear a terrible din, she *felt* it resonating through her bones. She flung the pillow off and sat up again, her baggy T-shirt slipping off her shoulder as she waited for the noise to start again.

'Mum-*my*, I can't sleep.' Henry was suddenly in the doorway, clutching his hands over his ears.

'No, me neith—'

There. Unmistakable. The stop-start din was coming from the wall adjoining next door and it felt like the entire house was shaking. Someone – *Craig*, no doubt – was drilling. It sounded as though he was about to burst through the wall at any moment. She leapt out of bed and shoved her feet into her slippers before taking Henry's hand.

'Come on, let's have breakfast,' she said, using all her restraint not to thump on the wall with the heaviest thing she could find. Craig was obviously doing it on purpose with the intention of getting a rise out of her. Well, he wasn't going to. He might well be doing DIY at an ungodly hour on a Saturday morning, but it wouldn't go on forever. No, the best thing to do was ignore him. Until she'd formed a plan to get rid of him.

———

With breakfast made and a grumpy Zoey having also been woken, her blank expression reflecting all their moods as she sat slumped over the kitchen table, Leah sipped her coffee and stared at her phone, wondering whether she should send a text to Gabe. He usually messaged her every day, but she'd not heard from him since he'd witnessed her screaming through the door at Craig a few days ago. She felt as though she owed him an explanation.

'Is it OK if we go to Dad's for dinner tonight?' Zoey said, almost sounding reluctant to ask as she spooned up her granola, scrolling through her phone with her free hand. 'He just texted asking us round, but we don't have to if you don't want us to.'

'*Cool!*' Henry said as he fiddled with his half-built Lego model. 'He can help me with this. I'm really stuck.'

Leah stared at her children for a moment – each of them fresh-faced and innocent, neither knowing the full horror behind their parents' divorce, though, at fourteen, she knew Zoey had picked up on things. She was determined to protect them as much as possible. Despite bin-gate and the early-morning drilling, maybe Liz and her mum were right – having Craig next door could ultimately work out for the best. The kids would be able to pop round and see him whenever they wanted, rather than having to wait at their grandparents' for him to never show up, and they'd still feel settled here with their bedrooms and familiar routine close by. While she hated the thought of her ex living next door, if it worked in Zoey and Henry's favour then she would just have to put up with her own discomfort.

'Sure, of course you can,' she replied with a smile. Besides, with the kids out for a few hours later, it meant she could ask Gabe round for a meal to make up for her behaviour the other evening. She'd cook him something special and get things between them back on track. Before she could overthink the situation and change her mind, she quickly tapped out a message inviting him over.

'You'll get to meet Gillian, Dad's new...' Leah trailed off. She had no idea if Craig had even told the kids he'd got a new partner. 'Dad's new friend,' she finished. If she was honest, the thought of another woman cooking and caring for her children turned her stomach. But then Craig had never been one for noticing their needs at any stage of their lives, so she figured that having her there could only be a good thing. And Gillian, while perhaps a little highly strung, seemed a decent sort. She had to remember that none of this was her fault. She'd simply been in the wrong place at the wrong time and fallen prey to Craig's advances. In time, Craig would likely cheat on her too.

'Actually, we've already met her, Mum,' Zoey said, peering up and pulling an awkward face. She glanced at Henry, her cheeks reddening. 'Do you mind?'

'She likes dolphins,' Henry said without looking up as he concentrated on forcing a piece of Lego into place.

'You've already met her?'

'Just... just once, a while ago,' Zoey said quietly. 'She got me a present.' She held up her wrist to show a cluster of cheap bracelets. Leah had noticed them before but just assumed she'd bought them in town when she'd been out with her friends. 'She got Henry some chocolate. I think it was to try and make us like her. I'm sorry, I should have told you.'

'That's... that's nice, love,' Leah replied, staring at them both for a moment. She forced a smile before getting up to clear the plates. She didn't want her children to feel disloyal about meeting their dad's new partner, though she also knew she was going to have to do a lot of lip-biting to make this work. But she was determined that, for the sake of the kids, she would. She simply had no choice.

———

It was gone midday and, while Zoey was at swimming club and Henry was in his room yelling at his PlayStation – partly talking to his friends online and partly because the thing was old and temperamental – Leah was staring at her bed. She needed to move it away from the wall that adjoined Craig and Gillian's bedroom in the hope that she wouldn't hear quite so much if it was positioned the other side of the room.

In reality, she knew this was unlikely, but it would make her feel better, and at least she'd be physically further away from them. She hated the thought that her ex was only feet away from her, cuddled up in bed with Gillian, their sex noises penetrating the wall, when once it had been her lying with her head on Craig's chest as he cradled her in a post-sex buzz.

Leah shuddered as she grabbed the bed frame and lugged it with all her force, a spasm of pain shooting through her lower back. The heavy bed only moved about six inches. Again and again, Leah used all her strength to gradually drag it away from the wall, stopping only to check her phone when she heard a text come in. It wasn't from Gabe.

Kids coming over later? Mum xx

Leah smiled and rolled her eyes. Her mother always signed off her texts with her name 'in case you don't know who it's from', she'd once told her.

They're going to Craig's for dinner xx

She flicked to the string of messages between her and Gabe, seeing that the one she'd sent earlier was still unread. She also saw that he'd been online only ten minutes ago.

Leah chucked her phone on the bed and went to straighten the picture that was previously hanging over her headboard, probably falling crooked from all the drilling and vibrations earlier. But then she decided it would be best to move it over her bed in its new position, so she unhooked it from the wall.

And that's when she saw the damage behind it – a plaster-cracking hole about half an inch wide, which had ruined the pale blue paint she'd applied only a couple of weeks ago.

'Oh my *God*,' she snapped, propping the picture against the skirting board. 'He *did* come right through.'

Leah stared at the hole, getting up close and squinting into it with one eye. It was only narrow, and she couldn't see much more than dust and bits of brick inside, but she knew that if she got a knitting needle or chopstick or similar, it would push right through to Craig and Gillian's bedroom. What the *hell* was he playing at? This was hardly putting up shelves. This was a blatant and deliberate invasion of her privacy.

She grabbed her phone, a sick feeling growing inside her. There was no way she could face another altercation on the doorstep.

What do you think you're doing? You've drilled right through the party wall. Make good immediately or I'll be taking legal action.

She was about to send the message but then thought better of it and deleted the part about legal action. Experience told her that Craig would love nothing more than an expensive legal battle, even if he didn't win – whatever winning would entail in this case. No, he'd simply enjoy the stress it would cause her, not to mention the financial cost. Even Liz's comparatively reasonable rates would be too expensive for her now.

Her hands were shaking as she swept up the mess that had dropped down onto her skirting board and carpet, her fingers fumbling with a bit of rolled-up cardboard as she stuffed it into the hole to prevent Craig spying. Had he intended to put a camera through? He wouldn't have banked on hitting a picture on her side, and if his intention was to spy on her, then he'd likely try again some other way. But why be so blatant about it?

To get a reaction out of you, that's why, she kept telling herself, trying to slow her frantic heartbeat. *He wants you to think that's what he's up to, to unnerve you.*

Downstairs, while she was waiting for the kettle to boil, Leah checked her phone again. Two blue ticks on WhatsApp told her that Craig had read her message but, as yet, there was no reply. *Perhaps he's at the DIY store buying filler right this moment,* she thought. No, more likely he'd downed tools and was at the golf club schmoozing some property investor to get involved with a shady deal, or out to lunch somewhere expensive with Gillian. She was so glad to be shot of that lifestyle.

She sloshed boiling water into her mug, flicking onto the messages between her and Gabe again. He'd still not read her message inviting him round later, yet he was online at that very moment. As much as she tried to ignore the sinking feeling inside, she knew it wasn't a good sign. He'd always been quick to reply. She dropped down at the kitchen table with her coffee, staring at her phone screen as Gabe came on and offline, her message sitting there with two grey ticks.

Should she message him again while he was online, she

wondered? He could hardly ignore her then. She clicked her phone off and slid it across the table. Of *course* she shouldn't. It was clear that she'd scared him off with her behaviour the other night.

'Hello, Daddy!' Leah suddenly heard Henry shout from the living room. Her skin crawled as she crept through the hallway and peeked in to where Henry was playing. She saw him jumping about in front of the window, waving his arms. 'Daddy's out there, look,' he said, turning to Leah when he saw her in the doorway. 'Can I go out and help him?'

Cautiously, Leah crept up to the window and saw Craig's back only a few feet away. He was bent over in his front garden digging a hole. A moment later, he stood up and turned, stretching out and grinning when he saw Henry through the glass. His eyes flicked to Leah, who quickly darted back into the shadows. But from the smirk on his face, she knew he'd seen her. Just as she'd seen the black and white checked and tasselled scarf wound around his neck.

CHAPTER THIRTEEN

Leah shoved her feet into her shoes and went out of the front door. Feeling more and more like she was under siege, she walked down the path and out onto the street. Craig was still in his front garden digging and he had his earphones in, so she knew he wouldn't hear her coming. A surprise approach, she'd decided – despite the adrenalin and fear surging through her – was needed.

But she stopped in the street, her eyes widening at the house on the other side of the road. A man was erecting a 'For Sale' sign in the front garden. Nothing particularly odd about that, as the owners had previously mentioned they were thinking of moving. No, the reason Leah suddenly felt repulsed was because it was her ex-husband's face leering out of the yellow and black sign being placed by the front boundary wall.

CRAIG FORBES – PROPERTY KING

Rex – Latin for king, she thought to herself, balling her fists and continuing round to next door's front garden. *The source of Gillian's nickname.* Craig didn't notice her as she approached.

He appeared to be digging a hole for a rose bush he had beside him in a pot.

'It's bad enough having you live next door to me, but now I have to stare at your face from my front window,' she said, standing only a few feet from him. She forced herself to stop shaking, to appear brave – the opposite of how she felt.

Craig didn't hear her or, if he did, he didn't acknowledge her.

'Craig!' Leah said in a raised voice.

Still no reaction.

She stepped forward and prodded his arm.

Slowly, he turned, giving her a slow look up and down before removing his wireless earphones and tucking them in his pocket.

'Leah,' he said slowly. Another sweep up and down her, his gaze lingering on her chest as his nose wrinkled. 'To what do I owe the pleasure?' He laughed, leaning on his spade.

'Where do I start?' she said, giving another glance across the street. 'What on earth were you doing this morning, drilling through my wall?' She folded her arms around herself, taking a step back. She didn't trust him not to lash out.

'Ah, that,' he said, laughing again. 'Did I come right through? Drill bit must have been too long. And anyway, it's *our* wall, don't forget. Shared.'

Leah forced down a swallow – only just holding back everything that wanted to burst out. 'Are you going to fix it? I've recently decorated and you've ruined it. Or is it some sick peephole?'

'Oh, Leah. You're still so angry, aren't you? I hope you don't act like this in front of my children.'

A deep breath prevented an outburst. 'Where did you get that scarf?'

At close range, there was no doubt it was Gabe's. It even had a few tassels plaited together along one edge – she'd watched Gabe fiddle with them on their first date. And if she sniffed it, she was sure she'd smell his cologne. It wasn't like the expensive brands Craig doused himself in. No, Gabe's preferred scent was far more subtle and earthy than that. And it suited him. She hated seeing Craig wearing his scarf and wanted to rip it off him. Or, better still, strangle him with it.

Craig touched the folds of fabric. 'It was a gift. Suits my new "man about town" look, don't you think?'

'What the hell are you talking about?' Leah scoffed. 'Man *prowling* about town, more like,' she mumbled under her breath. 'Who gave it to you?'

'Gillian. She has such good taste.'

'Well, it's actually my friend's scarf. He must have left it at yours the other night when...' The last thing she wanted to remember was the moment when her world turned upside down. 'I've come to get it for him,' Leah finished when Craig just stared at her. She held out her hand.

'Leah...' He shifted uncomfortably from one foot to the other, pulling a pained expression. 'Are you sure you're OK? You come storming round here accusing me of spying on you and stealing your *friend's* scarf.' He lingered on the word 'friend' in a mocking tone. 'Or should I say *boy*friend, or even *husband*? Who'd have thought, eh?' He smirked.

'He's not—'

'Because if he *is* your boyfriend, Leah, I'm not best pleased. You should have declared him to the court on the paperwork. You know the judge's decision relied on the facts about your position being accurate. Didn't your solicitor advise you? Liz Morgan might be a looker, but she's not got a great reputation, you know.'

'What are you *talking* about?' Leah felt her cheeks burning. She couldn't stand Craig knowing her business.

'I'd hate to think that you lied to the judge about having a boyfriend, even if it was just the early days of seeing him. Best you come clean now about your cohabitation intentions, then we can go back to court to clear it up. It could well have affected the judge's decision, and—'

'Oh for God's sake, just give me the scarf, Craig.' Leah couldn't help the tears pooling in her eyes. Liquid frustration and anger. 'I know it's Gabe's.'

'You're imagining things again.' He stared at her, grimacing. 'Unless you've come round about something to do with the children, then I suggest you get off my property. Or I'll be forced to call the police.'

Leah stared back, speechless.

'And I'll be calling them about theft, invasion of privacy and destruction of property!' she eventually retorted. 'You're not going to bully me any more, Craig.' She fought back all the old feelings – fear, helplessness and a sense that perhaps she had got it wrong, that maybe she *was* imagining everything.

'The wall will be fixed. But you go right ahead and call the police if you like. It will give me a chance to instigate a non-molestation order and get your harassment of me and my family logged.'

'Family?' Leah said, staring up at him disbelievingly. 'You blew a nuclear-sized hole in that a long time ago.' She stared at him for a second before turning to leave, managing to stumble on a loose brick in the path as she fled at speed, catching sight of Gillian's shocked face in the doorway as she broke into a run.

CHAPTER FOURTEEN

'Are you sure it's not just a similar scarf?' Jodi said as she opened the wine. When it was clear Gabe wasn't going to reply to Leah's invite, she'd messaged her best friend instead, asking if she was free. Since Jodi had arrived ten minutes ago, Leah had spewed out a catalogue of rage about Craig. 'Here, get this inside you. Let's go and sit down.'

They went through into the living room, each of them carrying their drinks and some chilli and cheese nachos Leah had taken from the oven. They sat next to each other on the saggy sofa with Leah reaching underneath a cushion and pulling out something hard.

'Great. Henry will be wondering where this is,' she said, staring at a piece of his new Lego model. He'd taken the box next door with him when they'd gone round to see their dad earlier. She expected them back by about half past nine. 'And to answer your question, I'm certain it was Gabe's scarf. He must have left it there when Gillian invited us for drinks last week-end. Craig is probably getting some weird kick out of keeping it.'

She shuddered at the thought, though something snagged in her mind as she recalled the evening. Gabe had knocked on her door and, before they'd gone round to Gillian's, he'd commented on her appearance, she remembered that. And she also remembered commenting on his, thinking how smart he looked in his navy shirt. 'Thing is, I don't remember him even *wearing* the scarf that night,' Leah whispered, crunching a tortilla chip. She frowned.

'Which means...?' Jodi said, grabbing a few chips held together with stringy, melted cheese.

'He was wearing a shirt,' she continued. 'He looked really good in it. But... but there was definitely no scarf.'

'Which *means*?' Jodi said again.

Leah stared at her. 'Which means he can't have left it next door. So how come Craig has it?'

'Which means that it can't be Gabe's scarf,' Jodi said, leaning forward and patting Leah's leg. 'How long have we known each other now? Going on ten years at least? It's fair to say we've been through some shit together... divorces, births, deaths, laughter and tears. The lot. And I've seen you crawl through hell and back because of him.' She flicked her eyes to the wall adjoining next door. 'But... and don't hate me for this... I don't want you to get all...'

Leah glared at her, raising her eyebrows and waiting for the blow she sensed was coming.

'...Well, all *irrational* again. Just let your bastard ex stew in his own juices of wrongdoing and let karma take care of the rest.'

Leah blew out through pursed lips. 'Irrational? Don't *you* start telling me I'm crazy and mad, or I really *will* start to believe I'm losing it.'

'So what's your explanation, then? I'm certain that Gabe doesn't have exclusive rights on black and white scarves. And I can't even believe we're wasting a child-free Saturday night discussing your ex.'

'Sorry,' Leah said, suddenly feeling stupid. 'You're right. It's

probably just coincidence.' She thought a moment. 'Unless...'
She saw the look on Jodi's face. 'OK, OK, I'll shut up about it.'

'Let me put some music on,' Jodi said, pulling up Spotify on
her phone and pairing it with Leah's Alexa. 'It'll take your mind
off things.'

Leah nodded and went to the front window to close the
curtains. It wasn't dark yet, but she wanted to shut out the
world. And that was when she saw the car pulling up on the
street and two familiar faces getting out, each of them laughing
and chattering to each other.

'Oh cool, Abby and Steve are here,' she said, standing on
tiptoe to get a better view. Her first thought was that she didn't
have enough wine in the house for everyone and that she'd have
to pop out to the shop to get some more. She'd always prided
herself on being a generous host. Her second thought was how
good it would be to see them and what a nice surprise that
they'd called round unannounced. Since the divorce was
finalised and she'd moved house, Leah had messaged Abby her
new address and invited them over several times, but she hadn't
had a reply. She figured they were just busy – as were many of
her and Craig's mutual friends, it had seemed.

'What's that?' Jodi said, drawing up beside Leah.

'We have company,' Leah said, heading for the door. 'Abby
and Steve are here.'

'Um, Lee,' Jodi said, pointing out of the window. 'I don't
think we have company at all.'

The women watched as the couple – with Abby in full
make-up and a smart dress and Steve also in going-out clothes –
walked up next door's front path. Abby was holding onto
Steve's arm and in her other hand was a bunch of flowers. Steve
was clutching a bottle of fizz. A moment later, the couple disappeared inside.

'Oh,' Leah said, whipping the curtains closed. She grabbed
the wine bottle from the coffee table and sloshed more into her

glass before topping up Jodi's. 'I got that wrong, then,' she said, flopping down on the sofa.

'I wouldn't worry about it,' Jodi said, her expression bordering on pity. 'Fuck 'em.' She raised her glass.

'To *real* friends,' Leah replied, clinking her glass. But she couldn't let it drop. 'I mean, the cheek of him! What the hell does he think he's playing at?' She shook her head slowly, knowing there was no answer to that question. 'I've known Abby since hairdressing college. We go way back. We've worked in salons together before, covered each other's shifts and—'

'Stop it,' Jodi said gently, putting her finger up to her lips. 'Remember what I said?'

Leah nodded, scowling. She poured more wine.

'Every time you have thoughts like this, another little piece of you dies inside and another little bit of him gets stronger. So stop it, OK?'

Leah laughed, then stuffed a fistful of nachos in her mouth. But then she froze, frowning as she listened.

'Alexa, pause,' she said. 'Did you hear that? Sounded like a car door banging.'

Jodi shook her head, but Leah was on her feet and at the window again, peeling back the curtains.

'Oh well, that's just great. Fran and Allie have just turned up next door now. Is he having a bloody party with all my friends, or something?' She shot over to the wall that adjoined the living room next door and pressed her ear against it. She heard noises but couldn't make them out, so she drained her tumbler of wine and put that up to the wall with her ear against it. 'Sounds like a boring party, if you ask me. And so much for him spending quality time with the kids. Henry wanted his dad to help him with a Lego model and—'

'Lee, *stop*. You're going to make yourself ill.'

'Or very drunk,' Leah replied, refilling her empty glass and knocking it back before topping it up. When she heard another car, she couldn't help looking out of the window again. Another couple of her friends were getting out of a taxi. And a short while after that, Michelle and Tony squeezed their car into a tight space opposite, right next to the For Sale board with Craig's face leering out at her.

'Zen-like calm,' Leah said, sitting down again. She wafted her hands in a downward gesture, albeit unconvincingly.

But she *was* bothered. As the two women chatted, with Jodi raising the volume of the music so that James Blunt had more of a chance of drowning out the sound of laughter and music that was now coming through the wall from next door, Leah found herself feeling more and more agitated. Craig and Gillian were having a party. All her friends were there – friends she'd known for years. And her kids were there too.

'What the hell was *that*?' Leah asked, jumping at the loud crash coming from next door. Suddenly, the music got louder.

'Calm down, just drunken antics, most likely,' Jodi said, rolling her eyes. 'Ignore. You know what Craig's like once he gets a few inside him.'

'But my kids are there. How can I ignore it?' She felt prickles of sweat erupting on her skin. 'I doubt very much Craig is looking after them.'

'Zoey's not stupid. Any sign of trouble and she'll be back here with Henry.'

Jodi was right – Zoey was a sensible girl and wouldn't stand for any nonsense.

'I'm going to take this round to Henry,' Leah suddenly announced, unable to relax. She reached for the Lego piece. 'It sounds like there's some kind of wild orgy going on next door. I didn't hear a peep when the previous neighbours lived there.'

'Don't be silly, Leah,' Jodi said, putting a hand on her arm. 'You'll just make yourself look stupid. Anyway, they probably won't even hear the doorbell with that din going on. The kids will be back soon.'

Leah glanced at her watch, hesitating. Eight forty-five. She knocked back the rest of her wine and stood up, looking back at Jodi from the hallway. 'Won't be a sec,' she said, slipping her bare feet into flip-flops that were left by the front door, completely unable to stop herself as she staggered outside.

CHAPTER FIFTEEN

Leah groaned and rolled over, screwing up her eyes. 'Oh, my *head*,' she mumbled, pulling the duvet up over her shoulders. Her skull thrummed in time with her pulse and a slash of pain seared across her forehead as the light seeped in through the curtains. As much as she wanted to go back to sleep, her mind was already whirring, pummelling her conscious thoughts with random snippets of... of...

'No-*oo!*' she said, sitting up. She gasped in a lungful of air as she clutched her face, shards of memory puncturing her brain. 'Dear *God*, please tell me it isn't real.' She screwed up her eyes – partly because she had a hangover big enough to split a rock and partly because of what had happened. Or rather, what she was trying to *remember* had happened.

She heard a noise. Jodi, downstairs... Yes, that's right... Jodi had stayed over because her partner was home, looking after Charlie. And they'd had drinks. A *lot* of drinks – well, *she* had.

And the kids... Oh God, their faces.

She dropped her head down into her hands as the memories dripped back, feeling sick in the pit of her stomach as she swung her legs over the side of the bed. The nausea ran deep and every part of her body ached. Then she saw her feet – black and muddy, her toenails encrusted with what looked like soil. She scowled, getting up and going to the mirror. Her cheeks were streaked with black mascara and her skin was blotchy and red. One side of her face was mud-covered, and, like her feet, her palms were muddy and stained grass green.

She knew last night hadn't ended well, but she had absolutely no idea how she'd managed to get into this state, let alone get into bed. Then she ran for the bathroom, only just making it in time as whatever was left of last night's booze and nachos came up.

———

'Give me the edited version,' Leah said, padding barefoot into the kitchen ten minutes later. She held a tissue at her mouth, feeling as though her insides had been through a mangle.

'Oh dear,' Jodi said, spatula in hand as she stood next to the hob. 'It's worse than I thought.'

Leah sat down at the kitchen table, the smell of bacon emanating from under the grill making her feel nauseous again. Jodi was frying eggs and had the kettle boiling. 'The kids...?' Leah asked nervously, wanting clarification of what she suspected.

'They're next door. They stopped over. Don't you remember?'

Leah nodded and groaned, holding her head. 'Yes,' she said. 'Kind of.'

'Hardly surprising,' she thought she heard Jodi say, and she couldn't disagree.

'Did everyone see?'

Jodi turned, gave a sombre nod. ''Fraid so.'

Leah groaned and dropped her head again, curling up her muddy toes. 'I honestly didn't think I'd had that much when I went round. It was that stupid loose brick on their path. I should sue!' She touched her cheek and winced.

'Wearing flip-flops while drunk didn't help. I put some ice on your face. The swelling's gone down a bit,' Jodi said, having a closer look.

Leah nodded again, too ashamed to look her in the eye. In fact, how would she look at anyone ever again? 'It was... it was just so...' She couldn't get the words out, but seeing her children standing either side of Craig in the front doorway, his hands on each of their shoulders – it had done something to her, all of them looking like the happy family that she'd once had. 'It was when Gillian came to the door that I...' Leah screwed up her eyes.

'That you lost it?' Jodi finished.

'*They're staying over with us,*' Leah said in a whiny voice as she imitated Craig. 'That's what he said. No, it's what he *told* me. Can you believe the gall of the bloody man?'

'The kids *wanted* to stop the night, Lee. They... they seemed to be having a really nice time at the party. Zoey asked you if it was OK, remember?'

The sequence of events was fuzzy, as though it had happened to someone else, and Leah had just been a passer-by catching a few snippets of the scene she'd caused.

'Did you go inside?' Leah asked.

'Briefly, after you'd fallen over. I explained to them that you were stressed about various things and had just wanted to bring the missing Lego piece round. I found it on the lawn and gave it to Henry, by the way.'

'You mean you found it where I'd fallen flat on my face in the mud with everyone watching after I'd sobbed my eyes out in front of Craig?' Leah's tone was bitter – but the bitterness was directed at herself. Everything in her mind was disjointed, like pieces of a smashed-up puzzle. What was worse was that everyone would think she was a terrible mother, when she knew the opposite was true.

'Look, get this inside you and you'll feel a lot better,' Jodi said, passing her a plate of toast, bacon and fried eggs. 'The kids will be home soon and you can have a talk with them. It'll all blow over, you'll see.'

Leah stared at her plate of food, grateful to Jodi even though it made her feel more nauseous.

'And did he reply... Gabe?' Jodi asked, sitting down opposite.

'*What?*' Leah froze, coffee mug halfway to her mouth.

'I tried to stop you, I really did, but... but you sent the texts anyway.'

Even though it hurt every fibre of her being, Leah ran upstairs to grab her phone. It was only when she was seated again that she opened WhatsApp, hardly daring to read what she'd messaged.

'Shit,' she said, dropping her phone onto the table. 'That's that, then.'

Feeling even more nauseous now, she got up to fetch a glass of water. She reckoned she needed about ten pints to rehydrate. While she was standing at the sink, she instinctively pulled up the blind, unable to help the gasp as she looked out into courtyard.

'What the *hell*?' Leah stood outside, her dressing gown pulled tightly around her, arms clamped around body as she stared down at the huge pile of garden rubbish. Brambles and sawn branches, large twigs and a ton of ivy was littered over her cobbles and mixed up with what looked to be general garden waste. 'Craig Forbes, I... I'm going to *kill* you!' she said loudly, going up close to the wall.

'Shhh, calm down, Leah,' Jodi said, trying to guide her back indoors. But she shrugged away.

'It's all going back over. Right now!' she said, pushing up the sleeves of her robe. She was filthy anyway and didn't care if she got even dirtier. This mess couldn't have come from anywhere else as, being on a corner, Craig and Gillian's garden was the only boundary she had with neighbours, apart from her own allotment behind her courtyard.

'I think there's some law that says neighbours can cut back your overhanging plants and trees, but they have to offer the waste back to you,' Jodi said, removing a large branch from Leah just as she was about to hurl it back over the wall.

'Yeah, *offer*,' she said through gritted teeth. 'I don't call this offering, do you? I call it fly-tipping.'

'Leah, wait,' Jodi said, trying to take the brambles from her. But the thorns snagged on Leah's arms and she yelped, snatching them back.

'What's all the noise?' a voice suddenly growled. A moment later, Craig's face appeared above the wall. 'I want to enjoy my garden in peace, if you don't mind, and...' He trailed off, looking Leah up and down and turning up his nose. 'Good grief, you look like death, woman. What are you doing?'

'Giving you back your rubbish, that's what.' Leah lifted up the brambles and attempted to get them up over the brick wall, but the thorns got caught on her robe and fell back down on her, scratching her face and neck as she wrestled with them.

'All perfectly legal,' Craig said calmly. 'Everything was over-hanging our garden. It was long overdue a cutback. By the way, the kids are staying here for a while.'

'But Henry has a party later,' Leah said, pulling a leaf from her hair. 'He needs to change and wrap the present before I take him.'

Craig was already shaking his head. 'No need,' he continued. 'He has some clothes here now, and Gillian has gone out with him to get a gift.'

Leah stared up at his smug face. 'But I've already bought a—'

'Leah, this is my contact weekend, if you remember.'

When have you ever adhered to that? she wanted to shoot back, but managed to bite her tongue. Instead, she gave him a terse smile and watched, relieved, as he jumped back down off whatever he was standing on.

'I swear, after everything he's done to me, I'm going to *murder* him,' Leah said, once he was out of earshot. She kicked at the pile of rubbish, knowing she'd have to have a bonfire on the vegetable plot to get rid of it all. She turned to go back inside, desperately needing some paracetamol, but froze as she heard her daughter's voice.

'Mum?' Zoey said as her head popped up over the wall. A deep frown was set between her eyebrows and her mouth hung open as her fingers gripped the coping stones.

'Oh... hi, love,' she said, glancing over at Jodi. She didn't need to ask if she'd overheard her comment. She saw it on her face. 'Are you still up for sorting your wardrobe out together later on?' She hoped her daughter would rather come home now that she'd had a night there.

'I should probably stay here,' Zoey said, biting her fingernail as she looked away. 'Dad wants me to as it's his weekend. Is it OK if I go shopping with Gilly this afternoon while Henry's at the party?'

'Shopping...?' Leah repeated, trying to remember when she'd last taken Zoey to the mall, spent time with her alone or treated her.

'Dad says we're getting pizza delivered and watching a movie later,' Zoey added through a pained expression. 'He says it's best if we sleep over here again tonight. But don't worry, Mum, I'll look after Henry.'

'It's school tomorrow,' Leah quipped back, feeling as if this was now a stand-off. She hated that her daughter was stuck between her and Craig – weapons in their war. 'What about preparing for the week? And your homework?'

Zoey glanced away for a moment, the frown on her young face deepening. 'Gilly said she's going to get me some uniform to keep here. And... and if you pass my school bag over, I can do my homework now. I've only got a little bit.'

Leah paused, studying her daughter's face. There was a troubled look about her, as though she wasn't at all comfortable saying any of this, but her father wasn't giving her much of a choice. The contact agreement stated that he could take them to school on Monday mornings.

'If that's what you want, darling,' Leah replied, not wanting to make it even more difficult for her. Plus, the banging inside her skull wasn't going to allow a full-on showdown. As Craig had pointed out, it was technically his weekend with the children.

'Thanks, Mum,' Zoey said, smiling at Jodi as her mum went to get the bag. When she returned, she took it and was about to pop down behind the wall again but hesitated and said, 'You're not really going to murder Dad, are you?'

CHAPTER SIXTEEN

The next morning, Leah couldn't help peeking out of the front window around the time she knew the kids would be leaving for school. She always dropped Zoey at the bus stop before taking Henry on to his primary school. But not today.

She'd not slept a wink last night and, instead, had lain awake, her eyes fixed on the cardboard-stuffed hole in the wall opposite as she'd listened out for sounds from next door. A couple of times during the evening she'd heard doors closing – Henry had a knack for slamming them unintentionally – and, earlier, she was convinced she'd listened to the muffled sound of two female voices on the other side of the wall separating her bedroom from Craig and Gillian's.

She'd got up and quietly removed the rolled-up cardboard from the wall, peering through the hole. All she saw was a vague pinprick of light the other side, mainly obscured by brick dust. But there was no mistaking the soft tones of Zoey's voice, punctuated by snippets of conversation from an older woman: Gillian. It was hard to hear what they were discussing – something to do with clothes and boys, she'd thought. Stuff a *mum* would talk about with her daughter.

'Very cosy,' she'd whispered, the stab of pain in her chest not going unnoticed. She'd tried to remember when *she'd* last sat on the bed and chatted with Zoey, gossiping and giggling, perhaps doing their hair and nails, but she couldn't recall. Then she'd shoved the cardboard back in the hole and got back into bed. Her head still thrummed, although maxing out on paracetamol had taken the edge off her fading hangover. As things stood, she never wanted to drink alcohol again.

And by the time she did finally drift off to sleep, Gabe still hadn't replied to her drunken text from Saturday night. What had she been thinking – accusing him of being friends with her ex? With the alcohol skewing her judgement, it had seemed like a reasonable explanation for Craig having Gabe's scarf. But now it didn't. She cringed as she remembered the messages that barely made sense.

I no what u did

traitor with my ex

you are scarf

I mjiss u love you xxp

She supposed she could pretend that she'd texted him in error, that it was meant for someone else, perhaps even claiming that Henry had got hold of her phone and played a prank. But the timestamp said 01.18 a.m., so that was unlikely. And even if it had been meant for someone else, it still didn't look good on her. No – she'd just have to ride out the consequences, which probably meant Gabe not wanting to see her ever again. And she could hardly blame him.

It was as Zoey and Henry came out of their father's house next door – each of them dressed smartly in what appeared to be brand-new uniform – that Leah's phone pinged with a message. But she was too distracted by what she was seeing to check the screen, watching as her kids walked down the front path, looking back over their shoulders and waving.

'Bye, Dad,' she saw Zoey mouthing and then a moment later, Gillian came down the front path dressed in smart work clothes. There was no sign of Craig.

On a whim, she dashed to the kitchen and grabbed a couple of chocolate biscuit bars from the tin, before running out of the front door and down the front path to the street. As she drew level with next door's drive, Gillian was reversing out her grey Audi, nearly running her over.

Leah patted the rear of the car to let them know she was there, coming round to the driver's side. 'Hi, hi...' she said breathlessly as Gillian wound down her window.

The other woman stared up at her, forking her large sunglasses on top of her head, revealing a scowl followed by a pitying look.

'I just wanted to give these to the kids for break time. They always take something.'

'Hi, Mum!' she heard Henry say from the back. Zoey was sitting in the front, cocooned in the big leather seat – nothing like Leah's ancient Mini.

'Hello, darling. How was the birthday party yesterday?' Leah said. She reached in through the window to pass the biscuit back to him, but Gillian raised her arm across the gap, blocking her way.

'They have snacks packed in their bags,' she said with a terse smile. 'Healthy snacks.'

Leah hoped Henry would reach forward and take his favourite biscuit, but he didn't.

'It was great,' he said. 'The going-home bags were amazing!'

'Yeah, we're sorted for food, Mum, but thanks,' Zoey said,

giving her a smile. 'We'd better get going, though.' She checked the time on her phone.

Leah stared at her daughter, returning her smile. She had an overwhelming urge to hug both of her kids and was about to open the rear door on Henry's side to give him a quick kiss at least, when Gillian started reversing out of the drive again, forcing Leah to jump backwards.

'Bye,' she called out, waving frantically. 'Love you!' But Gillian had put up the window. Leah saw Zoey mouthing something through the windscreen and make a couple of waving gestures, but she had no idea what she meant. She'd text her at lunchtime to find out.

———

It wasn't until she'd taken payment from her third client of the day that Leah remembered to check the message that had come in earlier. She went to the little staff room at the back of the salon and grabbed her bag, seeing that she'd also missed a few calls from her mum. Her heart thumped as she saw the earlier message was from Gabe. She screwed up her eyes as she tapped it open, hardly daring to look.

We need to talk

'God,' she muttered, unsure just how much talking it would take to undo the damage she'd done. Then she called her mum, who answered after only one ring.

'Where have you *been*, darling?' she said. 'I've been trying to reach you.'

'Sorry, Mum. I've had clients all morning. You should have called the salon line. Is everything OK?'

'It's your dad,' she said in a voice that made Leah think she was building up to something. 'He's in hospital.'

'Hospital?' Leah repeated frantically. 'What's happened? Is he OK?'

'Calm down, darling. He's fine but they're checking him out. I've just stepped outside for a moment, but I'm with him.'

'Mum, what *happened*?' Her mother had a way of minimising a crisis and skirting around facts.

'He had pains, darling, that's all. He's no spring chicken, you know. We all get pains. He'll be fine.'

'Pains *where*, Mum?'

'Just in his chest. Probably indigestion. I gave him some of my home-made herbal remedy earlier, so that'll help.'

It's probably what caused it, Leah thought, but decided to keep quiet. Her mum had a cabinet full of her so-called tonics, most of which she'd made herself. As a kid, she had been a guinea pig for her home-grown tinctures and potions and was only ever taken to the doctor if absolutely necessary.

'I'll come straight over,' Leah said, wondering if Charlotte was up for taking over her next couple of ladies. It was only for washes and blow-dries – nothing too complicated.

After Leah had spent the next few minutes arguing with her mother about it not being necessary, with Leah insisting it was, she delegated the rest of the day's clients and set off for the local hospital. But before she drove away, she replied to Gabe.

Yes let's talk. I'm sorry

———

'Dad... oh, *Dad*...' Leah said as she drew alongside her father's bed. He was still in 'resus' in A & E, dressed in a yellow and white hospital gown with a cannula in the back of his left hand and a pale grey hue to his skin. He didn't look well – not the vibrant and fit man she always pictured in her head when she thought of him. Seeing him lying there, it made her realise that her perception of him hadn't caught up with the present. For the first time ever, she thought he looked old.

'Hello, darling,' he said in that chipper voice of his, though it was slightly dulled. It reminded her of the actors in old black and white movies. The grey tufts of his usually neat hair were spiky and dishevelled, and he had a patch of dried saliva in the corner of his mouth.

Leah bent down and kissed his cheek. His skin felt cool and waxy. 'Do you need another blanket, Dad?' she asked, looking around for one. He shook his head.

'What happened? Did you call an ambulance, Mum?' She glanced over at Rita, who was wafting in and out of the curtained cubicle, chatting to any passing nurse or doctor who would listen to her. *He's thirsty... When's his scan... Are the blood results back yet?*

'No, we drove,' she said, looking anywhere but at Leah.

'Drove?' Leah turned to her father. 'What happened, Dad? Where were you when you felt ill?'

'Fuss about nothing,' her father replied, batting his hand in the air. Leah took it, giving his fingers a gentle squeeze. She had so many questions, but sensed she wasn't going to get answers easily. 'I'm fine,' he continued. 'I just want to go home.'

Leah was about to ask what had brought on his pains when a doctor came into the cubicle. She was wearing blue scrubs and looked in her early thirties. Her dark hair was swept up in a clip.

'How are you feeling now, Mr Ward?' she asked with a friendly smile. She glanced at the monitor behind the bed, studying the numbers.

'I've survived this long and served in the army for thirty-five years, so I think I've got a bit of time left in me yet,' he replied, avoiding the question.

'He looks really pale and not himself to me,' Leah interjected. 'Do you know what's happened to him?'

'You're family?' the doctor asked.

Leah nodded. 'His daughter.'

'I'm Doctor Khatri,' she said with a smile. 'Your father came in with chest pains and tingling in his left arm and fingers. We've run some blood tests so far and done a few ECGs. He's been down for a chest X-ray and is waiting for an echocardiogram now. Once we get all the results in, we'll have a clearer picture of what's going on.'

'Do you think he's had a...' Leah didn't want to say the words. 'A heart attack?'

The doctor made a sympathetic expression, raising her eyebrows. 'It's a possibility, but let's not jump the gun until we have the results. Meantime, we'll look after him and the nurses will be monitoring you regularly, Mr Ward.' She paused, watching as he made a face and held his left arm, rubbing at the skin.

'Fuss about nothing, if you ask me,' he said as the doctor left. 'If the stupid idiot hadn't wound me up, I'd never have—'

'Enough of that now,' Rita said quickly, fussing over him and offering him a sip of water as the doctor left the cubicle. 'Don't speak, just rest,' she added, leaving Leah even more puzzled about what had happened.

———

'Right, Mother,' Leah said in the hospital café after they'd bought a couple of coffees and sat down at a small table by the window. Her dad had been wheeled off by the hospital porter to have his heart ultrasound scan. 'What's going on? Tell me exactly what happened.'

Rita slowly stirred sugar into her tea, then adjusted the brightly coloured ethnic-style scarf she had tied around her hair

– only just managing to keep her masses of unruly waves under control. It only seemed ten minutes ago since Leah had trimmed it.

'Daddy just had a funny turn, that's all. You know what he's like.'

'More to the point, I know what *you're* like.' Her mother had spent months in denial about her split from Craig, not wanting to acknowledge the truth. Even when she and the kids had been forced to move into their place, her mother treated it as if she was just on a visit, as though she'd be happily skipping back to Craig at any moment. She was adept at avoiding reality. 'Were you at home? Out? Dad mentioned someone else was involved.'

Rita sipped her coffee, but Leah noticed the tremor in her hand – a tremor that wasn't usually there. 'We'd been out, just into town to get a few bits, that's all.' She smiled as if that was all the explanation needed.

'Dad said a "stupid idiot" had wound him up.' Leah used her fingers as quote marks. 'What did he mean?'

'Oh, you know what your father's like,' Rita replied. 'Can't leave him alone for a moment before he gets into some heated debate with someone. It's his trauma, darling. He saw some terrible things in Ireland that still haunt him.'

That much was true. Hypervigilant and mistrusting to the core, her father was a gentle giant most of the time. But his mood could flip in a second and turn him into someone unrecognisable.

'Who did he get into a heated debate with?' Leah asked, leaning forward across the table. She tried to fix her mother's gaze, but her eyes flicked nervously around the café.

Rita shook her head, releasing a few long curly strands of hair from beneath her scarf. 'No one,' she said, far too quickly for it to actually be no one.

'In a shop? On the street, or what?'

'Just outside some new shop in town. It was nothing really.'

'*Mum...*' Leah injected as much of a warning tone into her voice as she dared.

'OK,' she sighed, holding onto her coffee mug with both hands, staring down at the table. 'Dad was walking along the street minding his own business. He was on his way to the chemist. Then suddenly, someone appeared in a shop window as if they were lunging at him. Dad was triggered, thinking he was being attacked by the enemy.'

It sounded plausible, Leah thought. She'd seen similar before. 'He must have been really frightened.'

'I'm afraid he reacted by... by smashing his walking stick through the shop window. It was pure self-defence.'

Leah gasped. 'Oh God, poor Dad!'

Rita nodded. The way she held her breath told Leah there was more.

'Well, what happened? Was the person in the shop angry?'

Rita gave another nod.

'What did they say? Which shop was it?' She could drop by and apologise, help sort out and pay for repairs. Maybe even give them a free haircut.

'It wasn't a *shop* exactly,' Rita said, glancing up. 'More... more an estate agent.'

Leah felt goosebumps crawl up her body. Her mouth went dry as the realisation dawned on her. 'Estate agent?'

Rita gave yet another nod. 'Don't be cross, darling.'

'It was Craig, wasn't it?' Leah replied, covering her mouth.

Rita took a long sip of her coffee, daring to look her daughter in the eye. 'It would appear he has a new office in town. Quite a smart one, actually. I really do like the colour scheme that—'

'Mum, forget bloody colour schemes. What *happened*? If Craig is responsible for Dad having a heart attack, I'll... I'll—'

Leah's phone pinged on the table in front of her and when she looked down at the screen, she saw a message from Gabe.

Can you come to the boat tonight, 7 p.m.?

CHAPTER SEVENTEEN

Leah was relieved that it was still light as she climbed down the steep bank beside the bridge that led to the towpath. She'd parked in a lay-by further down the lane. She wouldn't want to be doing this in the dark – not because there was anyone else about to be wary of (though the thought of being in such a remote area also made her nervous), but rather because it had been raining all afternoon and the passage down to the canal was muddy and slippery. Plus, the towpath along this stretch of canal was particularly narrow. One foot wrong and she'd be in the greeny-grey murk of the water.

'All very romantic, but I'm not sure I'd want to actually *live* on a boat,' she muttered as she headed west along the path as Gabe had instructed. It was nerves talking, she knew, because when she'd first met him, the whole idea of him living aboard a narrowboat was appealing. Now it just added to her distress at having to face him. She felt stupid and ashamed.

A couple of moorhens flapped out of some reeds on the opposite bank, joining several others on the water. Leah smiled briefly, wondering if they were a family group, though she suddenly felt saddened that she wasn't with her own family.

No, they were still next door with their father. Staying overnight yet again.

After she'd finally got back to the salon earlier, once her dad had been discharged from hospital – thankfully no heart attack, stroke or any other issue found – Leah had called Jodi to see if she could sit with the kids for a couple of hours while she went to see Gabe. But Jodi was busy, and straight after she'd ended the call there'd been a knock on her front door. When she answered it, Craig was standing there with Zoey and Henry flanking him.

Leah had smiled at the children then looked up at Craig, who had his arms folded as though he was cross with her for just being in her own home. She braced herself for whatever was coming, almost flinching from his presence.

'Hi, guys,' she'd said as brightly as she could manage. 'Come on in, kids.'

She'd expected Craig to leave then, wondering why on earth he'd felt it necessary to walk them the few feet home. 'Zoey, you should have just used your key, love.'

'They've come to collect a few things,' Craig had said, sending a jolt through Leah before she'd even realised what was happening. Her children slipped past her, with Zoey giving her a plaintive look as she passed. Then she heard their feet thumping up the stairs.

'What do you mean?' she'd said, taking a step forward and closing the door ajar behind her.

'They want to stop over again tonight. They'll need their sports kits for tomorrow.'

'But it's not—'

'Don't argue, Leah. It's their choice.' Craig half turned to the street, huffing out one of his sighs – the same sigh that told Leah there'd be consequences if she caused a fuss. It had lost its power a little since the divorce, but still sent shudders through her; still had her thinking about her actions and how not to anger him. The fallout had never been worth it.

'If it's really what they want then...' she trailed off, shaking her head, wondering how much he'd pressured them into it, '...then fine, but I want them back tomorrow after school,' she'd finished, thinking that, actually, it would help her out if they stayed with him tonight. If things worked out between her and Gabe, all being well he might even ask her to stay on the boat – a romantic make-up evening. Wine, music, candles...

Craig's eyes had flicked behind her through the hallway and beyond as he waited for Zoey and Henry to return with their stuff.

'Looks like they'll be better off at mine and Gilly's anyway,' he'd said with a sneer, staring up at the front facade of the house. 'You need to get this place sorted, Leah. It's an eyesore on the outside, and frankly looks even worse on the inside. You're doing my property no favours.' He shook his head. 'You've really no idea about anything, have you?'

'I'm doing my best...' But Leah had stopped when she'd heard the kids coming back downstairs. Upset by his comment, she'd turned away from him, leaving him smirking at her as he walked off down the front path again, the kids calling out goodbye as they looked back over their shoulders.

———

'Ahoy, there!' Leah said ten minutes later as she finally approached the bows of *Blue Moon*, forcing herself to sound cheery. The swirling grey clouds above had turned a peachy orange shade towards the horizon, highlighting the hedges and the old bridge up ahead with golden flecks. Leah wasn't sure if the weather was clearing or gearing up for another heavy downpour. As she walked down the length of the narrowboat, eyeing the pretty pots of geraniums and nasturtiums on the roof, she hoped it was the former.

There was no immediate sign of Gabe on the rear deck, though she caught sight of a light on in the cabin below. It looked cosy, she thought, as she approached the end of the boat. She just hoped she could make things OK again between them. She'd hate things to end because of Craig.

'Hi there,' Leah said, suddenly spotting him. He was sitting half in and half out of the cabin on the top step, paintbrush in one hand and a palette in the other. He finished a few brush-strokes on the inside of the cabin door before looking up.

'Come aboard,' he said in a voice that gave nothing away.

Last time she'd visited, he'd held her hand as she stepped over the gap between the boat and the bank. This time, he didn't even get up. Leah swallowed and leant over, grabbing the roof rail before stepping onto the deck. There was a fold-up camping chair beside the tiller and a bottle of beer in the armrest drinks holder.

Gabe turned back to what he was doing.

'That's... that's beautiful,' Leah said, steadying herself as she crouched down beside him. 'Did you paint it all yourself?'

Gabe nodded. 'Roses and castles – traditional on the canals,' he replied, glancing at her. 'When I first bought her, it was all faded and peeling so I repainted it all. This is just a touch-up where the sun has got to it.'

'Nice work,' Leah said, wondering if she should give him a kiss. When he didn't stop what he was doing, she decided against it. He didn't exactly seem pleased to see her. She backed away and sat down in the camping chair, staring down at her feet for a moment, watching Gabe bring a painted rose back to life.

'Look, can I just say that I'm absolutely mortified by the messages I sent you,' she began. 'I was drunk and shouldn't have done it. The terrible thing is, I don't even *remember* sending them. I can't tell you how stressful it's been with Craig living next door. He was the reason I'd had a few too many. My friend had come over and it was supposed to be a nice evening, but...'

She looked away, catching sight of another moorhen family scudding along close to the opposite bank.

'...But it turned into a nightmare. After years of... of torment from my ex, of him making me believe I was crazy and a bad person, of putting up with it for the kids' sake, I thought I was finally free after the divorce from hell. How stupid was I, eh?'

She paused to tuck some flyaway strands of hair behind her ears, hoping Gabe might say something. He didn't.

'And now, he's... he's...' Leah tried to catch her breath, but it came out as a hiccup instead. 'He's drilled a hole right through my bedroom wall, dumped a load of rubbish in my garden, stolen my dustbin as well as your scarf, and now it seems he's hell-bent on taking the kids away from—'

Gabe suddenly swung round. Leah wasn't sure if his expression was that of pity or anger. Either way, it made her heart thunder, reminding her too much of Craig.

'Leah, stop,' he sighed. 'I don't really want to think about the messages you sent me or hear about the reasons behind them, if it's all the same to you.' He stared at her, waiting for a reply, but Leah didn't know what to say. Everything she'd planned to get out – all the excuses, reasons, apologies and owning her erratic and out-of-character behaviour – had dissolved.

'I'm sorry—'

'And I'm sorry you've got so much going on. It sounds tough. But the reason I chose to live on a boat...' Gabe paused, getting to his feet and retrieving the bottle of beer from the cup holder. He took a swig. 'Look, I had my own reasons for getting away from everything, simplifying my life by living this way and doing a job I'm passionate about. But suddenly it's starting to feel like things could be getting... complicated again.'

Leah sighed. He was trying to end it between them.

'I'm sorry,' she whispered. 'I didn't mean to make things complicated for you. But I understand that's how it looks.'

Gabe stared across the canal as the boat rocked gently in the wake of another narrowboat chugging by. He raised his hand and said a quick hello to the people on board – a couple in their sixties with a little terrier standing on the roof, yapping as they passed. When they'd gone, he turned to Leah, crouching down beside her.

'It's not how it looks, Leah, it's how it *feels*.' He placed a hand on her leg, sending shivers through her. She wasn't sure if it was a tender touch or a gesture that would end with him taking her hand and leading her off the boat. Or worse – his fingers creeping up around her throat. 'But there are things you don't understand.'

Leah stared down at his hand, noticing the patches of rough skin from all the manual work he did, the way a couple of his knuckles were slightly grazed and chapped. They were the opposite of Craig's soft, manicured hands, hands that weren't afraid to deliver a blow.

'I made you feel bad, and you didn't deserve that.'

Gabe opened his mouth to speak but closed it again. He stroked Leah's knee fondly, then reached up to gently sweep some hair off her face that had blown loose again. A breeze was getting up.

'Perhaps you should take some time to get over everything. Maybe you're not in the right place for a...' He turned his face away, narrowing his eyes as though he was bracing himself. 'For a relationship.'

'You're right,' Leah said, feeling her body tense.

Suddenly, she didn't want his hand on her, or for him to make kind gestures. She didn't want his cajoling and understanding words or his pity. And she certainly didn't want to be on his boat any more.

All she wanted right now was to be back at work, chatting to her ladies, having a laugh with her staff, and when she went home to her children, Craig wouldn't be living next door and the whole thing would have been a terrible nightmare.

'I never planned on meeting you,' Gabe said. 'The way it all happened... it caught me off guard, that's for sure.' There was a wistful look in his eyes.

Leah remembered when she'd set eyes on him that time, intrigued by how he was staying balanced up in the tree while brandishing a chainsaw.

'Look, no hands!' he'd quipped back when she'd called out to him to be careful in her parents' garden. She'd popped home for lunch and he was lopping a few trees for her mum and dad. They'd exchanged a few more words and then Gabe had gone back to work and Leah had gone back to the salon for the afternoon. When she'd arrived back with the kids later that afternoon, he was in the front drive loading up his van.

'We must stop meeting like this,' he'd said with a grin, removing his hard hat and hi-vis jacket. She noticed it had his name printed on the back. 'And see, I survived.'

Leah had enjoyed the feeling inside her as she stared at him, their eyes boring into each other, as though something was being reignited. A flickering flame of excitement that she'd first felt at that party Abby had dragged her to a couple of years ago. She'd sent the kids inside, telling them she'd be in shortly.

'Glad to see that,' she'd said. 'Rather you than me, though. I'm afraid of heights. Knowing me, I'd probably saw through the branch I was secured to.'

Gabe had laughed. 'I love it up there,' he'd confessed. 'It makes me feel safe, in an unsafe kind of way. I get to see all sorts.'

'And no one's going to argue with you while you're wielding that thing,' she'd said, glancing at the bright yellow chainsaw he was packing up.

'Very true,' he'd replied, his laugh doing something to Leah again. 'If there's ever a gory murder locally, I'll be top of the suspect list.'

They'd chatted a bit more, with Gabe asking how she liked living in the street, and Leah briefly explaining that she was only staying with her parents temporarily, that she was in the process of buying the house of her dreams and would soon be moving in. Gabe had asked where it was.

'It's got this patch of land out the back,' she'd told him. 'It's very overgrown and will need a lot of clearing. I'm going to turn it into a vegetable plot. Get some chickens, maybe some bees. You know, the full-on *Good Life* cliché.' They'd both laughed at that.

'Well, if you need a hand with the clear-up, let me know,' Gabe had said. 'I'll give you a card.' He'd rooted around in his glovebox before coming out of his van and scratching his beard. 'I seem to have run out. Let me put my number in your phone.'

It wasn't the first time Leah had noticed his strong hands. Stained with green sap and smeared with oil, she watched as his fingers deftly entered his details in her phone. Then, before she could say anything, he'd texted himself her number.

'Now I have yours too. For when I ask you out for a drink,' he'd said with a wink. Leah couldn't remember much after that, but she knew she'd stood there watching him pack up the rest of his kit. And she'd even given him a little wave as he'd driven off, before turning and going into her parents' house to make the kids' dinner. Somehow, at the end of the very long, dark tunnel that had been her life for so many years, Leah had sensed there was a tiny flicker of light.

'I guess I'll go, then,' Leah said now, hardly daring to look Gabe in the eye. Instead, she studied the delicate image on the cabin door, wishing she lived in the fairy-tale castle in the painting – a place where dreams really did come true. A place where Craig didn't exist.

Later, she couldn't remember if she'd given Gabe a hug or not as she left, or what he'd said to her, or what she might have said in return. All she was conscious of was getting off the boat and walking – no, *running* – away from *Blue Moon* back in the direction of her car along the muddy bank as fast as she could. And it wasn't the fading light that made her fall flat on her face as she scrambled up the slippery bank, rather the tears streaming down her cheeks, blurring her vision.

CHAPTER EIGHTEEN

Even before she'd opened her front door, Leah sensed something was wrong. She was churned up and unsettled from what had just happened, but something else added to her layers of unease as she stepped inside. A sixth sense kicking in that made her skin prickle.

She dumped her bag and keys on the hall table, half slipping off her jacket – which was caked in mud from her fall. Then she gasped, one arm still in a sleeve.

'What... what are you doing in my house?' she stammered, annoyed with herself that she wasn't ordering him out.

Through the door to her living room, she saw Craig sitting on her sofa, reclining with his hand draped over the back. He had one foot up on the seat with his shoe scuffing the fabric. He was idly flipping through a women's magazine and slowly looked up when he heard Leah's voice.

'You still reading this trash?' He knocked the magazine onto the floor. 'Christ, you look a state again. What have you been doing this time, mud-wrestling?' He huffed out a laugh.

'Why are you here? How did you get in?'

'My children live here, Leah. They invited me in.'

Leah slowly shook her head. Her entire body was shaking. Her mouth opened and closed several times, but nothing came out.

'Keep your hair on,' Craig went on. 'They're just getting some more belongings for the rest of the week. I said I'd help them carry their bags.'

'Rest of the week?' Leah whispered, hardly believing what she was hearing. 'No, Craig, they're back with me tomorrow, remember? You had them an extra night last night, so by rights, you've used up your midweek visit and shouldn't see them until a week Wednesday.'

'You're still so uptight and angry, aren't you?' He stood up and approached Leah, staring down at her. Even though he was only a couple of inches taller than her, it felt like two feet. 'The fact is, the kids prefer it with me and Gilly, so it makes sense that I have full residency.'

'You can't just go against the court order,' Leah told him. 'And don't even get me started on what you did to my father. He ended up in hospital because of you lunging at him, and—'

Craig laughed loudly, making Leah recoil. 'The stupid old fool put his walking stick through my front window. How is that *me* doing anything to *him*? I rushed over when I heard the sound of breaking glass.'

Leah thought back to what her mother had said happened. Had she got it wrong, or had her dad been muddled about events? Or the more likely option was that her father had spotted Craig's new agency in their town and had become incensed by the brazenness of the man. He'd been furious with him for treating his daughter so badly. If her dad had been triggered by seeing the new premises, he would have acted on impulse.

'That's *not* what happened,' Leah replied, though she knew

from experience there was no arguing with him. Craig was a bully, and her dad wasn't here to defend himself.

Leah was all ready to ramp up her defence and order him out of her house, but Zoey and Henry thundered down the stairs and appeared in the living room, each of them carrying a fully stuffed holdall. She went up to her children and cocooned them both in her arms, breathing in the scent of their day.

'Hey, my darlings,' she said, closing her eyes at their sweetness. Their innocence kept her going.

'Dad's got the new PlayStation at his!' Henry squealed, peeling himself away from Leah. 'And he bought me a gaming chair. It's awesome!'

'Wonderful,' Leah heard herself saying, though it cut deep. She'd never be able to afford anything like that for her son and knew that Craig had only done it to get one over on her and tempt Henry next door.

'How was school, Zo?' she asked her daughter, who stood with her head down and her eyes fixed firmly on the floor. She was visibly squirming. 'Oh... your ears,' Leah continued, reaching out and tucking Zoey's hair back. 'When did you get *those* done?' She tried not to sound upset, but they'd had an agreement that until she was sixteen at least, she'd stick with one piercing in each lobe. Now she had two extra studs in the cartilage.

'At the weekend,' Zoey said, without looking up. 'Gilly took me. Sorry, Mum. I can let them grow over if you don't like them.'

Leah shot a look at Craig, who stood there grinning and holding up his palms defensively.

'Nothing to do with me,' he said, looking at Zoey fondly. 'Girls' stuff. Far be it from me to interfere with all their shopping trips and pamper sessions.'

And that's when Leah noticed the expensive trainers her

daughter was wearing, as well as the nail varnish and rings she didn't recognise.

'Did you go to the extra swimming training at the weekend, love? The county gala is coming up soon.'

Zoey shrugged and pulled a pained face. 'Gilly said I didn't have to. I was tired from the party. We... we stayed up really late.' She glanced at her father with heavy eyes, hitching up her bag on her shoulder.

Leah forced a smile, praying no one mentioned her performance on the front lawn that night.

'Right, guys,' Craig said. 'Ready?'

Zoey didn't reply at first, hesitating when she realised Leah was still holding onto her arm. 'Is it OK with you, Mum, if we stay at Dad and Gilly's a bit longer? Gilly wants me to help her make a Mexican meal tonight. She's had all the ingredients delivered especially.' She let out a little sigh before leaning in and whispering in Leah's ear. 'I'll keep an eye on Henry for you. He's so excited about his new PlayStation.'

Henry jiggled impatiently from one foot to the other, bending forward under the weight of his bag. Craig took it off him, groaning and making a show of how heavy it was and sending Henry into fits of laughter.

'Sure,' Leah said, forcing herself not to glare at Craig. 'That's... that's fine, love.'

Leah watched as Craig ushered her children out of her house. It felt as though she was watching them being kidnapped and, without causing a scene she knew she'd later regret, there wasn't a damn thing she could do about it. But what she did know is that she'd be phoning her solicitor first thing in the morning.

———

Later that evening, Leah sat alone in her living room with the curtains drawn and her feet tucked up under her. She clutched a cushion to her chest, sipping on a glass of wine. She hadn't really wanted a drink – not after what the alcohol had caused her to text to Gabe the other night – but she needed something to take the edge off what she was feeling. And she wasn't about to text him again. In fact, he'd probably blocked her by now. She couldn't stand to check.

'Craig, Craig, *Craig*...' she said, digging the fingers of one hand into the soft stuffing of the cushion. She pretended it was her ex's face – that she was gouging out his eyes or twisting his smarmy cheeks, wiping the smirk off him for good. 'And how dare Gillian get my daughter's ears pierced without my permission.'

It sickened her that she hadn't been a part of the decision, that she was being undermined by someone who had no doubt started off as nothing more than one of Craig's random affair women. She worked for Craig's estate agency, so it was almost a certainty.

'*Cooking* together,' she said bitterly. '*Pamper* sessions,' she added in a mocking voice. When she went to get more wine from the kitchen, she went out of the back door in her socks and crept up to the wall between the two houses. She couldn't hear anything, so she dragged over a garden chair and stepped up onto it, peeking over the wall. The lights were on in the kitchen at the back of the big house, and she could just make out people busying about inside.

She watched for a few minutes as the figures flitted around the kitchen, behind the blinds that weren't quite drawn. There was Zoey – snuggled up in a soft fleece dressing gown that she didn't recognise, grinning as she chopped something on the large island unit. Several times, Gillian walked past, also in a robe, though hers appeared to be cream satin. The pair were obviously chatting together, and the way Zoey occasionally bobbed her head indicated there was music playing.

Leah stiffened, her fingers gripping the top of the wall as she held her breath. Craig came into the kitchen holding a glass of red wine – not wearing a robe like the others, but rather jeans and a branded T-shirt that she remembered buying for him. He'd never once worn it while they were together. She watched as he grabbed Gillian roughly from behind and wrapped his arms around her. She responded by tipping back her head and laughing as Craig planted a kiss on her mouth, trailing his lips down her neck. Zoey was about three feet away from them but remained focused on her chopping.

'For God's sake,' Leah muttered, knowing how uncomfortable that would make Zoey.

Then Craig went out of view for a moment and, a second later, Zoey and Gillian started dancing wildly – each of them waving their hands in the air and shaking their hips in time together. Leah's mouth dropped open as she witnessed what was obviously a well-rehearsed routine. Craig must have turned the music up because she could hear the beat of it through the window.

'How very cosy,' Leah whispered, trying to remember when she and Zoey had last had a kitchen disco, but she couldn't. She was pleased her daughter was enjoying herself, of course, but it cut deep that she wasn't a part of it.

Sure, they'd had fun over the years, she and the kids, mainly while Craig was working long hours or away on business (though she knew there hadn't been much actual business going on). And she couldn't deny that they'd made some good memories of them all together as a family – holidays, days out, celebrations. But since the divorce – since she'd been forced from the life that she'd envisaged for her and her children – she wondered if she'd become... well, not as *much* fun as she used to be.

She knew something had to change – and fast. Before her children slipped away from her completely. As she watched Zoey cavorting around the kitchen of the house next door with a woman who wasn't her mother, she made a pact with herself. She wanted Craig gone from her life for good. She just wasn't sure how she was going achieve that yet.

CHAPTER NINETEEN

'You have *no* idea how much I needed this,' Leah said as she sat cross-legged on the floor of Jodi's living room. There was plenty of space for the six of them in the modern detached house that Jodi and her partner, Nick, had bought through Craig's agency several years ago. Leah removed her sweater, revealing a T-shirt below – a testament to how warm a new house could be. Now they were well into October, the weather had turned chilly.

Despite her best efforts, Leah's thoughts had often drifted onto Gabe these last few weeks, wondering how he was – and if he was warm enough on the boat in this unusual cold snap. Each time her phone pinged with a message, she'd grabbed it, hoping it was him – perhaps offering to meet up, to talk things over, maybe try again.

But it never was.

She'd heard nothing from him since she'd walked away from his boat.

'Right, girls,' Jodi said, dropping down onto one of the floor cushions scattered around the big coffee table. 'Let the games begin!'

She peeled off cling film from the snacks they'd all brought and offered them round, while Abby shuffled and dealt the cards. It used to be that they'd meet up monthly at each other's houses, but in more recent times, their girl-only get-togethers had dwindled. Leah hadn't seen the others for what seemed like forever – though of course she'd spotted them all a few weeks ago going into Craig's house for what she now knew was a house-warming party. She'd since tried to put it out of her mind.

Though she had to admit, when Jodi had invited her to the gathering tonight, Leah had initially had second thoughts. She didn't want her business getting back to Craig if he was still in touch with the others. But then it could work both ways, she decided, and she might get some idea of what they knew about his reasons for moving next door.

'We've missed you so much at our get-togethers, Leah,' Abby said, taking an olive. 'And I can't believe none of us has seen your new place yet.' She glanced at the others and Leah swore her eyebrows rose slightly – though she couldn't be sure.

She wondered what Abby meant by *missing* her. She hadn't been told about any of their meet-ups for a long while.

'I know, it's crazy how time flies. I've been mad busy with gardening and decorating. The last of the summer just flew by, what with all the kids' activities and keeping them entertained and ferried about, as well as all the back-to-school stuff. But things are more settled now.'

Not all of that was at all true, of course, but Leah couldn't bear to reveal the reality – that Zoey and Henry had been spending more and more time with their father and Gillian lately, and, if she was honest, she was feeling more and more out of touch with what was going on in their lives.

She still saw them, of course, when they stayed the occasional night with her, but most of their free time now seemed to be spent with their father, and they'd gradually taken many of their toys and belongings next door. Leah had dealt with it by convincing herself that it was what the children wanted, that they enjoyed time with their dad and the lifestyle he offered, but she was also aware that Zoey's mood had changed. She didn't seem to be the happy and vibrant girl she once was. It had been particularly hard watching her children bring friends home from school, with Henry and his pals bouncing on the huge trampoline Craig had bought, as well as playing in the custom-built tree house. It must have cost a fortune.

'And what a coincidence that...' Michelle trailed off as though she'd had second thoughts.

Sensing what might be coming, Leah picked up her cards and made a groaning sound, trying to deflect attention. 'Oh well, that's me going to lose, with a hand like this.' She rolled her eyes and laughed, taking a couple of crisps.

'...A coincidence that... that you moved in right next door to Craig and Gilly,' Michelle finished, giving a glance around the group. Her expression was expectant.

Leah coughed loudly, putting up her hand just in time to catch the spray of crisps. 'Sorry, *what*?' she choked out. 'That's simply not true.'

'Bluffer,' Allie chipped in, immediately turning scarlet. 'I mean about the cards,' she added quickly.

'I guess it's convenient for the children, though,' Michelle continued in a pitying voice. 'Though if Tony and I ever split up – heaven forbid – then I'm not sure I'd want to have the minutiae of his new life shoved right under my nose. I'd want to get as far away as possible.'

'It really wasn't like that, Michelle,' Leah replied. She put down her cards and took a long sip of the cocktail Jodi had made. God only knew what was in it, but she didn't care. 'I wasn't the one to move in next to Craig. *He* moved in next to me. I had no idea about it.' Leah felt all eyes were on her. 'What?' she said, staring around when no one said anything.

'Sometimes it's hard to move on. We understand that,' Abby said, placing a hand on Leah's arm. 'But do you think it's healthy for you to be watching him all the time, monitoring what he's doing? And I say that out of love, Lee.'

'*Watching* him? Ha!' Leah couldn't help the exclamation as she leant back on her hands. She didn't know whether to get up and leave or stay and defend herself. 'I can assure you, it's totally the other way around. Craig even drilled a hole right through into my bedroom. I wouldn't be surprised if he'd intended on putting one of those little cameras through the wall if I hadn't spotted it and patched it up. If anyone's been spying on anyone, it's him spying on *me*.' Leah's voice wavered.

These were her friends, supposedly. Craig had only ever got to know them because of her. She'd met Abby, Michelle and Allie in Henry's school playground and, subsequently, they'd socialised as couples over the last three years.

'We understand, honestly,' Fran, Allie's partner, said.

She was the quietest of the group and also happened to work for another local estate agency. It was no secret that in the time since Leah had known her, she'd been cosying up to Craig in the hope he'd take her on. All of a sudden, she was seeing these so-called friends in a slightly different light.

'We know how tough it must have been for you to witness him meet someone else at work, but it's a close-knit business and I'm afraid it happens more often than you think.'

Leah couldn't help notice the loving look Fran gave Allie, the way they linked hands. Fran was a single mum to one of Henry's best friends when Allie came into her life – Fran had shown her around a rental property, and they'd hit it off straight away. However, no other partners were involved or cheating in their case. Leah wondered if everyone had known about Craig and Gillian's cosy work affair long before she'd found out, keeping their dirty secret.

'Right,' Leah said, resigning herself to being the scapegoat for now. She knew from experience that it was pointless defending herself if Craig had gone on the offensive first. He had a way of charming and convincing people of the most ridiculous things, especially when it came to selling houses. Manipulating their mutual friends to take his side would be child's play to him.

'Let's get on with this card game, shall we?' she continued, refusing to be drawn into anything further about her ex. It was bad enough having him live next door, let alone have him infiltrating her social life These friends had always been important to her.

'Leah, he showed us the video,' Abby said, a pained look on her face. 'Hand on heart, and I mean this in a kind way, but is your mental health OK since... you know, the divorce?' She mouthed the word 'divorce'.

Leah took another big glug of her cocktail, aware that all eyes were on her.

'And don't take this the wrong way because we all care about you, but he mentioned about your drinking, how you're struggling.'

'What video?' Leah made a point of putting down her drink.

'From the security cameras at his and Gilly's place,' Abby continued.

'I'm sure Leah doesn't need to worry about that now, 'Jodi chipped in with an uncomfortable look on her face. 'She's had enough on her plate lately.'

'No, no, it's fine, Jodi. I want to know what Abby's talking about.'

Abby grimaced, looking away for a moment. 'I mean, I kind of understand why you did it. If I'd been accused of something like that, I wouldn't be happy either. But I'm not sure—'

'Abby, will you please just tell me what you're talking about? I literally have no idea!'

'We all know you're a good mum – don't we, girls?' Abby

circled her gaze around the group. The others nodded in agreement.

'Let's drop it now,' Jodi said as she handed round a plate of snacks. 'Have one of these, Abby.'

'I just don't want her to hear it from anyone else, that's all,' Abby said, shifting her position on the cushion. She wrapped her long fingers around her wine glass and Leah couldn't help noticing her freshly manicured baby-pink nails. She balled up her own hands so her nails weren't on show.

'Hear *what*?' Leah insisted.

'And we all know how hard it is to bring up kids these days, what with all their demands and—'

'Abby, what?'

'I'm sure Craig didn't mean that you neglect them in a bad way, Leah. Just... well, he has the kids' best interests at heart. He's such a devoted dad. You can't disagree with that.'

Devoted dad echoed around Leah's mind until her brain caught up with what Abby had just said.

'*Neglect* them?' Leah barely whispered. She couldn't believe what she was hearing. Surely her friends – her school mum friends, of all people – knew that was a lie. She'd lay down her life ten times over for Zoey and Henry.

She shook her head, blowing out an exasperated sigh. So this was Craig's new tack – to make out that she was a bad mother.

'Abby...' Jodi warned, shooting her a look. She topped up everyone's glasses from the cocktail jug, hoping that would defuse the increasing tension. Everyone's glass except Leah's.

'The divorce took its toll on you, Lee. We understand that,' Abby pressed on. 'So it was inevitable that the kids would take a back seat for a while. Craig just wants to ensure they have stability going forward. Another break-up in their lives wouldn't be good for them.'

'Another break-up? What are you talking about?' Leah

tugged at the collar of her T-shirt as she broke out in a sweat. 'And for the last time, what video?'

Abby paused, her head tilted to one side, before she took her phone from her handbag. She opened Instagram and, before she knew what was happening, Leah had the phone thrust in front of her face and was watching a clip that, at first, she couldn't make out.

It was dark and grainy and shot from high up, though the person in the video was in a pool of light, their eyes glinting spooky reflections back at what was clearly a security camera. It only took another few seconds for Leah to recognise herself leaning over the wall – presumably the night she watched Zoey and Gillian cavorting about in next door's kitchen. Afterwards, she'd gone back inside and drowned her sadness in another glass of wine before going to bed with a pillow over her head so she couldn't hear the inevitable nightly noises from Craig and Gillian's bedroom.

'I mean... I sort of understand why you felt so upset, Leah, but... it was Henry who found all the rubbish you'd dumped over the wall into their garden. And he was so distraught that you'd thrown out his favourite action figures.' Abby pouted as she swiped through several Instagram photos following the video clip.

Leah saw a pile of rubbish – vegetable peelings, tissues, cellophane wrappers, teabags and all manner of kitchen non-recyclables – with the final photo showing a shot of three plastic action figures sitting on top of the mess, their bodies smeared with what looked like blood, though it was obviously tomato ketchup. She skim-read the caption beneath:

When your ex moves in next door... #bitter #divorce #exwife #nextdoor #backtocourtwego #leaveusalone

'This is utterly, *utterly* crazy,' Leah said, gasping. She'd already blocked Craig on her social media so hadn't seen any of these posts, but it was so typical of him to pepper his accounts with sympathy posts, as though *he* was the victim. 'I absolutely did *not* dump anything in Craig's garden, let alone throw out any of Henry's toys. In fact, I bought him those figures. I know how much he loves them.'

Leah rummaged in her bag for her phone, intending to text Craig and ask him what the hell he was playing at. But Jodi grabbed hold of her wrist and gently took it away.

'Trust me, Lee. Don't do it. Not right now.' She raised her eyebrows and peered over the top of her glasses, issuing what Leah knew was a friendly warning. She'd known Jodi for a long time and trusted her advice. And given her shotgun texting history with Gabe, she relented and put her phone away again.

'You're right,' Leah said, her mouth dry from rage. 'The idiot doesn't deserve my attention. But for the record, girls, what he's accusing me of is totally untrue.' She hung her head for a moment. 'Apart from having a look over the wall to... to check what the noise was. I heard loud music and it was keeping me awake.' Not quite true again, Leah knew, but she wasn't about to make herself look even more guilty. 'It's the lowest of the low to accuse me of neglecting my children.'

'Agreed,' Jodi said, picking up a card from the deck and ditching one from her hand. 'Your turn, Allie.'

Allie cleared her throat and, after shooting a quick glance at Abby and Michelle, she took her turn at the game.

'In that case, probs best not to mention the car,' Abby muttered under her breath. 'I'll get no thanks for it.'

Leah slammed down her cards on the table, harder than she'd intended. 'Car? What now?'

'Damaging personal property. You're lucky he hasn't got the police involved.'

'Please, let's just forget it,' Jodi said, getting visibly annoyed with Abby. 'I don't want the evening spoilt.' She turned to Leah.

'There's no way you can tell it's you in the video, so don't give it another thought. It was probably just teenagers causing trouble.'

'But it's his pride and joy,' Abby protested. 'Keying a car is never OK, but it had barely left the showroom.' She pouted, looking over at Leah. 'Though really, hon, I do understand your frustration.'

Leah stared at Abby then got to her feet and grabbed her bag. 'It seems no one is going to believe me, so I'm heading off now. Thanks for the invite, Jodi.' She bent down to give her friend a brief hug before glaring at the others.

'He really got to you all, didn't he?' she said, shaking her head as she left.

CHAPTER TWENTY

The house was dark, cold and far too quiet when Leah arrived home, grateful she'd only had half a drink and hadn't stayed over as planned. Numb, she dropped down onto her sofa, not particularly remembering the drive home from Jodi's house – apart from when she saw Craig's face leering at her as she passed three of his 'For Sale' boards on the route back.

'He's everywhere I turn,' she whispered, fiddling with the drawstring of her hoodie. She threw her head back and closed her eyes. What the hell was she going to do? A big part of her wanted to sell her house, move away – even if it was just to another area of town – but then why should she have to? Round and round her thoughts went, making her feel as though she was spiralling back into her old life.

Tonight, though, it seemed quiet next door and all the lights were off when she'd arrived home earlier. On top of everything, her mind was still spinning from Abby and Michelle's accusations, how they seemed to believe Craig's lies about her – though really, it came as no surprise. Craig was as convincing as they came.

'Neglecting my children,' she whispered, shaking her head

and sighing out hard. 'How could he *say* that?' Even though she knew it wasn't true, it was the lowest of the low. He knew where to hit her.

But Leah's tangled thoughts were interrupted by the doorbell ringing. She glanced at her watch. Eight fifteen. Odd, she thought, wishing she'd got round to installing the video doorbell she'd bought a while back.

It rang again – several times in quick succession.

She wasn't expecting anyone, though a pang of hope shot through her that it might be Gabe dropping by, wanting to smooth things over between them. She got up and cautiously went to open the front door, keeping it on the chain.

'Oh...' she said, shocked to see Craig standing there, staring at her. 'Are the children OK? Where are they?' She gripped the door, eyeing him through the gap. 'Craig?' she said when he didn't reply. He was swaying and his eyes appeared glazed, while his shirt was half untucked from his jeans and his hair ruffled. 'Where are the children?'

'Kids are fine,' he finally said, expressionless, swaying again. 'Can I come in?'

Leah's heart thumped. She could smell the booze on him even through the small gap in the door. 'What for?'

Craig put out a hand, leaning on the wall. 'Jus' let me in, Lee,' he slurred.

Sighing, Leah closed the door and took off the chain, opening it fully. Something was wrong and she just prayed it wasn't to do with the children. 'Tell me where Zoey and Henry are?' she said as he tripped up the step into the hallway.

He leant back against the wall. 'Got anything to drink?' He grinned, reaching out a hand and stroking her arm. Leah shied away, closing the door, though not locking it. He wouldn't be staying long.

'You're drunk,' she said. 'I don't think you need any more

alcohol. If you don't tell me where the kids are, I'll have to call Gillian.'

'They're...' He thought a moment, as if he couldn't quite remember. 'They're at the cinema with Gilly.'

'But it's past Henry's bedtime.'

'Chill, Leah. Like I said, they're fine.'

'But you're clearly not.' Leah sighed again, staring up at him. 'What is it you want, Craig?' Her voice wavered as she spoke, knowing how quickly his mood could turn.

'Jus' to see you,' he said, drawing closer. 'Is that such a crime?'

Leah narrowed her eyes at him. 'I know you too well,' she said. 'You might as well tell me why you're here and cut out the cr—'

'Don't be like that, Lee,' he said, putting his arms around her waist. Leah recoiled, slipping through into the living room to get away from him. He followed her. 'You want the truth?'

She turned, making sure she kept a good distance.

'I miss you,' Craig said when Leah remained silent. 'All the good times we had.'

Leah breathed in sharply, shuddering from his words. She certainly hadn't been expecting that. 'Like I said, you're drunk. Hopefully in the morning you won't even remember you said that.' She silently wished she could erase it from her mind too.

'I'm serious,' Craig said, dropping down onto the sofa. 'Things aren't the same with Gilly. It's not like we had.'

Leah felt a pang of guilt for poor Gillian – the woman who had taken her place. She'd be devastated if she knew Craig was here, insinuating such things.

'That's up to you to sort out with her,' Leah replied. She wanted none of his nonsense. 'I suggest you go home and make yourself a strong coffee.'

'How about you make me one?' Craig said, tilting his head to one side. His cheeks were flushed from the alcohol and he had a sheen of perspiration on his skin. 'It'll give us time to...' He looked her up and down. 'You know... talk.'

'There's nothing to talk about,' Leah said, folding her arms. 'Why aren't you at the cinema with Gillian and the children?'

He shrugged. 'Because I wanted to go to the pub instead.'

'Did you two have a row?'

'You always were a mind reader,' Craig said, standing up. He approached her again, taking her by the shoulders and pulling her close. 'And you always understood me. It could work out quite nicely, what with us living next door to each other, don't you think?'

Leah froze. She wasn't sure if it was fear that fixed her in place, making her completely unable to extract herself from his touch, or something else. Something far more sinister and worrying as she stared up into his eyes.

'Gillian need never know. Our little secret.'

'Craig!' she said, finally finding the strength to release herself from his grip. 'No. Just absolutely no. You've got a bloody nerve.'

'You don't mean that,' he said, advancing on her again. 'I know you still have feelings for me.'

Leah stumbled backwards, bumping into the wall. As he approached her again, she wanted to scream, to run – do anything to get out of this situation. But as he lunged towards her, arms outstretched and making a grab for her, she managed to drop down and slip out from beneath his grip. Craig swung round – a devastated and hurt look on his face – making Leah flinch, waiting for the blow she was used to receiving.

'You need to go now,' she said as sternly as she could manage when he just stood there staring at her, a doleful look in his eyes. 'After everything, if you think you're going to make *me* your affair partner, then you can think again.'

'But, Leah—'

'Go home, Craig. Sober up and sort it out with Gillian.'

Leah slipped past him and went into the hallway, holding the front door open wide. She needed him gone before she broke down. She was barely holding it together.

'Fine,' he replied after a moment, heading towards the door. 'But don't ever think I don't care about you, Lee, because...'

But she didn't wait to hear the rest. As soon as he was over the threshold, she shut the door, double-locking it, before leaning back against the wall and covering her face with her hands, wondering what the hell had just happened.

CHAPTER TWENTY-ONE

As the kettle boiled, Leah stared out into the darkness of her little courtyard, rattled by Craig's visit. She had no idea if it was the booze talking or if he really did regret their divorce and wanted her back.

She shuddered at the thought, jumping as the security light came on outside. But then she saw Cecil sloping past, winding his way towards the back door. She opened it and let him in, pausing to gaze out. She'd not sat out in her pretty courtyard with a coffee now for weeks – not since *he'd* moved in next door. And she'd not bothered to water her pots or sweep the old cobbles like she used to. She couldn't stand the thought of Craig watching her every move from his window above, laughing and mocking her as she made her home her own while he stared down from his grand place that was five times more expensive. Or worse, that he was imagining them reuniting or having some kind of sordid affair.

The only space outside offering any kind of privacy was the vegetable garden beyond the wall. He couldn't see all of it from his upstairs windows, though certain parts were visible. She'd spent more and more time tending to it the last few weeks, partly to block out the void left by the kids not being around as much – and at least she could hear Henry's voice over the wall when he played out with his friends, occasionally the beat of whatever music Zoey had playing in her new bedroom – but also because tending to the garden soothed her, gave her some peace from her overwrought mind.

Leah made herself a mug of chamomile tea and, on a whim, took it outside. The security light lit her way over to the old wooden door in the wall, which she shoved open, going through into the darkness beyond. It was as if the air itself was different within the old Victorian garden, somehow easier to breathe.

Over in the far corner, she heard the content roosting sounds coming from her hen house. She only had four birds so far, but since they'd arrived from the rescue place a week ago, they'd already been good layers. She stumbled over the long grass between the beds she'd been digging, rattling the wooden gate to the coop that she'd made. She was proud of herself for constructing it out of timber she'd found lying about, with chicken wire from the local hardware store to keep out the couple of foxes she knew prowled about at night locally. Their plaintive and eerie screeches had woken her more than once.

'Night night, ladies,' Leah said quietly to the hens. She heard rustling and clucking coming from within their shelter and continued walking around the perimeter of the garden, feeling like a security guard checking everything was secure. A couple of times she stumbled on the uneven ground, her slip-on shoes not much use out in the long, wet grass – though the nearly full moon and ambient light from the town provided some visibility.

She stopped when she reached the point closest to the road – a patch of thick, brambly hedge with an old, disused gateway buried within it leading out on to the road beyond. It wasn't a busy street by any means, and would have once been used as access for the gardeners when they came to work, growing vegetables for the Old Vicarage back in its heyday when this part of town was a separate village. She needed to get it cleared, opening up the access to make it easier to bring in a bigger rotavator next year. She had grand plans for the growing season in the spring.

But then Gabe was on her mind – how he would have been the one she'd ask to help chop back the hedge. He'd have had it done in no time with his equipment, perhaps accepting a home-cooked meal instead of actual payment. His rates weren't expensive, she knew that from her parents. In fact, after they'd swapped numbers at her mum and dad's place back in the summer, she'd gently probed what her parents knew about him, how they'd found him for their tree work.

'Oh, a flyer came through the door at just the right time. And he seemed like a nice chap,' her mum had said, fiddling with her hair and blushing a little. 'Very charming, in fact. Plus, his rates were... well, they were almost too good to be true compared to the other quotes we'd had.'

Leah had nodded, filing the information away and not really thinking much more of it.

Until now when, she admitted, she really needed his help.

But it wasn't just that. No. She missed him like mad and had had to restrain herself from messaging him on several occasions. It was clear he didn't want to hear from her. He would have been in touch himself if he did. It hurt like hell, but it wasn't any more complicated than that. Though the thought of contacting him still niggled away at her daily.

Leah flicked on her phone torch to help guide her around the rest of the allotment. She ended up sitting on a tree stump near the fruit cages, nursing her mug of hot tea, staring at the big pile of garden rubbish she'd been accumulating for Bonfire Night. It was already huge.

A few weeks earlier, she'd naively imagined her and the kids making a guy, setting light to the big pile of wood – home-made toffee apples at the ready and eating ketchup-doused hot dogs as they watched the flames. Her fantasy had gone on to include Gabe as he ran back from lighting the fireworks, then slipped his arm around her as they all stood close, huddling up to keep warm, their eyes glittering with the bright colours in the sky.

But the whole dream had gone up in smoke.

Now she sat alone, staring at the great pile of rubbish – the latest addition being all the branches and garden waste that Craig had dumped in her courtyard. And what ridiculous behaviour, she thought, knowing that he'd deliberately planted the mess of kitchen rubbish on his side, complete with Henry's toys, and photographed it to make it appear like she'd done it. When would it stop? What if it never did? How many months, years or decades of her life would she have to hold her breath, waiting to see what stunt he pulled next?

It was a small town and word would soon spread about her being the crazy ex, the woman who couldn't move on, obsessed with her former husband and his new woman. Her business would likely suffer as clients got wind of the rumours and her friends would drift away even more. Meantime, Craig would be seen as the hero, the good guy who saved his children from neglect at the hands of their mentally unstable mother.

Leah clamped her teeth together as her mind created a future for herself that didn't exist yet, but so easily could. She knew the way that man worked. All too familiar with his sick ways, she knew he'd never forgiven her for finally finding the courage to leave him for good. And she could hardly believe the nerve of the man, coming round drunk and implying they should have an affair – all part of his manipulation tactics, no doubt.

She'd tried dozens of times to escape him over the years. On the fourth attempt, she'd packed a small bag each for her and the children and hidden their belongings in the boot of her car in readiness. Passports, bank statements and copies of mortgage documents plus a spare phone charger were in there, along with a change of clothes each and basic toiletries.

'I'm leaving,' she'd said one winter's evening when Craig had come in from work. Her first mistake was telling him.

Henry was a toddler and Zoey only just eight. She'd already fed and bathed the children and wrapped them up in their dressing gowns, warm socks and slippers. She had snacks and drinks in the car and absolutely no idea where she would take them. Probably a cheap hotel – she didn't care. But she was ready and determined, and nothing, not even Craig, would talk her out of her decision.

'Don't be ridiculous,' he'd said, dumping down his work bag. She remembered his snide laugh, the reek of women's perfume as he pushed past her in the hall.

'I mean it, Craig. I've had enough.' She'd followed him into the kitchen while the kids were watching TV. Leah gripped her car keys, knowing that all she needed was her children and she was ready to go.

So what was stopping her? What had rooted her to the floor?

It was the look he'd given her as he swung round to face her – a look of bereavement, almost as though she'd glimpsed his soul behind the mask. A person she rarely, if ever, saw.

Saying nothing, he'd unscrewed the whisky bottle he was holding and, as he usually did when he got home, he poured a large drink.

He put down the bottle and walked over to her, taking a large sip as he drew near, his face pressed up close to hers.

'I swear to God, Leah, if you walk out of that door now and leave me, I will kill myself. What will you tell the children then? That Daddy is dead because of you?'

Then he'd spat in her face.

She'd recoiled from the smell of his breath, taking a step back. But Craig moved closer, his cheeks red and seething as his hand grabbed hold of her waist, slipping up her body, over her stomach, her breast, and up onto her neck. While taking another swallow of drink, he forced her back against the wall with his knee pinned between her legs to stop her moving.

And then he'd squeezed, his hand strong as his fingers dug into Leah's neck until she could hardly breathe. Red-faced and choking, she grabbed his arm, trying desperately to pull it away, but the fight for oxygen took over as her vision blurred and her hands fell limp.

All she could think of in those terrible moments was the children – and, if she died, how they would be left with only him.

She must have managed a nod – some kind of gesture that he recognised as acquiescence.

It was enough.

He released her.

Leah had dropped to her knees, coughing and gasping, her head pounding as though it was about to explode. Her car keys were lying on the kitchen floor beside her, and she saw his hand reach down and pick them up.

'You won't be needing these now, will you?' he'd said, confiscating them for the next three months, not allowing her to leave the house unless it was to take the children to school.

Now, sitting on the tree stump, Leah took another sip of her tea. But it had gone cold. She stared at the bonfire, her dreams of a cosy night around it with the children and Gabe destroyed.

She missed him so much.

On a whim, going against every grain of sense she had left, she took her phone from her pocket and tapped out a brief message to him, telling him her news and how she was getting on with the garden, knowing she'd probably regret sending it when he didn't bother to reply. But she knew she'd regret it more if she didn't at least try to make contact.

When she saw the two grey ticks appear on her screen, indicating the message had been delivered, she got up and walked over to the bonfire, hurling her mug into the pile of branches and twigs. It smashed against the wood. And the only thing Leah could imagine burning in it now was Craig.

CHAPTER TWENTY-TWO

Leah turned over in bed, restless and unable to sleep. She pulled the duvet up over her head, still feeling disturbed by what had happened at Jodi's as well as Craig's subsequent visit. Sleep had been fitful at the best of times lately, her senses on high alert for her ex's next stunt – but this was different. Something inside the house was keeping her awake. Something close by.

There it was again. A buzzing noise. In her sleepy state, it took her a few moments to realise it was her phone vibrating on her bedside table. She forced her eyes to focus on the clock, seeing that it was 3.30 in the morning.

The children. Was something wrong?

She sat up and grabbed her phone. Through blurry eyes, she saw that the screen was filled with alerts; another couple flashed in as she stared at it, her phone vibrating in her hand. Dozens of texts and WhatsApp messages, all from numbers she didn't recognise. She scrolled through them to make certain there was nothing from Zoey – perhaps one of them was home-sick or feeling poorly – but there wasn't.

So who was bothering her at this time of night?

She opened WhatsApp first – seventy-four new alerts. As she opened the first few messages, it was hard to take in what she was seeing, as though her brain was shutting out the full horror of what was being sent to her. One minute she was asleep, and then *this*?

Dirty slut wants it

...followed by a picture – a close-up of a man's face with his drool-covered tongue sticking out.

The next message consisted of only a picture – a naked man in front of a mirror, his head cropped from the photo.

Want a good fucking bitch

...the next one read, followed by a series of emojis.

Cumming round yours now...

Suck this...

You need a good spanking...

The vile messages went on and on, the content getting worse and worse, not to mention the sexually explicit pictures.

Leah screamed and threw her phone onto the duvet. Her breathing quickened – short, sharp shots of panic burning her lungs. She began to sweat, and her arms tingled with pins and needles as her heart raced in her chest.

More messages lit up her screen.

'Oh my God, oh my *God*,' she cried, not knowing what to do. She dared to open the latest message and the words 'I know where you live' sent shivers through her.

Then her phone began to ring – a number she didn't recognise. She rejected the call but it rang again, this time from an unknown number. Call after call came in and more messages every few seconds – so fast that she didn't even have time to go to her settings to block the numbers.

In the end, she turned her phone off completely. With her knees drawn up under her chin, Leah sobbed. Deep, guttural, pathetic cries of frustration and fear. Snot and tears soaked into her duvet as her body shook from despair.

He must have put my number on some seedy sex hook-up site, she thought desperately – and not only that, but in the middle of the night. Sleep deprivation had been one of his favourite punishments, and now it was revenge for her rejecting his advances earlier.

'I... I could... *kill* him for this...' she sobbed over and over, terrified for her safety as well as the children's. She knew now it was time to go to the police, before she did indeed commit murder.

———

The engine started on the third go – the rattling sound making Leah worry she'd wake the entire street. And she certainly didn't want anyone next door knowing she was going out in the middle of the night. Her hands shook as she gripped the wheel, edging her car out of its tight space on the street.

Fifteen minutes later, she was standing in the waiting area of the police station under the glaring fluorescent lights while the custody sergeant dealt with a drunk man at the desk who was being held up by two officers either side of him.

Leah's legs felt weak, and she knew she looked a state – red eyes, unbrushed hair and wearing whatever clothes she found discarded on her bedroom floor from when she'd been working in the vegetable garden earlier. She clutched her phone to her chest, turning it round and round while shifting from one foot to the other. She'd left it turned off as she couldn't stand to see what else had been sent to her.

Suddenly the man in front of her leant forward and vomited all over the floor – a deep, belly-crunching retch as he spewed up the contents of his stomach, mostly alcohol, judging by the stench. Leah jumped back so her feet didn't get covered in it.

She turned to face the waiting area, populated by several other drunk people, plus a woman with bruises on her face and a child in tow, and a glum teenage boy sitting alone, tapping on his phone as he sat with his legs splayed out in front of him.

'Yes, miss,' the officer finally said when the man who had vomited had been escorted away. 'Mind where you tread there. Cleaner's on the way.'

Leah sidestepped the yellow puddle and approached the desk. She glanced behind her, not wanting anyone to hear.

'I... I'm being harassed,' she said, leaning towards the Perspex screen separating them. Seeing the officer there – his broad shoulders inside his uniform, his expression dour yet oddly comforting, as though years in the force had set a permanent expression of 'nothing will surprise me now' into his features – relaxed Leah slightly.

She was safe; it would all get sorted out.

'Harassed in what way?'

'By my ex-husband. He... he lives next door and I think he's put my number online.' Leah glanced behind her again. The small child was almost asleep, resting her head on what Leah saw was her mother's pregnant stomach. 'On a sex hook-up site,' she said quietly, leaning even closer to the screen.

The officer gave a small nod and tapped something into his computer. 'How did you discover this?'

Leah held up her phone. 'I daren't even switch it on. It'll go berserk with disgusting messages and pictures. People were phoning me in the middle of the night. I have no idea who they are. I'm scared.'

'And what makes you think it's your husband?'

'*Ex*,' Leah corrected. 'Believe me, it's exactly what he'd do. He wants to make my life miserable.'

'Would you mind showing me the messages?' the desk sergeant said.

Leah hesitated then nodded, pressing the power button and waiting.

'Hook-up sites, you say?'

Leah nodded again, handing her phone over with the latest messages on screen. About thirty more had come in since she'd turned it off.

'I see,' the man said, his bushy eyebrows lifting above the rim of his black glasses. 'Most unpleasant.'

'How do I stop it? What can you do to help me? I need my phone for work, for the kids... for everything. Will you go and visit him and insist he takes down whatever he's done?'

'Whoa, slow down there, miss,' the officer said with a smile, handing back her phone. 'We take this sort of thing very seriously, but there's a process. Let me get some details before we go jumping to any conclusions about how this has happened. You may have been hacked, for instance.'

Leah laughed, trying not to roll her eyes. She didn't want to rile the police. 'No. It's my ex. Trust me on that. He moved next door, and he's been intent on making my life a misery ever since.'

'I see,' the officer said wearily. 'Right, let's start with your name and address, shall we?'

———

The next day, Leah was grateful for the hairdryers and general noise in the salon drowning out her thoughts. Though even after three strong coffees she was still struggling with exhaustion. She'd not slept a wink once she'd got back from the police station and had watched it get light, listening to Craig and Gillian having early-morning sex at around 6 a.m., followed by the vague sound of Henry's excited voice in their bedroom later as the four of them readied themselves for the day ahead.

Then she'd waited for her children to come out from next door, all ready for school – their rucksacks packed with books, pencil cases and lunch boxes. It was a comforting ritual she'd grown into when they weren't staying with her.

'What the *hell*?' she'd suddenly said, leaning forward on her bedroom windowsill, straining to see next door's drive. She'd frozen from shock for a moment before rallying herself and dashing downstairs and outside. It had been Craig taking the kids to school that morning, and she'd run up to his vehicle, barefoot and still in her dressing gown. She'd banged on the driver's window.

Craig had jammed on the brake and scowled at her through the glass. He'd taken his time before winding it down. 'What now, Leah?'

'I should be asking *you* that!' Leah had glanced at each of her children – Zoey in the front as usual, Henry in the rear. 'What on earth are they wearing?'

'Uniform,' Craig had said, making no effort to hide his smirk. Both children had a pained expression on their faces, Zoey more so – almost apologetic, and certainly sad.

'But *what* uniform?' Leah had spat, feeling bad that their children had to witness this scene. She calmed her tone. 'It's... it's not their usual one.' She cast her eyes over their dark green blazers, with Henry wearing grey shorts and a green and yellow cap. Zoey looked uncomfortable in her long pleated skirt and yellow silk cravat.

'They're going to private school now. The other ones were useless.'

'*What*? You can't just send them to a different school without consulting me. And especially not halfway through term!' She'd offered a smile to the kids, trying to indicate that everything would be OK, that they didn't have to do this. 'Zoey, Henry, get out of the car. I'll take you to school this morning. Your *actual* school.'

The children had willingly gathered up their bags and gone to open their car doors, their relieved expressions telling Leah what she already knew – that they didn't want to change schools at all.

'No!' Craig snapped, flicking the switch on the central locking. 'Stay where you are, both of you. You're going to St Philip's, like we agreed. It's all arranged. You'll have a much better standard of education.' He'd swung round to address Henry. 'You want to go to a good university, don't you?'

'He's seven, for God's sake, Craig. University is the last thing on his mind.' Leah had yanked at the car door handle then, but it was locked. 'Let them out. You can do what you like to me, but do *not* involve our children in your pathetic grudges.' She'd leant in through the car window, trying to speak quietly but also so she had a chance of reaching the central locking button on the dashboard.

'St Philip's provides a top-class education for five- to eighteen-year-olds,' Craig said robotically, sounding as though he was reading from the prospectus. 'Are you saying you want to deny our children that?'

'Don't be ridiculous. Their current schools are rated outstanding. They love them. More to the point, I don't want to deny them their friends and familiar surroundings.' Leah lunged for the central locking switch, but Craig had batted her arm out of the way and put up the electric window, trapping a clump of her hair and pulling it from her scalp as he'd reversed out of the drive. As she'd stood there clutching at her head, the last thing Leah saw was Henry sobbing in the back of the car, his hands pressed up against the glass.

CHAPTER TWENTY-THREE

'It's not *quite* what I was hoping for,' Margaret, one of Leah's regular clients, said later the same morning as Leah held the mirror behind her. 'It's... it's a lot shorter than I asked for.' She had a disappointed look on her face. 'And the colour hasn't taken, has it? There are loads of greys still.' She ran her fingers through the roots.

Margaret was Jimmy's grandmother and she'd already mentioned to Leah about the family gathering that evening, how she wanted to look her best. Leah had taken the opportunity to ask about the possibility of Jimmy helping to clear the hedge in the vegetable garden, but Margaret had proudly told her that her grandson had got a new job with a local building company and that he'd be busy working on the site.

'I'm so sorry you feel it's not right,' Leah said, knowing she'd been distracted by earlier events with Craig. 'There's no charge this time, and I'm very happy to do another colour for you if you want to book in again. All on the house.' She smiled, hoping that was enough.

'It's my anniversary dinner tonight and all the family will be there. I'd wanted to... to look nice,' Margaret said, standing up and pulling off her protective gown. There were tears in her eyes, and when Leah offered to make her a cup of tea, she rushed out of the salon without another word.

'Everything OK?' Sally mouthed over the noise of the hairdryer.

Leah pulled an exasperated face, close to tears herself. On top of the night's goings-on, she was agitated beyond belief that Craig had sped off with their children, taking them to a strange school. It had all been cooked up behind her back.

'I've had better mornings,' Leah confessed when Sally flicked off the dryer. 'I'll send her a bunch of flowers.'

'It wasn't that bad, don't worry,' Sally continued, glancing up as she wafted a can of hairspray around her client's head.

Leah wasn't sure she agreed, and felt wretched on Margaret's behalf. Over at the little reception desk positioned near the salon entrance, Leah checked the diary. She had two more cuts to take her up to lunch and then a gap of a couple of hours where she'd planned on getting some paperwork done. However, as things stood, she had no intention of going through the accounts. No, she had something far more pressing to attend to.

———

At one o'clock, she told Sally and Charlotte that she'd be out for a while. She trusted them entirely to hold the fort for a couple of hours. There was no way she could just sit back and do nothing about Craig's latest stunt.

Having dashed home quickly to grab what she needed, Leah put the address of St Philip's School into Google Maps on her laptop and memorised the twenty-four-minute route, not wanting to switch on her phone.

She gripped the wheel as she sped along the bypass out of town, the engine of her old Mini straining as she turned off a roundabout. A few miles further on and the road narrowed, twisting and winding through the countryside. Several times she had to pull over into a gateway for a car coming in the opposite direction to pass, and once she had to reverse back to a passing place.

As she drove on, the lane grew even narrower, with grass and weeds poking through the tarmac. The little car juddered along in second gear – she daren't go any faster in case—

'Oh *God!*' she squealed, jamming on the brakes. Coming round a blind bend was a huge tractor, twice the height of her car. She flashed her headlights and pressed her hand on the horn in case the farmer hadn't seen her from up in his cab. Thankfully, he slowed to a halt, waiting as Leah reversed back to a gateway.

'Apart from anything, I am *not* doing this journey twice a day for the next ten years,' she grumbled, once the tractor had passed, the farmer giving her a polite wave. She was grateful to her dad for giving her the 1970s Mini, but it had no modern safety features and wouldn't be up to this drive regularly.

Fifteen minutes later, Leah slowed as she searched for the school's entrance. The lane had widened again and was bordered by black estate railings with parkland either side. Then the verge opened up into a sweeping driveway, flanked by a smart green sign with gold-painted lettering.

'St Philip's Preparatory and Senior Schools,' Leah read. Thankfully, the gate was open so she drove straight in, though the security cameras at the head of the drive didn't go unnoticed – and neither did the other security patrol warning signs, given what she was about to do.

At the end of the long, straight drive was a grand building that was clearly once a country house, though the more modern buildings attached to it gave away its current status as a school. As did the signs indicating the various departments – Science,

Medical Centre, Bookshop, School of Art, Sports Centre – Leah noticed as she pulled into the parking area.

'Sports Centre,' she said to herself, imagining an Olympic-sized pool and the top-notch training Zoey would no doubt receive. 'And probably opportunities to compete at national level,' she whispered, wondering if she was doing the right thing.

The place certainly looked impressive, she thought, getting out of the car and looking around. And there was no denying it was a far cry from their state schools – but it was also a far cry from their friends and everything they were familiar with.

Putting these thoughts from her mind, she brushed herself down, conscious she had hair stuck to her black leggings, and strode up to the building's impressive entrance, her handbag slung over her shoulder.

The place was eerily quiet as she pushed her hand against the polished brass plate on one side of the big double doors, venturing into the foyer, which seemed more like a plush country hotel than a school. The furniture was lavish and antique, and the floor was covered in thick burgundy carpet, which Leah's flat work pumps sank into.

'Hello, may I help you?' came a voice from behind a carved wooden counter. Leah hadn't spotted the woman as she'd entered, distracted by the opulence of the place. The fees must cost a fortune each term.

'Hi, yes. I'm Zoey and Henry's mum. They're new... today, actually.'

'Ahh, yes, Mrs Forbes. Welcome to our school. Your husband indicated that you might... arrive.' The woman looked her up and down.

'Oh, he did?' Leah decided not to correct the woman about her mistake – that she wasn't Mrs Forbes any more. 'There's been a bit of a mix-up, you see. Both children have impor-tant... dental appointments this afternoon, so I've come to collect them. Craig got the dates muddled. We meant for them to start tomorrow.'

'I see,' the woman said, frowning and leafing through a large leather-bound notebook on her desk. 'There's nothing noted here about an early pick-up.'

Leah shook her head. 'Oh, Craig, you silly thing,' she said with a laugh, cringing at the posh accent she found herself putting on. 'He's been so distracted by work lately. I would have sent the au pair, but she's not well today, so here I am!'

'I'm sorry, Mrs Forbes, but without prior authorisation, you understand I can't just release the children. Especially as we haven't met you before.'

'But they're *my* children,' Leah said, her accent slipping again. 'And... and they're getting braces fitted. Both of them, today. They can't possibly miss the appointments.'

'But Henry's only seven,' the receptionist said, looking puzzled.

'His teeth are... advanced for his age. You can check with the dentist, if you like.' Leah rummaged in her bag and pulled out her dead phone, pretending to look for the number. She was banking on the receptionist believing her.

'That won't be necessary, but I really can't allow the children to leave until I get confirmation from their—'

A deafening bell suddenly sounded around them, vibrating through the entire school. Within seconds, the corridors, stairs and lobby area were filled with streams of children trying not to break into a run as they strode in pairs or groups through the reception area, clutching books and bags as they chattered excitedly.

Leah suddenly felt as though she was adrift on a rough sea as she spun round, searching the faces. From the corner of her eye, she was aware of the receptionist saying something, but she couldn't hear what.

'Zoey!' Leah called out, raising her arm.

Her daughter swung round, glancing her way. She rushed up to Leah, elbowing past the other kids, making a couple of them scowl and shove her back.

'Oh, *Mum*,' Zoey said, her face crumpling from relief. She was close to tears as she threw her arms around Leah's neck.

'It's OK, love,' Leah said, hugging her briefly. 'Where's Henry?'

'I... I don't know,' she said, choking back a sob. 'He was crying when we arrived. He was taken off somewhere. To the juniors' bit, I think.' Leah pointed to the main door.

'Right, come with me,' she said, grabbing her daughter's hand as another bell sounded. The children remaining in the lobby area rushed off, squealing about being late. 'Let's go and get him.'

'Mrs Forbes! Wait!' Leah heard a voice calling out after them as she and Zoey pushed through the large doors to outside. But she ignored the receptionist's protests, scanning around until she saw a sign indicating the Junior Department as they began to run. When they rounded the corner of the main school, a smaller, modern building came into view with about thirty kids close to Henry's age charging about the playground.

'Henry!' Leah called out as she approached the metal railings, her hands gripping the bars. Her eyes flicked from one face to the next as she tried to spot her son.

'Mum, he's over there – look!' Zoey pointed to a tree close to the fence, where Henry was standing alone watching the other children play. They both ran up to him.

'Darling... it's OK. I've come to get you.'

Henry's face lit up as he turned at the sound of his mum's voice. Then his chin quivered and he started to cry.

Frantically, Leah looked around. There was a gate on the other side of the playground, with two teachers standing beside it, monitoring the playtime, so that route wasn't an option.

'Here,' Leah said, pointing to a knotty stump sticking out of the tree trunk. 'Henry, can you step on that to climb over the fence? I'll help you.'

Henry was agile and used to climbing and, in no time, he was making his escape. It was as he was getting his other leg over the railings that the whistle blew three times in quick succession and a teacher yelled out.

'Hey, you! Stop! What are you doing?'

Then Leah heard the receptionist's voice from the main school hollering at them as the two staff in the playground ran towards the fence.

'Quick!' Leah said to Henry, grabbing his shoulders and waist as he rolled himself over the top of the fence. He half fell, half dropped down to the other side, landing on his knees, but soon had himself upright. 'Run!' she instructed her children, grabbing their hands as they charged back towards the car park.

As they approached her old car, with Leah grateful she'd not bothered to lock it, they yanked open the doors and hurled themselves inside.

'Hit the locks!' Leah said, starting the engine and reversing out of the space. The Mini's wheels spun in the gravel as she floored the accelerator and sped off down the drive, leaving three members of staff standing in their wake, their hands on their hips and one of them already on her phone.

CHAPTER TWENTY-FOUR

After Leah had dropped the children back at their usual schools, having spoken to each of their sympathetic and concerned head teachers about what had happened and leaving instructions for no one, apart from her or her mum, to take them from the school, she drove slowly back to the salon. She felt churned up, drained and at the end of her tether.

From what she'd been told, Craig hadn't bothered to inform their schools that he was removing Zoey and Henry, and instead they'd been marked absent without authorisation. The school secretary hadn't been able to reach either parent – Craig hadn't answered their calls and they couldn't contact Leah because she'd still not dared to switch on her phone.

Before she went back into the salon, having parked in the small staff area at the back of her row of shops, she gathered up the green and yellow uniforms that the kids had changed out of and put them in a bag in the boot of her Mini. While she was driving, they'd managed to wriggle into their old school uniform that she'd brought with her from home. She'd have a chat with them later about what had happened, try to put a positive spin on it somehow so they didn't think their father was a complete idiot.

'You've gone too far now, Leah,' she suddenly heard from behind her as she was locking up her car. She froze, hardly daring to turn round as she recognised the voice. The hairs on the back of her neck prickled.

She gasped as Craig grabbed her upper arm, roughly swinging her round.

'How dare you remove my children from their new school,' he growled, his face close.

Leah cried out, yanking herself away from his grip. Thankfully, she knew there was a security camera aimed approximately at where they were standing.

'How dare *you* send them to a new school without consulting me!' she spat back. 'I'm the resident parent, despite you luring them to your house these last few weeks. As far as these decisions go, it's down to me which school they attend.'

'I should report you to the police for kidnapping,' he snarled. 'Do you know how much it will have damaged my reputation, the people in a school like that witnessing your deranged behaviour? The member of staff was in pieces when she phoned me to tell me my children had been snatched. Luckily for you, I managed to dissuade her from calling the police. I was forced to tell her that you'd escaped from a psychiatric ward and that I'd deal with it.'

'Psychiatric ward?' Leah said, turning to go. 'Repu*tation?*' She blew out incredulously. 'That's all you care about, isn't it, your stupid reputation. I bet you were hoping to meet some rich parents at St Philip's, and flog them one of your crooked bits of land with its non-existent planning permission.' Leah stopped in her tracks, squaring up to Craig. She jabbed a finger at his face. 'And believe me, if you *dare* to take those children out of school without my knowledge or permission, you'll find yourself right back in court.'

She retreated, visibly shaking and bracing herself for his comeback. But there was none. Instead, he stared at her with a strange look in his eyes – the same look he'd given her the night before. His silence unnerved her. And so did the way he moved a couple of steps closer – slow steps, with his hands coming up towards her arms again, though this time in an unthreatening way. Instinctively, Leah took a couple more steps back herself – but it was that *look* in his eyes that prevented her from legging it into the salon.

'Oh, Leah...' Craig said, dragging out her name.

She scowled, rooted to the spot.

'All this... *stuff* between us. I don't like it.' His voice was heavy with regret. 'Not one bit.' His hands reached out and gently took her shoulders, pulling her closer. 'What happened to *us?*'

She looked down at the ground, not wanting to be sucked in by his eyes. Eyes that reminded her of when they'd first met, when things were good and there wasn't even a sniff of the trouble to come. But she realised it was all part of his game plan – playing on her empathy.

Don't fall for it... she screamed in her head, urging herself to run.

But for some reason, she didn't.

Instead, she forced herself to say something – *anything*. 'And *I* don't much like it when—'

But she was unable to finish what she was saying because Craig pulled her right into his arms and brought his mouth down on hers, his warm lips engulfing her as he kissed her – a full-on, passionate kiss with one hand cupped behind her head and the other around her waist. She felt his moans resonating through her.

Every emotion swept through Leah in those short moments – guilt, remorse, sadness, happiness, hope and despair, as well as anger and love, familiarity and a sense of coming home. She wanted it to stop – *oh how she wanted that* – but she found herself completely unable to do anything except stand there and respond to him. It was as though her entire body and soul had time-slipped into the past, as if by doing nothing it would obliterate all that was wrong between them and make everything all right again.

She was lost in his embrace – completely and utterly drowning in Craig.

Then something clicked inside her.

She raised her arms and pushed back sharply against his shoulders, sending herself staggering backwards. She sucked in a lungful of air – gasping as though she'd been held underwater, which wasn't far from the truth. Her eyes grew wide as she doubled over from shock, staring up at him, wrapping her coat tightly around her and grabbing onto her handbag as the strap slipped off her shoulder.

Slowly, cautiously, she stepped backwards, retreating from him.

He watched her, standing there with a self-satisfied look on his face.

Or *was* it that?

No. It wasn't his usual look of smugness and one-upmanship. It was something else entirely. From where she was standing, it looked an awful lot like... *regret*.

Leah spun around and ran, but she stumbled on a loose paving slab, just managing to save herself from falling flat on her face.

Against her better judgement, she stopped, turning back to face him.

'It's *you* who'll be getting a visit from the police,' she said, wiping her sleeve across her mouth. 'I've reported you for putting my number on those vile websites.'

As she headed through the back door of the salon, she swore

she heard Craig laughing. But she didn't stop to find out. She just needed to get away.

CHAPTER TWENTY-FIVE

'*Mum*... you have no idea how glad I am to see you,' Leah said later as she arrived home from work, taking off her coat. Somehow, she'd got through the afternoon in a rush of clients and paperwork and, for the first time in a long time, the house seemed warm and cosy and there was a delicious smell coming from the kitchen. She silently thanked her mum for being there.

'Don't worry, darling, they're both upstairs safe and sound,' Rita said.

Leah had explained everything to her mum on the salon phone earlier, asking if she could come a bit early to fetch the kids from school. She didn't want Zoey waiting around for the bus in case her father lured her into his car.

'Thanks, Mum,' Leah said, following Rita into the kitchen. It was the glass of wine she saw on the table first, and another one for her mum, half-finished already.

'Bottoms up, love, and you'll feel better in no time.'

Leah couldn't deny that it was exactly what she wanted, but it was the other item on the kitchen table that was disturbing her. She picked it up.

'Where did this come from?' she said, glancing at her

mother and picking up the scarf – *Gabe's* black and white check scarf that she'd seen Craig wearing a few weeks ago.

'Now don't be cross, darling,' Rita said, brandishing a wooden spoon. 'He didn't stay long.' She cleared her throat.

'Who?'

'Craig. I think he felt bad about it.' Rita flicked her hair back as she glanced away, and Leah noticed she was wearing lipstick – a much paler and more subtle shade that the scarlet she usually wore. It made her appear... *younger*, she thought.

Leah scoffed and dropped the scarf as though it was infected. 'Fat chance of that. No, he's up to something else.'

She ran the back of her hand across her mouth, reminded of earlier. She'd already decided she'd tell *no one* about what had happened by the car. That way, she could pretend it hadn't. She shuddered as she remembered how her body had briefly responded to Craig's kiss.

'From what I can gather, darling, he realised there'd been a mix-up. He told me that he'd spotted that gardener chap working in the vegetable plot from his upstairs window earlier. He decided to bring the scarf round so... so I could give it to him.' She cleared her throat again.

'Wait... *what*?' Leah's mind ran over what her mother just said. And it wasn't about Craig feeling 'bad'. She doubted he was capable of that. '*Gabe* was here?'

'Well, he must have been, darling, though by the time I went outside to give him the scarf, he was gone. But it looks as though he's done a good job on the hedge. Though I'm not sure what you'll make of... of the other thing that's happened out there.' She made a pained face.

'What are you talking about, Mum?'

Leah didn't wait to find out, but instead shoved her feet into her old slip-ons by the back door and headed straight to the vegetable plot. It was already getting dark but there was still just enough light to see her way – and enough to see that the overgrown hedge that had been blocking the gateway to the road had been cleared.

'He's done a good job,' Leah said, her heart fluttering as she inspected the work. She wasn't sure if it was a good sign that Gabe had been round, or if she should feel miffed that he'd not let her know he was coming – though her phone was still switched off. She thought back to the last text she'd sent him, wondering if he'd replied with an offer of help. She couldn't keep her phone turned off forever and decided she'd chase up the police later to see what they were doing about it.

As she looked at what Gabe had done, she noticed how he'd begun neatening and laying the remaining hedge either side of the gate in the traditional way, and the care he'd taken to remove the huge pile of rubbish, adding it to the ever-growing bonfire. Then her thoughts drifted to Guy Fawkes Night, him with her and the kids standing around the flames, all of them cosy and happy.

She shook her head. That was never going to happen, though she hoped they could still remain friends. In reality, he was probably going to pop the bill through her door at any moment. It was just another job to him. She had to accept that.

Leah sighed and turned, heading back to the house. She needed to put everything out of her mind for one evening and take care of her children and enjoy the food her mum had made. The kids deserved some peaceful family time after everything that had happened. And so did she.

But as she passed through the courtyard on the way back to the house, Leah clapped her hand over her mouth, halting suddenly.

'Oh my *God*!' she said quietly, determined not to alert Zoey and Henry to yet more trouble. She wasn't sure she could take any more today.

In the six-foot-high brick wall that separated her courtyard from Craig's garden, there was a hole. A *huge* hole. In her rush to see the work Gabe had done on the hedge, she'd not noticed it on the way past. But there was an opening – at least the width of a doorway – with what appeared to be a temporary door made of chipboard fixed in place.

Leah scowled at it before kicking it hard, anger building inside her chest. The board didn't budge, so she launched herself at it with both hands, shoving against it. Still it didn't move. She marched back into the kitchen.

'What do you think, darling?' Rita said, waving the wooden spoon about. 'Good job done in the veggie garden. You'll have so much fresh produce next year.'

'What on *earth* has happened to my wall?' Leah said, toning down her voice. It wasn't her mother's fault that Craig had knocked it down.

'I hoped you knew about it, darling,' Rita said, offering a taste of the food she was making. 'That it was some arrangement you and Craig had together – an access point for the children to come and go, perhaps. Seems reasonable under the circumstances, I suppose.'

Leah shook her head, too distracted to be bothered with food. She paced about the kitchen. 'I had no idea,' she said. 'And I doubt very much that Craig has done it for the children. No, he's up to something yet again. I'll tell you what, though, this time he's overstepped the mark. I seriously can't take any more.'

'Darling,' Rita said to her, raising her eyebrows in a warning and waving the wooden spoon towards the door. 'Enough now...'

Henry was standing there, Lego model in his hand, his eyes wide and searching as he stared at his mother. His mouth puckered and twitched, and Leah noticed him rocking slightly, his shoulders beginning to draw inwards.

'Is... is... is... Mummy getting ill in the head again?' he said with a stammer that she'd not heard in a long while. He went up to his nana and pressed himself against her side, not taking his eyes off Leah. 'D-daddy said she... she was mental.'

'It's fine, Henry. Don't worry, I'm not ill,' Leah said, forcing herself to remain calm. She went up to him, embracing him as she closed her eyes. 'Mummy's just got a few grown-up problems at the moment. But it'll all be fine. None of it's your fault. OK?' She tilted his chin with her forefinger and kissed the top of his head. 'Shall we eat now? Nana's made us a lovely dinner.'

Henry nodded, finally giving Leah a limp hug back. Then Zoey came downstairs and the four of them sat around the kitchen table while Rita made small talk, with every clatter of the cutlery jangling Leah's nerves.

CHAPTER TWENTY-SIX

The next morning, Leah woke suddenly. The remnants of crazy dreams swirled around her head. She'd had her hands around Craig's throat as she'd tried to strangle him, although in the dream it had been *her* who couldn't breathe, *her* whose head felt as though it was going to explode. This had blurred into another dream where she and Gabe were making love – the pair of them pressed up against the brick wall in her courtyard, each of them kissing passionately, tearing the other's clothes off. But then they'd fallen backwards as the brick wall crumbled and they'd landed on their backs in Craig's garden, with him laughing down at them, a sledgehammer in his hand.

She gasped for breath as she sat bolt upright, becoming conscious of a noise. Several noises, in fact, though it took a moment for her brain to untangle them and realise it wasn't still the dream.

Screaming, shouting, banging. The sound of raised voices – one male, one female. It was coming from Craig and Gillian's bedroom next door. They were having a blazing row, by the sound of it.

The other noise was more subtle and further away – a deep, resonant, rumbling vibrating through the fabric of the house.

Leah got out of bed and put on her robe, tying it around her waist as she went to the front window. All looked normal in the street – apart from the new 'Sold' sign stuck beneath Craig's mugshot on the 'For Sale' board opposite.

She froze when she heard another scream from next door – reminded of how things had been between her and Craig. Then she went across the landing into the bathroom. She opened the little frosted window and peered out. There was no one in the courtyard directly below, though in the daylight she could now clearly make out the remains of brick dust and rubble from where her wall had been torn into the day before. She'd be phoning her solicitor as soon as they opened.

The rumbling was louder now – a growling sound resonating through the chilly morning air. She pushed the window open further and gasped when she caught sight of the scene in her vegetable garden. At least three bright yellow diggers were trundling through the garden, along with a team of men in hi-vis jackets and hard hats – some operating the machinery, while others were marking up the ground with bright tape and spray paint.

For a second, Leah felt frozen, catching glimpses of the diggers churning up her precious vegetable beds with their chunky caterpillar tracks and clawed buckets as they came down on the earth, gouging out trenches.

'Craig, what the hell's going on?' she yelled through the open window in the direction of his house. But she knew he wouldn't hear – not least because of the noise of the diggers, but also because of the row that still seemed to be raging next door. Her fingernails dug into the windowsill as she watched on in horror.

When she was finally able to stir herself, Leah rushed back to her bedroom and threw on her jogging bottoms and a sweatshirt, then ran down the stairs and shoved her feet into her boots. She marched across the cobbles and through into the walled garden, brushing her hair away from her face as the breeze whipped it about.

'What's going on?' she called out to the team of workmen invading her property. None of them looked up; rather they were preoccupied with the diggers as they rumbled over the land, scooping up mounds of earth, or busy marking out areas with tape and surveying equipment. And then Leah saw someone she knew, coming through the newly cleared gateway. She rushed over.

'Jimmy! Jimmy, do you know what's happening? Why are you all here? You need to stop them right now. *Please*. This is my garden.'

Jimmy peered at Leah from beneath his hard hat, his mouth opening and closing several times before he spoke. His eyes flicked around the site, as though he was searching for someone.

'Hi, Mrs Forbes,' he said, shifting from one foot to the other. He dropped a huge coil of blue plastic piping on the ground. 'I got myself a proper job at last.' His grin was hesitant.

'I'm pleased for you, Jimmy, but for the love of God, what's going on here? Please stop them! They're destroying everything.'

Jimmy looked away, his expression pained. 'I'm just following my orders. You'd better speak to Bill. He's the site manager. He's gone to pick something up from the supplier, but he'll be back in half an hour.'

Leah let out an exasperated sound, knowing Craig was behind all this. She thanked Jimmy and ran back across the garden to her courtyard, stumbling on the cobbles and twisting her ankle as she came to a sudden stop.

The chipboard in the demolished wall had been removed and the gaping hole to next door's garden exposed. Craig was striding towards it from his side with another person next to him

– a woman dressed in green combat trousers and sturdy boots, with a navy zip-up fleece bearing an embroidered logo. She appeared older than Leah, wore no make-up and her hair hung down over each shoulder in two long, grey plaits. She was carrying a large plastic crate of some kind.

'They're this way,' Craig said, allowing the woman to walk through the opening first.

'Get out!' Leah said, darting in front of the woman before she reached the doorway to the vegetable garden. 'Both of you, leave now! You're trespassing, and I'll be calling the police if you don't go. Craig, you had no right to knock through the wall. What the hell were you thinking?'

Craig gestured to the woman to continue. 'You're blocking our way, Leah. Please step aside.'

'Pfft!' was all Leah could manage as she felt a mix of fear and anger building inside.

'Go right ahead and call the police, then,' Craig sighed. 'I have a right of way over your...' Craig looked around with a sneer. 'Over your backyard in order to gain access to my land.'

'What land? What are you talking about? This is just more of your nonsense.' Leah hugged herself in an attempt to stop shaking.

Craig raised his arm and pointed to the vegetable plot. Then he headed for the gate again, stepping around Leah.

'I said, get off my property!' She didn't care what the woman thought of her, whoever she was, as she hurled herself at Craig, shoving into him. Something inside her had boiled over.

Craig staggered backwards but kept his cool. He raised his hands in a conciliatory way before taking his phone from his pocket. He tapped on it several times then held it to his ear. Leah was so stunned that in the few seconds that followed, she couldn't move or say anything. Terrified of the repercussions, her heart thumped and her mind whirred as she prayed she was still in the middle of her nightmare.

'Hello, is that Alvington police station?' Craig said after asking to be put through to the local force. 'Yes, I want to report an assault.' His voice was infuriatingly calm. 'My neighbour is refusing right of way across her property to gain access to my land. She's become violent.' A pause. 'Yes, yes, she just shoved me and now she's blocking my way.' Another pause. 'No, if I do that, she'll attack me again. Yes, I've tried being reasonable. I need to gain access immediately as there are building works going on.' Craig stared at Leah. 'Thank you. In that case, I'll wait until the officers arrive.'

The woman with the crate retreated towards Craig's garden, a concerned look on her face. 'Is there another way I can access the coop?' she said, glancing nervously at Leah. 'I don't want the hens to become stressed.'

'*Hens?*' Leah repeated, hardly believing what she was hearing. '*Your* land? Craig, have you completely lost your mind?'

Craig looked at the woman apologetically. 'Like I warned you, she has mental health issues. If you go round to the front of my house and take the next two right turns, you'll see the rear of the plot where the builders have access. You can remove the birds peacefully that way.'

'What do you mean, remove the birds?' Leah approached Craig again. Her hands flew about in front of her face as she gestured wildly. 'Please, don't take my hens,' she begged the woman.

'Well, we can't have them bulldozed now, can we?' Craig said. 'Margaret is from the RSPB and will ensure their welfare. I have no need for them on my land.' He nodded and called out a thank you as the woman walked off, the huge plastic crate banging against her side as she went.

'But they're *my* chickens,' Leah protested. 'And it's *my* vegetable plot. Why are you doing this, Craig?' She let out a whimper, fighting back the tears.

'It's not a vegetable plot, Leah, it's a building plot,' Craig continued. 'And despite what you may think, it's not yours. It's one hundred per cent legally mine.'

Each one of Craig's words sounded triumphant.

Leah shook her head. She wanted to laugh but couldn't find it in her, not even a hysterical one. She folded her arms and stood squarely facing him, torn between wanting to run into the plot again to stop the destruction she could hear going on, but also knowing she needed answers from Craig.

'That's rubbish, and you know it,' she told him. 'The vegetable garden belongs to my property and has done since the house was split into two in the 1950s. My solicitor handled it all. Check the title deeds.'

'I think you might want to appoint a better solicitor,' Craig said with a smirk. 'She's got a great body, though.' A strange sound came from the back of his throat. 'I suppose you could always sue her for negligence. That's why they have insurance, after all.'

Leah shook her head. 'What are you *talking* about?'

'There was an old covenant in the deeds to both properties, Leah, and, for some reason, your solicitor chose to overlook it.' His voice was mocking. 'Perhaps she instructed the intern to go over the documents and they were only given an inexperienced skim. Or maybe her mind was elsewhere. I don't know, and frankly, neither do I care. But there's irrefutable proof that the legal owner of *my* house also owns the plot of land and has a right of way across your courtyard. There was also pre-existing planning permission, and I'm building four houses on the plot, due for completion in six months, so you'd better bloody get used to me coming and going.'

Craig's laugh made Leah squirm. It was the same laugh he'd used on her many times over the years. She'd first encountered it when she'd been getting ready to go to his best friend's wedding, only a year after they'd got married themselves. It was as if a switch had flicked inside the kind and charming man she'd first met, as though his mask had slipped clean off his face, exposing someone monstrous beneath.

Leah had only given birth to Zoey three weeks prior to the wedding they were attending, and she was concerned that she'd not lost any baby weight at all – at least that's what it had felt like when she'd tried to squeeze into the dress she'd planned on wearing.

'The zip won't do up and my boobs won't stay in. I'll leak milk the moment Zoey so much as whimpers, and my stomach still looks like a bouncy castle.' She'd felt so despondent and had turned around from the mirror then to see Craig's reaction, hoping for a bit of sympathy. But instead, he was laughing at her.

Not just a sympathetic chuckle with a few words of encouragement about soon getting back in shape, or that she looked beautiful as a new mum.

No. Craig had spewed out a laugh that sounded like pure poison, his eyes appearing dead inside. She'd thought, at that moment, it was what pure evil looked like.

'Craig?' She'd felt tearful and her cheeks had flushed. 'Is it that bad?'

'You look disgusting. I won't be seen out with you.' Then he'd refused to speak to her for the rest of the day and evening at the wedding, choosing instead to surround himself with the slim and pretty bridesmaids, leaving Leah wearing leggings and a loose top that made her feel frumpy while she took care of baby Zoey.

'Four... *four* houses,' Leah said, feeling herself sway. She clutched her head for a second, then without thinking rationally, she charged up to Craig and kicked him hard in the shin bone. Before she could stop herself, she raised her right leg towards his groin and kneed him hard. Craig doubled over in pain, while Leah grunted and howled as she pummelled his back. Then she grabbed handfuls of his hair and pulled as hard as she could, tearing clumps from his scalp.

A second later, she felt several pairs of strong hands on her upper arms and her shoulders, swiftly pulling her away from Craig. Her legs buckled and her feet twisted sideways as she went down, crying out in pain as both her arms were clamped firmly behind her back. When she looked up, spitting out the hair that had got caught in her mouth, she saw the faces of two uniformed police officers staring down at her.

CHAPTER TWENTY-SEVEN

Leah sat at her kitchen table, her head bowed, shoulders hunched as the officers' eyes bored into her – along with Craig's icy stare as he leant against her kitchen counter, his arms crossed. She hated that he was inside her house, but the police had wanted to speak with them both and the children were next door with Gillian getting ready for school.

She picked at her fingernails under the table, praying that she didn't dissolve in tears.

'She completely flipped out at me, Officer,' Craig said. To anyone else, he sounded entirely reasonable and calm. His voice was smooth and confident – someone you'd listen to in a crisis. 'I'm afraid Leah is no stranger to mental health issues. She's clearly going through a bad patch again.' He let out a sigh that could be mistaken for caring.

'*What?*' Leah whipped her head up. 'I don't have bloody mental health issues! You're the only mental one around here.' She took a sharp breath, hearing how deranged she sounded. While Craig was smartly dressed in his work suit, she was in her dirty old gardening clothes with her hair still wild from tossing and turning all night and her face burning red from rage.

'Oh, Leah,' Craig said in a fake voice that made him sound kind. 'Are you not taking your pills any more?' He shook his head and looked at the two constables. 'When we were married, I always had to remind her. Without her meds... well, her temper gets the better of her. I'm worried about psychosis.'

'Psychosis? Pills?' Leah half stood up but one of the officers stepped towards her. 'For fuck's sake,' she muttered.

'Remain seated, please,' the officer said.

Leah looked at each of them. 'Look, he's lying. There's nothing wrong with my mental health. Apart from *him*.' When she jabbed her finger towards Craig, her entire arm shook. If they didn't do something to help, she knew things would only get worse for her and the children. Craig was not a good loser.

'You two were *married*?' the officer asked, sounding doubtful.

'It's complicated,' Craig replied, wiping his hands down his face, making himself appear exhausted and at the end of his tether. 'Well, it wasn't at all complicated until she decided to buy the house next door to mine,' he added. 'Point is, Officer, there's not a lot I can do about my ex living next door to me, my partner and my children, but I *do* object to her making my life difficult. I really don't want to go the legal route as I know she can't afford it, so if you could talk some sense into her, that would be most welcome. I'm not being unreasonable.'

'If I can just speak,' Leah said, holding up a hand, but Craig's voice dominated hers.

'I'd like nothing more than for us to get on, especially for the children's sakes, but it's been one thing after another since she moved next door to us. I can only assume she did it so it was easier to harass me. I know the divorce was hard for her, but she has to accept that I've moved on and I'm with someone else now.' He sighed, shaking his head.

Leah felt sick. What a performance. The voice inside her screamed, begged, pleaded for her to stay calm, not to upturn the table and lunge at Craig. It urged her to stop and think before she spoke. She knew she was only one wrong move away from arrest and a night in a cell.

'You're incredible!' she spat. 'I've had enough of you and your lies. And I'm sick to death of your games. How *dare* you make up this rubbish about me? Fine – take me to court. I don't care! I'll happily explain how you're trying to con me out of my garden so you can no doubt pull yet another shady property deal. I'll tell the judge everything you've done to me, including putting my phone number on that disgusting website!'

'If you could calm down, please, miss,' the other officer reminded her. 'We're happy for you to discuss this down at the station with us if you prefer. Mr Forbes has already indicated outside to my colleague that he doesn't want to press charges for assault, and, under the circumstances, if you remain reasonable, we will also not pursue the matter further.' The officer glanced at his watch and spoke into the radio hissing and crackling at his shoulder. He clearly had better things to be doing with his time.

'Check at the police station if you don't believe me,' Leah said. 'I had to report him for the stunt he pulled. I had all these sick messages and... and...'

'Miss?' the officer said, raising his eyebrows.

Leah slumped forward on the table, her head cradled in her arms. She felt like a naughty child. Somewhere from deep inside her depleted reserves, she found it in herself to nod.

'OK,' she said, dragging her head up. She felt a couple of hot tears dribble down one cheek. 'But please... Craig, can I ask that you stop whatever you're doing in my... in the vegetable garden. *Please?* Let me check with my solicitor first. I know there's been a terrible mistake and—'

'This is what I get, you see,' Craig said, flapping his hands at his sides. He paced up and down Leah's small kitchen, acciden-tally knocking a tea towel onto the floor and treading on it. 'She turns on the waterworks and makes me feel guilty.' He shook his head. 'Leah, my builders are on a tight schedule. Just because you foolishly purchased a property to spite me, which has now legally backfired, is hardly my problem. Any fanciful ideas of growing your own potatoes and collecting eggs from hens just went up in smoke, I'm afraid.'

Leah glanced up at the officers in turn, each of them giving her a nod.

'OK,' the older officer said. 'Mr Forbes, I suggest you call a halt to the building works for a day or two so that your ex-wife can take legal advice regarding the land, given that it's a civil matter.' He opened up a small tablet. 'We just need to take a few details of the incident and then we'll be on our way. However, if there is further violence towards Mr Forbes, then... Well, I'm sure you don't want an arrest on your record.'

The other officer glanced at his watch again as Leah reluctantly nodded. 'Thank you,' she said, her heart thumping so hard she thought it might burst from her ribcage.

———

As soon as she arrived at the salon for work, Leah called Liz Morgan, her solicitor. As usual, she was told that Liz wasn't available so she'd left a message for her to call back urgently. The day had passed in a blur of clients and deliveries, with her mother stopping by unexpectedly in the afternoon to check how she was.

'I can't talk now, Mum,' Leah had said, cancelling the glare she was about to give her over the head of her client. Instead, she turned on the hairdryer but saw in the mirror that her mother had taken up residence in the waiting area, pretending to flip through magazines while watching her out of the corner of her eye. She couldn't help noticing that she seemed nervous, on edge, as though something had happened. As soon as the client had paid and left, Rita pounced on her daughter.

'Is it Dad?' Leah said, suddenly wondering if there was bad news. She'd barely had time for her father since his hospital scare and felt terrible that she'd let her own problems outweigh her dad's ill health.

'Your father's... *fine*,' Rita said, flapping her hand in a dismissive way. 'He'll outlive us all. If you ask me, this PIST is all nonsense—'

'Mum, it's *PTSD* and it's absolutely *not* nonsense.'

'You're not the one who has to live with it,' Rita said in a low voice, guiding Leah towards the staff room by her elbow.

'And neither are you,' Leah said, once they were inside. 'Anyway, what's up? You're acting strange.'

'Am I?' her mum shot back. 'I'm not.' She fiddled with her hair, her colourful bangles and bracelets jangling on her wrists. Leah noticed one of her nails was broken, something her mother would never normally tolerate, and her make-up was far from perfect, plus her clothes seemed creased and dishevelled. It was a rare day when Rita didn't look immaculate.

'Then why are you here?'

'To see if you're OK, of course. Can't a mum check in on her daughter?'

Leah stared at her mother, narrowing her eyes. Something was up, she just wasn't sure what.

'OK, OK... I'll admit it.' She held up both palms in a self-defence gesture. 'I went to see Craig this afternoon.'

'*What?*'

'I didn't want you to hear it from anyone else in case you... in case you thought I was meddling.' She looked away briefly. 'And I was... *seen*,' she whispered.

'Seen by who? What are you talking about? And why on earth did you go to see Craig?' When Rita didn't reply, Leah continued. 'Mum, I truly appreciate everything you do for the kids and the extra stuff around the house to help me – I honestly couldn't manage without you. But I really wish you'd leave the issues with me and Craig out—'

Leah stopped when she saw her mother's tears. She couldn't remember the last time she'd seen her cry.

'Mum? Oh, *Mum*... I'm sorry. Here, sit down.' She pulled out a chair and helped her down onto it. 'Was he rude to you? You seem... really upset.'

'I just wanted to make things easier for you, darling, in case there's any chance you two might get back together. I... I thought I was doing the right thing, Leah. Honestly, I did. But then... Oh God, I can hardly stand to think of it.' She covered her face.

'Mum, *what*? Did he say something to hurt you?'

Rita looked up from behind her hands. 'He made *advances* to me, darling, that's what.' She whispered the word 'advances'.

'Craig came *on* to you?'

Her mother gave a tiny nod, not looking her in the eye.

'I'll bloody kill him,' Leah said, pacing about the small staff room. 'He's really, *really* gone too far now. How dare he do that to you!'

Rita reached for her daughter's wrist and grabbed it with bony fingers. 'No, no, it's fine. I... handled it. But that gardener man of yours saw it and, well, you know. I just wanted to tell you first.'

'Gabe was there?' Leah said, dumbfounded.

Her mother nodded again, still not looking at her.

'What the hell was he doing there?' Leah asked, her mind racing.

'I don't think Gabe realised I was there at first. He burst in through the living room French doors, stopping suddenly when he saw us.'

'Gabe saw Craig making a pass at you, is that what you're saying?'

Another small nod from Rita.

'Then what happened?'

'I didn't stick around to find out, darling. But as I left, I heard an almighty fight break out between them.'

'Good God,' Leah muttered, grabbing her coat and bag ready to leave. 'Mum, go home to Dad. You look in shock. I'm *so* sorry this happened to you. I'm going to fix it.' Could things honestly get any worse, Leah wondered, as she dashed out to her car.

CHAPTER TWENTY-EIGHT

After she'd left work, Leah stopped off to pick up Henry from his friend's house where he'd gone directly from school, then she drove to the pool to meet Zoey after her swimming training. She always walked to this particular session after school with several friends. Leah pulled into the car park just on time.

'Come on, come *on*, Zo...' she said as she and Henry waited in the car outside the pool entrance, parked on double yellow lines. She tapped her finger on the steering wheel as a few of Zoey's friends dawdled out of the sports centre doors, munching on snacks as they went off to meet their mums.

Leah was eager to get home – to confront Craig about upsetting her mother and check if there'd been further destruction to the vegetable plot. And later, once the kids were in bed, she planned on bracing herself and turning on her phone to call Gabe. She wanted to ask him what had happened earlier. He'd obviously stood up for her mum, and she was grateful for that, but she couldn't help wondering why he'd gone to Craig's house in the first place.

She opened the car door quickly and stuck out her head.

'Bethany, hi...' she called. 'It's Leah's mum,' she added when the girl looked over to the car.

'Hi, Mrs Forbes,' she said, waving.

'Do you know if Zoey will be long changing?'

'Zoey?' Bethany said, frowning. 'She wasn't in training today, sorry.' She shrugged and walked off.

Leah got out of the car and ran over to the girl. 'What do you mean, she wasn't in training?' Leah's mind flipped back to this morning – all a bit of a blur with the police coming out. The kids had stayed at Craig's last night and she'd gone out to meet them on the drive as she usually did before they'd left for school. She'd been rattled and upset from what had happened but had wanted to give them a couple of treats as well as a clean swimming kit for Zoey. She'd said hello to Gillian, but she hadn't replied, only giving her a brief glance. Leah couldn't be totally sure, but she wondered if she'd caught sight of a bruise on Gillian's cheek – that, or it was badly applied make-up, or perhaps a shadow.

'Was Zoey in school?' Leah asked, trying not to panic.

'We had maths together earlier,' the girl said, sidestepping around Leah as her mum tooted the car horn. 'Yeah... she was there.'

Leah thanked Bethany and went back to her car, telling Henry she'd be back in a moment. She walked briskly inside the pool building, heading into the changing room where only a couple of girls were left packing up their belongings. She asked them the same questions she'd asked Bethany – and got the same vague answers as the girls put on their coats and left.

'Mrs Mallory,' Leah said to the swimming coach who came into the changing room as she was heading out. 'Where's Zoey?'

The woman made a shocked expression. 'Oh...' she said. 'She wasn't in training today. Well, she *was*... and then she wasn't.'

'*What*?'

'She said she'd texted.'

'Where did she go?'

The coach cleared her throat and rolled her eyes. 'Kids,' she said. 'She went off with a man. It's OK, she knew him.'

Leah stared at her, stunned, though she didn't need to hang around for any more answers. Craig had taken her. She thanked the coach and dashed back out to the car, where Henry was repeatedly kicking the seat in front of him, an agitated look in his eyes. She started up the engine and sped home.

―――

'Darling, do you promise me that you'll wait here? Just watch the telly and don't move, not even if the doorbell rings or anything.'

'What if the house burns down?' Henry said, sitting cross-legged on the sofa with a bag of crisps in one hand and his Lego spaceship in the other.

'Well, yes, then it's OK to come out of the front door. But not for any other reason, OK?'

Henry stared at the ceiling for a second. 'What if there's a flood?'

'Yes, leave the house if there's a flood, too.' Leah headed for the door.

'What if aliens come?'

'They won't, Henry. Just eat your crisps and watch TV. I'll be back in five minutes. I just need to see Daddy quickly.'

Leah had seen Craig's car on the drive beside Gillian's when she'd arrived home and, as she headed to the front door, she called out to Henry that she wouldn't be long. Once she was outside, she marched round to Craig's house, trying to contain the rage burning inside her.

. . .

Leah banged on the Old Vicarage's front door. She waited a few moments and then thumped again, rapping with the iron door knocker too. When no one answered, she peered through the big bay window to the side but couldn't see anyone. She went back onto the path again, peering around the other side of the house to check that both cars were still there. They were. She banged on the door again.

After a few moments, Leah thought she heard someone just behind the door, though still no one answered her repeated knocks.

'Craig, it's me, Leah. Open up. I need to speak to you,' she said through the letter box.

Nothing.

She knocked again. 'Craig, I know you're in there. Or Gillian, if you can hear me, please open the door. I need to talk to Craig.' Then she added, 'I'm not here for a fight,' though deep down, she knew she was.

'Leah?' came a quiet voice through the door.

'Yes, it's me, Gillian. Is Zoey there with you? Did Craig pick her up early from swimming?'

The door opened, and Gillian stood the other side of it. It took Leah a moment to even recognise her – she somehow appeared smaller than she had earlier in the day, and her hair was a mess and her clothes weren't the usual designer outfits she usually wore. Instead, she was dishevelled and dressed in baggy pale grey sweatpants and a stained T-shirt. Her feet were bare, and it didn't look as though she was wearing a bra.

'Come in,' Gillian said flatly, staring down at the ground. She was stooped and hunched, flinching as Leah came past her into the hallway. And that's when she saw that the bruise she'd suspected earlier had bloomed into a yellowy-green and purple patch around her left eye, plus she also had a split lip and marks on her neck.

'Jesus,' Leah said, not taking her eyes off Gillian's face. 'Did *he* do this to you?' She wanted to reach up and gently touch her face, feeling as though she was looking at a mirror image of herself over the years, but instead she glanced down the hallway, expecting Craig to come roaring out of one of the rooms in a rage.

Gillian said nothing. Instead, she closed the front door behind them, checking up and down the street first.

'Is Zoey here, Gillian? She wasn't at swimming. I think Craig picked her up.'

Gillian shook her head weakly.

'*What?* Then where is she? Where's Craig?' Leah marched through to the sitting room at the back of the house, expecting to see him reclining beside the fire, reading the newspaper and sipping on a whisky, pretending to be lord of the manor like he clearly thought he was.

But he wasn't there.

Leah turned back to Gillian, who looked even more distraught and ghostlike. Gently, Leah took hold of her arms, conscious of how she jumped from her touch, though she didn't pull away.

'Gillian, please speak to me. Do you know where Zoey is?'

Gillian stared at her then shook her head. Then she nodded. Then she shook her head again. 'Yes... I... I saw a text... She's... she's safe. She's fine.' Her words were gossamer thin as she leant against the wall, looking as though she was about to pass out.

'Thank God,' Leah said, though she was also concerned about Gillian. 'What's he done to you?'

'Please... come... will you come into the kitchen?' Gillian whispered. She seemed terrified, as though she hardly dared speak. 'I... I need to ask for your help.'

CHAPTER TWENTY-NINE

'Oh, thank God you're home,' Leah said when she got back, setting eyes on Zoey. She wasn't sure if she was shaking from what had just happened next door, or if it was from relief that her daughter was safe, sitting snuggled up with Henry on the sofa, the pair of them watching TV and looking as though they'd each scoffed three bags of crisps, judging by the empty packets beside them. Zoey was still munching on one. But Leah didn't care about that. She was just grateful that her little family was together and that she'd locked the front door to the world outside.

'Chill, Mum,' Zoey said, offering her a crisp. 'I'm fine.'

'I was so worried when you weren't at swimming.' Leah took a crisp and forced it down, her throat closing up drily as she swallowed. 'Mrs Mallory said you'd gone off with a man. I thought... I thought Dad must have fetched you but then Gillian told me he hadn't.' Leah closed her eyes for a second, thinking about what else Gillian had told her. She had to concentrate on her children, on looking after them. Nothing else mattered.

'I didn't feel well before swimming. I couldn't get hold of you, Dad or Nana so I called Pops to come and fetch me from the pool. It was really nice to see him. He seemed... well, he seemed like he needed cheering up. He told me stories of when he was in the army and how he'd first met Nana.'

That much Leah knew. Gillian had somehow, in her distressed state, managed to tell Leah that she'd seen a message from Rita come in on Craig's phone, saying that Ronald had fetched Zoey from the pool. Naturally she was relieved that Zoey was safe, but it was more *how* the message had come to light that disturbed Leah, and why Gillian was looking at Craig's phone in the first place.

'How are you feeling now, love?' Leah said, perching on the arm of the sofa and stroking Zoey's hair. She reached out and did the same to Henry, but he pulled away, not taking his eyes off the TV. 'Clearly not feeling too sick any more,' she said, tapping the crisp packet.

'Fine now,' she said, her eyes also fixed on the TV. 'Pops got us hot chocolate and we went for a walk. Then he brought me home.'

Leah swallowed, puzzled. Her dad never usually did things like that. It was always her mum who picked up the kids from school or clubs and looked after them. He loved his grandchildren, of course, but in his own particular way. 'That's nice,' she said, hoping Zoey might elaborate. She didn't.

'Anyway, where have *you* been, Mum? When I came in, Henry was crying and calling out for you. He really needed the loo but refused to get off the sofa because you'd told him not to move a muscle. He said you'd been gone ages.'

'Oh, Henry,' Leah said, feeling terrible. 'I'm so sorry. Have you been to the bathroom now?'

Henry nodded.

'I don't think I was gone *that* long, was I?' Leah said, looking away. She glanced at her watch. But it was true – she'd been next door talking to Gillian for far longer than the five minutes she'd promised Henry. In fact, it had been nearly an hour.

Later, when both children were fed and had bathed – Leah hadn't been able to eat a thing – and Henry was asleep and Zoey was hunched over her desk in her bedroom doing her homework, Leah went outside to assess the damage. While the police officers had told Craig to halt the building work for now, she knew it was likely he'd ignored them. It was heartbreaking to think that all her good work in the vegetable garden had been destroyed.

None of his claims about him owning the land were fair, but she also knew that Craig always trod just on the right side of the law. He wouldn't have knocked through the garden wall or turned the vegetable plot into a building site if he hadn't been within his legal rights. It upset her that he'd gone about it this way, though this evening's turn of events – seeing Gillian in that state – had left her feeling numb and helpless.

Of course, Leah had phoned her solicitor at least half a dozen more times throughout the day, leaving message after message as well as sending an email about Craig's claims regarding ownership of the land, the planning permission and the right of way, how something must have been missed or gone wrong during the conveyancing process, and for Liz to urgently call back.

But she hadn't heard a thing, with the firm's receptionist telling Leah over and over that Liz Morgan was in court all day and she would phone when free. She couldn't help wondering if her solicitor already knew about the error and was concocting a plan to throw Leah off the scent.

It was chilly outside and dark now, too, but the courtyard

light allowed her to pick her way through the churned-up ground of the vegetable plot, though she was careful where she trod, seeing trenches had already been dug for pipework.

Her eyes cast around what had, until recently, been her beloved vegetable garden, complete with chickens and neatly laid sets of onions and garlic, and even terracotta cloches for the rhubarb forcing next year, as well as the asparagus bed she'd been excited to uncover. All of it gone. Destroyed in a couple of hours.

She walked on further, catching sight of the bright yellow diggers lined up beside the gateway entrance the other side of the plot – all except one. The largest machine stood at an awkward angle not far from the bonfire, which was still smouldering from the builders lighting it earlier in the day, she assumed. Its caterpillar tracks were caked in thick mud and its bucket suspended in mid-air; a hard hat was hanging on one of the levers in the cab.

Leah couldn't bring herself to look at the semi-burnt pile of wood she'd built up over the weeks. She didn't want to deal with the thoughts it would trigger – the romantic and now ridiculous-seeming notion of her, Gabe and the kids having a fun evening of fireworks around it. Her dreams of a happy-ever-after had literally gone up in smoke.

She walked back towards the house, her feet dragging, but, when she reached the courtyard again, she stopped to unlock the number-coded padlock on the door of the brick store – the small building where she kept gardening equipment and other tools.

Except the padlock was already unlocked, hanging loose on the catch. She saw that the dials were set to the code she'd always used – the date of her and Craig's wedding anniversary. She'd never got around to changing it.

'I must have forgotten to lock it,' she said to herself as she opened the rickety old door.

Inside were bamboo canes for the beans she was going to grow, old clay flowerpots, her many pairs of worn gardening gloves, the old petrol chainsaw that her dad had given her for clearing the plot when she'd first moved in, though she'd never dared to use it yet, plus an old lawnmower, as well as an assortment of rakes and shovels, and a bag of compost dumped in her wonky wheelbarrow.

'I may as well get rid of it all now,' she said. 'I won't be doing any more gardening.' Then her eyes settled on a gap on the crooked shelf. 'Odd,' she said, trying to recall what had been there. Then she remembered. The old metal jerrycan her dad had given her when he'd dropped off the chainsaw. He'd explained about two-stroke fuel and had put a sticker label on the petrol can so she knew what it was.

Thinking about where she may have left the can or if she'd even moved it seemed insignificant in the light of everything that had happened. She felt numb, broken and drained.

And it wasn't simply because her garden had been destroyed.

No, her anguish ran deeper than that.

Leah leant back against the rough brick wall, her knees buckling as she dropped to the floor. With her arms hugging her legs, she buried her face and cried. It wasn't self-pity, rather an unfathomable pain that seemed permanently stitched into the fabric of her being – a pain that had built up over many years but was now finally being released.

———

Later, Leah sat on her bed wrapped up in a soft robe with her wet hair piled up on her head in a towel. She held her phone, turning it over and over in her hands. There was no option but to switch it on and face whatever messages had come through since she'd reported the incident to the police.

Though when she finally plucked up the courage to hit the on button, fewer new messages than she'd anticipated pinged in. Perhaps the police had given Craig a warning after all.

She rested her head back against the headboard, taking a few slow, deep breaths and then, steeling herself, she deleted all the disgusting texts. She'd intended getting herself a new number if necessary, though it was an annoyance she could do without. The salon had a landline but many of her clients liked to speak to her personally, calling her mobile to make appointments.

Once she was satisfied that her phone was clean, she went to tap out a message to Gabe. In their WhatsApp string, she saw a missed message from him that he'd sent in reply to hers from a few days ago. It was friendly and he'd offered to come and clear the gateway, but when she hadn't responded, he'd come and done it anyway.

But she still had no idea why he'd visited Craig earlier, nor why, according to her mother, they'd had a fight. And the mix-up with the scarf was equally baffling. None of it made sense. She typed:

Hi, sorry for radio silence, had an issue with phone. Can you call me when you're free? Also, I miss you. L xx

———

'Hello?' Leah said, after waking suddenly and lunging for her phone.

'Did you delete my number already?' the voice said with a laugh. 'You sound like you don't know who it is.'

Leah sat up, rubbing her eyes with one hand. 'No, no, I'd just drifted off. Sorry...' she said. 'It's been one of those days.'

'It's nice to hear your voice,' Gabe said, though with a cautious note.

'You too,' she replied, her mind racing through everything she'd planned to say.

'How have you been?'

'Oh, you know...' she said in a so-so kind of way. 'A few things going on.' She paused, hoping he might reciprocate. He didn't. 'What happened between us... I wanted to explain but then things got tricky here and—'

'Your message said you had phone problems?'

'It's too complicated to explain but I couldn't use it for a while. I think it's sorted now.'

'Complicated indeed,' he said in a wry voice. 'And for what it's worth, I've missed you too.'

Leah's heart clenched. She couldn't deny that she'd developed feelings for him during the time they'd known each other. In fact, until now, she hadn't realised just how strong those feelings had been. Hearing his voice had thrown her off the reason for getting in touch.

'What was it that's so urgent?' Gabe asked. 'Do you have more work for me?'

'No, but thank you for doing the hedge, though...' She trailed off, not wanting to explain about the building works and the land. 'You must let me know what I owe you.'

'When I didn't hear back from you, I wasn't sure if I should just go ahead,' Gabe replied. 'And there's no charge.'

'That's kind, thank you,' she replied. 'Look, I know it's getting late, but are you free to come round tonight?' She wanted to see him face to face, read his expression and gauge his body language when she asked about him visiting Craig.

There was a pause – a pause during which Leah got off the bed and went to the window. In the street below, she saw the 'For Sale' board opposite with Craig's face smirking out of it. The stick-on 'Sold' sign had slipped and either the wind or passing youths had damaged the post, because it now stood at an awkward angle.

Leah drew the curtains.

'Sure,' Gabe replied. 'Is everything OK?'

'Thanks,' Leah replied, more flatly than she'd intended and without answering his question. 'I appreciate it.'

CHAPTER THIRTY

It was the following afternoon when Leah heard the screams.

She was at home, cooking – though cooking wasn't entirely accurate, as in reality she was microwaving a frozen spaghetti Bolognese for herself. And neither did she have much of an appetite or inclination to eat it – knowing she'd have to force it down.

First thing that morning, she'd phoned the salon, telling Sally that she wouldn't be coming into work today. A day off, she'd decided, was needed. Her mum was fetching the kids from school and taking Leah to swimming training and then going on with Henry to a birthday party at the soft play centre. Rita hated it there but had offered to do it, sounding unusually saccharine when she'd called.

Leah strained her ears again. The first scream had come at the same moment the microwave pinged and she wasn't entirely sure what it was she'd heard. But once the machine stopped and she'd taken out her meal, there was no doubting the piercing and urgent shrieks of... of a *woman*. And it was easy to tell that the noise seemed to be coming from the back of her house, given that the window above her sink was ajar to let in some fresh air.

Leah dashed to the window to look out. There was no one in the courtyard and she couldn't see anything through the gap in the wall into next door's garden. The builders hadn't been on site today either – small blessings, she'd thought earlier.

She shoved on her shoes and went outside, waiting for another scream.

And there it was, coming from the vegetable garden – or building plot as it now seemed to be. She'd still not heard anything back from her solicitor's office, despite more attempts to contact Liz. She'd even been round to the office that morning with the intention of seeing Liz face to face, but, unusually, the office was closed with not even the receptionist there to answer the door when she'd rung the bell repeatedly.

'Hello?' Leah called out as she went into the walled garden. 'Who's there?'

It took a moment to take in what she was seeing as her eyes scanned around – the destruction still making her want to weep. But as her eyes settled and focused, she realised that Gillian was on her knees beside the smouldering bonfire at the far side of the garden. She was screaming and rocking backward and forward, her hands clutching at her head as animal-like noises spewed out of her.

'Gillian?' Leah cried, running over, stumbling on the uneven ground. 'What's happened?'

'Oh my God, oh my God, oh my *God*...' Gillian kept repeating, punctuated every so often by a wail.

When Leah reached her side, her first instinct was to pull Gillian to her feet – she was sitting too close to the smouldering remains of the fire, which was still throwing out a large amount of heat – but she was a dead weight and wouldn't stand up. Leah grabbed her by the shoulders and shook her instead, trying to get some sense out of her.

'What's happened?' She stared down at Gillian. The woman was hysterical, tears streaming down her mascara-streaked and bruised face. Her cheeks were puffy and her eyes red and sore. Her hair was a mess and she was wearing the same dirty clothes that she'd had on yesterday.

'Gillian, please, tell me what's going on,' Leah said, feeling her anxiety levels rising.

'Look!' Gillian said – a half-scream, half-cry. She pointed with a shaking hand at the bonfire. 'Oh my God, no, I can't stand it... *Nooo...*'

Leah looked down at the fire, her eyes scanning the blackened pile of wood, pallets and other general building rubbish.

'What is...?' she said, about to continue. But then she stopped, clapping her hands over her mouth. 'Oh... Christ, *no...*' she whispered behind her palms. She turned round, bending over as her stomach suddenly cramped and the cup of tea she'd had half an hour ago splattered onto the muddy ground, along with bits of toast she'd managed to eat first thing. She dry-retched a few more times, spitting out as she wiped her mouth on the back of her sleeve.

Gillian had somehow managed to stand up by herself, staggering over to Leah. 'We have to call the police,' she wailed. 'Help me! We need to get him out! He might be alive!'

Leah stared at the body – its charred head, the arm sticking out of the remains of the fire, the melted, tarry clothes clinging to its torso. There was no way this person was alive. She stood there staring at it for what seemed like an age, though in reality it was only a few seconds.

'Oh, *Gillian...*' she finally whispered, clutching onto her arm as they held each other for support. Twists of smoke spiralled upwards into the grey sky, plus the occasional crackle and upward rain of sparks as another part of the bonfire ignited.

Leah turned and took Gillian by the shoulders, looking her in the eye. 'I want you to listen to me, OK?'

Gillian nodded frantically.

'Did Craig eventually come home last night?'

The nod turned into a shake. 'No.'

'And did you report him missing to the police, like I suggested?'

Leah thought back to when she'd gone next door looking for Zoey, and how upset Gillian had been. Through her tears, she'd managed to tell Leah how Craig had been getting more and more angry over the last few weeks, accusing her of having an affair, not letting her go out when she wanted. And someone – she didn't know who – had tipped him off about spotting her in the local pub with a man. It was then that he'd started hitting her.

'After he'd come back from seeing the police at yours this morning, he... he threatened to... to *kill* himself. He said every-thing was messed up because of me, that it was all my fault,' Gillian had sobbed. 'I begged and begged him not to, said I'd do anything he wanted, but he wouldn't even speak to me. Then he left for work.'

Leah had tried to explain to Gillian that that was how Craig operated, that it was abusive behaviour and he was doing it to manipulate and control her. But Gillian had been so upset, she wasn't taking it in.

'He must have come home from the office sometime during the day,' Gillian had said, sipping the tea Leah had made for her. 'Everything was a mess – cushions thrown around, a painting half hanging off the wall, things from the coffee table swept onto the floor. And several mugs were smashed in the kitchen. When I came home from work, his car, phone and keys were still here, but there was no sign of him.'

Now, beside the bonfire, Gillian was nodding again. 'Yes, yes, I reported him missing, like you said. In the early hours of the morning.'

'Good,' Leah replied. 'Let the police deal with him. What-ever happens, I want you to know this is *not* your fault, Gillian, OK? But I also want you to prepare yourself... for... for the worst.' Leah glanced down at the body again, hardly able to look at his face – the sight of the shiny burnt skin making her want to throw up again.

'Does... does it look like Craig?' Gillian asked, covering her mouth.

'It's impossible to tell,' she said, sighing heavily. She turned away, trying not to retch again. 'But you're right, we need to call the police.'

Gillian tore at her hair, pacing about again. 'I can't stand it!' she screamed. 'It's all my fault. We have to save him. Help me pull him out!' Her knees buckled again as she dropped down at the edge of the fire.

'Gillian... no...' Leah had to shout to be heard above her screams. She knew it was futile. 'Stop! You'll get burnt.' Gillian was yanking on the charred arm of the body.

And that's when Leah spotted someone watching them. A woman on a grey horse wearing black riding boots and a padded jacket was peering over the newly cleared gateway. There wasn't much of a footpath, just a muddy verge where the machinery had been brought in. A car hooted its horn at her as it passed, making the horse snort and step sideways. The woman tried to calm the horse, tightening the reins.

'Are you OK in there?' she called out. 'I heard screaming.' Her eyes darted about, lingering on Gillian kneeling beside the bonfire.

'Yes, yes, we're fine,' Gillian called back, suddenly standing up and somehow managing to sound normal. 'Just... it's just a little accident, but we're fine.'

Leah didn't think that was particularly accurate, but they didn't need this woman sticking her nose in.

'There'll be another accident if you don't watch out,' Leah warned the woman. 'It's a narrow verge.'

Another car swerved to avoid her as it came past, its engine revving as the driver slammed it into first gear again after braking.

'Thank you, though,' Leah called out, waving as the woman nudged her heels against the horse's sides and rode off, looking back over her shoulder a couple of times.

'Oh *Leah*, I can't stand it,' Gillian spluttered through snot and tears when she'd gone. She lunged at the body in the fire again, and in turn, Leah lunged at her, pulling her away. A charred branch suddenly dislodged, causing a flare-up of flames around the body.

'Stop!' Leah ordered. 'It's too late to do anything. We have to call the police.'

They both stared down at the unidentifiable corpse. Nothing seemed real; it didn't seem possible that it was the father of her children lying dead in the fire – that Craig had finally followed through with his threat.

'I told him he'd gone too far yesterday morning,' Gillian continued, touching her bruised cheek. 'That the way he was treating you... the mother of his children... it wasn't right. I said he should allow you time to speak to your solicitor about the land, sort it out amicably. For the kids' sake at least.'

'Thank you for fighting my corner,' Leah whispered.

'He argued with everyone. He'd even had a run-in with Bill, the site foreman, before he left for work yesterday.' Gillian hugged her arms around her. 'They'd had a big row about having to halt the works, how it would screw them over financially. When Craig came back inside, he was steaming angry. He was threatening all sorts.'

Leah sighed heavily. 'I can vouch for his temper,' she said, grabbing hold of Gillian to stop her pacing about. 'And then he took it all out on you?'

Gillian nodded, chewing her fingers. She didn't know what to do with herself.

'Do you have your phone on you? Mine's inside.'

Gillian shook her head.

'Let's go up to the house and call the police. And you need to be in a fit state to speak to them.' Leah glanced her up and down. 'You can put some clean clothes on. Everything will be OK.'

Gillian stared at her, her face crumpling. 'How... how can you be so... *calm*, so... *together*? Rexie is *dead!*'

Leah took her by the shoulders again. Their faces were close. 'I can assure you, Gillian, I'm not in the least bit calm.' Then she took her by the hand. 'Come on. The sooner we call them, the sooner it will all be over.'

And as the women walked away, Leah glanced back over her shoulder, watching as the biggest plume of flames yet roared up from the pyre and the charred head of the corpse dropped backwards in the heat.

CHAPTER THIRTY-ONE

The living room in the Old Vicarage suddenly seemed huge, cavernous. *Ridiculous, even*, Leah thought as she sat rigid on the edge of the uncomfortable sofa. *Who needs a room this large*, she wondered, her mind all over the place, trying to distract herself. Her eyes flicked over the lavish furnishings – nothing like she'd ever choose, even if she could afford it. It reeked of too much money and wanting to show off. In other words, it reeked of her ex-husband.

Dead, she thought, her stomach churning.

She'd wished for it enough times over the last few weeks.

Gillian wailed again.

And then she saw Craig's sweater thrown over the arm of a chair – the cuffs turned up and one of his hairs on the dark blue lambswool V-neck he'd always worn to work in the colder months. She felt sick again seeing it.

'Can I get you something?' the constable asked Gillian, leaning towards her on the sofa. He was young and nervous and kept talking into his radio. He was the first officer to respond to their emergency call and, after assessing the scene outside, he'd radioed for backup. 'A cup of tea or glass of water while we wait, perhaps?' It prompted another sob from Gillian followed by a frantic nod.

'Yes, yes, yes,' she said, suddenly scowling as if she wondered what, exactly, they were waiting for.

Leah couldn't recall why, in the blur of everything, but for some reason, the French doors to the garden were wide open. Perhaps Gillian had opened them when they'd come back inside. She'd been doing random things – such as putting on her shoes and coat then taking them off again. Turning the television on and flicking through dozens of channels before switching it off again. Then she'd tried to use her phone but ended up dropping it on the floor and, at one point, she'd gone into the kitchen and opened the fridge door, staring into it as though looking for a snack. Leah had followed her into the kitchen and closed the fridge door behind her when she'd walked away, her arms hanging by her sides.

'Tea...' Gillian whispered, as if it was the first time she'd ever heard the word.

'Cures everything,' Leah replied, kicking herself for being thoughtless. 'I'll make it,' she said, standing up when the officer looked at her expectantly.

'The FLO will be here soon,' he commented, explaining that she was a family liaison officer, trained to deal with this type of situation.

Family, Leah thought.

The constable's uniform seemed too small, as though his overworked biceps and shoulders wanted to burst out. He'd taken off his outer jacket but still seemed constrained, not to mention overburdened by various bits of equipment attached to him.

Leah went to the kitchen and returned shortly with a tray and three mugs. 'There's sugar and milk,' she said to the officer. 'Help yourself.' She stirred in a couple of teaspoons of sugar for Gillian and added milk. 'Here you go,' she said, sitting down next to her. When she didn't take the mug, Leah put it back on the tray. And then the doorbell rang, making Gillian jump, just at the same moment as a group of police officers traipsed through the back garden past the open French doors – all of them dressed in white suits and carrying metal cases of equipment.

Leah headed to the front door to answer it. As expected, it was another officer – a woman in her late thirties this time, with a kind smile on her face. Her head was tipped slightly to one side, making her short blond ponytail just visible around the side of her neck.

'Mrs Forbes?'

'Yes,' Leah replied without thinking. 'I mean, no. Yes, I was. But not now. I'm the ex-wife. Gillian lives here. She's in the sitting room.' She stepped aside and allowed the officer in, feeling, fleetingly, as though the house was hers and she was welcoming a guest. The scent of lilies from the vase on the central table was pungent – sickly-sweet from flowers that were past their best.

'I'm PC Megan Graham, the liaison officer. I'll be staying a while and explaining everything that's going on. And I'll be the point of contact going forward. Nice place,' she added, taking off her hat. 'A forensics team has gone round the side already,' she said, wiping her feet vigorously. 'The gate was open.' She had a small bag with her and silenced her radio as they entered the living room.

'PC Wentworth,' the younger male officer said, standing up as she entered. He looked relieved to see her. 'And this is Gillian,' he said, sitting back down in a different spot to allow the FLO to be near her. 'I'm afraid she's had rather a nasty shock.' He glanced between Gillian and the FLO.

The officer introduced herself to Gillian, her voice soothing and confident. 'I'll be here to look after you, answer any questions you may have about what's going on outside, and to keep you informed of progress.' She leant forward and peered up at Gillian, who was sitting rigid, staring at her cup of tea on the coffee table in front of her. 'And meantime, you can tell me what's happened. Does that sound OK?'

Gillian suddenly lifted her foot and kicked over the tea, sending it all over the carpet. The empty mug plopped onto the soft pile, undamaged. Leah leapt up and returned from the kitchen with several tea towels, dropping to her knees to clean up the mess.

'I understand that it's a very stressful time for you, Gillian. I know it's confusing and upsetting. The more information we can gather at this stage, the better. It will help us going forward with whatever investigation follows. Are you OK with your friend being present for now?' She glanced at Leah.

Friend, Leah repeated in her head. She tried to assimilate that definition with everything that had happened the last few weeks. Certainly, when she'd first met Gillian and before she knew Craig was her partner, while she may not have thought they'd ever be *best* friends, she'd believed that, as neighbours, they'd get along just fine.

But maybe now, even after everything, there was potential for a friendship of some kind. They certainly had more in common that they'd first realised.

Gillian managed a nod. She sat with her shoulders pulled inwards and her hands clasped between her legs. Since they'd discovered the body, she'd changed into clean jogging bottoms and a white sweater. Leah hadn't seen her without make-up before, but she'd managed to wash her face from earlier. The bruising shone out.

'Is... is he alive?' Gillian said in a voice that didn't sound like hers. 'Rexie?'

'Let's wait until we hear from the detective inspector in charge of the scene, shall we?' PC Graham said.

'Where's... where's the ambulance?' Gillian asked. 'I told them to send one.' Her face was covered in worry lines.

Leah noticed that PC Wentworth had stepped outside the French doors and was talking on his radio. When he came back inside, he closed the doors behind him. He also drew the curtains and went to flick on the light.

Perhaps in readiness for when they remove the body, Leah thought.

'Paramedics and ambulance are at the scene,' he said, hitching up his trousers before he sat down again.

'If there's anything they can do,' PC Graham said, 'please be assured, they'll do it.' She reached out and patted Gillian's hand. 'I know it's a dreadfully worrying time for you.'

'But is it... is it Craig in the fire? We had a row yesterday and he stormed off. I felt awful about it. And now... and now this,' she said, letting out another sob. 'I reported him missing last night when he didn't come home. I was so worried.'

PC Wentworth took down notes on her tablet.

'I couldn't stand it if our last words were angry.'

'We'll have more information once the team have done their work. There's a forensic pathologist at the scene too.' Another pat on the hand from the FLO. Then she added sugar and milk to the remaining mug of tea and offered it to Gillian. 'Have a sip of this.'

'Forensic pathologist?' Leah said, but then stopped herself. She wondered how much they could tell from an incinerated body. Not much, she didn't think. The more she thought about it, the more her head spun.

'Excuse me,' she said, getting up and dashing to the downstairs toilet. She shut the door and leant back against it. She screwed up her eyes but that didn't prevent a couple of tears trickling down her cheeks.

What if Craig really was *dead*? How would she break it to the children? And she'd have to tell her parents, Craig's remaining family up north, their mutual friends – and what about his business, his staff, his properties, his stuff – his *everything*? As his ex-wife, the responsibility for most of those things didn't lie with her any more, but it was still all too ghastly to contemplate.

She heard herself weeping as though it was someone else. Pain that had been stored up far too long.

She stayed in the toilet until there was nothing left to cry, and then she went to open the door, praying with all her might that when she did, she'd see Craig standing there in the hall by the vase of lilies, flicking through his mail, scowling at her when he turned around, a jar of maraschino cherries in his hand.

CHAPTER THIRTY-TWO

The next couple of hours passed in a blur. A couple of other officers came and went, and PC Graham, along with the original officer, asked them questions about what had happened from the moment Gillian had discovered the body in the bonfire up to her calling the emergency services. They also enquired about the preceding couple of days, each of them taking down notes. Or at least they tried to ask questions. Gillian wasn't making much sense.

Leah added her side of the story, too, saying how she'd heard the screams and had gone outside to investigate. They grilled Gillian about her argument with Craig, where her bruises had come from, but she was vague about the details, her face reflecting the pain she felt inside. Leah knew all too well the guilt that was left behind after one of Craig's meltdowns.

It reminded her of when friends had asked her if she was OK, how she'd got the bruises, why she never socialised much any more or didn't reply on their WhatsApp group messages. She'd brushed them all off with excuses, saying she was just clumsy, that she was fine or tired or busy with work – not wanting to betray Craig. Despite everything he'd done, her loyalty was fierce.

Then the officers turned their focus to Leah's involvement with Craig and how she'd come to be living next door to her ex-husband.

'How long have you got?' she said.

'As long as it takes,' was PC Wentworth's reply. 'The short version will do for now.'

'Living next door to him wasn't intentional, I can assure you,' Leah said. 'Let's call it an unfortunate coincidence. Since he moved in, things haven't been easy.'

Both officers looked up from their tablets.

'Can you explain?' PC Graham asked, sipping on the fresh tea that Leah had made. Every step she'd taken between the fridge, sink and kettle had seemed laborious, as though a great weight was dragging her into an abyss.

'Our divorce was... was acrimonious,' she explained. 'Craig moved next door to continue controlling me. He's never got over me leaving. It's as simple as that.'

Gillian made another whimpering sound but contained it by sipping on her tea. Leah noticed her hand shaking as she raised the mug to her lips.

PC Wentworth nodded. 'I understand there's been police involvement recently between you and your ex-husband,' he said in a way that wasn't posing a question but was certainly expecting an answer. He glanced at his tablet. 'Early yesterday morning, I see.'

'I'm afraid so, yes,' Leah replied. 'And also on one other occasion.'

There was silence for a moment as she wondered if she was required to expand on that or if they already had the details. Maybe they were testing her. After all, none of this situation reflected well on her – her ex-husband reported missing after countless rows and two instances of police involvement. And then a body turns up in the bonfire she'd made on her land.

'Craig put my phone number on... on a hook-up website. I got dozens of disturbing calls and messages so I reported him. You can check at the police station, if you like. I haven't had an update about the case yet, but I presume an officer must have warned him because it's stopped now.'

'Sorry to hear that,' PC Wentworth said, clearing his throat.

'And then Craig called the police on *me* yesterday morning because I tried to stop him coming into my courtyard. He wanted to take my chickens. It was all to do with a land dispute. I've been trying to speak to my solicitor, but she's dropped off the face of the earth.'

Leah felt her heart rate rising at the thought of just these two incidents, let alone everything else that had happened since they'd become neighbours.

'OK, so let's focus on the last day or two for now,' the officer said. 'When was the last time you saw your partner, Gillian?'

It was as though Gillian didn't hear the question, because she suddenly stood up and went over to the French doors, touching the curtains. She turned round to face the officers, a vacant look on her face. 'Why are these closed? Is it night already? Are you staying for dinner?' Her voice was weak and fragile, and she suddenly seemed small against the swathes of fabric behind her, as though she was on stage. The bruise on her face had fully bloomed now, and several more had come up, as well as marks on the side of her neck. Fingermarks.

'Don't worry, we don't need any food,' PC Graham said kindly, following her over. 'Why don't you come and sit down again?' She guided her by the elbow and Gillian began to follow, but then she stopped.

'Is it Craig in the bonfire? Is he dead?' She dropped to her knees and covered her face, sobbing with her head bent down to the carpet. 'I... I... loved him, you know. I really did...'

'I know, it's OK, it's OK,' the female officer said. 'Come and sit down.'

This time, Gillian allowed herself to be led back to the sofa, where Leah helped her down and covered her up with a throw. She was shaking as Leah handed her a tissue.

'I last saw Craig when he left for work, just before I took his children to school,' she said when she'd composed herself again. She flashed a look at Leah. 'He wasn't here when I got home, but I saw that he'd been home at some point during the day. When he didn't come back all evening, I reported him missing. I was worried because he... he'd... already threatened he was going to hurt himself. And he hadn't taken his phone, his keys or his car.' Gillian suddenly sounded much more together. 'It's just not like him.'

Leah thought it was exactly like him but kept quiet for now.

'Did he take his wallet?' the officer asked.

'I... I don't know that,' she replied.

Leah swallowed. His wallet? They'd not checked for it last night when Leah had come looking for Zoey. Gillian was in a terrible state and the focus had been on comforting her. She'd needed someone to talk to – someone who *understood*. Someone who knew what to do.

'We went out in my car and drove around searching for a bit, but we couldn't see him anywhere,' Leah chipped in. 'I even stopped at the local pub to check,' Leah added, glancing at Gillian.

Gillian stared back, looking vacant.

'I told her that Craig had most likely taken off just to worry her, that he'd probably got drunk somewhere and checked into a hotel for the night. It's what he often did when I was married to him.' She shrugged. 'I said she shouldn't be too concerned.'

'He's disappeared before?' PC Graham asked.

'A number of times,' Leah replied. 'The first time was when I told him I wanted a divorce. That was years ago now. He was angry at first but then he seemed like a broken man, crying and begging and everything. It was all an act, of course. Then he stormed out. I was frantic with worry because the last thing he'd said to me was that he was going to kill himself, that he couldn't live without me and the kids.'

Gillian hiccupped out a sob, covering her nose with the tissue.

'When he didn't return by late evening, I panicked and went out looking for him, driving around all his usual places. I phoned his friends and family and sent loads of texts, begging him not to hurt himself, to come home. His phone went to voicemail, so I left messages, telling him how much I loved him, that I'd do anything to make it work between us. I couldn't stand for the kids not to have a dad, for them to grow up believing it was my fault he'd killed himself.'

'And what happened?' PC Wentworth asked. 'How was he found?'

'Oh, he called me the next morning, all bright and breezy. He told me his phone had run out of battery and that he'd got drunk and had been sleeping it off at a friend's house.' Leah paused. 'Then he asked if I really meant what I'd said in my messages, that I loved him and wanted to make it work.' She sighed. 'Turns out it was a woman's house he'd stayed at, of course. But he'd got what he wanted.'

'Which was?'

'Me, of course.'

There was a knock on the French doors, making Gillian jump again. PC Graham went to see who it was.

'Ma'am,' she said as she opened the door. A cool breeze wafted down the length of the living room and a woman, mid-forties with mousy shoulder-length hair cut into a precise bob, stepped inside. She was slim and wearing black trousers and a dark, waist-length wool coat with the collar turned up and a pale green blouse beneath it. She wore no make-up or jewellery but somehow still seemed anything but plain. Her features were delicate and refined, yet steely and determined too – as if she'd seen everything in her time.

'Uh-oh, pale carpet,' she muttered, retreating to the doorway to kick off her shoes – ugly, practical things, Leah noticed. And very, very muddy.

'Hello, ma'am,' PC Wentworth said, standing up as the woman approached.

'Hello,' she said, her eyes flicking between Leah and Gillian. 'I'm Detective Inspector Carla Nelson. I'm in charge of the scene outside and the ongoing investigation. Can you tell me who called the emergency services?' she asked, taking a seat in a small armchair at right angles to Gillian.

Gillian flicked up her hand. 'Me, Gillian Harris.'

DI Nelson leant forward, forearms resting on her legs as she spoke. Leah was tempted to huddle forward too, the five of them forming a powwow, but she remained sitting upright. There was clearly news.

'I wanted to update you on progress so far. Our forensics team have been working away and are keen to find out as much as they can before it gets dark. The light is already going. It's normal for them to pick through and photograph everything meticulously, as well as leaving markers for items of interest. So don't feel concerned if you've seen anything like this from the upstairs windows.'

Leah nodded.

'But I'm sorry to say that the person you discovered in the bonfire is sadly deceased.'

Another sob came from Gillian as she covered her face and rocked back and forth. Leah shifted closer to her and stroked her back. DI Nelson bowed her head out of respect before continuing.

'Because of the nature of the injuries and the fire damage, it's hard to get much in the way of identification yet, but we understand that you reported your partner missing last night and you're concerned the deceased is him, Craig Forbes. Is that correct, Gillian?'

'Yes, yes, that's right,' Gillian said, sniffing. She wiped her nose on her sleeve.

'We do always keep an open mind when it comes to identification, so I'd advise you to—'

'But who else would it be?' Gillian suddenly blurted out. 'I swear I saw a watch on him that looked like Craig's.'

DI Nelson nodded and waited a moment. 'I understand. But the watch was badly burnt and, without expert analysis, it's hard to confirm a make and suchlike at this stage.'

'So are you saying it's *not* him?' Gillian asked hopefully.

DI Nelson made a face that indicated she wasn't sure, but it was clear something else was on her mind. 'After initial scene evidence was gathered, our forensics team removed the body from the extinguished fire. A small part of the person's back was unharmed by the flames.'

'Wait... are you saying it's Craig or not?' Gillian clutched the edge of the sofa expectantly. Leah knotted her hands together until her knuckles went white.

'What I'm saying is that we still don't know. However, the person was wearing a workman's high-visibility jacket – you know, the luminous ones you often see.'

Leah frowned. That didn't sound like something Craig would wear.

'While most of it was melted and destroyed by the fire, there was a more intact section on the back, where a name was printed on the jacket. Sometimes workers do this so they can be spotted easily on site. I was wondering if...' DI Nelson cleared her throat. As experienced and calm as she seemed, Leah imagined such a task was never easy. 'I was wondering if the name Gabe meant anything to either of you?'

CHAPTER THIRTY-THREE

As she got into the car, Leah wondered if she was feeling steady enough to drive – and if she would even remember the way to her parents' house given her state of mind, let alone not have an accident. All she wanted was to fetch her children and get back home.

The detective's words were still ringing in her ears.

Gabe... Dear God, no. What the hell had they discovered?

She'd decided she wouldn't say a word to the children yet about what had happened. Gillian was still worried it might have been Craig in the fire, and Leah had been trying to think of a reason why he'd be wearing Gabe's hi-vis jacket. She couldn't.

The discovery had certainly thrown everything into confusion, and Leah had no idea how much detail police forensics could glean from such a badly burnt body or what they'd be able to piece together about events leading up to the death. From the way DI Nelson was talking, she now realised it was probably quite a lot.

Leah managed to get the key into the ignition on the fourth attempt. She started the engine. PC Graham was still with Gillian, as was DI Nelson, though she said she'd be leaving soon and would be in touch with each of them in the morning. She said that they'd both be required to come into the station to make formal statements. And then that had been that. For now.

In fact, Leah had been surprised at how easy it had been to walk out of Gillian's house and seemingly return to normal life.

'Normal,' she whispered to herself as she pulled out of the parking space. Then she shouted it at the top of her voice, turning on the fan full blast to demist the screen. 'Nothing's *ever* been normal!' Several passers-by stopped and stared as she roared off down the road.

Tears rolled down her cheeks, her blurry vision making it hard to see as she drove.

Hold it together, she told herself. *Block it all out.*

She laughed bitterly. Old habits died hard, that was for sure. It was her best skill, hiding in deep denial, and now she was grateful for it. It was what had got her through years of marriage to Craig.

It had been a question of survival.

And yet from the outside, they'd appeared to be the perfect family. Loving parents with two adorable children. A home – clean and warm, and always good food on the table. Craig with his business, the local big man in estate agency, respected and trusted, providing for his family. 'King of Property', a piece in the local paper once dubbed him.

'Property,' Leah whispered now as she drove. That's all she ever was to him.

But this time, the tears weren't for the past, or for when her children had caught her applying make-up to hide the bruises or had heard raised voices. No, this time she was crying for her future – her *lost* future.

This time her tears were for Gabe.

She pulled over into an empty bus stop, yanking on the handbrake. It was dark and every street and car headlight turned into crazy starbursts in her eyes. She was finding it hard to see.

'Oh, Gabe, no... *Please don't let them say it's you...*' She leant her head forward on the steering wheel and sobbed again.

'You didn't deserve this,' she said, rummaging in her bag for her phone. Maybe it wasn't true. Maybe the police had got it wrong and the letters on the jacket were unclear. Perhaps it was Gary written on the back, or some other name beginning with G.

But deep down, she knew it was Gabe's jacket. She'd seen him wearing it when they'd met outside her parents' house, when he'd been packing up his van. She remembered his smile, his strong arms, and how his hair was damp from sweat after a day's graft. He'd turned to put his equipment away and she'd noticed the name written in capitals across the back of his jacket – GABE. She'd even commented on it, asking if it was short for Gabriel. Then came the inevitable angel joke that he must have heard dozens of times before.

In the car, she called Gabe's number, waiting for it to connect. But it didn't. It went to voicemail. She tried three more times and on the last attempt, she left a message.

'Hey, Gabe, it's... it's me. Could you give me a call? I just want to know you're OK. Thanks, bye.'

She tucked her phone back in her bag and took out a tissue, peering into the rear-view mirror to clean her face. 'I couldn't *not* check on him,' she whispered to herself, blowing her nose. Then she put the car into gear and drove off to her parents' house.

'Hello, dear,' her father said in the kitchen ten minutes later. Leah had a key to their house but had rung the bell before she let herself inside, calling out that it was her from the hallway. 'Wasn't expecting to see you,' he went on, wiping his hands down the apron he was wearing. 'Thought your mother said we were having the children to stay overnight. She said you weren't well.' He stirred something on the hob then turned round to face her. 'What is it with everyone not being well?'

Leah made a puzzled face. 'I'm OK, Dad. Who else isn't well?'

'Your mother. She's had a migraine since yesterday.' He rolled his eyes, jumping as toast popped out of the toaster.

'I didn't know,' Leah said, taking off her coat and dropping down onto a chair at the little table. It was only a small kitchen with outdated beige cabinets that she knew her mother hated. 'More to the point, how are *you* feeling now, Dad?' she asked, more concerned about her father's health. While she knew her mum suffered with migraines from time to time, she also knew that they sometimes appeared very conveniently – allowing Rita to get out of something she didn't want to do, or to gain sympathy and attention if she was feeling ignored.

'Marching on and chipper, my dear daughter,' Ronald said, waving the wooden spoon at her.

Despite his stoic tone, Leah sensed a sadness beneath. A couple of baked beans dripped off the spoon and onto the floor, so she grabbed some kitchen roll and wiped them up, saving her father the trouble.

'Wish I could say the same about you, though,' he added, watching her. 'You've got a face like a wet weekend. What's up?'

Leah let out an involuntary sigh as she sat back down. Her father was always direct.

'In your own time,' her dad said, glancing across at her as he put the toast onto two plates and slathered them with butter. Then he dolloped baked beans on each and added a large pile of grated cheese on top. 'That'll have to do,' he said with a tight grin, putting the plates on the table. 'I'm no chef. Kids!' he called out of the door towards the living room. 'Tea's up!' He shuffled back to the cutlery drawer and took out what he needed, then made two glasses of orange squash.

'Thanks for this, Dad, you're a star,' Leah said, her heart warming as Zoey and Henry tumbled into the kitchen. She gave each of them a hug, squeezing them both a little harder and longer than usual.

'My fave,' Henry said, dragging out a chair and grabbing his knife and fork before he'd even sat down. Zoey was less enthusiastic about the food but thanked her grandad by going up to him and giving him a hug. Her head landed on his shoulder for a moment and Leah couldn't help noticing that she closed her eyes for a second as he hugged her back.

'Come on, eat up, then,' he said, urging Zoey to sit. 'Don't let this culinary masterpiece go cold.'

Leah watched on as her children tucked into their food. Her dad put the kettle on and made a questioning face at her, holding up a mug. Leah nodded. 'I'll just pop upstairs to see how Mum is,' she said, slipping out of the room. She heard mild protests from her father as she left, about how it wasn't a good idea, but he was drowned out by Zoey and Henry's chatter.

She tapped on her mother's bedroom door. 'Mum?' She opened the door a crack. 'Are you asleep?' The room was dark and smelt of her mother – mainly a blend of lavender and rosemary with the rich scent of the other essential oils she used when she had a migraine. But there was something else too – a fusty, unwashed base note that she didn't recognise. It wasn't like Rita.

'Mum?' she said, going in. The curtains were drawn and Leah tripped on something as she made her way to the bed. She bent down to retrieve the discarded clothing – again it wasn't like her mother not to hang up what she'd been wearing.

She heard a groan coming from beneath the covers. 'Mum, are you OK?' she said quietly, sitting down on the edge of the bed.

Another moan. 'What do you want?' her mum said, uncovering her arms and trapping the sheets tightly around her slim body. 'I've got a migraine.'

Leah reached out and flicked on the bedside lamp. Rita screwed up her eyes and groaned louder. 'Ouch,' she said, draping an arm over her brow. 'Why did you do that?'

'Because I need to talk to you, Mum.'

'I don't want to talk,' Rita replied in a voice that Leah barely recognised. It made her sound like a stubborn child.

'I'm sorry you've got a migraine. What do you think triggered it?'

'How would I know?' she said, struggling to sit up. She plumped up the pillows behind her.

'Mum...' Leah sighed. She wasn't sure how to approach what she needed to ask without making her clam up entirely. 'Can you tell me more about what happened when you went to see Craig yesterday?'

'Such as?' Rita reached over to her bedside table for a glass of water and took several long swigs. She wiped the back of her hand across her mouth, forgetting that she was wearing red lipstick.

'How did he seem? Did he mention if he was going away anywhere?'

'I've already told you what happened. He made a pass at me, that gardener chap arrived, and then I left.'

'That's the heavily edited version, I feel,' Leah said, crossing her legs.

'Believe what you like,' Rita replied, pulling the bed sheets higher up her chest. She was wearing a cream petticoat and Leah noticed how thin she seemed – her skin loose on her bones, freckled after many years of tanning.

'But why did you go round in the first place, Mum?' She had to visit the police station in the morning and wanted to find out as much information as possible. The last thing she needed was to appear obstructive or as if she was hiding something.

'You'll just say I'm a meddling old fool,' Rita said with a pout. 'You know that I wanted to try and smooth things over with you and Craig. You'd been through enough. Don't think I don't know what that man is really like, darling, because—'

'Trust me, Mum, you don't know.'

Rita frowned, clutching the sheet under her chin between her long, slim fingers. 'What is that supposed to mean?'

Leah looked away. 'I never told you the half of what he did to me. And now is really not the time to go over it. But take it from me – our divorce wasn't because he left the toilet seat up one time too many or was lazy around the house.'

'I know it was an unhappy marriage, darling,' Rita said pensively, studying her hands. 'Are you saying there was someone else involved?'

Leah snorted a laugh. 'He had many affairs over the years, Mum,' she said matter-of-factly. 'But even that didn't cause the most damage. Nor was it the physical stuff, though I feared for my life several times.'

Rita held out her hands. 'Look at the state of these, will you?' she said, as though Leah had just commented on the weather, not her abusive ex. 'I've been letting myself go. I need to book in for a manicure.' She shook her head, picking at the remaining adhesive on one fingertip where a long, pointed fake nail had been stuck.

Leah sighed. 'Your hands still look lovely, Mum. You *always* look lovely.' She reached out and held her mum's fingers, stroking the tip of one of her bright pink nails. She laughed. 'You're the only sixty-three-year-old I know with glittery gold stripes on their falsies,' she said. 'And believe me, I know a lot of sixty-three-year-olds.'

'Don't mention my age, darling,' Rita said, pulling her hand away. 'And I'm not like the women who come into your salon.'

'No,' Leah said, managing a laugh. 'You're certainly not.'

They sat in silence for a moment.

'So go on, what was it, then?' Rita asked.

Leah frowned, tipping her head sideways.

'What was it that did most of the damage if it wasn't his affairs or him hurting you?'

'I lost myself, Mum,' Leah said. 'Bit by bit, he eroded the person I was. Eventually, it got to a point where I didn't believe I was even *worth* saving.' She paused, not wanting the conversation to take this turn. 'Anyway, he can't have taken all of me because some shred inside me reignited – a tiny spark in a burnt-out fire.' She winced at the analogy.

'Oh, darling,' Rita said, reaching out and touching her arm. 'I had no idea you felt like that.'

'I know you didn't, Mum.' Leah took a sip of her mum's water. 'But look, what's important now is that you tell me everything that happened while you were at Craig's yesterday.' Leah knew there was every chance that the police would pay Rita a visit once they found out that her mother had been there. 'And I want to know what Gabe said, too. And more importantly, what he *did*,' Leah finished. 'You said he and Craig got into an argument?'

Rita drew up her legs and hugged her arms around them, resting her chin on her knees. She peered up at Leah. 'It was terrible, darling,' she said, shuddering. 'I honestly thought they were going to kill each other.'

CHAPTER THIRTY-FOUR

Leah knew she'd never sleep. Everything that had happened in the last couple of days churned around her mind, not making any sense. As she'd parked outside her house earlier, after bringing the children home from her parents' house, she'd noticed that Gillian's car was missing from the driveway. Craig's four-wheel drive was still there, covered in a silvery dew. When she glanced up at the big house, there were no lights on. She assumed Craig still hadn't turned up or Gillian would have let her know. He'd been gone over twenty-four hours.

It was quiet upstairs now, with both of the children asleep. Leah cradled a tumbler of whisky in her hands as she sat on the sofa, though she hadn't drunk any of it yet. While she wanted nothing more than to obliterate her thoughts, she also needed to stay alert, keep her wits about her.

She thought back to what her mother had said, which differed very little from what she'd told her originally when she'd come into the salon. According to her, she'd called in at the Old Vicarage to reason with Craig, to ask him to go easy on Leah and consider a reconciliation – though this baffled Leah as she'd never divulged any of Craig's recent behaviour to her mother. She was used to drip-feeding her the details, and it had stayed that way since their divorce.

Then her mother had recounted how Craig had offered her a drink. When Rita had refused, he'd approached her and grabbed her by the waist, pulling her close. Then Gabe had come in through the French doors and Craig had shoved her away. According to Rita, that was when she'd left, hearing raised voices between the two men, followed by the sound of something crashing as she closed the front door.

'How long were you there, Mum?' Leah had asked.

'Couldn't have been more than five minutes,' she'd replied.

After that, Gabe and Craig had been alone together, Leah thought, taking a sip of the whisky. She dialled Gabe's number again, but it went straight to voicemail. She didn't leave another message. Then she texted Gillian and asked if she was OK. A reply came back almost immediately.

At a friend's house for the night. Can't stand being at home alone. Speak tomorrow.

She put her phone down beside her, unsure how long had passed before she moved again – maybe only a few minutes, or it could have been several hours – but Leah just sat, staring into space, her consciousness only aware of the bare minimum as her mind processed everything.

Her mind drifted back to a family holiday they'd taken about five years ago. Zoey had been beside herself with excitement about going to the seaside and Henry, only three at the time, had slept through the entire drive to Norfolk. They'd rented a cottage only a few minutes from the sea and Leah had packed the car with buckets and spades, inflatable toys, picnic chairs, board games and all manner of other things to make a happy holiday.

Even Craig had seemed excited at the prospect of getting

away from work for a few days, managing to put on a pair of shorts and sandals when the rain had finally stopped.

To this day, Leah wasn't sure what had triggered him. Had it been something she'd said or done, a look she'd given him, perhaps, that he'd misconstrued?

He'd come in from a long walk along the pebbly beach alone, while Leah and the children had been painting pictures in the cottage kitchen. The weather had turned foul, and Craig was soaking wet.

'What's all this mess?' he'd snapped.

'Craig, don't,' she'd dared to say. Her first mistake.

Craig had glared at her, before picking up the watercolour she'd painted and ripping it in two. Zoey didn't say a word; rather she'd just slipped away into the living room and put the TV on loud. When Henry started grizzling, Craig had ordered him to join his sister.

'Who is he?' Craig had demanded, getting up close to Leah.

'Who is *who*?' Leah had backed away.

'The man you've had round while I've been out.' He'd pressed himself close to Leah, shoving her against the closed door. 'You reek of him.'

'Craig, *don't*,' she'd said, trying to wriggle free from his grip. He was hurting her. 'I've been with the children. Of *course* I've not had anyone here.'

He'd stared into her eyes and, for a second, Leah wondered if she saw something of the person she'd fallen in love with – the man who had once been capable of kindness and respect. Though as every year had passed, that man had slipped further and further away.

'I can't take you being like this any more,' Leah had dared to say.

Her second mistake.

She remembered willing herself to shut up, to keep quiet and placate him for the sake of the children, but something had switched inside her. 'I'm filing for divorce when we get home. Living like this is no good for the children and it's certainly no good for me.'

To her surprise, Craig hadn't retaliated in the way she'd expected. She'd managed to prise herself from his grip and went to put the kettle on – anything to regain some normality. When she turned round, Craig was sitting at the table crying – a silent weep at first, which quickly turned into louder sobs, his hunched shoulders shaking as his tears fell onto Zoey's painting.

'Oh, *Craig*...' Leah had said, putting a hand on his back, wondering if they could work it out. But he'd pulled away and disappeared upstairs for several hours, shutting himself in the bedroom.

Later, when Leah had made dinner for everyone and Craig still hadn't come down, she'd gone upstairs to fetch him, hoping he would be civil enough to join her and the children for food. But he wasn't there.

Instead, on the bed, she'd found a letter – similar to the dozens of other handwritten notes she would receive from him over the years – some short, some long, some personal, while others were so cold and emotionless, they could have been meant for anyone. But they all had one thing in common – that Craig was going to kill himself. And this would be followed by a period of him going missing, only for him to reappear when Leah had professed her undying love for him.

Now, with her mind numb and exhausted, she wasn't even conscious of going up the stairs – though she must have at some point as she found herself on her knees, rummaging through several boxes shoved in the landing cupboard that hadn't been unpacked from the move.

'There,' she whispered, pulling out the grey box file. She wasn't sure why she'd kept all the notes and letters he'd written over the years – perhaps it was so she could remind herself of what he was like if she'd ever doubted herself, or maybe there was a sentimentality attached that she couldn't let go of – the relics of her marriage.

Leah slipped one of them into her pocket, then shoved the box and its remaining contents back in the cupboard. Tomorrow she'd be going to the police station to give a witness statement – and she would show them the note. She wondered if they'd have identified the body by then, if they'd be breaking the news to her that the charred remains were Gabe – she'd already told DI Nelson that they'd been dating – or if it was Craig. She knew that whatever happened, they were going to want to know more about when she'd last seen each of them.

CHAPTER THIRTY-FIVE

Leah wore plain black trousers with a cream sweater. It was chilly first thing, so she'd put on her padded jacket for the short drive, though now she sat with it bunched up on her knee in the police station as she waited to be called through. She'd made herself known to the desk sergeant.

The waiting area was busier than it had been the other night. There were several women with young children whining on their laps, and two teenage lads joking about something on their phones. An older couple sat slightly apart from everyone else, the pair of them holding hands and looking concerned.

They reminded Leah of her parents – two parts of a whole. To anyone who didn't know them, Rita and Ronald seemed wildly different, though they complemented each other in a way that made up for their differences. Leah was proud of them for making their decades-long marriage work. More than she'd achieved.

As she looked around, she was hoping to spot Gillian, but she wasn't sure what time she'd been asked to come in. When she'd texted her earlier, she hadn't received a reply, and Gillian's car was still missing from her driveway this morning.

'Miss Ward?' a voice called out.

Leah looked around and saw a young female uniformed officer standing in an open doorway to the left of the glass-fronted reception desk. She held it open as Leah gathered her coat and bag.

'Hi, yes, that's me,' she said, suddenly feeling nervous.

'This way,' the officer said to her with a smile. 'And no need to look so worried,' she added. 'DI Nelson said to put you in interview room three. I'll take you down.'

She followed the officer down the long corridor, stepping aside as a couple of people came in the opposite direction – another officer with someone behind him that Leah couldn't immediately see.

'Gillian!' Leah said as they passed, spotting it was her. 'Has Craig come back? How are you doing?' She reached out a hand, touching Gillian's arm. It wasn't a grab, but Gillian recoiled as though it was. She looked up from behind the curtain of her unbrushed hair – her gaunt face and her vacant eyes shocking Leah. And the stare she gave her was deathly cold – piercing and empty. Venomous, almost.

'Gillian?' Leah said, taking a few steps after her as she continued walking back towards the waiting room. 'What's happened? Are you OK?'

'Miss Ward, this way please,' the officer who had summoned Leah said, beckoning her on. Leah watched, her mouth hanging open, as Gillian disappeared out of sight.

The constable held the interview room door open and told Leah to take a seat inside. The small room was drab and smelt vaguely of sweat, as though it had recently been occupied by someone who hadn't washed in a while.

'They won't be long,' the officer said, leaning against the wall. She kept glancing through the small square of wired glass in the door.

They, Leah thought, wondering if the other detective who'd been at Gillian's house yesterday would also be present.

'Did you manage to find a parking spot OK?' the young woman went on, struggling for chit-chat. 'It's a nightmare out there since they decided to dig up the car park. Nothing wrong with it if you ask—'

The door suddenly swung open, and DI Nelson strode in with a man following close behind her, who Leah recognised as her colleague from yesterday.

'Morning, Leah,' the detective said brightly, dropping several files on the table that she'd been clutching against her chest. In her other hand she held a paper cup of coffee. She placed it down on the laminated table carefully and then took off its lid. 'Thanks for coming in,' she said as she sat down, the other detective mirroring her actions almost exactly. 'You remember DC Flynn Marshall.'

Leah nodded, squeezing her hands into her padded jacket nestled on her lap.

'Do you want to hang that up?' DI Nelson asked as the constable left the room, shutting the door behind her.

Leah draped it over the back of her chair, thinking she ought to do as she was told.

'Right, hopefully this won't take too long at this stage,' DI Nelson continued with a smile. 'I know we went through events yesterday, but this is more of a fact-finding mission, to make a full record of events from your side.' She looked at Leah over the top of a pair of red-framed glasses that she'd just put on, somehow transforming her rather mousy and unremarkable appearance into someone you'd look twice at. 'That sound OK?'

Leah thought it was odd that she was asking, and wasn't sure that she had a choice, but she nodded anyway, which, for some reason, provoked a broad smile from the detective.

'Oh, and there's no word back from the pathologist on the ID of the deceased yet.' She tapped a pen on her front teeth as she peeled open a manila folder a few inches, scanning whatever was written inside.

Leah nodded again. Her mouth was dry, and her heart banged against her ribcage. The sound of her blood pulsing through her ears was almost deafening.

The detective put down her pen. 'Just so you understand, Leah, you're not under caution at this point. And we won't be digitally recording what you say. But we'll both be taking detailed notes, which will form your statement of events. And we might ask you questions along the way to make sure everything is covered. Then we'll get you to read through and sign it as a true and accurate account. OK?'

'At *this* point?' Leah said, wishing her voice hadn't croaked.

'Yes,' was all the detective said as she opened up an official-looking pad with 'Witness Statement' heading it, along with the constabulary logo and various other boxes for details to be filled in. She wanted to tell them that she hadn't actually witnessed anything, so what use was she going to be? But she decided to keep quiet.

'Okey-dokey,' DC Marshall said, suddenly piping up. 'Tell us again in your own words what happened yesterday, Leah. What led up to you discovering that human remains had been found in the bonfire?'

Leah wondered how far back she should go. To when she was microwaving the spaghetti, or was that part irrelevant? And if she did start there, should she tell them why she'd taken a day off work, hence her heating up the spaghetti at home in the first place? And if she did that, then surely she needed to go back even further and provide details about her and Craig, their divorce, everything he'd been doing to her since he'd moved next door, as well as pretty much the entirety of their marriage. It would take the rest of the day and a whole notepad to do that.

'I heard screams,' Leah said quietly. 'I was in my kitchen with the window open and suddenly there was screaming.' She wondered if she should speak slowly, given that DI Nelson was writing by hand. DC Marshall was tapping on the keyboard linked to his tablet, so seemed to be faster.

DI Nelson glanced up, adjusting her glasses. She sniffed and nodded, apparently waiting.

'So I went outside. Then I realised the screams were coming from my vegetable garden.'

'By vegetable garden, you mean...?' DI Marshall asked, his fingers hovering over the keys.

'The walled garden behind my house. My ex bulldozed it because he decided it was *his* land.' She then described what had happened between her and Craig.

'That must have made you very angry,' DI Nelson suggested.

'It would make anyone angry,' Leah replied, frowning. She recounted how she'd found Gillian by the bonfire and how events had unfolded. 'Then we came back inside and called 999. We were both very shaken.'

'Was anyone else apart from Gillian with you at the bonfire?' DI Nelson asked.

'No,' Leah said. 'Oh, wait. Actually, there was a woman going past on a horse. She keeps it in a nearby field. I've seen her around before. She heard Gillian's screams and stopped to ask if we were OK.'

'And what did you tell her?'

Leah thought for a moment, picturing the horse getting agitated, the cars speeding past. 'We told her we were fine. That there'd been an accident, but everything was OK.'

'I see,' DI Nelson commented.

'She was on a horse on a busy road. It was dangerous. We didn't want to bother her,' Leah added, hoping that might help. The detectives wrote everything down.

'You've already indicated that you know someone called

Gabe, the name on the back of the deceased's jacket. Would you tell us again how you know him?'

Leah nodded. 'Yes. Gabriel Holland. Gabe and I were... are... were... well, we were dating.' She thought back to the night before last, when he'd come round at her request. After what had happened between them, she was more confused than ever now.

'How did you meet?'

Leah paused, wondering what to say. She decided on the simple version. 'He... he was doing some tree work for my parents. We met while he was packing up his van.'

'And when did you last see Gabe?'

'Is this relevant?' Leah asked, suddenly feeling as though this was less of a statement and more of an interview. She wondered if she needed a solicitor, and then her thoughts were on Liz Morgan and how she still hadn't been in touch.

Neither detective said anything.

Leah shook her head and stared at the ceiling as she felt her cheeks burn red. 'Um, it was a while ago now.'

She wished there was something in the room to focus on – a picture on the wall, a pot plant, a coffee machine or even a different colour paint to the drab grey of the walls. None of it helped her state of mind.

'I saw him a few weeks ago,' she said. 'He lives on a canal boat, and I went there. He wanted to talk.' She paused, watching as both detectives made notes. 'Well, he wanted to end our relationship, actually.'

'And why did he want to end things?'

'He didn't think I was ready for a relationship after my divorce,' Leah said, glad to have moved away from more recent events. 'He saw me get really angry at my ex one time. I think it was all too much for him, having Craig living next door to me.'

'So that was the last time you saw Gabe?' DI Nelson asked.

'Yes,' Leah said quietly, feeling herself sweat. 'Though

Mum said she saw him more recent—' She stopped. There was no reason to bring her mother into this.

'You mother saw him?'

'Actually, I'm not sure,' Leah said. 'I'd have to check. Mum gets confused. I don't think she even knew that we were dating, to be honest. She always harboured a hope that Craig and I would get back together.'

'I see,' DI Nelson said, glancing at her colleague. She tapped the pen on her teeth again before sitting back in her chair. 'So let me check I've got this right. You were dating a man named Gabriel Holland? And your ex-husband is called Craig Forbes?'

Leah nodded. 'Yes.'

'As you know, our forensics team removed the remains of a body from a fire on your property, wearing a jacket with the name Gabe printed on the back. And Craig Forbes, your ex-husband, the man you admit to feeling anger towards, has been reported missing,' DI Nelson said. 'How does all that sound to you, Leah?'

Leah stared at them. The first time she tried to speak, it came out as a croak. Then, finally, she managed to say, 'It doesn't sound good, does it? Not good at all.'

CHAPTER THIRTY-SIX

The towpath wasn't as muddy as it had been the last time she'd walked along it. Though now, Leah wasn't walking – she was running. After she'd finished at the police station – with the detective warning her it wouldn't be a good idea to leave the area for the time being as they may want to speak to her again soon – she'd dashed home and changed into jeans and trainers, getting back in her car and driving to the lay-by where she'd previously parked when she'd been to see Gabe aboard *Blue Moon*.

She nodded a hello to a couple out with their dog, pressing herself against the hedge as they passed on the narrow towpath. *Hurry up*, she thought, waiting for them to walk by as their dog sniffed at her legs.

When they'd gone, she continued, jogging towards where she'd last seen Gabe.

Though it wasn't *where you last saw him, was it?*

Her thoughts were all over the place. She'd *lied* to the police. And she'd had good reason to. Inviting Gabe to hers the other evening had been a terrible mistake and had left her vulnerable with her feelings all over the place. But there was no way she could have admitted that to the police.

'Damn,' Leah said ten minutes later as she stopped, leaning forward, hands resting on her knees as she panted. 'I swear it was here.' She stared along the stretch of canal where she thought *Blue Moon* had been moored. Except there was no boat there now. The bridge up ahead seemed familiar, and so did the thicket of reed on the opposite bank where she'd seen the moorhens, with the ploughed field behind it.

She stood, hands on her hips, glancing up and down the length of the canal as far as she could see. Had Gabe moved the boat a few weeks ago, to be nearer to town perhaps? Or had he only recently vacated the mooring, after he'd fought with Craig?

Either way, she turned to go.

It was as she was walking back to the car that she encountered a boat chugging towards her. The man steering the boat raised a hand and greeted her and there was a woman on deck beside him. She recognised them from when she'd been on the deck of Gabe's boat, just before he'd ended things with her, and the couple had said a cheery hello.

'Hi,' Leah said, stopping and turning around to walk alongside the boat on its slow journey. 'I don't suppose you've seen *Blue Moon* on your travels, have you?'

The woman was already nodding.

'He's moored up in the marina, love,' the man said. 'Engine troubles,' he said with a laugh. 'There's always something or other with these things.' He patted the roof of his vessel.

'Weston Fields marina?' Leah asked, stopping now as there was no point following them further. The man confirmed it was and Leah thanked him and hurried back to her car.

———

Leah drove off from where she was parked, speeding up along the country lane. The Mini's engine strained as she changed up and down through the gears, taking a couple of blind bends as fast as she dared. She wasn't a hundred per cent certain of the best route to the marina and had to reverse at one point to take a missed turn. But that petered out into a dead end, and she retraced her path, cursing that there was no reception on her phone to check the map.

It was as she passed the end of a long, private farm track that she slowed to a stop, remembering the shortcut. A couple of years ago, she and the kids, along with her parents, had been walking along the canal in search of a pub they'd been recommended. Her father, seeming to think he was leading a military operation, had insisted on taking the shortcut – a public footpath and road across farmland. The kids had moaned and grumbled about the long walk in the heat, but she remembered passing by the marina at the time.

Now she stared up at the faded sign pointing down the track.

'Wells Wood Farm and Dairy. Private Road. No Public Access to Marina. Footpath Only,' she read out. 'Hang it,' she muttered, reversing back a few feet and flicking on her indicator. She didn't care if she was trespassing. If she was stopped, she'd make up some excuse about being lost. She just needed to get to Gabe's boat as fast as she could.

She sped down the single-width track, praying she didn't meet anyone coming the other way, bumping over a couple of cattle grids as she passed from one field to the next.

'I swear it's this way,' she said, beginning to doubt herself as the track twisted downhill, leading into woodland. 'Any minute now,' she muttered, hoping that she'd round the next bend and see the marina car park. But instead, she found herself heading deeper into the dark woods with the light fading and the trees closing in around her.

Leah glanced down at the dashboard to check her fuel, knowing it was getting low, as she rounded a sharp bend, stepping on the accelerator and speeding up again as she pulled out of it.

'Oh Christ!' she screamed suddenly, jamming on the brakes as hard as she could.

She felt the skid of her tyres as the old Mini juddered to a sudden stop. Her breaths were sharp and shallow, and her heart thumped as she dared to open her eyes. She'd only caught a glimpse of the fallen tree before she'd jammed on the brakes, certain she was going to plough right into it.

But by some miracle, she'd managed to stop the car a couple of feet short of the big trunk that spanned the width of the road. It must have come down in the storm the week before.

As her heart rate subsided, Leah got out of the Mini. She leant on the door, sucking in the cool, damp air of the woods as she stared at the tree. While she'd avoided the main trunk, she shuddered as she saw the lethal branch sticking out at right angles, the end of it only a couple of inches from her windscreen in line with the passenger seat. If Zoey or Henry had been in there and she hadn't managed to stop in time...

Leah shuddered, refusing to think of such a terrible thing. Instead, she got back in her car and manoeuvred a three-point turn to head back. She'd just have to go the long way round.

Twenty minutes later, she pulled up in the marina car park and got out, heading over towards the office and the metal gateway leading to the moorings. She'd visited before, when Gabe had first taken her out on his boat, so she knew roughly where to go. Though if his boat was in for repair, she supposed it could be in the workshop.

'I'm looking for *Blue Moon*,' she said to the first person she spotted – a lad who clearly worked there, given his overalls and greasy hands. He was striding towards the long boat shed carrying a toolbox. He appeared to be in a hurry.

'That way,' he said as he continued walking. 'Bay twenty-three, I think,' he added.

Leah thanked him, knowing the office was manned during the day and that they were tight on security. Last time she'd been here, the gate to the moorings had been locked, and Gabe had met her and let her through. But luckily, this time someone had left the metal gate slightly open, the catch not having caught properly, and she was able to push it open.

She walked briskly along the boardwalk, wondering what to say to Gabe if he was aboard, how she would face him after the other night. It didn't really matter, she supposed – she just wanted to set eyes on him and make certain he was OK, fill him in on everything that had happened. After that, she supposed the police would contact him.

Leah's heart thumped as she approached bay twenty-three, spotting the painted white lettering against a navy background each side of the bows – *Blue Moon*. From the front, the boat appeared closed up and uninhabited, with its grey tarpaulin sheeting fixed tightly in place over the foredeck. But as she went down the walkway along the side of the boat, she noticed that the pots of pansies on the roof had dribbles of water draining away from them. Someone had recently given them a drink.

'Hello?' she called out when she reached the rear deck. The tiller handle extension wasn't in place and the folding chair Gabe usually kept on the deck wasn't there either. Leah didn't see any shoes or boots, and there were no empty mugs or cans as evidence of him sitting out and having a drink as he liked to do. The rear doors of the boat were closed and the hatch above them pulled across. But then she noticed that there was no padlock on the bracket.

'Gabe?' she said, stepping aboard. The boat rocked a little as she stood on the deck, and she waited in case it alerted him to a visitor. But no one came out, so she knocked on the hatch instead. 'Gabe, are you in there? It's me, Leah.'

Nothing.

Leah looked across at the boats either side of *Blue Moon* but there was no sign of anyone to ask if they'd seen him. Tentatively, she slid back the hatch a few inches and peered down below. It was dark inside so she opened the double doors, going down into the cabin. She noticed that Gabe had done a good job touching up the colourful rose and castle paintings on the woodwork.

'Gabe, are you in there?'

She wondered if he might be in the tiny bathroom or perhaps taking a nap in the cabin towards the front, but as she went down the steps and through the rest of the boat to check, she soon realised there was no one on board.

As she stood staring down at the neatly made double bed, she took her phone from her bag and dialled Gabe's number. It was worth another try. But before it even had a chance to ring or go to his message service, she suddenly felt the boat rocking, followed by a couple of loud bangs coming from the rear of the boat. Quickly, she walked back towards the galley, seeing that any daylight from the open doors was gone.

Someone had shut them. And then she heard the rattling of keys and the sound of the padlock clicking into place.

'Hey!' she called out, rushing up to the doors and thumping on them. 'Gabe! I'm in here. It's me, Leah! Wait!' To her horror, she felt the boat rock again and then, through the side window, she saw a pair of legs dressed in jeans and work boots walk along the length of the boat on the boardwalk. She ran alongside them, banging on the cabin windows as she went, yelling out that she was inside. By the time she got to the third window above the seating area, the legs stopped.

A figure bent down and a face peered through the glass, cupping their hands against the window.

'Oh, Gabe, thank *God*. Let me out. I'm locked in!'

For a moment, Leah thought Gabe hadn't seen her and was going to walk off again, but to her relief, he came back on deck and unlocked the doors.

'Leah?' he said, coming down the steps. 'What on earth are you doing here?'

It only took a split second for her to run up to him and throw her arms around his neck. She didn't care what he thought of her – for breaking into his boat or for the tight hug she was giving him – or anything else, for that matter. 'I thought you were *dead*. Thank God, oh thank *God* you're here.'

She felt the soft up-and-down judders of his chest as he softly laughed, cradling her in his strong arms.

'Dead?' he finally said, releasing her so he could see her face. 'Why on earth would you think that?'

Leah looked up at him. 'Where do I even begin?' she said, dropping down into the swivel armchair next to the small wood-burning stove. With her voice shaking, she filled him in as best she could.

Gabe crouched down in front of her and took hold of her hands. He didn't speak – just stared into her eyes.

'And... and so I thought it could have been *you* in the fire,' Leah said. She took a huge breath in and sighed. 'I couldn't stand it – especially after what happened between us the other night. It was so...' She trailed off in case he didn't feel the same way.

'That's absolutely *terrible*,' he said, frowning deeply. 'What a shock for you. I'm so sorry. But as you can see, I'm very much alive.'

'I'm so relieved,' she said. 'Though I almost didn't make it here alive myself.' The adrenalin from the near accident was only just fading. 'There was a tree down and I nearly drove into it.'

'On Wells Wood Farm?'

Leah nodded.

'It's next on my work sheet to clear,' Gabe replied. 'I'm still catching up with fallen trees from the storm. Thank God you're OK.'

'And on top of everything, Craig's gone missing,' Leah told him. 'Gillian's reported it to the police.'

Gabe was silent, briefly glancing out of the cabin window. 'Missing?' He rubbed his beard. 'When was he last seen?'

Leah studied his expression, but it remained neutral, giving nothing away. 'That's what I wanted to ask you.'

'Me?' Gabe replied immediately. He stood up again and paced up and down the length of the living area.

Leah saw his shoulders hunch up around his ears as he shoved his hands in his jeans pockets. And she saw, too, the anguished look on his face as he dropped down in the matching chair the other side of the little stove.

'Have you seen him in the last couple of days?' Leah asked, her mother's words echoing through her mind.

No reply.

'Gabe, the police are all over this. Craig disappeared at the same time a body was found on my land wearing your jacket. I was at the police station this morning giving a statement, for heaven's sake. I feel sick with it all. If you know something, please tell me.'

Gabe just sat there, staring down at the floor. Leah heard the soft rasp of his breathing and felt the gentle rock of the boat as another vessel slowly chugged out of the marina.

'Do you know something? Please, for Christ's sake,' Leah said a few moments later when he still hadn't replied. 'Gabe, what's going on?'

Finally, he looked up at her. 'Leah,' he said solemnly. 'There's something I need to tell you.'

CHAPTER THIRTY-SEVEN

Leah stared at him, incredulous. 'Let me get this perfectly straight,' she said, standing up but then sitting down again when she realised how light-headed she felt. 'You've been working for *Craig* all this time?'

'That's not exactly how I'd put it,' Gabe responded, the same anguished look on his face as when he'd first confessed. 'Not *working*, as such. And not all this time, either.'

'But you took money from my ex in return for... for...' Leah could hardly bring herself to repeat what Gabe had just told her. Whether she believed he was remorseful, as he claimed, was irrelevant at this point. She hadn't got anywhere near forgiveness yet – if she ever would. She was still struggling with Gabe lying to her – especially after the other night. She'd invited him round to find out why he'd been at Craig's house, but instead, passion had taken over. She'd made herself vulnerable to him and he'd betrayed her trust. It was clear now that he didn't have feelings for her – he'd just been trying to distract her.

'Leah, really, it's not what you're thinking.' Gabe tipped his head back against the leather headrest and closed his eyes. His hands swept up over his face and he groaned, dragging them down again.

'It sounds an awful lot like it to me, Gabriel Holland.' Using his full name somehow distanced herself from him emotionally. 'Basically, what you're saying is that my ex-husband paid you to *spy* on me. Is that right?'

'Spying makes it sound more sinister than it was. He told me he just needed some information.'

Leah let out a short laugh. 'Really? You couldn't fucking make it up. Did you have a pair of binoculars up that tree, is that it? Did you watch me get changed in my parents' house? Make a note of what I had for breakfast?'

'I know how bad it all sounds but...' Gabe stood up and went to the little galley, lifting the kettle off the two-burner stove. He filled it with water and then lit the gas.

'Making bloody tea isn't going to make this any better,' Leah snapped.

Gabe turned off the gas.

'But I'll have one anyway. I'm thirsty.'

Gabe relit the stove.

'I want to know everything,' Leah said, glaring at him as he stood with one hand on the kettle handle and the other shoved in his front pocket. 'From the beginning.'

He nodded. 'The last thing I want is to upset you, Leah.'

'It's a bit late for that.' Leah's mind was all over the place. 'Is this why you ended our relationship? Did Craig tell you to do it?'

'*No*, not at all,' he replied. 'That genius piece of thinking was all my doing.'

Leah stared out of the cabin window, watching another boat chug past.

'Look, Craig approached me several months ago. It was totally random. I had no idea he was your ex-husband. Or that *you* were his ex-wife.'

'Go on.' Leah folded her arms, refusing to look at him as he spoke.

'I was doing some tree work at a property that he was valuing to put on the market. As he was leaving, we got chatting out the front. He wanted to know about the type of work I did and my rates, that sort of thing. Then he asked for my card as he often had potential clients who needed their gardens sorting out before they went up for sale.'

'I'm listening,' Leah said, still not looking at him.

'He told me he knew of a tree-lopping job. He wanted me to cold-call on a particular property and go in with a very low quote to ensure I got the work. He promised to make up the difference in cash.'

'For heaven's sakes,' Leah muttered, staring down at her feet.

'He went on to tell me that if I was up for it, I could earn a couple of grand extra on top of the tree job.' Gabe paused, clearing his throat. 'At the time, I was really short of cash, Leah. Several big clients hadn't paid up and I'd got bills coming in. Plus, I'd got into the habit of sending my mum a chunk of money each month. She's seventy-eight and lives alone and I don't get to see her as often as I'd like. It was guilt money, I suppose, and I didn't want to let Mum down.'

The kettle whistled and Gabe took a moment to pour hot water onto two teabags. He let them steep.

'I was curious, I admit. And when I asked what the extra work entailed, Craig told me – and these were his words, Leah, not mine – he told me it was to "keep tabs on my psycho ex". It turned out that the tree work was at your parents' house.'

'Jesus Christ,' Leah said, flopping back in the chair.

'He wanted me to find out if his ex-wife was seeing anyone. And he wanted photos of places you went, who you met up with, and a log of any addresses and vehicle number plates.

Anything that I could find out about you, basically. I thought it would only be for a couple of days.'

'That must have made for some fucking interesting reading,' Leah said. '*Not.*'

'Before I started, I had no idea it was you or what he'd put you through. And to begin with, Craig seemed like a decent enough guy. Before I started the job, I'd been to his office, and we even went to the pub. He told me he'd been screwed over in a terrible divorce and that you'd lied to him throughout. I suppose I felt sorry for him.'

'Pah!' Leah exclaimed, hardly able to contain herself. 'Yeah, he's a charmer, all right.' She took the mug of tea Gabe handed to her, sipping that instead of exploding.

'Ultimately, he said he wanted to know where you were moving to. He said you weren't allowing him to see the children and he believed you might take them overseas without his permission.'

'And you *believed* this bullshit?' Leah said, swinging round to face Gabe, who was still standing by the stove.

'Initially, yes,' he replied. 'I had no reason not to, and as I said, I didn't know who you were at that point. Once I'd seen you... well, all that changed. Plus, I admit, initially it touched a raw nerve. One of my brothers was married to a woman from the States and this exact situation happened to him. He hasn't seen his children in years. It's very sad.'

'But you asked me out on a *date*... when I was still living at Mum and Dad's. And you *still* didn't tell me...' Leah's mind flashed back to the other night at her house. She shuddered.

'That was my idea, just so you know. I genuinely wanted to get to know you better. And that's when everything changed. After we'd been on a couple of dates, I couldn't help falling for you.'

'So it was *you* who told him where I'd moved to?' Leah

groaned when Gabe nodded. 'And how did Craig even *know* that Mum and Dad's tree needed work?'

'I've actually no idea about that.' Another pause. 'I'm genuinely so very sorry, Leah. If I'd known that... If I'd...' He trailed off, unable to find the right words.

'I'm speechless. You fed private information about me to my abusive ex-husband. How Craig must have been laughing at me. I bet he could hardly contain himself when the Old Vicarage came up for sale. He probably pressured Carrie and Josh into selling up.'

'What I was going to say, Leah, was...' Gabe put his tea on the counter and came over to Leah, kneeling down in front of her again. 'If I'd known I was going to fall in love with you, I'd never have done any of it.'

Silence as Leah stared down at him.

'Fall in *love?*'

Gabe nodded, not taking his eyes off her. 'Yes. It's why I ended things with you.'

'You broke it off with me because you were in *love* with me?' Leah stood up abruptly. 'Oh well, that makes perfect fucking sense. I genuinely do not understand men any more.' She paced up and down the cabin, trying to take in everything he was telling her.

'When you messaged me the other day,' Gabe continued, 'telling me your news, I was so happy to hear from you. Even though I knew it could never work out between us now, I wanted to do something nice for you, to make it up to you even in just a small way. I replied to you, but I didn't hear back, so I decided to clear the gateway and sort out the hedge anyway. To make life a little easier for you.'

'That was big of you,' Leah said, sitting down on the step beneath the door hatch. She clasped her mug with both hands.

Gabe returned to the leather swivel chair again, swinging

round to face her. 'In fact, I came round the day before yesterday to finish the job but—'

'I wouldn't have bothered, if I were you,' Leah said. 'For a start, Craig has destroyed my vegetable garden. His bulldozers made easy work of that. And the whole area is a crime scene now anyway.' Leah put her mug on the counter and cradled her head in her hands. She suddenly looked up. 'But what?'

Gabe swallowed, sipping his tea, a thoughtful look on his face.

'But I didn't end up finishing the job, as it turned out.'

'Why? Too busy cosying up to my ex, were you?'

'No. But I did see him.'

'So I hear,' Leah snapped, remembering what her mother had told her.

'I'd already told Craig a few weeks ago that I wouldn't be helping him with his... his *spying* any more. We were dating and it didn't sit right with me.'

'I do love a man with morals.'

'But Craig still hadn't paid me what he'd promised. When I came to finish your hedge two days ago, I saw his car was on the drive, so I knocked on the front door. There was no reply. When I was round the back of your place, I spotted the hole in the wall and went through into his garden. The French doors were unlocked.'

'So you were out of pocket for spying on me? My heart bleeds for you. Doesn't surprise me in the least, by the way. I don't ever recall Craig settling a debt on time.'

'For what it's worth, I was going to donate the money to a domestic violence charity. There was no way I was going to keep it for myself.'

Leah nodded, unable to argue with that. '*Was*? I'm assuming Craig didn't give you what he owed you? Too busy trying it on with my mother, I imagine.' She blew out between her lips and shook her head, appalled by the thought of it.

Gabe appeared puzzled for a moment, opening his mouth several times to speak before changing his mind.

Leah watched him, remembering how her mother had described the sound of Craig and Gabe fighting as she'd hurried to leave. Clearly, Gabe had come out of the fight relatively unscathed, looking at him now. But then she went cold at the thought of what Gabe was about to tell her. Perhaps Craig hadn't come out of the fight quite so unscathed. Perhaps he hadn't come out of it at *all*.

'No, he didn't pay me what he owed me,' Gabe finally said in a quiet voice. He tapped his forefinger on the side of his mug before continuing. 'And I don't know what you mean when you say he was trying it on with your mother. He wasn't—'

'Hang on, wait,' Leah said, grabbing her phone from her bag when she heard it ringing. No Caller ID was displayed on her screen, but she answered it anyway. A few moments later, she hung up, the colour draining from her face.

'Leah?' Gabe said, standing up and coming over. 'What is it?'

'That was DI Nelson, the detective in charge of the case,' she said, dropping her phone back in her bag. 'She wants me to come into the police station this afternoon.'

'Has there been a development?'

'I don't know,' she said. 'But they want to interview me under caution.' Leah stared up at him. 'They're treating the case as murder.'

CHAPTER THIRTY-EIGHT

'Let's begin,' DI Nelson said, checking the video camera was operating.

Since Leah had taken the detective's phone call, her stress levels had risen to new heights. Her heart had thrashed out an unsteady beat as she'd left the boat and driven to the police station, with the cruel words she'd hurled at Gabe as she'd left still ringing in her ears. He'd offered to come with her, but she'd refused, though not before she'd told him exactly what she thought of him for what felt like a huge betrayal.

But by the time she'd parked the car, she was already regretting her words. If he was indeed telling the truth, then Gabe was simply yet another person caught up in Craig's web of deceit and manipulation. How easily her ex-husband charmed his victims. How easily he lied his way into the minds of others. Craig was infiltrating her life, encircling her. She felt under siege.

Now, as she sat in front of the detectives in a heightened state of anxiety, she sensed the change of tone in DI Nelson's voice. While it wasn't as friendly as it had been earlier, it wasn't antagonistic either. It was somewhere between the two, which unnerved Leah even more. She couldn't read her at all.

DI Nelson folded her arms across the files set in front of her on the desk and leant forward. She'd already explained to Leah what was going to happen as well as making sure she understood her rights.

'This interview is being video-recorded in room five at Alvington police station. I'm Detective Inspector Carla Nelson, and also present to assist with the interview is Detective Constable Flynn Marshall. Sitting opposite DC Marshall is Rebecca Bernard, duty solicitor. Would you please tell me your full name and date of birth, please?' DI Nelson said while looking at Leah.

Leah turned to her solicitor. She'd had such a short time with her before the interview, she'd barely had a chance to fully ascertain why she'd been brought back in. Further questions about the body discovered in the walled garden was what she'd been told. But why? She'd already made a statement about everything she knew. The solicitor gave her a nod and a small smile.

'Yes, I'm Leah Mary Ward and my date of birth is the thirteenth of March 1983.'

'Thank you, Leah. As you know, you're being interviewed under caution. You are not under arrest and may leave at any time. But to do so may result in you being arrested for further questioning. And as already explained to you, anything you do say now may be used against you as evidence in a court of law.'

Leah felt as if she was underwater with the detective's words bubbling around her. She heard her talking about cautions and rights and courts and investigations and that she didn't have to say anything if she didn't want to. She found herself nodding and looking at her solicitor again, blindly putting her trust in this woman who she'd met barely twenty minutes ago.

'Yes, I understand,' Leah said, though she wasn't sure she did. She clasped her hands in her lap, fiddling with her fingers.

'You told us in your witness statement earlier how Gillian discovered a body in the bonfire on your property and how, with your support, that led to her calling the police.'

Leah nodded. It seemed the safest thing to do. But suddenly her mouth opened and the words came tumbling out. 'But what if it's *not* my land? Craig swore it's his. I don't know whose it is any more, to be honest.'

'Would that make you feel better?' DC Marshall suggested. 'If it wasn't your land?'

Leah hung her head. 'No, that's not what I'm saying. It just feels like you're trying to blame me for something.'

The detective watched her for a moment before continuing. 'We established earlier that your relationship with your ex-husband is... strained. Is that a fair assessment, would you say?'

Leah wanted to laugh hysterically but held it in. 'Yes.'

'Land Registry records show that Mr Forbes bought his property *before* you purchased yours, Leah, though you've previously claimed the opposite. With that in mind, do you agree it was *you* who moved in next door to him?'

'What? That's impossible!' Leah shook her head. She didn't understand. 'I watched their removals van arrive *after* I'd moved in.'

'Have you ever asserted to anyone that you wanted to kill your ex-husband, Leah?'

Leah felt her cheeks burning. 'If I have, I didn't mean it literally.'

'But you have said that you wanted to kill him?'

The solicitor leant over and whispered to Leah.

'It's fine,' Leah replied. 'I don't need to say "no comment" as I didn't mean that I *actually* wanted to kill him.'

'Would you answer the question, please, Leah? Have you ever said you wanted to kill your ex-husband, Craig Forbes?'

'Why? Is he dead? Have you found him?' Leah clapped a hand over her mouth. 'And, anyway, who told you I said that?'

'Please answer the question,' the detective repeated.

Leah glanced at her solicitor. 'No comment,' she finally replied, assuming that Gillian must have heard her over the wall. Was that why she'd shunned her earlier in the day when they'd passed in the corridor? Did Gillian believe she'd killed Craig?

'Have you ever been physically violent towards your ex-husband?' DI Nelson went on to ask.

'No!' Leah replied. 'It was the other way around.'

'A couple of days ago, two of our officers were called out to your property to break up an altercation between you and Mr Forbes. The officers' report states that when they arrived, you were attacking your ex. They witnessed you kick him in the groin and repeatedly thump him.'

'Yes, but that was because he was bulldozing my garden.' Leah felt herself welling up. 'It was... After everything he's done to me, I just flipped. I couldn't help it.'

'You couldn't control your anger, is that what you mean?'

'A saint wouldn't be able to control their anger if they'd had to put up with what I've had to since he moved in.'

'Can you give an example?' DC Marshall asked.

'How many do you want?' Leah glanced at her solicitor, who gave her a nod. 'OK... let me think. He drilled a hole right through my wall into my bedroom.' She held up her hand, counting on her fingers. 'He paid someone to spy on me, which is how he knew where I was moving to, by the way. I can only assume that he must have completed his property deal first and rented it out to the previous owners for a few weeks before they moved overseas – no surprise, given that's Craig's business.

'I have to listen to him through the wall having sex, and he turned up at my house one night drunk, implying we should have an affair...' She stopped, clearing her throat. 'He stole my dustbin – not to mention he stole my *children* during *my* contact time, when he'd barely bothered to see them before he moved next door. And he sent them to a different school without my permission.' She counted onto the next hand. 'And he's told everyone I have mental health issues.

'He's opened up a branch of his estate agency business in town purely to annoy me, and everywhere I go I see his face leering out of the "For Sale" signs. He scared my dad half to death and put him in hospital with a suspected heart attack, and he's stolen most of my friends, telling them lies about me damaging his car and dumping rubbish in his garden.'

Leah dropped her hands into her lap when she ran out of fingers.

'Oh, and he's been in my house when I wasn't there, and he's knocked a huge hole in my garden wall, saying he has a right of way over my courtyard to get to *his* land, even though it's mine.

'More recently, as you know, I've had to report him for putting my phone number on a sleazy hook-up site.' Leah drew in a breath, but then continued, even when she saw DI Nelson about to speak. 'And to add insult to injury, he accosted me at the back of my salon a few days ago and… and forced a *kiss* on me.' There, she'd said it.

'That's a lot of pent-up anger, Leah,' DI Nelson said, making a few notes. 'You say he forced a kiss on you? We've already collected and are reviewing various CCTV footage from the vicinity of your salon and your ex-husband's new premises. Have a look at this, if you would.'

The detective tapped on her tablet several times, then turned the screen to face Leah.

Leah stared at it, stunned when, after a few moments of looking at a view of the empty alley at the back of her salon where she'd parked her car, she saw herself captured by the camera's narrow angle. Craig then approached her. As she watched the footage, she stifled a sob, cupping her hand over her mouth as she saw Craig lean forward and kiss her.

Except it appeared nothing like she remembered.

'Does this look as though he forced himself on you, Leah?'

'Well...' She trailed off. 'It may not *look* like it, but that's what he did.'

'I'd say that's a recording of a woman quite enjoying a kiss, wouldn't you?'

The DI replayed it and Leah sat there, shaking her head as she saw herself raise her arms at Craig then wrap them around his neck as she fell into his kiss. One of her legs hooked up behind her and she turned her head sideways as he pressed himself against her. They'd staggered off screen before the point where she'd shoved him away.

'But that's not how it happened at all. Do you have any footage of when we were standing further to the left? That's when we were arguing. He'd put my kids in another school and I'd just been to get them. It was awful. I was upset.'

'Not too upset to enjoy a kiss with your ex-husband, though?'

Leah said nothing. 'No comment' would only add to her guilt.

'You mentioned your mental health issues just now. Have you received treatment for this? A formal diagnosis?'

'I've taken antidepressants in the past, but after what I've been through, who wouldn't?' She looked at her solicitor for support, but the woman remained blank-faced. 'I'm not crazy, if that's what you're thinking.'

'Do you often lose your temper?' The detective clasped her hands under her chin, leaning her elbows on the edge of the table.

'No,' Leah said quietly. 'Very rarely.'

DI Nelson opened the file again, angling it so that only DC

Marshall was able to see the contents. She pointed to something, which they both took a moment to read.

'Do you recognise this, Leah?' DI Nelson slid a photograph in a plastic sleeve across the table.

Leah stared at it for a moment. 'It's a petrol can. It looks like the one Dad gave me a while back.'

'And this?' The detective produced another image.

'It's a label. Dad's handwriting. It was on the can.' Leah's tone was weary, terse, exasperated. There was no use denying the facts.

'They were both discovered in the vicinity of the bonfire and the petrol can was empty. Do you know how the items got there?'

'No,' Leah said quietly. 'But I noticed the jerrycan was missing from my shed. Someone must have taken it.'

'Was the shed locked? Had there been a break-in?'

'It had a coded padlock, which was unlocked when I last went inside.'

The detective made some notes and then she referred DC Marshall to another document in the folder.

'Going back to the website incident you mentioned, Leah. We have the follow-up report on file now. The website owners confirmed that a post containing a phone number was indeed put up at approximately 1.20 a.m. on the night you made the complaint against your ex-husband.' DI Nelson opened the file again and showed Leah a printout of what appeared to be an email. There was a number highlighted in yellow. 'Is this your phone number, Leah?'

'Yes.'

'The website's policies and terms of use forbid the posting of direct contact information such as phone numbers and addresses, so it was taken down within a couple of hours, once flagged. Their technical contact provided an IP address from which the post was made. Subsequently, our IT team has located the specific internet service provider and we're in the process of requesting further, more detailed information from them. Would you please state who provides your telephone and broadband services?'

'I'm with BT,' Leah replied.

'Which we already know is the provider used to access the website. According to Gillian, their household is signed up to a completely different ISP. Did you put your own phone number online, Leah, in order to blame your ex-husband for it?'

'*No!* No, I certainly did not. No comment. But no. Just no!' Leah stared up at the ceiling, sighing out. This was ridiculous.

'What type of device do you use, Leah? Android or Apple?'

'I have an ancient Dell laptop and a not very new Samsung phone.'

'Do you know what type of devices your ex-husband uses?'

'That's easy,' Leah said confidently. 'He'd never use anything except Apple. The latest phones *and* computers. I can say that with certainty. Craig has to have the best of everything.'

'Thank you for confirming. We know that the post on the website was made from an Android device.'

Leah shook her head as her mouth fell open. 'Maybe he bought a different phone. Or used Gillian's. I don't know. He's not stupid, and he's hardly going to incriminate himself.'

'OK, moving on from that for a moment. In your witness statement, you mentioned that you last saw Craig on the morning two of our officers came out to your property. Is that correct?'

'Yes.'

'And I've noted that you mentioned the possibility of your mother having seen your ex-boyfriend, Gabriel Holland, more recently than you last saw him?'

'I... I don't know. I think I was confused.'

The detective nodded, staring at Leah for a moment.

'You stated that you last saw Gabriel Holland on the day he

ended your relationship when you visited him on his boat a few weeks ago. You said you couldn't be sure of the exact date.'

Leah stared down at her hands, picking at the skin around her thumb. 'Yes,' she said, regretting the lie for a second time. 'And... and Mum didn't actually *see* him,' Leah added. She was hearing the words come out of her mouth as if she had no control over them whatsoever, as though a different person was speaking.

'Can you explain further?'

'Mum went...' Leah crossed and uncrossed her legs, then folded and unfolded her arms. 'Mum went to Craig's house, but she didn't actually go inside. She saw another car on the drive, so she left, not wanting to interrupt.' Whatever happened, she didn't want her mum dragged into this. She wouldn't deal with it well and, furthermore, she didn't want her father getting unnecessarily stressed. He'd end up in hospital again.

'I see,' DI Nelson replied. 'And you've just remembered this?'

Leah nodded. 'Sorry.'

'So it's been a few weeks now since you saw Gabriel Holland and two days since you saw your ex-husband?'

Leah's cheeks burned a deeper shade of red and tears pooled in her eyes. She didn't think she could keep up the lie any longer. 'I... I don't know. I'm not certain of anything any more. Maybe... It's all unclear and I'm...'

But then she stopped, staring at the table where the detective was tapping her pen as she scanned the file. The repeated sound of it made her want to swipe it onto the floor. She took a deep breath.

'Have you ever been cheated on, Detective?' she found herself asking.

DI Nelson looked up.

'I see you're wearing a wedding ring,' Leah continued, glancing at DI Nelson's left hand as she waited for an answer.

Then she looked directly into her eyes. 'Have you ever been so badly deceived and lied to that you don't know what's real and what's not any more?'

Behind the steely stare of a professional, she swore she caught a glimmer of something – noticed a slight twitch under one eye as her pupils widened. She saw a mother, a wife, a woman betrayed.

'Interview temporarily suspended at 4.23 p.m.,' DI Nelson suddenly announced, flicking off the recording device and gathering up her files. She stood up abruptly and swept out of the room.

————

'And when we went back into the interview room, the detective asked if I'd killed my ex,' Leah said into her phone. 'Then she asked if I knew who it was in the fire.'

Once she'd arrived home after being released from the interview, having stopped off on the way to pick up the children, Leah had made sure they were fed and washed before settling them in bed. It was the bravest act she'd ever had to put on, though once she was alone, she'd clutched a sofa cushion and buried her face in it as she broke down in tears.

But the self-pity didn't last long. She'd made a cup of tea, knowing she needed to speak to someone – someone who would offer support. That's when she found herself dialling Gabe's number, praying he'd pick up – especially after everything she'd said to him earlier.

He did. On the second ring.

'What did you reply?'

'After I'd had a word with my solicitor in the break, I just said "no comment" to everything. That was her advice. I'd made a statement and then she read it out to the detectives on my behalf. It basically said that I didn't know anything. Then they let me go. The solicitor said they didn't have enough to charge me with and were just trying it on. It was so surreal, Gabe, I don't know how I'm going to get a wink of sleep.'

'You're in shock,' Gabe replied. 'Go easy on yourself. Take a hot bath and eat something if you can.'

Leah said that she'd try.

'Where are the children?'

'They back here with me now. Mum's been really good. I'm not sure how I'd have got through this without her.'

Gabe remained silent.

'Are you there?'

'Yeah,' he said quietly, as though something was on his mind. 'Though my battery's getting low, if I suddenly disappear. Did they give any indication about identifying the body yet? Or where Craig might be?'

'No,' she replied. 'Only that there was nothing official back from pathology, though I got the impression they have an idea.'

'They were testing you.'

'Mmm,' Leah agreed, her mind still swimming from it all. 'When I was on your boat earlier, you were about to tell me what happened when you went to collect your money from Craig. Mum said she heard you both fighting, Gabe. What happened?'

Silence.

'Hello, Gabe, are you there?' Leah stared at her phone screen. 'Gabe?' she said again, before chucking it down beside her. He'd finally run out of battery.

CHAPTER THIRTY-NINE

Leah knew there was no way she would sleep, and neither did she feel inclined to take Gabe's advice and have a hot bath and some food. Instead, she'd paced about the house, feeling agitated and anxious, not to mention frustrated when he'd not called back to continue their conversation. She needed to know exactly what had happened when Gabe had gone to see Craig for his money.

She'd tried to call him back several times, of course, but it hadn't connected. From what she knew so far, it sounded as though he was the last person to see Craig before he went missing. She knew her mother was prone to exaggerating and her witnessing harsh words between Craig and Gabe, or even raised voices, could have been misconstrued by her as a fistfight. Either way, she didn't want her mum caught up in it all, especially as she'd left in a hurry anyway.

On a whim, Leah dialled Gillian's number, but it rang out. Craig's car was still sitting on the Old Vicarage's drive when she'd come home earlier, but she hadn't noticed if Gillian's car was there or not. She'd been focused on Zoey and Henry.

She went out into the courtyard and peered through the hole in the wall.

A light was on next door. Gillian must be home.

It wasn't the kitchen light she saw, but a softer glow seeping through the door from the hallway – perhaps a lamp, or maybe the flicker of the TV.

On a whim, she went back through her house and then out the front, going up next door's path and knocking on the door. She didn't think it was too late to disturb her, under the circumstances, and she doubted Gillian would be asleep given everything that had been going on. She wanted to know what had happened at the police station and ask why she'd ignored her in the corridor. If she'd upset her somehow, she wanted the chance to put things right. The kids would be fine left alone for a few minutes.

But there was no reply. Leah knocked again and rang the bell. Still nothing.

She peered through the living room window, but it was dark inside.

Guessing Gillian had the TV turned up loud in the sitting room at the rear of the house, she went home and out into her courtyard again, checking around the back. This time, the light she'd spotted had been turned off.

On an impulse – glancing over her shoulder – she crept into next door's garden and up the couple of steps to the French doors. She didn't want to be accused of snooping, though it suddenly felt exactly like that. She cupped her hands against the glass. No sign of anyone. Then Leah slowly turned the handle, expecting the doors to be locked. But they weren't.

Without thinking, she pressed down further on the handle and slowly pulled open the glass-paned door. Calling out to Gillian would have been the right thing to do, she knew that, but then it also seemed like the wrong thing to do. She convinced herself it was because she didn't want to disturb

Gillian or scare her half to death. She would just check every-thing was OK, that Gillian was safe, and then she'd go home again. It was neighbourly.

Leah stood in the dark drawing room, hugging her arms around her body. She'd already changed for bed and was wearing pyjama bottoms and a T-shirt with flimsy slippers on her feet.

The first thing she noticed was the smell.

The lilies, she thought, catching the sickly scent of them rotting in their water. The drawing room was cold and dark, but she didn't want to turn on the light. Instead, she used the torch on her phone, padding quietly through the room and into the hallway, greeted by an even stronger odour. Sure enough, the flowers' heads were wilting and brown, and the remaining water in the glass vase was slimy and green.

She decided to check upstairs, her feet sinking into the plush pile of the carpet with every step, turning left when she reached the landing. She stopped and listened in case Gillian was in the shower – but all she heard was the sound of her own breathing.

Inside Craig and Gillian's bedroom, it was similarly dark and the curtains were half closed. She remembered what Gillian had said about the pattern, how she disliked the birds staring at her and now, with the light from the street catching the fabric, she tended to agree. Their eyes looked sinister.

'Hello?' Not a whisper as such, but not far off.

The huge bed was empty and neatly made up with the rest of the room also clean and tidy, just like it had been when Gillian had first shown her around. It didn't look as though the police had done any kind of search on the property yet. From what she'd learnt earlier, they were currently focusing their investigation on the remains found in the fire, rather than Craig's disappearance.

But Leah was in no doubt that they'd be all over Gillian's

house before too long if Craig didn't turn up in the next day or so – and, given the questions they were asking her earlier, they'd be all over her house too. And then Gabe was on her mind again and whatever had happened when he'd come round for his money.

Leah walked slowly across the bedroom towards the en suite shower room, stopping when she saw the damage to the wall – the spot where Craig had drilled through. The ugly hole with brick dust staining the wall beneath it was in the middle of pristine white paintwork and not even in a place where a painting or shelf would be hung. It was obvious he'd done it purely to antagonise her.

She looked away, tentatively pushing open the door to the bathroom. She didn't want to disturb Gillian if she was in there. But, like the rest of the house, it was dark and empty inside. Leah pulled the light cord, catching a whiff of various scented products.

She looked around, scanning the room where her ex-husband washed every day, almost sensing the ghost of him in there. Hanging on the back of the door were two dressing gowns – one cream satin and the larger one grey towelling. She ran her fingers down the smooth fabric of Gillian's robe, pulling it off the hook and draping it over her shoulders, sliding her arms into each sleeve. She tied the belt around her waist and looked at herself in the mirror above the his-and-hers basins.

She looked nothing like Gillian, of course, even wearing her silky robe, but then again, she didn't think she looked anything like herself either. Staring back, she saw a gaunt woman with thin lips, dark circles around her eyes and hair that badly needed styling – ironic, given her job.

On a whim, she opened the bathroom cabinet, her eyes scanning the items inside – several boxes of medications, the blister pack of Gillian's pill lying on the shelf, cotton buds, make-up remover and various other toiletries that weren't pretty enough to display on the open shelving. Then she saw a lipstick and took it out, opening it up. It was a deep scarlet – nothing like she'd ever wear – but she swiped it across her lips anyway, doing a bad job of applying it.

She posed in the mirror, pouting at herself as she imagined Craig coming up behind her, sliding his hands around her waist and nuzzling her neck with his mouth.

You look beautiful... he'd say. *Are you ready for dinner?*

Leah laughed silently, her mouth wide and her teeth bared as she tipped back her head.

How had things come to this? Maybe she *was* losing her mind.

She gripped the edge of the basin, leaning forward and staring at herself in the mirror. What the *hell* was she doing? She needed to get a grip. She needed to get *out*.

She tore off the robe and hung it back on the hook, grabbing a tissue and wiping it across her mouth. But all it did was smudge red into her skin, making her look like a clown. Then she left the bathroom and went back down the stairs again, stopping in the hallway. The lilies caught in her nostrils again, making her want to sneeze.

Leah stared at the doors leading off the hallway and, instead of heading back through the drawing room and out of the French doors where she'd come in, she decided to quickly check the kitchen in case Gillian was in there. Again, she opened the door slowly so as not to startle her.

But as before, it was empty, which left her puzzled about the light she'd seen through the window. She was beginning to think she'd imagined it.

The kitchen felt cold with only the moonlight glinting in through the blinds and reflecting off Gillian's shiny glass-topped table. Like the rest of the house, it was pristine – every surface polished and smear-free, the floor mopped and clean enough to eat off.

Then something caught Leah's eye – on the floor, over by the skirting board opposite the run of kitchen cabinets. A small sparkle in the moonlight.

She walked over and bent down, picking it up. About an inch long, she studied it for a second before realising what it was.

A false nail – long with pink polish and a glittery gold tip.

Leah stared out of the window, between the slatted blinds and up at the moon as a cloud scudded in front of it.

'*Mum*,' she whispered as she studied the nail again, taking a closer look to make certain. There was no doubt it was hers. And that's when she saw what appeared to be a smear of dried blood on the underside. Horrified, she slipped it inside her pyjama pocket, relieved that she'd found it before the police had searched the house. Now she just wanted to get home and back to the children.

It was as she turned round to go that she screamed, suddenly stopping in her tracks before backing away until she was pressed up against the sink.

'Hello, Leah,' a voice said through the darkness.

CHAPTER FORTY

'*Craig?* What the hell are *you* doing here?'

'Shouldn't I be asking you that?' He made a noise – somewhere between a growl and a laugh.

Leah didn't like the way he was approaching her; didn't like the way the moonlight cast eerie slices of light over his face. She took a sideways step.

'Where have you been? The police have been looking for you. Gillian is worried sick.'

'That's not your business any more, is it?'

Leah's mind hummed with confusion and fear. 'I saw the bruises on Gillian's face. Did she find out what kind of man you are, is that it?'

Shut up, shut up! she screamed in her head. She couldn't afford to antagonise him.

Craig took another couple of steps closer into a pool of moonlight, giving Leah a better look at him. He also had a bruise on one cheekbone and a small cut on the side of his neck that looked red and raw. She remembered what her mother said about Gabe and Craig fighting.

'What are you doing in my house, Leah?' He came closer.

She turned her head sideways. He smelt revolting. Her heart drummed frantically in her chest as she felt his hands slip around her wrists. And suddenly she was back there, in their family home, feeling terrified for her life, for her kids' lives, and it seemed as if no time had passed – as if she hadn't even escaped and wasn't really divorced at all.

'I... I'm sorry, Craig,' she said, her voice shaking. 'I was looking for Gillian. To see if she was OK.'

'Liar,' he spat, tightening his grip and yanking her arms.

Leah fought back the cry of pain. He always hated it if she made a fuss.

'You... you should let the police know you're OK.'

He released her and walked away, pacing up and down beside Gillian's glass table, pushing his hand through his hair – something he always did when he was stressed. 'You've complicated things, Leah. You always were a nuisance, weren't you?'

'I... I'm sorry. I'll just go home and won't say a word. It's your business, Craig, and I won't tell anyone I saw you.'

He laughed, sending shivers down Leah's spine. Then his face fell serious. 'Why is there police tape all over my building site? What's been going on?'

Leah resisted saying anything about who owned the land. She didn't care about it any more. Didn't want to grow vegetables where someone had died.

'There's... there's been some kind of accident. Gillian... she found... a body in the bonfire. She was so upset. She thought it was you. That's why I came to check on her.' She prayed that was enough to placate him.

That noise in his throat again – a deep thrum that made Leah want to curl up into a protective ball. She'd heard it too many times before.

'Once the investigation is over, you'll... you'll be allowed to carry on with the build.' Leah inched towards the door. Craig might be slim and wiry, but she knew he wasn't a runner. If she got a head start, she'd be able to make it back to her place without him catching up. She'd lock herself in and call the police.

She stepped another couple of feet away from him.

'How's that boyfriend of yours?' Craig took a pace closer, cancelling out her head start.

'I don't have a boyfriend,' she replied, wanting to tell him how he'd ruined that for her. But she didn't. She needed him as calm as possible.

'Lying bitch.' He was up in her face again.

Leah flinched. This wasn't going to work. 'Why don't you call Gillian and tell her you're home? She's staying with a friend.'

Another step away from him.

'With a man, most likely. She's just like you.' His eyes turned glassy, staring. 'You're all the same, you women.'

'*What*? What are you talking about, Craig? She's a good person and she's worried about you.' She reached out to touch his shoulder gently in the hope it might calm him, but he pulled away.

'Enough, Leah. Don't think I don't know what you're doing.'

His body tensed – his jaw clenching, his pupils dilating – and, despite his proximity, she knew it was now or never. She had to get out.

She spun round and ran, her slippers sliding on the kitchen floor as she pushed off. She darted out of the kitchen and through the hall, knocking into the table with the vase of lilies, sending them crashing to the tiles. When she burst through into the living room, she glanced back over her shoulder to see how close he was.

But Craig wasn't there. He wasn't pursuing her.

It threw her off guard for a second, making her wonder if she'd completely imagined his presence, but she wasn't taking any chances and turned again, charging down to the other end of the drawing room to the French doors. Once there, she grabbed one of the brass handles, knowing there was no time for fumbling. As soon as Craig realised her intention, he'd be after her.

She pressed down on the lever. No movement.

She tried the other one, then both at the same time.

Still nothing. The handles were rigid, unlike when she'd come in and they'd been easy to open.

Frantically, Leah rattled both handles over and over, shoving against the glass doors and even kicking at them with her slippered foot. They didn't budge.

She turned, knowing she'd have to get to the front door. She let out a whimper when she saw Craig standing in the doorway, blocking her exit.

'Going already?'

Leah's breathing was shallow and painful as her heart struggled to keep up with the adrenalin raging through her.

'The... the kids,' she managed to get out. 'They're at home. I only... I only popped round quickly. I need to get back to them.' She held his gaze as she walked towards him, trying to appear confident. As she was about to slip past him, he shoved his arms out wide, preventing her from leaving the room.

'You left my children alone?'

'It was only going to be for a few min—'

The blow was swift and hard, the back of his fist connecting with Leah's temple. Her head bounced off the door frame and she staggered backwards, stumbling into a side table at the end of the sofa. She lost her balance and went down, her hip catching on the table as a lamp fell on top of her.

'Oww... no...' She held her head and tried to push herself up with the other hand, but Craig kicked her arm away and she dropped back onto the carpet. He loomed above her, shaking his head. Then he spat on her, the globule landing just under her eye.

Instinctively, Leah drew her knees up and rolled onto her side, hugging her legs and burying her face between her arms. She screwed up her eyes, hardly daring to breathe.

She had no idea how long she stayed like that. The only sounds she heard were when Craig shut the door and moved across the room. She sensed he'd sat down, hearing the creak of the sofa, and dared to open one eye to confirm this. He was sitting about six feet away from her, leaning forward on his forearms with his hands clasped together. One finger was tapping rhythmically against the back of the other hand while he stared down at her, barely even blinking.

CHAPTER FORTY-ONE

'What went wrong, Leah?'

Slowly, she unfurled herself and opened her eyes. Craig was sitting back in the sofa – more relaxed now, almost looking as though he was chilling with guests.

Leah slowly sat up, praying this was her chance to talk him round, to persuade him to let her go home. She couldn't stay like this forever. She needed to get back to the children.

'Wrong?' she said, slowly easing one hand closer to her hip.

'What went wrong with *us*?'

'Oh. I...' she said, stalling for time. 'We were good once, weren't we?'

She hated that that was actually true. They *had* been good once. A team with a vision, big hopes for their future, plans for their family. But those thoughts had no place in her mind now. Regrets weren't going to get her out of here – though what he said still ate away at her.

Tentatively, she felt around the pocket of her pyjama bottoms.

Damn. Not there.

Her phone must have fallen out when she'd run from the kitchen, or perhaps when she'd gone down after he'd hit her.

'We can still be good parents together, surely?' she said.

Slowly, ever so slowly, she got to her knees and put one foot out, then the other until she was standing. Craig didn't move. Just watched her, that look in his eyes she knew too well – the same one he'd given her many times after he'd run out of rage and wanted to reconcile. Something in her heart twinged.

Leah's gaze flicked to the floor, near where she'd fallen.

'Lost something?'

When she turned, Craig was holding up her phone, waving it about. He laughed.

'Can I have it?' she said, going over to him and holding out her hand. He whipped the phone away, holding it up over his shoulder.

'Uh-uh,' he taunted. 'You won't be needing it.'

'What are you talking about? Give it to me. I'm going home to the children.'

'You can try.'

Leah glared at him before turning and running to the hallway, knowing before she even got there that the front door would be locked. She grabbed the handle and turned it anyway. But she was right – he'd locked her in and, short of smashing a window, there was no way out.

Frantically, her eyes scanned about, spotting a cast-iron umbrella stand beside the door. She pulled out the umbrellas and threw them on the floor, lifting the heavy stand before wielding it back over her shoulder. Her arms and stomach muscles trembled from effort as she aimed it at the foot-wide glass panel to the left of the door, not knowing if she'd even fit through the gap once the glass was smashed.

Screwing up her eyes, Leah used all her strength to hurl the iron stand at the window.

But nothing happened.

It was still fixed rigid above her shoulder. When she turned her head, Craig was standing there gripping the object in his fist.

'Don't go yet, Leah. In fact, don't go at all.' He prised the umbrella stand from her grip, setting it back in its place. Then he grabbed her upper arm, digging his fingers into her flesh. 'Come.' He dragged her back into the drawing room and flung her down on the sofa. It felt warm from where he'd been sitting.

'Our children are next door alone, for Christ's sake.' She rubbed her arm where he'd hurt her. 'I need to get back to them.' She tried to stand up, but Craig's hands rammed against her shoulders, shoving her back down. He loomed above her, only reacting when a shrill ringtone sounded.

He pulled Leah's phone from his back pocket, staring at the screen. He flashed her a look.

'Your stupid boyfriend,' he spat. 'Perhaps I should have a word with him, tell him that he won't be seeing you again.'

'I told you, Gabe is not my boyfriend,' Leah retorted, lunging for her phone. He pushed her back down again.

The phone stopped ringing. A few moments later, it pinged.

Craig stared at the screen. 'What does this mean?' He held the phone out for Leah to read the text message.

Sorry, phone charger problem. Call me back asap. There's something you need to know xx

'How sweet,' Craig said. 'Kisses.' He reached out and belted Leah around the head.

Stunned, she closed her eyes, waiting for the room to stop spinning.

'You dirty bitch.' He paced about the room, restless. 'I should have known he couldn't be trusted with a whore like you.'

'I know you paid him to watch me.' Leah's head thrummed

as she spoke. 'You can't buy people, Craig. Gabe has morals. When he realised what you were doing, he saw you for the pathetic coward you are. I hope he knocked you out cold when he punched you.'

Craig stopped and swung round. There was a sickening grin on his face.

'Punched me?' He laughed loudly. 'I assure you, Leah, you'd have been thoroughly disappointed in him. *He* was the coward. He didn't even raise a finger to me when I challenged him. I refused to give him his money, so he left.'

'That's not what Mum said,' Leah shot back, instantly wishing she hadn't mentioned her mother. Craig had never liked her, though he had always been two-faced – slagging her off behind her back then acting like the perfect son-in-law in front of her. And Rita had lapped it up. It was the reason she was so cut up about her and Craig divorcing – no more charming, successful son-in-law to brag about. If she'd heard some of the things Craig said about her, she wouldn't have thought so highly of him.

'Your mother needs to calm down,' Craig said, shaking his head. 'Whatever that boyfriend of yours told you he saw, he's lying. And whatever Rita has spouted off has come from the mind of a frustrated old woman.'

Leah stared at him. Confused.

He was making that face – his *lying* face, where his eyes never quite met hers and his chin pulled back into his neck. And she'd never thought of her mother as *old* before. In fact, she'd gone out of her way to preserve her youth and never looked anything but glamorous. People were always amazed they were mother and daughter.

The skin under Craig's eye twitched and his ears burned red.

More signs, Leah thought, staring up at him.

'You're lying. Mum saw you hit Gabe and how he fought

back. She told me all about the fight,' Leah said in a calm voice, suspecting that whatever Gabe needed to tell her, it was to do with this. 'And she also told me why she'd come to see you.'

Craig froze.

Leah stood up, pushing back her shoulders and holding her head high.

'I'm angry as hell at her, by the way. She was bang out of order. And so were you for even entertaining her.'

Leah hated the thought of her mother trying to convince Craig to give it another go for the kids' sakes, and heaven forbid that Rita had suggested it was what Leah actually wanted.

'Everything that comes out of that woman's mouth is poison. She's deluded.'

'I know what my mother told me, Craig. And it's exactly the sort of thing she'd do. But yes, I agree with you on this one. Her motives were indeed deluded. And you need to keep your hands off her. It's frankly disgusting.'

For the briefest of moments, Leah thought she spotted something that looked like shame flicker in Craig's eyes. But it was gone as fast as she'd noticed it.

'Well, since she's confessed, you might as well know that it was entirely her fault. She started it.' He walked over to the window and stared out into the front garden. He let out a laugh. 'It was on your birthday, actually. Your thirty-fifth, I think. Everyone was round at ours – you'd made a cake, put out food and decorations, and the music was on.'

'What's my birthday got to do with anything?'

Then the shrill ringtone from Leah's phone again. Craig fumbled as he silenced it, throwing it on the floor in anger. She thought he was going to stamp on it, but it slid under the sofa.

Leah took a step closer to where it had fallen.

'The kids were playing up that day, Henry especially,' Craig continued. 'You'd been too preoccupied with organising the party to notice he needed attention. Typical of you – too wrapped up with yourself to notice anyone else's needs.'

'Craig, what are you talking about? I spent our entire marriage focusing on everyone except me!'

He tracked the headlights of a car as it cruised past the house. Then he whipped round to face her. 'I found her upstairs crying, Leah. What was I supposed to do, ignore her?'

'Who was upstairs? What the hell are you talking about?'

Turn around again, for God's sake turn around...

Leah eyed the floor. She saw the corner of her phone poking out from under the sofa. She'd heard that you only needed to dial two of the nines to be connected.

'Your mother, Leah. She was in our bedroom.'

Leah stared at him, trying to remember. The party was only a vague collection of fragments in her mind. Even though it was her birthday, having organised the whole thing she'd have been too distracted and exhausted to notice where everyone was.

Her fingers itched to grab the phone, but she also wanted Craig to finish what he was saying.

'Why was she crying?'

'I'd only gone upstairs for clean clothes. Henry had managed to get chocolate ice cream all over me. I went into our bedroom and took off my dirty shirt, then into the en suite to put it in the wash basket. Your mother was in there, sobbing in front of the mirror.'

'What was wrong with her? Had someone upset her?'

But Leah couldn't get the image of Craig standing naked from the waist up next to her weeping mother out of her mind.

'She told me that she needed some attention, that she was lonely and wanted to feel young and special again. What was I supposed to do?'

Leah didn't say a word. *Couldn't* say a word. Even grabbing her phone had gone from her mind. She tried to speak but only a couple of croaks came out.

'I know what you're thinking, Leah, but it wasn't like that. I did it purely to comfort her. In hindsight, I know I should have changed the sheets afterwards, but we were in a rush to get back downstairs before we were missed.'

Leah stared at him, completely unable to move.

CHAPTER FORTY-TWO

'You slept with my *mother*? At my *birthday* party? In *my* bed?'

Leah covered her face, dragging her hands down as she shook her head.

'She was surprisingly good, actually. After that, it became something we both enjoyed regularly. A bad habit, I suppose.' He shrugged.

This is not real, Leah screamed in her head. *This is not happening...*

'You look shocked,' Craig said after a few moments of silence.

Leah stood staring at him. Every cell in her body was stinging and raw.

'You bastard,' she whispered. 'I put up with some hellish shit from you over the years, but this is the lowest of the low.'

'What can I say, Leah? Sometimes you didn't want sex. You were always tired.'

'That's right. Make it my fault. You wore out *that* bloody excuse on all your other affairs.' Leah paced about. If she didn't, she'd do something she'd regret. 'But my mother, Craig. My *mother*.'

'I don't know why you're so upset. You just told me that you knew about it.'

'*Knew?*' Leah yelled. 'My mother told me that she'd come here to talk some bullshit to you about us getting back together. Then she said that you'd made a pass at her.' She scoffed out a laugh. 'I didn't know you'd been fucking her for four years!'

'Has it been that long?' he said, making a thoughtful face.

But Leah was doing her own thinking, despite her mind feeling like a wet sponge.

'He saw you, didn't he? Gabe. When he came to ask for his money, he saw you and my mother at it together.'

Craig shrugged.

'I can read you like a book, Craig Forbes.' Leah pushed her hands through her hair. No wonder Gabe had been stalling what he had to tell her. 'Then what? You got angry at him? You threatened him because you didn't want your dirty little secret to get out? What *happened*?'

Her mind ran through the possibilities. If Craig's depraved mind could hide something as immoral as this, then he was surely capable of... *anything*.

She shuddered, remembering her mother's false nail on the kitchen floor.

'You upset her, didn't you?' she whispered, eyeing him as they skirted around each other. She just needed to get near her phone. 'Don't forget I know you inside out. You'd have been thoroughly ashamed that Gabe caught you with my mother, that he'd witnessed one of your twisted fantasies playing out. Did you make fun of her? Insult her? If it had been one of your blond twenty-somethings from the office, no doubt you'd have been bragging about it.'

'Upset your mother? Oh, she managed that all by herself,' he said, smirking. 'She's just a stupid old woman.'

Leah's eyes flashed to the mark on the side of his neck – a

perfectly round bruise with a small cut sliced in the centre. A cut that could easily have been made by a pointed fingernail.

'Did you *attack* her? Did she have to defend herself from you?'

No wonder Rita had been upset when she'd come round to the salon that afternoon. And she'd made up the story about Craig making a pass at her to cover herself in case Gabe told her what he'd witnessed. But Gabe hadn't managed to say anything yet because he knew how devastated Leah would be.

'The stupid woman went crazy. It was self-defence.'

'And why did she go *crazy*, Craig?' Leah approached him slowly. 'What did you do that would drive my sixty-three-year-old mother to attack you? Or perhaps it was self-defence on *her* part?' Despite being furious with her mother, Leah was now grateful that Rita had been to her martial arts classes regularly. She might be angry as hell with her, but she didn't want her hurt.

From the corner of her eye, Leah noticed that she was only about three feet from her phone. Right now, nothing else mattered apart from calling the police and getting home to her children.

As Craig was pacing about, agitated and spewing out ridiculous excuses, Leah made her move. She dropped down and lunged for her phone, managing to grab it and make a dash for the door. If she could just get into the downstairs toilet, lock herself in, that would buy time.

'Get back here, bitch!'

A hand clawed at her shoulder, grabbing her T-shirt just as she was in the doorway. She half swung round but managed to yank herself away to the sound of ripping fabric. As she rounded the corner into the hall, she slipped on the tiles, slowing herself down a pace. The toilet was near – only a few feet away now.

Her head whipped back as Craig grabbed her hair.

Leah screamed as pain tore through her scalp.

'Get off me!'

She twisted round under his arm and lifted her right knee sharply, just missing his groin as he folded backwards. His hold on her hair loosened for a second and she swiped his arm away with a swift chop, breaking free.

'I'm going to *kill* you!' he shrieked.

As Leah lunged for the toilet door handle, Craig caught her by the arm, swinging her around and grabbing the other arm tightly so she was facing him with her body pressed up close. Sensing she was about to knee him again, he kicked her feet from under her and swept her sideways, picking her up and carrying her back into the drawing room with his arms latched around her middle.

Leah wriggled and writhed, thumping him as hard as she could. He hurled her down onto the sofa, but she immediately scrambled to her feet, landing on the floor when he shoved her down again.

Defeated and exhausted, she knelt in front of him, panting in and out sharply, hair stuck all over her face as she lowered her head.

She was done, empty, broken. No more fight inside her. She sobbed – a deep pain coming out that had been buried for years.

It was hopeless. Had always been hopeless. It had taken her years to escape and divorce him – but the tragedy was, she'd not escaped him at all. Everywhere she turned, Craig was there. He was pernicious, rooting himself in her life in every way possible.

She now realised she'd never be free. She was stupid to have thought otherwise.

It was time to give up. Surrender.

Time to do what she'd always done best.

'Kill me, then,' she said quietly, looking up at him through the tears. She swept her hair off her wet face then clasped her hands under her chin, almost in prayer. Craig had a demented look in his eyes as he stared down at her, but she knew it reflected the look in hers. 'Get on with it if you're going to do it.'

Craig remained strangely quiet. Watching her.

By some miracle, Leah still had her phone clutched in her hand and she fingerprinted it open, her arms shaking from fear. She managed to get onto the dial screen before he spoke.

'Leah...' he said, his voice heavy. He let out a sigh.

A sigh she recognised. A sigh that made her feel as though she'd come home.

She looked up, seeing something in his face – something familiar and warm that tugged at her heart, unravelling her. The same feeling that had allowed her to be reeled back in every time she'd tried to leave, hoping things would be different this time.

Yes, that was it.

Hope.

It was a hard feeling to give up.

A drug.

They stared at each other – Craig towering above Leah as she knelt beneath him, looking up through matted hair, her lips smeared red from earlier.

And she felt herself falling.

Falling into his heart again as he held out his hands to her.

Slowly, she closed her phone screen and slipped it in her pocket, putting one hand and then the other in Craig's warm palms. His fingers clamped round hers as he helped her stand up. They were only inches apart, staring into each other's eyes for what seemed like an age.

Getting to know one another all over again. Just as they'd done before, time and time again.

'Oh, Craig,' Leah said, feeling the tightness in her body relax a little. Familiar and easy. Staying was easier than going. It would put an end to the fighting, the attacks, the anxiety and the pain. If she relented, it would all be over. Their family back together. Peacetime.

Except this time, she didn't know if he'd have her back.

But it was her only chance of freedom. She had to try.

He took a step away, a slight scowl returning to his face, though they were still holding hands. Leah did that thing he liked – her forefinger gently stroking his palm. Slow and rhythmic, soothing him.

'I... I've missed you,' she managed to whisper. '*Really* missed you. Life without you... it's not... it's not *life*, Craig. What we had – it was so special.'

Craig made a growling sound deep in his throat. He gave a short nod, his eyes flicking around the room as though he wasn't sure what to think.

'You're right. It *was* special,' he finally replied.

'We can fight all we like – and God knows, we're good at it – but we'll never have that feeling with anyone else. You know it as well as I do,' Leah continued, drawing him closer. She pressed up against him. 'We have children together, Craig. That's as special as it gets.'

She felt her hands being squeezed in return, then felt his body respond against her as she pressed herself closer. She closed her eyes as he spoke.

'I've never stopped loving you, Leah. Everything that's happened...' He paused, pulling a pained expression as he tried to think of the words. 'I never meant to hurt you, but you must know that none of it was my fault. Every time I thought I was going to lose you, I panicked. What was I supposed to do?'

Leah listened intently. She'd heard his script many times before. She smiled up at him, opening her eyes again.

'I understand,' she said. 'It was so hard for you. And I know I wasn't easy to live with, that we had our struggles, but...' She trailed off, staring at the floor, wondering how she was going to get the words out. They burned deep inside her –

had been smouldering there since forever. 'But you're the only man for me. Without you by my side, life is meaningless. Sure, I've tried to make a go of it alone, but it's not the same. And the children miss you terribly. We need our family back together.'

Craig took a deep breath as though he couldn't help himself, his chest puffing outwards.

'You really mean that?'

Leah thought she saw a flicker of disbelief under one eye – a minuscule twitch, but she couldn't be sure.

'I've never meant anything more in my life. Perhaps we had to go through all this to realise what we had.' She leant her head against his chest, catching the erratic beat of his heart in her ear. She let out a little laugh. 'And we own one hell of a house between us now.'

Craig returned the laugh. 'We do indeed,' he crooned, planting a kiss on the top of her head. 'Could this really be a new beginning, do you think? Are you really committed?'

'Oh, Craig,' Leah replied, wrapping her arms tightly around his waist. 'You have no idea how much I am. Since you kissed me outside my salon, it's all I've thought about. No other man matches up. If that makes me a bad person, then I don't want to be good.'

'My darling wife,' he said before bringing his lips down on Leah's mouth, cupping her face gently in his hands. Leah wasn't about to protest that technically she wasn't his wife any more – instead, she fell into his embrace, allowing herself to drown in his kiss.

Then, suddenly, there was a loud crash.

The sound of breaking glass.

Craig jerked backwards and Leah let out a little scream, clinging onto him.

'Jesus Christ,' Craig yelped. 'What was that?' Something had landed on the floor beside him.

Leah gasped as she tried to gather herself, not knowing what was happening.

'What the hell—' Craig yelled as he saw the brick and broken glass on the carpet beside him.

Someone had smashed the front window and was climbing in, shards of glass shattering around them as they pushed through.

'Gabe!' Leah shrieked when she saw who it was, stumbling as Craig shoved her in front of him.

'What's going on, Leah?' Gabe cried. 'Get out of the way. Keep back, he's dangerous!' His eyes flicked from her to Craig and then back again. She saw something in them – the hurt, the disbelief.

'No, Gabe – stop!' Leah pleaded as he lunged towards them. 'You don't understand. Please... leave us alone. Go away!' She held up her hands in defence, but Gabe sidestepped her and squared up to Craig, who was shielding himself behind Leah.

'Don't you understand the meaning of divorce?' Gabe barked at him. Then he held out his hand for Leah to take, but she just stood there, staring at it. 'She wants nothing to do with you. Let her go.'

'You're a bit too late, Tree Boy,' Craig sneered, pulling Leah closer. 'We're getting back together.' Another throaty sound rumbled in his chest as Leah slid her arms around his waist, clinging onto him again.

'Leah?' Gabe said, turning to her. He took a step towards her, extending his hand more, a concerned look on his face. 'What's going on? Tell me this isn't true. What about *us*?'

Craig scoffed.

'It's true, Gabe,' she confirmed, only managing to meet Gabe's shocked stare for a second. Just enough time to notice the confusion and hurt. 'There is no "us". Craig and I love each other. We always have done. So...' She forced herself to look at him. 'So you need to leave. I'm choosing Craig. I want to be with him and you have to understand that.' She gave him her hardest stare, ignoring the knot in her stomach.

'Do as she says, Tree Boy,' Craig barked. 'Before I call the police and report you for criminal damage. My solicitor will be sending you a bill for this mess.'

Gabe held up his hands, looking wounded. 'He's danger-ous, Leah. You're making a huge mistake. Don't you see, this is classic abuse – him reeling you back in? It'll happen over and over. You really need to listen to me. I came to tell you that—'

'Get out of my house!' Craig boomed. He took his phone from his pocket. 'I'm calling the police.'

'No need. I've already called them,' Gabe shot back. 'Leah, I've just been to your mother's house,' he continued, giving her a pleading look. 'You *have* to listen to me...'

'Gabe, no, stop,' Leah begged, imploring him with her eyes. 'I already know about Mum. It wasn't Craig's fault. I've moved on from all that.'

'Leah, no, you don't understand what I'm saying,' Gabe pressed on, his voice urgent. 'Your mum saw Craig... She saw him *kill* someone... He's crazy and dangerous!'

Leah staggered as Craig shoved her aside, watching in horror as he threw a punch at Gabe, missing him completely. Gabe ducked to the side before bringing his own fist up and connecting with Craig's jaw.

Craig lurched sideways, knocking into a small table and sending ornaments and books crashing to the floor. Regaining his balance, he charged at Gabe, arms outstretched as he roared in anger.

'Stop! No!' Leah screamed, dragging Craig back by his shirt. 'Leave him alone! Let's just get out, Craig. The police are coming, for God's sake. Do you want to be arrested? Let me help you!'

Craig froze, his arm poised to take another swipe at Gabe. He turned to Leah. She'd never seen him look so scared.

'Did you hear that?' Leah said, taking Craig's hand. 'Sirens. It's now or never, darling. We have to get out. Let me help you. *Please.*'

Craig swallowed, hesitating as Leah wrapped her arms around him.

'I know exactly what to do,' she whispered in his ear. Then she led him to the French doors, which Craig unlocked, taking the key from his pocket with a shaking hand.

'No – get back, Gabe!' Leah screamed out as he came after her.

'Please, Leah, wait. You're making a terrible mistake...' Gabe begged. But when Leah lashed out at him again, he backed away with his hands raised.

Then, as she and Craig stepped out into the night, the police sirens growing ever louder, she paused briefly, looking back at Gabe through the doorway, praying he saw the fear in her eyes.

CHAPTER FORTY-THREE

Leah's old Mini started on the third attempt, the engine juddering to life in a cloud of smoke. Craig sat in the passenger seat, cursing Leah's plan to leave in her ancient old car as he did up his seat belt.

'We should have taken my car,' he snapped. 'It'll be much quicker than this heap.'

'I doubt the police will be looking out for my car,' Leah said, revving the engine and pulling out of her parking spot. 'And besides, your keys are back in your house.' Her legs felt like jelly and she was barely able to keep her feet steady on the pedals.

When they'd fled the Old Vicarage, they'd gone back through Leah's house and she'd grabbed her car keys and a proper pair of shoes. In the hallway, she'd briefly listened out for the children upstairs, but everything was silent. She hated leaving them alone, but she had no choice. They were far safer here. Besides, she trusted Zoey if there was an emergency. Right now, she had one of her own to deal with.

'Christ, hurry up. They're coming!' Craig ordered, swinging round in his seat to look back. In the rear-view mirror, Leah saw the blue flash of police car lights not far behind her as she sped to the end of the street. She barely stopped at the give way sign, swinging out onto the main road that would take them out of town.

'What's your plan?' Craig demanded, the fear in his voice obvious. 'Where are we going?' He kept glancing over his shoulder. But the blue lights were in the distance now, presumably because the police had stopped at the Old Vicarage.

'I have a friend... Sarah,' Leah said, while focusing on the road ahead. 'She has a little cottage in the countryside not far from here that she lets out on Airbnb. I sometimes clean it for her as I need the extra cash. I have a key on my fob and the place is empty at the moment. No one will find us there.'

'Good girl,' Craig said. He reached out and patted Leah's thigh, making it harder for her to concentrate. 'That was quick thinking.'

'It'll give us time to figure out what to do next while we lie low. Mum will come round for the children, so don't worry about them.' It came as no surprise to Leah that he'd not even mentioned Zoey and Henry.

'OK, OK,' Craig said. 'Christ, watch out!' he added, as Leah nearly hit the kerb as she rounded a bend. 'Can't this thing go any faster?'

'Do you want me to get caught on a speed camera?' Leah replied. 'Once we're out of town, I'll speed up.' She gripped the wheel so hard, her knuckles turned white.

'You've got your sensible head on today, my darling,' Craig said. 'But we don't have any clothes or supplies. All I have is my wallet and phone. That's why I came back to the house.'

Up ahead, Leah spotted the black and white of a national speed limit sign, indicating they were approaching the edge of town. She knew exactly where she was heading, reckoning on it taking about twenty minutes. The longest journey of her life.

What would be at the end of it, she wasn't yet sure.

'The cottage has everything we'll need for now. I... I

recently put in a fresh welcome hamper. And we'd better turn off our phones so the police can't track us,' Leah said, glancing down at hers on the little console between them. It had to be done.

As they left the street lights of Alvington behind, heading out into the countryside, Leah pressed the accelerator down harder. She glanced at the speedometer – fifty miles per hour and the Mini was already rattling.

'You do know that what Gabe said was a lie, don't you?' Craig said. 'He's just a jealous idiot trying to cover up all *his* wrongdoings. I hope the police are arresting him right now!'

'I know, I know...' Leah replied, looking out for the turning she knew was coming up. She just wanted to get off the main road and couldn't focus on who'd done what or who was guilty or at fault. None of that mattered any more.

'Are you certain of the way?' Craig asked. 'Do you want me to drive?' He hated not being in control.

'No, we can't afford to stop now. And I know this car's quirks. It's not like yours.'

Leah spotted the sign and indicated right, though there were no other cars in sight.

'How much further?' Craig asked a few minutes later as they sped along the country lane. They were about six miles away from the town now and it was so dark that Leah struggled to see the road in the weak light thrown out by the Mini's headlights.

'Not too far,' she replied, praying she remembered the way. She glanced down at the fuel gauge. With everything that had been going on, she'd not had a moment to go to the petrol station and the needle was well into the red zone now. She gripped the steering wheel even harder, praying she had enough to get where she was heading.

'I'm so grateful to you, Leah, for helping me. You know I never wanted things to turn bad between us. Being with

Gillian...' Craig gripped the door handle as Leah took a bend too fast, stepping on the brakes suddenly as the Mini lurched sideways. 'Jesus, be careful, woman.'

'What about Gillian?' Leah pressed down hard on the accelerator again. There was a stretch of straight road before the next turn. 'What are you going to tell her?'

Not far now... not far now... Leah repeated over and over in her mind, barely listening to Craig as he replied. She had no idea what would happen when they got to where she was heading, or what the result would be. All she knew was that she had to try. The future was hopeless otherwise.

She stepped on the brake again as the turning loomed up fast, swinging the Mini down an even narrower lane.

'Gillian became unbearable to live with. It was a mistake moving her into my house,' Leah heard Craig continue. 'She rarely listened to me. She was always complaining about something. Ungrateful woman. I was barely able to keep her under control. Not like you, Leah. We'll be a proper team again, won't we?'

'Mmm,' Leah agreed, frowning as she leant forward to get a better view of the road. The drizzle had started up again and she didn't want to miscalculate. 'Yes, yes, we will be...'

'It was why I left. I couldn't put up with her stupid nonsense any more. She'd started blaming me for hitting her, but what did she expect? It was an impossible situation for me.'

'Where did you go?' Leah asked, still focusing ahead. 'Everyone was... worried about you.'

'I had to get away for a night or two. For some peace. An old friend picked me up and I stayed with her. She's always been so good to me.'

Leah gave a brief nod as she slowed the Mini and took another turn. Only one more junction to go, and then they'd be there. *Almost safe now*, she told herself. *Or not* – but she didn't want to think about that. She was doing this for herself and her children.

She glanced at the petrol gauge again, praying it would hold out for the next couple of miles.

'Christ, woman, be careful!' Craig shrieked as she misjudged another bend.

'I'm scared the police are going to catch up with us,' Leah said. 'Just hold on and let me drive. I'm doing this for you. For *us*, remember?' She glanced across at him and, even in the dim light of her dashboard, she saw his face was ashen.

They drove on in silence, the only noise coming from the straining engine and the squeaking wipers as they dragged back and forth across the windscreen. The drizzle had turned to heavy rain.

'Here it is,' Leah said, relieved to see the sign pointing down the track. 'Thank God,' she muttered, speeding up again once she'd made the turn.

'It's a farm?' Craig asked, reading the sign, but Leah didn't reply.

She pressed the accelerator harder on the straight as they headed down the hill, praying that she'd make it around the bend at the bottom.

'Will it be safe for us here?'

Leah remained silent, easing her foot down further on the pedal. The Mini rattled and shook as it bumped over a cattle grid, making Craig grab hold of the dashboard.

'Jesus Christ!' he called out. 'Are you sure you know where we're going?'

The engine strained loudly as Leah pressed the pedal to its limits, bracing herself for the turn ahead as they bumped over the second cattle grid. Gripping the wheel as tightly as she could, she yanked it hard to the right, feeling the wheels skid on the loose dirt as they sped around the sharp corner.

'Leah, for God's sake!'

But Leah ignored him, flooring the accelerator as she sped away from the open lane and into the woods. She glanced down at the speedo, watching the needle creep up towards sixty... sixty-five... The rain sheeted down and Leah struggled to see as the wipers flashed across the glass, but she continued on, ignoring Craig's comments as she focused on her driving.

One final burst of power and the Mini's engine strained so much that Leah thought it might explode. She'd never driven it this fast – but then she'd never fled for her life before either.

She gritted her teeth and pushed pack in her seat, her arms outstretched and rigid as she gripped the wheel, her fingers numb from the pressure. Her right foot was on the floor, but she pressed harder anyway, squeezing every last ounce of power from her car.

They rounded the final curve of the lane at full speed and then Leah saw it – thanking God it was still there, that Gabe hadn't yet cleared it away as she'd feared.

Leah drove directly at the fallen tree, following the exact same path as she had before, knowing she only had a second to react.

'Watch out!' Craig yelled.

But Leah had no intention of watching out.

With a final blast of power, she sped at the tree, stepping on the brake only at the very last moment as soon as she heard the branch smashing through the passenger side of the windscreen.

Then everything went black.

CHAPTER FORTY-FOUR

Leah didn't know where she was. She heard a sound she didn't recognise – a regular beep-beep pulsing through her head. Her eyes were closed, though she sensed bright lights through her eyelids. She was lying on her back and her arms were down at her sides.

Perhaps she was dead.

Her mind was fuzzy and sore, and there was a pain in her right shoulder. In fact, her entire body hurt.

She opened her eyes but screwed them up again. Everything was so bright.

'Darling?' she heard a voice say. A familiar voice, though she couldn't work out who it belonged to. Then she felt something warm on her arm. The touch of a hand.

She opened her eyes again, forcing herself to look this time. There was a ceiling above her, fluorescent lights glaring down. She turned her head to one side, wincing at the pain.

'Mum?'

'I've been worried sick about you, darling. Oh, sweetheart,' she said, planting a light kiss on Leah's cheek.

'What... what happened?' She forced her mind to work, to piece the shards together.

She'd been driving... the sheeting rain... the darkness... the tree.

'Don't think about that now,' Rita said.

Leah let out a whimper as images filtered back.

Craig...

She screwed up her eyes again and turned away from her mother, remembering.

'What are *you* doing here, anyway?'

'You've been in an accident, darling. Apparently, a farmer found your car smashed into a fallen tree.'

'Where are Zoey and Henry?' She tried to sit up but flopped back down from the pain.

'They're fine, Gabe is looking after them. He's been really helpful and kind.'

Leah let out a little sigh. *Gabe...*

'And they're OK?'

Rita nodded. 'Don't you worry,' she said, squeezing her hand. 'But Leah, darling, there's something I need to confess. This has made me realise how precious life is and—'

'Stop, Mum. I don't want to hear it right now.' Leah turned over to face the other way, staring at the blood pressure monitor. 'You didn't need to come.' Her voice was cold.

Rita covered her face. 'You know, don't you?'

Without looking round, Leah nodded. She felt her mother's hand on her arm again.

'Don't touch me.'

'I don't expect you to forgive me, Leah. But I'll do whatever it takes to make it up to you.'

Leah didn't reply. Instead, she screwed up her eyes, thankful that her mother couldn't see her face, the tears wanting to escape.

'If you'll just listen to me, it's important, Leah. I went to

Craig's house to end it with him. The guilt was destroying me. I couldn't stand what was I doing to you, to your father, to the children. Not to mention what I was doing to myself. I've been so selfish.'

'My heart bleeds for you, Mum.' Leah sighed, turning to face her mother again. 'But you didn't end it with Craig, did you? And Gabe saw you both together.' She winced at the pain in her collarbone.

Rita pursed her thin lips – the first time in a long time Leah had seen them without lipstick. She hung her head.

'You know how persuasive Craig can be, darling.'

'Jesus, Mum. Does Dad know?'

Rita nodded. 'He's known for a long while. It was... like this unspoken thing between us. It's why he reacted so badly that time outside the agency window, when he saw Craig.'

'I hope you're proud of yourself, Mother.'

'I never expected to get swept up by Craig's charms again. I swear I was trying to protect you.'

'Protecting me would have been not to have an affair in the first place.'

'Darling...' Rita trailed off. 'You know Craig's way.'

'Craig's way?' Leah said, spotting a glass of water on the table beside her. She tried to reach it but her arm was in some kind of splint. Rita passed the glass to her, holding it to her lips.

She screwed up her eyes as she sipped, gasping as an image of the branch smashing through the windscreen flashed through her mind. Blood and glass everywhere.

'What did the police tell you?' Leah asked. She had no idea what had happened after the crash.

Rita didn't say anything for a moment. Instead, she sat with her hands in her lap, her fingers busy. Pick, pick, picking at her brightly painted nails. She'd had her manicure redone, Leah noticed, though seemed intent on ruining it.

'I'll be doing the right thing and turning myself in,' Rita

announced. 'It's one thing keeping such a terrible secret over the years, but it's quite another knowing I killed a man.'

'What are you talking about, Mum?' Leah turned her head again. Her mother's face was crumpled with anguish.

'I didn't mean to kill Craig, but it was self-defence. I had no choice, but I did it and now I'm confessing. I'll be turning myself in.'

'Mum, stop it, you're making even more of a fool of yourself.'

'Why won't you believe me?' Rita said. 'I deserve my punishment.'

Leah closed her eyes, exhausted and in pain. 'The police won't be interested in your drama.'

Rita was silent again. Leah watched as her mother's sharp eyes flicked all over the cubicle.

'I... I think they *might* be interested, actually.'

Leah prepared herself for whatever else was coming. 'Interested in what, Mum?'

Rita gave a few precise nods, her hands folded neatly in her lap. 'When Gabe caught Craig and me together... well, he burst in through the French doors around the back. He seemed to be on a mission.'

'Craig owed him money.'

'Apparently so. Although... although once Gabe realised what was going on, I think the money slipped his mind.' She hung her head briefly.

'I'm sure it did.' The thought of her mother being caught in the act with her ex-husband made her feel nauseous.

'Craig suddenly acted as if I was dirt on the bottom of his shoe. As if I meant nothing to him.'

'Now there's a surprise.'

'He shoved me away and hopped about trying to get his clothes on. Gabe was not impressed at what he'd witnessed. Craig liked to be creative with our lovemaking and we were—'

'For God's sake, Mother, spare me the details.'

Rita cleared her throat. 'This is hard for me too, darling. Gabe was so shocked by what he'd seen that he told Craig he was going to tell you everything.'

'And Craig got angry?'

'Oh yes,' Rita said. 'Angrier than I've ever seen anyone. And Gabe was angry on your behalf, that much was clear.'

'Is that when you left?'

'No, darling. No, I didn't leave then like I originally told you.' Rita bowed her head again. 'Craig lashed out at Gabe, saying he'd kill him before he had a chance to tell anyone what he'd seen. Gabe remained quite calm, actually. He wasn't up for a fight like Craig wanted. He said he was going to finish the work on your hedge.'

'I see,' Leah said, listening intently, despite the pain in her head.

'After he'd gone, Craig was pacing about the room, punching things and sweeping ornaments off the mantelpiece. I've never seen anyone in such a rage. And then he got angry at me, blaming *me* for starting it all between us.'

Leah listened. The behaviour sounded familiar.

'He couldn't let it go. He said he was going outside to "sort out that bastard once and for all". Those were his words.'

'That sounds scary, Mum.'

Rita nodded. 'I tried to stop him, honestly I did. But he stormed outside after Gabe, telling me to go home. Only his words were a lot stronger than that, I can assure you. But Leah, I didn't go straight home. I waited maybe ten or fifteen minutes, wondering what on earth to do. It was all such a mess. Then I went out to find Craig. At first, I couldn't see any sign of him, but then I went into the vegetable garden and sure enough, there were two men over the other side of the plot. Craig was kneeling on the ground next to a digger and the other

person... Oh, Leah... he was... under... under*neath* the digger.'
She stifled a sob.

'Mum, what? What are you saying?' Leah struggled to sit up, but the pain forced her down again.

'By the time I'd got closer, I saw that he was completely crushed under those huge muddy caterpillar tracks. He was wearing this bright luminous jacket thing and his work helmet had popped right off. It was awful, Leah. I've heard some gruesome things in my time from your father's army stories but this... this was *real*, right in front of me.'

'Did Craig know you were watching?'

'Not at first. But then he saw me. Well, it was as though he saw me but didn't *see* me, if you know what I mean. Like he was in another world. There was pure hatred in his eyes.'

'Then what did he do?'

'The digger was already running so Craig jumped into the cab and... and he reversed,' Rita said. 'Then he used the metal bucket to... to shovel him up. I didn't see the person's face. And then he tipped him onto the fire.' She covered her mouth with her hand, shaking her head.

'Oh, Christ, no.' Leah's mind raced. 'Did you see anything written on the work jacket, Mum?'

'There was something. A name, I think, but I couldn't read it. Craig was swearing and raging about still wanting to kill Gabe.' Rita reached out and took her daughter's hands. 'He dragged more wood on top of the body and then he had a can of petrol – it was that jerrycan your father gave you a while back. He doused him with it, as well as all the smouldering wood. I had to run back, it flared up so fast. The flames were huge. Even if he was still alive, he didn't stand a chance after that.'

'Craig must have mistaken whoever it was for Gabe,' Leah said quietly, thinking. Her head ached with it all.

'After that, I followed Craig back inside, begging him to

phone the police, but he kept shoving me away. So I told him that *I* was going to call the police.'

'And did you?' Leah was confused, knowing she couldn't have done.

'No,' Rita confirmed.

'Mum?'

Rita had tears rolling from her eyes now. 'He came at me, Leah. Like, really came at me. We were in the kitchen and I thought he was going to kill me too. I felt it in his energy. He had something in his hand, though I couldn't see what it was. It could have been a knife, a rolling pin – anything. Then, as he lunged at me, something in me just flicked. Like a switch turning me into automatic mode. The tiger in me coming out. My sensei said this would happen if we needed it, as long as we'd practised enough.'

Leah didn't say a word.

'I got him here.' Rita tilted up her chin and touched an area of her neck. 'With the vagus strike that I'd been taught. I only meant to stun him so I could get out of the house. But he went down instantly. This move... it can stop the heart. I'd only ever practised on dummies before, but sensei assured us it can slay a man, Leah. I checked for his pulse but there was none. Not that I could find. No response at all. So... and I'm not proud of this... I panicked. I gathered up all my stuff, making certain I'd got everything, and I left. I'd *killed* him.'

'And that's when you came to the salon to see me?'

Rita sighed. 'After a while, yes. I drove to a lay-by first, expecting the police to come and arrest me at any moment. But they didn't. They never came for me at all. So when I'd calmed down a little, yes, that's when I came to the salon.'

'Jesus, Mum.' Leah rested back on her pillow. 'You should have called the police straight away. You'll be in so much trouble now. And you didn't take everything when you left, actually. You must have broken a nail. I found it on the kitchen floor.'

Rita was about to say something, but the cubicle curtain whipped open and Leah saw DI Nelson step inside, with two uniformed officers flanking her. She gave Leah a glance before turning to Rita.

'No need to say it all again,' the detective said. 'I heard everything loud and clear. Rita Ward, I am arresting you on suspicion of perverting the course of justice. You do not have to say anything, but it may harm your defence if you do not mention, when questioned, something which you later rely on in court. And anything you do say may be given in evidence.'

Rita sat perfectly still for a moment and then gave a brief nod, standing up with her shoulders squared and her chin up. She picked up her handbag and bent down to kiss Leah on her forehead.

'I'm so sorry, darling,' she whispered, before being led out by the two officers.

CHAPTER FORTY-FIVE

'Do you need any more pain relief?' the nurse said as he came into the cubicle to check Leah's blood pressure and temperature. He glanced at the detective, having just crossed paths with the uniformed officers as Rita was led out. He seemed unfazed, perhaps used to a police presence from time to time. A & E was busy beyond the curtains, with the occasional moan of a patient, the beeping of machines, phones ringing and medical staff rushing about. Leah's nurse maintained his calm and reassuring manner.

'Yes, please,' she said, touching her shoulder. 'It really hurts.'

'We'll get you down to X-ray shortly,' the nurse said. 'We're pretty certain you've broken your collarbone and your wrist.' He glanced over at the police officer as he wrote up Leah's notes, putting the file on the table beside the bed. 'You were lucky, by all accounts,' he continued, adjusting her pillows.

'Lucky?' Leah didn't feel lucky. Not until she knew what had happened to Craig.

She took the pills given to her then leant back and closed her eyes. But all she saw were the wipers flapping across the rain-soaked windscreen, the headlights shining on the fallen tree, and then the car filling with broken glass, branches and leaves. Blood had splattered everywhere.

She opened her eyes again, gasping from the memory.

'Are you up to talking?' came a voice.

Leah had almost forgotten that DI Nelson was there.

Leah pressed the button on her bed so she was sitting upright. 'Yes,' she said, nodding. 'What time is it?'

DI Nelson sat down in the plastic chair next to the bed and glanced at her watch. 'One forty,' she said. 'The night is still young,' she added with a small smile.

Leah stared at the ceiling as she tried to piece together events. Fragments colliding.

'I was in a car accident...' she said, a vacant tone to her voice.

'That's why I'm here, Leah,' the detective said.

Leah looked at her. Held her breath.

'Do you remember who else was in the car?'

Leah thought for a moment. 'Craig was in the passenger seat.' She let out a sigh. 'We've just got back together.' She fixed her eyes on the ceiling again. 'We... we realised that we still love each other, that we should never have split up.'

'You'd got back together?' The detective sounded incredulous, frowning. 'I'm afraid there's some bad news, Leah.' She cleared her throat. 'Craig didn't make it. The branch sticking out from the fallen tree... It came through the windscreen on his side. He suffered massive head and chest injuries. I know it's no consolation, but it would have been quick.'

Leah let out a little sob. Only *she* knew that it was a sob of relief.

'I'm so sorry. For you and your children.' DI Nelson was silent for a moment. 'As the nurse said, you *were* lucky. If you'd not managed to stop exactly when you did, the front of your Mini would have hit the main tree trunk and your injuries would have been far, far worse. Or even...' She trailed off.

Leah nodded and closed her eyes. Under the bed sheets, the fist of her good hand clenched. Despite the relief, a single hot tear forced its way from her eye. She'd risked everything – even her own life – but it had paid off.

She was finally free.

'Am I in trouble?' Leah asked, the tear running down her cheek and onto the pillowcase. 'I was the one driving. Craig told me he wanted us to get away, to spend a romantic night together. He said he knew somewhere we could go, that everything would be good between us again, that he was sorry for everything he'd done to me. He's always been so persuasive, so I believed him. I just wanted things back to normal again, for me and the kids.' Another sob. 'But then it was raining, and we got lost. Craig was getting angry and yelling at me, and then suddenly there was this huge tree in the road as I turned the corner and... Oh God...' She covered her face and let the tears come.

DI Nelson listened, watching Leah's distress. 'It was a freak accident that couldn't have been predicted, Leah. The tree was on private land and you'd have had no idea it was there, let alone that a random branch would directly hit Craig. You mustn't blame yourself.'

'I tried to stop sooner, but it all happened so fast. I only had a second to react.'

'There'll be an inquest, of course, but don't worry about that for now. Just focus on getting better.'

Leah nodded.

'I'm truly sorry you had to go through all this,' DI Nelson said.

'I hope you never do,' Leah replied. 'I saw it in your eyes, you know. When we were in the interview room, and I asked you if you'd ever been cheated on.'

'I don't think my story compares to yours, Leah.'

'You just never think it will happen to you. That if you only did this or that differently, tried harder, became a better wife...' She trailed off, holding her bad wrist. 'All things considered, I came out lightly. I'm still alive.' She paused. 'Lucky, right?'

DI Nelson stared at her, a slight frown flickering on her brow.

Leah held her gaze, sensing some kind of understanding passing between them.

'Dan's not violent,' the detective said.

'Neither was Craig to start with.'

DI Nelson sighed, uncrossing her legs. 'He's left me, anyway. Gone to be with the other woman.'

'I'm sorry to hear that.'

'Don't be. She's welcome to him.'

'Kids?'

'Twins. One of each.'

'They'll be OK,' Leah said, reaching out her good hand and taking hold of the detective's. '*You'll* be OK.'

The two women looked at each other again, a future of possibilities fleetingly caught in each other's eyes.

'And so will you, Leah. So will you.' DI Nelson stood to leave just as the nurse peered around the curtain.

'You've a visitor, Miss Ward. Shall I send her in?' he asked.

Leah watched as the detective left the cubicle, and then she nodded at the nurse. 'Yes, yes, please do.'

Gillian stood at the cubicle entrance, holding the curtain open. Her face was pale and gaunt, and the bruises on her face had burst into a rainbow of mauve, yellow and green. Her hair was tied back in a limp ponytail.

'Hello,' she said meekly, stepping inside. She closed the

curtain behind her, her eyes darting about and an uncertain expression on her face.

'Gillian... hi.' Leah pressed the button on her bed a couple more times. The painkillers were starting to kick in now, and the nurse had given her something extra through the drip.

'Is it OK me being here?'

'Of course.' Leah pointed to the chair next to the bed.

'I wasn't sure if I should come after I was so rude to you at the police station.'

Leah watched as Gillian slipped off her padded coat. Underneath, she was wearing a plain grey sweatshirt over black leggings. A far cry from the woman she'd first met on the street alongside the removals van.

'I'm glad you're here,' Leah said. 'DI Nelson has just left.'

Gillian nodded. 'I saw her in the corridor.'

'Did she say anything?' She wasn't sure how much Gillian knew.

'No.'

Slowly, Gillian sat down, perching on the edge of the chair.

'I've been staying with a friend but came home earlier this evening.' She took a tissue from her bag and dabbed at her nose. 'It's silly, but part of me hoped that Craig would be home by now. You know – apologising, promising that he'd change.' She let out a pathetic laugh.

'I know,' Leah said. 'Believe me, I do.'

'But when I got home, there was no one there. Just more mess. I feel so alone.'

'Oh Gillian, I'm so sorry.'

'Then Gabe knocked on the door. He's looking after Zoey and Henry.'

Leah nodded, closing her eyes at the thought of Gabe. She'd never be able to erase the look on his face when she told him she still loved Craig.

'He didn't really tell me much, apart from that you and Craig are back together.'

Leah opened her eyes. She shook her head. 'No,' she mouthed quietly. 'No, we're not.'

Gillian looked confused. 'But Gabe said—'

Leah put her finger up to her mouth. 'Shhh...'

She thought for a moment, wondering how best to break the news.

'I was in an accident. Craig was in the car with me and...' She took a deep breath. 'It was raining... I was driving fast... there was a tree.' Another pause. 'He's dead, Gillian.'

Gillian stared at her, unmoving. The sounds of the busy ward went on around them as both women sat in silence. Her mouth opened but nothing came out.

'*Dead?*' she finally said. Her expression was blank.

Leah nodded several times. She took Gillian's hand in hers, giving it a squeeze. 'We're free,' she mouthed.

'My God,' she replied, tears collecting in her eyes. Then she squeezed Leah's hand right back.

CHAPTER FORTY-SIX

The next day, Leah left the hospital, blinking in the afternoon sunlight as she waited for her taxi.

Her right arm was in a plaster cast and a sling, and she'd been discharged with strong painkillers for her fractured collarbone that, she was told, would heal on its own in time. She had an appointment to come back for a review in a week.

She stayed silent on the short journey home.

The front door wasn't locked, and her house was eerily quiet when she stepped inside. When she'd got out of the taxi, she thought she'd seen a face at Gillian's front window but couldn't be certain. All she wanted was to be with her children, though when she discovered the house was empty, she wondered if Gabe had taken them to his boat.

She sat down in her living room, feeling teary and empty, but almost immediately there was a knock at the door. She went to open it.

'Gabe...' She glanced behind him, expecting to see Zoey and Henry. But they weren't there.

'They're next door with Gillian,' he replied, as though he'd read her mind. 'She told me about the accident. Are you OK? And I'm... I'm so sorry.'

Leah looked up, trying to read his face. She gave a little nod. 'Thank you. And thank you for taking care of Zoey and Henry.'

Then Gabe spotted her arm. 'Uh-oh. You're right-handed.' He gently touched the cast.

Leah rolled her eyes. 'I should have broken the left one.' She opened the door wider. 'Do you... do you want to come in?'

Gabe followed her into the living room, but went straight into the kitchen to make some tea.

'Thank you again for everything,' Leah said when he returned. 'And thank you for saving my life.' She didn't think he'd ever understand how much she meant that.

Gabe looked puzzled.

'When you smashed the window,' she explained.

'You can thank my phone for running out of battery for that,' he replied, still looking bewildered. 'After we'd got cut off, it took an age to get any power back into it. My charger has a loose cable, so I had to fix it. When I finally called you back, you didn't answer. I really had to speak to you, Leah.' He paused, taking a sip of tea. 'There's something I've been trying to tell you and it couldn't wait any longer.'

Leah listened, sipping her own tea.

'When I couldn't get hold of you, I drove over, but you weren't here,' he said. 'Then I heard screams coming from next door so I went outside and looked through the front window. When I saw Craig with his hands around your throat, I grabbed a loose brick from the path and smashed the window.'

'That brick and I have history.'

'But then I realised that you two were... that you'd been *kissing*.'

Leah bowed her head, breathing in the steam from her mug. 'It wasn't like that.'

'It's fine, honestly.' Gabe held up a hand and looked away briefly. 'Your business.'

They sat in silence until Gabe reached out across the sofa to take her hand. Leah pulled away.

'What I'd wanted to tell you, Leah... It's not going to be easy to hear. Your mother, she—'

'I already know,' she interjected. 'And yes, he got to her too. He got to *everyone*. It took a lot to say no to Craig.'

'Indeed.' Gabe was thoughtful for a moment. 'He even convinced you to get back together with him.'

'No... he didn't.' She gave him a look. 'Mum came to see me in A & E earlier,' Leah continued. 'There's something I don't understand. When Craig got angry after you'd caught them together, Mum said you went out to finish the hedge.'

Gabe nodded. 'That's right. It's what I'd come round for in the first place. Then when I saw Craig was home, I went round for my money.'

'But you didn't finish the hedge, did you?'

'I wanted to grab a drink and something to eat before I started work, so I took my tools down to the gateway then walked to the local shop. Plus, I needed some thinking time.'

'Was there anyone else in the garden? Or building site, should I say.'

'Just a lad finishing up. Jimmy, he said. The site manager had told him to clear up some stuff and he was working alone. It had started to drizzle so I offered him my hi-vis work jacket. I'd got another one in the van that I was going to grab when I returned from the shop.'

'Oh God, *Jimmy*?' Leah said, a concerned look sweeping her face. 'And did you return?'

'Yes and no,' Gabe said. 'When I came back, I got as far as the gateway but realised that Craig was there, messing about with the JCB. He looked angry as hell so I thought, you know what? I'm not getting involved with any more aggro today, so I left. He didn't see me. I figured I'd pick up my tools another time. I've explained all this to the police.'

'Christ,' Leah said, dropping her head down. 'He thought it was you.'

'I don't understand.'

'Craig saw your name on the back of the jacket and crushed *Jimmy* with the digger, thinking it was you. You're both a similar build and have the same hair. Plus Jimmy had a hard hat on. With the drizzle, the smoke from the fire... not to mention the red mist in Craig's eyes, he... he... didn't realise it *wasn't* you. Oh, how *awful*. The poor boy. His poor family. An innocent lad caught up in this mess.'

Gabe reached out and pulled Leah into his arms. At first, she resisted but then she buried her face against him, allowing the tears to come.

'Let me go and get the children,' he said when her tears had subsided. 'They'll be so pleased to see you. And... and if it helps, I can stay when you tell them.'

She nodded and sniffed. 'Thank you.' Breaking the news about their dad would be the hardest thing she'd ever had to do.

Leah went to the window and watched as Gabe walked down the path, glancing back over his shoulder and giving her a smile. She couldn't smile back – not yet. Though something inside her stirred – something that would take time to set free.

While he was gone, Leah looked in the mirror above the fireplace, wiping her face with her sleeve. She still looked gaunt, pale and exhausted – but this time when she saw herself, she thought there was a glimmer of something in her eyes that she hadn't seen in a long while. Something that made her not seem quite so lost any more. She thought, perhaps, that it was what hope looked like.

EPILOGUE

ONE YEAR LATER

Leah walked along the towpath, shining the torch in front of her. Zoey and Henry were itching to run off ahead – or rather, Henry was, but Zoey was doing a good job of making sure he didn't fall into the canal. It was only 6 p.m. but being early November, it was already dark. It had been bright and sunny all week, frosty too, and Bonfire Night was equally chilly, with all of them wrapped up in thick coats, scarves, gloves and boots.

'It's not much further,' she called out to the children. Though 'child', for Zoey at least, was beginning to seem inappropriate. She was almost a young woman, with a recent win and personal best in the county swimming gala yet another achievement for her daughter.

Despite the loss of her father in the accident, she'd thrown herself into her schoolwork and sport – her way of coping, Leah supposed. The counsellor at school had been invaluable, helping her work through her emotions and grief. She had her good days, and bad ones, too – as did Leah – and Henry was processing his loss in his own way. As the questions gradually came about Daddy dying in the car crash, Leah answered them as best she could, as well as protecting them both from the brief flurry of news reports.

It had been tough for all of them, but they were gradually making progress.

'Ahoy there!' Leah called out as they approached the rear deck of *Blue Moon*. The lights were on inside the boat, and Gabe had strung fairy lights all over the cabin sides and bows, making it look like a floating grotto. He was sitting on the deck when they arrived, a steaming hot drink in his hand. He'd lit a small brazier on the bank too.

'Come aboard,' he said to Zoey and Henry. It was their first visit to the boat. Leah had been cautious about involving them too soon, especially as she'd taken her time rebuilding things with Gabe. Her counsellor was helping her work through forgiveness – Gabe had been a victim too – as well as unpicking her reluctance to trust, resetting her boundaries. It had been a slow process, but Gabe's patience and understanding helped.

She wasn't someone's ex-wife any more. She was Leah.

'Oh, this is wicked!' Henry exclaimed, taking Gabe's hand as he stepped over the gap between the bank and the deck. Zoey followed him on, standing between the wooden doors of the cabin, gazing around.

'Look, Sprat, fireworks!' She pointed to the sky where red and gold rain showered above them. Another few cracks and bangs peppered the night with colour.

'It's so cool,' Henry said, clapping his hands as he craned his neck to watch.

'Welcome aboard,' Gabe said, giving Leah a kiss as she stepped onto the deck. It felt a little crowded with the four of them in the small space, but cosy too. 'It's good to see you.'

'Here, I brought some goodies,' she said, handing him a bag.

'Sausages, whisky and marshmallows,' he said, peering inside. 'You know me too well.'

'It might be a bit dark for a sundowner, but I thought a

whisky and ginger would warm us up,' Leah said with a laugh. 'And there's hot chocolate in there for the kids.'

Gabe saluted and went into the cabin.

'This is so cool, Mum,' Zoey said, hitching herself up so she was sitting on the edge of the roof. She slid around so her feet were dangling over the water side of the boat. The sky above their town, only a mile or so away, was lit up by firework displays and the glow of bonfires.

'It's lovely, isn't it?' Leah said, wondering if she should pay a visit to the marina when they left tomorrow and have a quick look in the office window. There were always a number of boats advertised for sale.

Gabe came out with frothy hot chocolate for Zoey and Henry and a drink for him and Leah. He lifted Henry onto the roof next to his sister so he could watch the fireworks with her.

'Just don't fall in, Sprat,' Zoey replied, putting an arm round him. 'I'm not jumping in to rescue you.'

Leah and Gabe sat down in the two camping chairs either side of the tiller, huddling under the tartan blankets he'd put out.

'I've made up all the bunks,' Gabe told her. 'It's cosy for the kids, and we'll be in the front cabin.'

Leah smiled. 'I was just pondering getting a boat,' she told Gabe. 'Nothing huge, but I think they'd love it. Weekends away, days out, that kind of thing.'

'I can help you look, if you like. Thirty-two feet would be about right. I know Jeff down at the marina. I'll ask him to keep an eye open.'

'Thanks. And it's not as if I can't afford it, either.' Leah lowered her voice. 'The first completion money came through yesterday.'

Gabe nodded, looking thoughtful. 'Have they moved in yet?'

Leah nodded. 'They seem like a nice family. And Gillian

called me earlier, saying that two of the other properties had full asking price offers during the week. The fourth house will be ready to market soon.'

'You've worked so hard to get it all done.'

'I didn't really have a choice,' Leah said. 'Sally's been amazing, taking over the running of the salon while I've project-managed the builds. I couldn't have done it without you, though,' Leah said, raising her glass. 'Your knowledge and contacts have been invaluable. Here's to teamwork!' She clinked her glass with Gabe's beer bottle. 'I expected to have broad beans and asparagus in the vegetable garden this year, but instead, I've got four houses worth half a million quid each.'

'Will you be selling your place soon?'

'Probably, when I've converted it back into one property. Perhaps next spring. I was thinking of living there long-term, but I don't think I can. Too many ghosts.'

'Is your dad still doing OK?'

Leah grinned. 'Oh, he loves having me and the kids next door. He's quite happy pottering with all the jobs in the Wash House that I never got round to doing. It makes him feel useful. I've not mentioned about us all moving yet, but wherever I buy, it'll have room for him.'

'Does he ever hear from your mother?'

Leah made a face. 'Occasionally, like me. Her suspended sentence has still got a few months to run, as have her community service hours. I don't think they'll get back together, and I think that's right for Dad. He's starting to enjoy life again. He's joined the local bowls club and goes to the history society, too.'

'Good for him.'

'Mum sees the kids every couple of weeks. I'm never going to cut her off from them.'

'But you're cutting her off from yourself, right?'

'She was fifty per cent of what happened with Craig, but she's still my mum.' Leah kept her voice down. 'He manipulated everyone. Gillian fell prey to him, most of my friends, other estate agents. Even *you* were sucked in. It was a huge shock finding out that he'd been sleeping with Liz, my solicitor. After that, he'd got her over a barrel.'

Gabe let out a wry laugh. 'If there were any last laughs to be had, you certainly got them.'

Leah agreed, staring up into the night sky as another shower of rockets broke into a thousand glittering stars.

'I'll always make sure Mum's looked after financially. I've got more than enough for me and the kids, what with Craig's investments, his business and all the property.'

'Part of me almost feels sorry for Liz, but then she was married too,' Gabe said. They'd gone over what had happened many times.

'Craig blackmailing her into not filing the decree absolute, threatening to tell her husband about their affair if she did, certainly backfired on him. When he died, I was still his wife, but I had no idea. I blindly trusted that Liz had done all the proper paperwork.'

'Karma works in mysterious ways,' Gabe whispered.

'Turns out Craig was right about the land belonging to his property, though. Liz had completely missed the covenants in the old deeds. Too busy sleeping with Craig to focus on work, probably. Anyway, I'm glad she's been struck off. The irony is, she'll have to hire someone for her own divorce now.'

Leah stared up at the sky as another burst of rockets exploded.

'And as Craig's wife, you inherited everything.'

'Yep. He hadn't even changed his will. I was still the main beneficiary.'

'How's Gillian getting on with managing the estate agencies?' Gabe asked. They'd socialised with her and her new partner, Mark, several times. He seemed pleasant, though Leah never mentioned anything to her about it being the bald man she'd spotted her with in the pub a little over a year ago.

'She's doing well,' Leah said. 'She's rebranded the whole business. Frankly it's a relief that she's changed all the signage. It means I don't have to stare at *his* face every time I see a "For Sale" board now.' She looked up at Zoey and Henry on the roof, chattering excitedly, hot chocolates cupped in their hands. She smiled. 'Did you get the loot?' she added in a whisper.

Gabe nodded. 'All safely stored in the bows.'

'Hey, guys,' Leah called out. 'Come and get one of these.' She reached into her bag and pulled out two packets of sparklers and a lighter, handing them to Zoey and Henry. Zoey rolled her eyes, trying to imply she was too old, though Leah noticed the excitement on her face.

'I didn't forget us,' Leah said, tearing open another packet and lighting a couple from the tea lights Gabe had put out. She waved hers around, her eyes dazzled by the trail left behind.

'I've not had one of these in years,' Gabe laughed, drawing shapes in the air. 'This one's for you,' he said, swirling a big love heart over and over.

Leah grinned – something she'd not done often enough lately. 'Right back atcha,' she said, drawing a heart shape of her own.

———

Half an hour later, Gabe emerged from the cabin with cooked sausages, fried onions and hot dog rolls. Everyone was on deck, helping themselves and squirting on tomato sauce, getting messy in the process. Then Gabe went to stoke the brazier on the bank until it glowed bright, its flames licking up into the night.

'Bring your food onto the towpath, you two,' Leah said to her children. Gabe had disappeared down the towpath to the front of the boat, where he climbed into the bows. 'Come and get warm by the fire.'

'This is *wicked*, Mum, thanks!' Henry said, wiping sauce off his chin. 'Best Bonfire Night ever.'

'Yeah, Mum, it's all right actually.' Zoey smiled, looking up at her and resting her head against her mum's shoulder as she bit into her hot dog.

Suddenly, there was a shout from the front of the boat. 'Ready, you lot?' Gabe called.

'Ready!' they all chimed back.

There was the flicker of a lighter flame and then Gabe ran back down the length of the boat to where they were standing. Leah handed him his hot dog and pressed herself against him as he slipped an arm around her.

The four of them stood there, huddled together as the huge all-in-one firework erupted into the sky in a fountain of colour and bangs and squeals and sparks in an impressive display above the canal. It seemed to go on forever.

Zoey and Henry clapped and laughed – the first time in a while that Leah had seen them truly happy. Gabe hugged her close as the fireworks rained above them.

Leah glanced up at him and saw the flames reflected in his eyes. And within his eyes, she was reminded of *another* fire – the fire that had raged inside her for just one night a couple of years ago.

She saw herself and Gabe – when they'd first set eyes on each other. There had been a fire there, too, though this one was between them. Such a cliché, and they'd both laughed about it since.

Leah had never intended going – *a friend of a friend of a friend was having a party*, according to Abby, all excited, and Leah was invited. *Hell,* everyone *was invited*.

She almost couldn't be bothered, but another Saturday night alone was worse than tagging along to a gathering where she didn't even know the host. Craig was away on another of his so-called business trips. He didn't know, but she'd already read the messages between him and Suzie, whoever Suzie was. But it was clear that business wasn't on the agenda.

It was when her mother had offered to have the kids overnight that Leah made up her mind. She *would* go to the party. She hadn't got anything to wear and had gone straight from work on a whim – underdressed and underwhelmed. But it didn't matter. She'd gone there to drink, to dance and to forget. Yet another weekend alone and feeling miserable was not happening.

And it turned out that forgetting had been easy given the wine she'd had to drink, though at the time it had taken all Leah's resolve not to give in.

He'd come over, they'd chatted, they'd danced, and then they'd gone outside for some fresh air. When Gabe had kissed her, it was a few moments before she'd pulled back.

'I can't,' she said, gasping. 'I'm married.' They'd seemed like the hardest words of her life.

Afterwards, she'd gone home, blocking him from her mind. But somewhere inside her, a spark from that night had remained alight, ready to be reignited when they'd met again on her parents' drive a year later.

'Karma is mysterious indeed,' Leah whispered up at Gabe now, planting a kiss on his lips as they stood behind the children.

He returned the kiss fondly, staring down at her and pulling her closer.

And the fire inside Leah ignited all over again as she imagined the home she would buy for them all and the fires they'd keep on burning.

A LETTER FROM SAMANTHA

Dear Reader,

Thank you so much for reading *The Ex-Husband* – I do hope you enjoyed the story and following Leah on her journey. If you'd like to be kept up to date with all my new releases, you can click on the link below for news (you can unsubscribe at any time).

www.bookouture.com/samantha-hayes

It's said that divorce and moving house are right up there in the list of most stressful life events – and certainly when coercive control and abuse underpin the reasons for the marital split in the first place.

When I wrote this book, I wanted to give my main character a new beginning and renewed hope of finding her happy ever after once she'd finally escaped her ex-husband. She certainly deserved it, don't you think? But of course, a psychological thriller wouldn't live up to its name if danger, fear and tension weren't lurking from the first page.

So I asked myself: what would be Leah's worst nightmare after she'd got her much-anticipated fresh start? After her difficult divorce, what would be the one thing that made her feel as though she hadn't ever escaped at all? And that's when I decided to ramp up the stakes and have her ex-husband move in next door.

We've all heard stories about nightmare neighbours, but combined with the serious issue of domestic abuse, Leah finds her ex not only invading every aspect of her life, but her family and friends also fall victim to Craig's manipulation. It was sheer desperation that drove Leah (literally) to take matters into her own hands and risk her life for a final chance at freedom.

If you enjoyed reading *The Ex-Husband*, then I'd be so very grateful if you could leave a quick review on Amazon to let other readers know about my book. It really helps spread the word. Meantime, I'm busy working away on my next novel – and do feel free to follow me on social media (links below).

Finally, if you or someone you know have been affected by issues surrounding domestic violence, emotional abuse or coercive control, then help is available through several charities. The National Centre for Domestic Violence can be reached at *www.ncdv.org.uk* and Women's Aid have a website here *www.womensaid.org.uk* and The National Domestic Abuse Helpline phone number (UK) is 0808 2000 247. Please do reach out if you need help.

With warm wishes,

Sam x

www.samanthahayes.co.uk

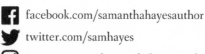

facebook.com/samanthahayesauthor

twitter.com/samhayes

instagram.com/samanthahayes.author

ACKNOWLEDGEMENTS

Huge thanks and gratitude to my amazing editor Jessie Botterill for being so brilliant and enthusiastic about this book! I'm so very grateful to Sarah Hardy, Kim Nash, Noelle Holten and Jess Readett, the amazing publicity team at Bookouture, who tirelessly promote my books, and to Seán for his eagle-eyed copy-editing, and to Jenny for proof-reading – thank you all! And, as ever, a massive thanks to the entire team at Bookouture for everything you do.

Big thanks to Oli Munson, my agent extraordinaire, for encouraging words – and, well, everything! As well, of course, thanks to all the staff at A. M. Heath.

A special thank-you to Martyn Eagles, to whom this book is dedicated. He kindly participated in the Book Aid for Ukraine charity auction and was the winning bidder on my lot – a selection of signed books, plus this book dedication. So this one's for you, Martyn! Thank you for your contribution to such a worthwhile cause.

And massive thanks to all the bloggers, reviewers and book lovers around the world who take the time to read, review and shout out about my books. I truly appreciate it – and I love reading all your comments and seeing all the creative Instagram posts!

Last but not least – much love to my dear family, Ben, Polly and Lucy, Avril and Paul, Graham and Marina, and Joe.

Sam xx

Made in United States
North Haven, CT
17 July 2022

21476737R00211